To Frances Gordon,
with love.

My special thanks go to Alice Fisher,
whose assistance in helping me research this novel
was invaluable.

Lives of great men all remind us
We can make our lives sublime,
And, departing, leave behind us
Footprints on the Sands of Time.

HENRY WADSWORTH
LONGFELLOW

The dead do not need to rise.

They are a part of the earth now and the earth can never be conquered for the earth endures forever, it will outlive all systems of tyranny. Those who have entered it honourably, and no men entered earth more honourably than those who died in Spain, have already achieved immortality.   ERNEST HEMINGWAY

AUTHOR'S NOTE

This is a work of fiction. And yet . . .

The romantic land of flamenco and Don Quixote and exotic-looking señoritas with tortoise-shell combs in their hair is also the land of Torquemada, the Spanish Inquisition and one of the bloodiest civil wars in history. More than half a million people lost their lives in the battles for power between the Republicans and the rebel Nationalists in Spain. In 1936, between February and June, 269 political murders were committed, and the Nationalists executed Republicans at the rate of a thousand a month, with no mourning permitted. One hundred and sixty churches were burned to the ground, and nuns were removed forcibly from convents, 'as though,' wrote the Duc de Saint-Simon, of an earlier conflict between the Spanish government and the church, 'they were whores in a bawdy house'. Newspaper offices were sacked and strikes and riots were endemic throughout the land. The Civil War ended in a victory for the Nationalists under Franco and, following his death, Spain became a monarchy.

The Civil War, which lasted from 1936 to 1939, may be officially over, but the two Spains that fought it have never been reconciled. Today another war continues to rage in Spain, the guerrilla war fought by the Basques to regain the autonomy they had won under the Republic and lost under the Franco regime. The war is being fought with bombs, bank robberies to finance the bombs, assassinations and riots.

When a member of ETA, a Basque guerrilla underground group, died in a Madrid hospital after being tortured by the police, the nationwide riots that followed led to the resignation of the Director General of Spain's police force, five security chiefs and two hundred senior police officers.

In 1986, in Barcelona, the Basques publicly burned the Spanish flag, and in Pamplona thousands fled in fear when Basque nationalists clashed with police in a series of mutinies that eventually spread across Spain and threatened the stability of the government. The para-military police retaliated by going on a rampage, firing at random at Basques' homes and shops. The terrorism that goes on is more violent than ever.

Dealing with two turbulent weeks in 1976, this is a work of fiction. And yet . . .

Chapter 1

Pamplona, Spain 1976

If the plan goes wrong, we will all die. He went over it again in his mind for the last time, probing, testing, searching for flaws. He could find none. The plan was daring, and it called for careful, split-second timing. If it worked, it would be a spectacular feat, worthy of the great El Cid. If it failed . . .

Well, the time for worrying is past, Jaime Miró thought philosophically. *It's time for action.*

Jaime Miró was a legend, a hero to the Basque people and anathema to the Spanish government. He was six feet tall, with a strong, intelligent face, a muscular body, and brooding dark eyes. Witnesses tended to describe him as taller than he was, darker than he was, fiercer than he was. He was a complex man, a realist who understood the enormous odds against him, a romàntic ready to die for what he believed.

Pamplona was a town gone mad. It was the final morning of the running of the bulls, the Fiesta de San Fermín, the annual celebration held from 7 July to the 14th. Thirty thousand visitors had swarmed into the city from all over the world. Some had come merely to watch the dangerous bull-running spectacle, others to prove their manhood by taking part in it, running in front of the charging beasts. All the hotel rooms had long since been taken, and university students from Navarra had bedded down in doorways, bank entrances, cars, the public square, and even the streets and pavements of the town.

The tourists packed the cafés and hotels, watching the noisy, colourful parades of *papier mâché gigantes*, and listening to the music of the marching bands. Members of the parade wore violet cloaks, some with hoods of green, others garnet, and still others wearing golden hoods. Flowing through the streets, the processions looked like rivers of rainbows. Exploding firecrackers running along poles and wires of the tramways added to the noise and general confusion.

The crowd had come to attend the evening bullfights, but the most spectacular event was the *Encierro* – the early morning running of the bulls that would fight later in the day.

Ten minutes before midnight in the darkened streets of the lower part of town, the bulls had been driven from the *corrales de gas*, the reception pens, to run across the river on a bridge to the corral at the bottom of Calle Santo Domingo, where they would be kept for the night. In the morning they would be turned loose to run along the narrow Calle Santo Domingo, penned in the street by wooden barricades at each corner until at the end they would run into the corrals at the Plaza de Hemingway, where they would be held until the afternoon bullfight.

From midnight until 6.00 a.m., the visitors stayed awake, drinking and singing and making love, too excited to sleep. Those who would participate in the running of the bulls wore the red scarves of San Fermin around their throats.

At a quarter to six in the morning, bands started circulating through the streets, playing the stirring music of Navarre. At seven o'clock sharp, a rocket flew into the air to signal that the gates of the corral had been opened. The crowd was filled with feverish anticipation. Moments later a second rocket went up to warn the town that the bulls were running.

What followed was an unforgettable spectacle. First came the sound. It started as a faint, distant ripple on the wind, almost imperceptible, and then it grew louder and louder until it became an explosion of pounding hoofs, and suddenly bursting into view appeared six oxen and six enormous bulls.

12

Each weighing 1,500 pounds, they charged down the Calle Santo Domingo like deadly express trains. Inside the wooden barricades that had been placed at each intersecting street corner to keep the bulls confined to the one street, were hundreds of eager, nervous young men who intended to prove their bravery by facing the maddened animals.

The bulls raced down from the far end of the street, past the Calle Laestrafeta and the Calle de Javier, past *farmacias* and clothing stores and fruit markets, towards the Plaza de Hemingway, and there were cries of '*¡Olé!*' from the frenzied crowd. As the animals charged nearer, a mad scramble began to escape the sharp horns and lethal hoofs. The sudden reality of approaching death made some of the participants run for the safety of doorways and fire escapes. They were followed by taunts of '*cobardon*' – coward. A few in the path of the bulls stumbled and fell and were quickly hauled to safety.

A small boy and his grandfather were standing behind the barricades, both breathless with the excitement of the spectacle taking place only a few feet from them.

'Look at them!' the old man exclaimed. '*¡Magnífico!*'

The little boy shuddered. '*Tengo miedo, Abuelo*. I'm afraid.'

The old man put his arm around him. '*Si*, Manuelo. It is frightening. But wonderful, too. I once ran with the bulls. There's nothing like it. You test yourself against death, and it makes you feel like a man.'

As a rule, it took two minutes for the animals to gallop the 900 yards along the Calle Santo Domingo to the arena, and the moment the bulls were safely in the corral, a third rocket would be sent into the air. On this day, the third rocket did not go off, for an incident occurred that had never happened in Pamplona's 400-year history of the running of the bulls.

As the animals raced down the narrow street, half a dozen men dressed in the colourful costumes of the *feria* shifted the wooden barricades and the bulls found themselves forced off the restricted street and turned loose into the heart of

13

the city. What had a moment before been a happy celebration instantly turned into a nightmare. The frenzied beasts charged into the stunned onlookers. The young boy and his grandfather were among the first to die, knocked down and trampled by the charging bulls. Vicious horns sliced into a baby's pram, killing an infant and sending its mother down to the ground to be crushed. Death was in the air everywhere. The animals crashed into helpless bystanders, knocking down women and children, plunging their long, deadly horns into pedestrians, food stands, statues, sweeping aside everything unlucky enough to be in their path. People were screaming in terror, desperately fighting to get out of the way of the lethal behemoths.

A bright red truck suddenly appeared in the path of the bulls and they turned and charged towards it, down the Calle de Estrella, the street that led to the *cárcel*, Pamplona's prison.

The *cárcel* is a forbidding-looking two-storey stone building with heavily barred windows. There are turrets at each of its four corners, and the red and yellow Spanish flag flies over the door. A stone gate leads to a small courtyard. The second floor of the building consists of a row of cells that holds prisoners condemned to die.

Inside the prison, a heavyset guard in the uniform of the *policía armada* was leading a priest garbed in plain black robes along the second floor corridor. The policeman carried a sub-machine-gun.

Noting the questioning look in the priest's eye at the sight of the weapon, the guard said, 'One can't be too careful here, Father. We have the scum of the earth on this floor.'

The guard directed the priest to walk through a metal detector very much like those used at airports.

'I'm sorry, Father, but the rules –'

'Of course, my son.'

As the priest passed through the security portal, a

14

shrieking siren cut through the corridor. The guard instinctively tightened his grip on his weapon.

The priest turned and smiled back at the guard.

'My mistake,' he said as he removed a heavy metal cross that hung from his neck on a silver chain and handed it to the guard. This time as he passed through, the machine was silent. The guard handed the cross back to the priest and the two continued their journey deeper into the bowels of the prison.

The stench in the corridor near the cells was overpowering.

The guard was in a philosophical mood. 'You know, you're wasting your time here, Father. These animals have no souls to save.'

'Still, we must try, my son.'

The guard shook his head. 'I tell you the gates of hell are waiting to welcome both of them.'

The priest looked at the guard in surprise. 'Both of them? I was told there were three who needed confession.'

The guard shrugged. 'We saved you some time. Zamora died in the infirmary this morning. Heart attack.'

The men had reached the two farthest cells.

'Here we are, Father.'

The guard unlocked a cell door, then stepped cautiously back as the priest entered the cell. The guard locked the door again, and stood in the corridor, alert for any sign of trouble.

The priest went to the figure lying on the dirty prison cot. 'Your name, my son?'

'Ricardo Mellado.'

The priest stared down at him. It was difficult to tell what the man looked like. His face was swollen and raw. His eyes were almost shut. Through thick lips, he said, 'I'm glad you were able to come, Father.'

The priest replied, 'Your salvation is the church's duty, my son.'

'They are going to hang me this morning?'

The priest patted his shoulder gently. 'You have been sentenced to die by the garrotte.'

15

Ricardo Mellado stared up at him. 'No!'

'I'm sorry. The orders were given by the Prime Minister himself.'

The priest placed his hand on the prisoner's head and intoned: '*Di me tus pecados . . .*'

Ricardo Mellado said, 'I have sinned greatly in thought, word and deed, and I repent all my sins with all my heart.'

'*Ruego a nuestro Padre celestial para la salvación de tu alma. In el nombre del Padre, del Hijo y del Espiritu Santo . . .*'

The guard listening outside the cell thought to himself: *What a stupid waste of time. God will spit in that one's eye.*

The priest was finished. '*Adiós*, my son. May God receive your soul in peace.'

The priest moved to the cell door and the guard unlocked it, then stepped back, keeping his gun aimed at the prisoner. When the door was locked again, the guard moved to the adjoining cell and opened the door.

'He's all yours, Father.'

The priest stepped into the second cell. The man inside had also been badly beaten. The priest looked at him a long moment. 'What is your name, my son?'

'Felix Carpio.' He was a husky, bearded man with a fresh, livid scar on his cheek that the beard failed to conceal. 'I'm not afraid to die, Father.'

'That is well, my son. In the end none of us is spared.'

As the priest began to hear Carpio's confession, waves of distant sound, at first muffled, then growing louder, began to reverberate through the building. It was the thunder of pounding hoofs and the screams of the running mob. The guard listened, startled. The sounds were rapidly moving closer.

'You'd better hurry, Father. Something peculiar is happening outside.'

'I'm finished.'

The guard quickly unlocked the cell door. The priest stepped out into the corridor and the guard locked the door behind him. There was the sound of a loud crash from the

16

front of the prison. The guard turned to peer out the narrow, barred window.

'What the hell was that noise?'

The priest said, 'It sounded as though someone wishes an audience with us. May I borrow that?'

'Borrow what?'

'Your weapon, *por favor*.'

As the priest spoke, he stepped close to the guard. He silently removed the top of the large cross that hung around his neck, revealing a long, wicked-looking stiletto. In one lightning move he plunged the knife into the guard's chest.

'You see, my son,' Jaime Miró said, as he pulled the sub-machine-gun from the dying guard's hands, 'God and I decided that you no longer have need of this weapon.'

The guard slumped to the cement floor. Jaime Miró took the keys from the body and swiftly opened the two cell doors. The sounds from the street were getting louder.

'Let's move,' Jaime commanded.

Ricardo Mellado picked up the machine gun. 'You make a damned good priest. You almost convinced me.' He tried to smile with his swollen mouth.

'They really worked you two over, didn't they? Don't worry. They'll pay for it.'

Jaime Miró put his arms around the two men and helped them down the corridor.

'What happened to Zamora?'

'The guards beat him to death. We could hear his screams. They took him off to the infirmary and said he died of a heart attack.'

Ahead of them was a locked iron door.

'Wait here,' Jaime Miró said.

He approached the door and said to the guard on the other side, 'I'm finished here.'

The guard unlocked the door. 'You'd better hurry, Father. There's some kind of disturbance going on out –' He never finished his sentence. As Jaime's knife went into him, blood welled out of the guard's mouth.

Jaime motioned to the two men. 'Come on.'

17

Felix Carpio picked up the guard's gun, and they started downstairs. The scene outside was chaos. The police were running around frantically trying to see what was happening and to deal with the crowds of screaming people in the courtyard who were scrambling to escape the maddened bulls. One of the bulls had charged into the front of the building, smashing the stone entrance. Another was tearing into the body of a uniformed guard on the ground. The red truck was in the courtyard, its motor running. In the confusion, the three men went almost unnoticed. Those who did see them were too busy saving themselves to do anything about them.

Without a word, Jaime and his men jumped into the back of the truck and it sped off, scattering frantic pedestrians through the crowded streets. The *guardia civil*, the paramilitary rural police decked out in green uniforms and black patent leather hats, were trying in vain to control the hysterical mob. The *policia armada*, stationed in provincial capitals, were also helpless in the face of the mad spectacle. People were struggling to flee in every direction, desperately trying to avoid the enraged bulls. The danger lay less with the bulls and more with the people themselves as they trampled one another in their eagerness to escape, and old men and women were pushed aside under the feet of the running mob.

Jaime stared in dismay at the stunning spectacle. 'It wasn't planned for it to happen this way!' he exclaimed. He stared helplessly at the carnage that was being wreaked, but there was nothing he could do to stop it. He closed his eyes to shut out the sight.

The truck reached the outskirts of Pamplona and headed south, leaving behind the noise and confusion of the rioting.

'Where are we going, Jaime?' Ricardo Mellado asked.

'There's a safe house outside Torré. We'll stay there until dark and then move on.'

Felix Carpio was wincing with pain.

18

Jaime Miró watched him, his face filled with compassion. 'We'll be there soon, my friend,' he said gently.

He was unable to get the terrible scene at Pamplona out of his mind.

Thirty minutes later they approached the little village of Torré, and skirted it to drive to an isolated house in the mountains above the village. Jaime Miró helped the two men out of the back of the red truck.

'You'll be picked up at midnight, the driver said.

'Have them bring a doctor,' Jaime replied. 'And get rid of the truck.'

The three of them entered the house. It was a farmhouse, simple and comfortable, with a fireplace in the living room and a beamed ceiling. There was a note on the table. Jaime Miró read it and smiled at the welcoming phrase: *Mi casa es su casa*. On the bar were bottles of wine. Jaime Miró poured drinks.

Ricardo Mellado said, 'There are no words to thank you, my friend. Here's to you.'

Jaime raised his glass. 'Here's to freedom.'

There was the sudden chirp of a canary in a cage. Jaime Miró walked over to it, and he watched its wild fluttering for a moment. Then he opened the cage, gently lifted the bird out and carried it to an open window.

'Fly away, *pájarito*,' he said softly. 'All living creatures should be free.'

Chapter 2

Madrid

Prime Minister Leopoldo Martinez was in a rage. He was a small, bespectacled man, and his whole body shook as he talked. 'Jaime Miró must be stopped,' he cried. His voice was high and shrill. 'Do you understand me?' He glared at the half dozen men gathered in the room. 'We're looking for one terrorist, and the whole army and police force are unable to find him.'

The meeting was taking place at Moncloa Palace, where the Prime Minister lived and worked, five kilometres from the centre of Madrid, on the Carretera de Galicia, a highway with no identifying signs. The building itself was green brick, with wrought iron balconies, green window shades, and guard towers at each corner.

It was a hot, dry day, and through the windows, as far as the eye could see, columns of heat waves rose like battalions of ghostly soldiers.

'Yesterday Miró turned Pamplona into a battleground.' Martinez slammed a fist down on his desk. 'He murdered two prison guards and smuggled two of his terrorists out of prison. Many innocent people were killed by the bulls he let loose.'

For a moment no one said anything.

When the Prime Minister had taken office, he had declared, smugly, 'My first act will be to put a stop to these separatist groups. Madrid is the great unifier. It transforms Andalusians, Basques, Catalans and Galicians into Spaniards.'

20

He had been unduly optimistic. The fiercely independent Basques had other ideas, and the wave of bombings, bank robberies and demonstrations by terrorists of the ETA organization, Euzkadi ta Azkatasuna, had continued unabated.

The man at Martinez's right said quietly, 'I'll find him.'

The speaker was Colonel Ramón Acoca, head of the GOE, the *Grupo de Operaciones Especiales*, formed to pursue Basque terrorists. Acoca was a giant, in his middle sixties, with a scarred face and cold, obsidian eyes. He had been a young officer under Francisco Franco during the Civil War, and he was still fanatically devoted to Franco's philosophy, 'We are responsible only to God and to history.'

Acoca was a brilliant officer, and he had been one of Franco's must trusted aides. The Colonel missed the iron-fisted discipline, the swift punishment of those who questioned or disobeyed the law. He had gone through the turmoil of the Civil War, with its Nationalist alliance of Monarchists, rebel generals, landowners, church hierarchy and the fascist Falangists on one side, and the Republican government forces, including Socialists, Communists, liberals and Basque and Catalan separatists on the other. It had been a terrible time of destruction and killing in a madness that pulled in men and war matériel from a dozen countries and left a horrifying death toll. And now the Basques were fighting and killing again.

Colonel Acoca headed an efficient, ruthless cadre of anti-terrorists. His men worked underground, wore disguises and were neither publicized nor photographed for fear of retaliation.

If anyone can stop Jaime Miró, Colonel Acoca can, the Prime Minister thought. But there was a catch: *Who's going to be the one to stop Colonel Acoca?*

Putting the Colonel in charge had not been the Prime Minister's idea. He had received a phone call in the middle of the night on his private line. He recognized the voice immediately.

21

'We are greatly disturbed by the activities of Jaime Miró and his terrorists. We suggest that you put Colonel Ramón Acoca in charge of the GOE. Is that clear?'

'Yes, sir. It will be taken care of immediately.'

The line went dead.

The voice belonged to a member of the OPUS MUNDO. The organization was a secret cabal that included bankers, lawyers, heads of powerful corporations and government ministers. It was rumoured to have enormous funds at its disposal, but where the money came from or how it was used or manipulated was a mystery. It was not considered healthy to ask too many questions about it.

The Prime Minister had placed Colonel Acoca in charge, as he had been instructed to, but the giant had turned out to be an uncontrollable fanatic. His GOE had created a reign of terror. The Prime Minister thought of the Basque rebels Acoca's men had caught near Pamplona. They had been convicted and sentenced to hang. It was Colonel Acoca who had insisted that they be executed by the barbaric garrotte Vil, the iron collar fitted with a spike which gradually tightened, eventually cracked the vertebra and severed the victim's spinal cord.

Jaime Miró had become an obsession with Colonel Acoca.

'I want his head,' Colonel Acoca said. 'Cut off his head and the Basque movement dies.'

An exaggeration, the Prime Minister felt, although he had to admit that there was a core of truth in it. Jaime Miró was a charismatic leader, fanatical about his cause, and therefore dangerous.

But in his own way, the Prime Minister thought, *Colonel Acoca is just as dangerous.*

Primo Casado, the Director General de Seguridad, was speaking. 'Your Excellency, no one could have foreseen what happened in Pamplona. Jaime Miró is –'

'I *know* what he is,' the Prime Minister snapped. 'I want to know *where* he is.' He turned to Colonel Acoca.

'I'm on his trail,' the Colonel said. His voice chilled the

22

room. 'I would like to remind Your Excellency that we are not fighting just one man. We are fighting the Basque people. They give Jaime Miró and his terrorists food and weapons and shelter. The man is a hero to them. But do not worry. Soon he will be a hanging hero. After I give him a fair trial, of course.'

Not we. I. The Prime Minister wondered whether the others had noticed. *Yes*, he thought nervously. *Something will have to be done about the Colonel soon.*

The Prime Minister got to his feet. 'That will be all for now, gentlemen.'

The men rose to leave. All except Colonel Acoca. He stayed.

Leopoldo Martinez began to pace. 'Damn the Basques. Why can't they be satisfied just to be Spaniards? What more do they want?'

'They're greedy for power,' Acoca said. 'They want autonomy, their own language and their flag –'

'No. Not as long as I hold this office. I'm not going to permit them to tear pieces out of Spain. The government will tell them what they can have and what they can't have. They're nothing but rabble who . . .'

An aide came into the room. 'Excuse me, Your Excellency,' he said apologetically. 'Bishop Ibanez has arrived.'

'Send him in.'

The Colonel's eyes narrowed. 'You can be sure the church is behind all this. It's time we taught them a lesson.'

The Church is one of the great ironies of our history, Colonel Acoca thought bitterly.

In the beginning of the Civil War, the Catholic Church had been on the side of the Nationalist forces. The Pope backed Generalissimo Franco, and in so doing allowed him to proclaim that he was fighting on the side of God. But when the Basque churches and monasteries and priests were attacked, the Church withdrew its support.

'You must give the Basques and the Catalans more freedom,' the Church had demanded. 'And you must stop executing Basque priests.'

23

Generalissimo Franco had been furious. How dare the Church try to dictate to the government?

A war of attrition began. More churches and monasteries were attacked by Franco's forces. Nuns and priests were murdered. Bishops were placed under house arrest, and priests all over Spain were fined for giving sermons that the government considered seditious. It was only when the Church threatened Franco with excommunication that he stopped his attacks.

The goddamned Church! Acoca thought. With Franco dead it was interfering again.

He turned to the Prime Minister. 'It's time the bishop is told who's running Spain.'

Bishop Calvo Ibanez was a thin, frail-looking man with a cloud of white hair swirling around his head. He peered at the two men through his pince-nez spectacles.

'*Buenos tardes.*'

Colonel Acoca felt the bile rise in his throat. The very sight of clergymen made him ill. They were Judas goats leading their stupid lambs to slaughter.

The bishop stood there, waiting for an invitation to sit down. It did not come. Nor was he introduced to the Colonel. It was a deliberate slight.

The Prime Minister looked to Acoca for direction.

Acoca said curtly, 'Some disturbing news has been brought to our attention. Basque rebels are reported to be holding meetings in Catholic monasteries. It has also been reported that the Church is allowing monasteries and convents to store arms for the rebels.' There was steel in his voice. 'When you help the enemies of Spain, you *become* an enemy of Spain.'

Bishop Ibanez stared at him for a moment, then turned to Leopoldo Martinez. 'Your Excellency, with due respect, we are all children of Spain. The Basques are not your enemy. All they ask is the freedom to –'

'They don't ask,' Acoca roared. 'They demand! They go around the country pillaging, robbing banks and killing policemen, and you dare to say they are not our enemies?'

24

'I admit that there have been inexcusable excesses. But sometimes in fighting for what one believes –'

'They don't believe in anything but themselves. They care nothing about Spain. It is as one of our great writers said, "No one in Spain is concerned about the common good. Each group is concerned only with itself. The Church, the Basques, the Catalans. Each one says fuck the others."'

The bishop was aware that Colonel Acoca had misquoted Ortega y Gasset. The full quote had included the army and the government; but he wisely said nothing. He turned to the Prime Minister again, hoping for a more rational discussion.

'Your Excellency, the Catholic Church –'

The Prime Minister felt that Acoca had pushed far enough. 'Don't misunderstand us, Bishop. In principle, of course, this government is behind the Catholic Church one hundred per cent.'

Colonel Acoca spoke up again. 'But we cannot permit your churches and monasteries and convents to be used against us. If you continue to allow the Basques to store arms in them and to hold meetings, you will have to take the consequences.'

'I am sure that the reports that you have received are erroneous,' the bishop said smoothly. 'However, I shall certainly investigate at once.'

The Prime Minister murmured, 'Thank you, Bishop. That will be all.'

Prime Minister Martinez and Colonel Acoca watched him depart.

'What do you think?' Martinez asked.

'He knows what's going on.'

The Prime Minister sighed. *I have enough problems right now without stirring up trouble with the Church.*

'If the Church is for the Basques, then it is against us.' Colonel Acoca's voice hardened. 'I would like your permission to teach the bishop a lesson.'

The Prime Minister was stopped by the look of fanaticism

in the man's eyes. He became cautious. 'Have you really had reports that the churches are aiding the rebels?'

'Of course, Excellency.'

There was no way of determining if the man was telling the truth. The Prime Minister knew how much Acoca hated the Church. But it might be good to let the Church have a taste of the whip, providing Colonel Acoca did not go too far. Prime Minister Martinez stood there thoughtfully.

It was Acoca who broke the silence. 'If the churches are sheltering terrorists, then the churches must be punished.'

Reluctantly, the Prime Minister nodded. 'Where will you start?'

'Jaime Miró and his men were seen in Ávila yesterday. They are probably hiding at the convent there.'

The Prime Minister made up his mind. 'Search it,' he said.

That decision set off a chain of events that was to rock all of Spain and shock the world.

Chapter 3

Ávila

The silence was like a gentle snowfall, soft and hushed, as soothing as the whisper of a summer wind, as quiet as the passage of stars. The Cistercian Convent of the Strict Observance lay outside the walled town of Ávila, the highest city in Spain, 112 kilometres north-west of Madrid. The convent had been built for silence. The rules had been adopted in 1601 and remained unchanged through the centuries: liturgy, spiritual exercise, strict enclosure, penance and silence. Always the silence.

The convent was a simple, four-sided group of rough stone buildings around a cloister dominated by the church. Around the central court the open arches allowed the light to pour in on the broad flagstones of the floor where the nuns glided noiselessly by. There were forty nuns at the convent, praying in the church and living in the cloister. The convent at Ávila was one of seven left in Spain, a survivor out of hundreds that had been destroyed by the Civil War in one of the periodic anti-Church movements that took place in Spain over the centuries.

The Cistercian Convent of the Strict Observance was devoted solely to a life of prayer. It was a place without seasons or time and those who entered were forever removed from the outside world. The Cistercian life was contemplative and penitential: the divine office was recited daily and enclosure was complete and permanent.

All the sisters dressed identically, and their clothing, like everything else in the convent, was touched by the symbolism of centuries. The *capuche*, the cloak and hood, symbolized innocence and simplicity, the linen tunic the renouncement of the works of the world, and mortification, the scapular, the small squares of woollen cloth worn over the shoulders, the willingness to labour. A wimple, a covering of linen laid in plaits over the head and around the chin, sides of the face and neck, completed the habit.

Inside the walls of the convent was a system of internal passageways and staircases linking the dining room, community room, the cells and the chapel, and everywhere there was an atmosphere of cold, clean spaciousness. Thick-paned latticed windows overlooked a high-walled garden. Every window was covered with iron bars and was above the line of vision, so that there would be no outside distractions. The refectory, the dining hall, was long and austere, its windows shuttered and curtained. The candles in the ancient candle-sticks cast evocative shadows on the ceilings and walls.

In four hundred years nothing inside the walls of the convent had changed, except the faces. The sisters had no personal possessions, for they desired to be poor, emulating the poverty of Christ. The church itself was bare of ornaments, save for a priceless solid gold cross that had been a long-ago gift from a wealthy postulant. Because it was so out of keeping with the austerity of the order, it was kept hidden away in a cabinet in the refectory. A plain, wooden cross hung at the altar of the church.

The women who shared their lives with the Lord lived together, worked together, ate together and prayed together, yet they never touched and never spoke. The only exception permitted was when they heard mass or when the Reverend Mother Prioress Betina addressed them in the privacy of her office. Even then, an ancient sign language was used as much as possible.

The Reverend Mother was a religeuse in her seventies, a bright-faced robin of a woman, cheerful and energetic, who gloried in the peace and joy of convent life, and of a life devoted to God. Fiercely protective of her nuns, she felt more pain when it was necessary to enforce discipline, than did the one being punished.

The nuns walked through the cloisters and corridors with downcast eyes, hands folded in their sleeves at breast level, passing and re-passing their sisters without a word or sign of recognition. The only voice of the convent was its bells – the bells that Victor Hugo called 'the Opera of the Steeples'.

The sisters came from disparate backgrounds and from many different countries. Their families were aristocrats, farmers, soldiers . . . They had come to the convent as rich and poor, educated and ignorant, miserable and exalted, but now they were one in the eyes of God, united in their desire for eternal marriage to Jesus.

The living conditions in the convent were spartan. In winter the cold was knifing, and a chill, pale light filtered in through leaded windows. The nuns slept fully dressed on pallets of straw, covered with rough woollen sheets, each in her tiny cell, furnished only with a straight-backed wooden chair. There was no washstand. A small earthenware jug and basin stood in a corner on the floor. No nun was ever permitted to enter the cell of another, except for the Reverend Mother Betina. There was no recreation of any kind, only work and prayers. There were work areas for knitting, book binding, weaving and making bread. There were eight hours of prayer each day: Matins, Lauds, Prime, Terce, Sext, None, Vespers and Compline. Besides these there were other devotions: benedictions, hymns and litanies.

Matins were said when half the world was asleep and the other half was absorbed in sin.

Lauds, the office of daybreak, followed Matins, and the

29

rising sun was hailed as the figure of Christ triumphant and glorified.

Prime was the church's morning prayer, asking for the blessings on the work of the day.

Terce was at nine o'clock in the morning, consecrated by St Augustine to the Holy Spirit.

Sext was at 11.30 a.m., evoked to quench the heat of human passions.

None was silently recited at three in the afternoon, the hour of Christ's death.

Vespers was the evening service of the church, as Lauds was her daybreak prayer.

Compline was the completion of the Little Hours of the day. A form of night prayers, a preparation for death as well as sleep, ending the day on a note of loving submission: *Manus tuas, domine, commendo spiritum meum. Redemisti nos, domine, deus, veritatis.*

In some of the other orders, flagellation had been stopped, but in the cloistered Cistercian convents and monasteries it survived. At least once a week, and sometimes every day, the nuns punished their bodies with the Discipline, a twelve-inch long whip of thin waxed cord with six knotted tails that brought agonizing pain, and was used to lash the back, legs and buttocks. Bernard of Clairvaux, the ascetic abbot of the Cistercians, had admonished: 'The body of Christ is crushed . . . our bodies must be conformed to the likeness of our Lord's wounded body.'

It was a life more austere than in any prison, yet the inmates lived in an ecstasy such as they had never known in the outside world. They had renounced physical love, possessions and freedom of choice, but in giving up those things they had also renounced greed and competition, hatred and envy, and all the pressures and temptations that the outside world imposed. Inside the convent reigned an all-pervading peace and the ineffable sense of joy at being one with God. There was an indescribable serenity within the walls of the convent and in the hearts of those who lived there. If the convent was a prison, it was a prison in God's

Eden, with the knowledge of a happy eternity for those who had freely chosen to be there and to remain there.

Sister Lucia was awakened by the tolling of the convent bell. She opened her eyes, startled and disoriented for an instant. The little cell she slept in was dismally black. The sound of the bell told her that it was 3.00 a.m., when the office of vigils began, while the world was still in darkness.

Shit! This routine is going to kill me, Sister Lucia thought.

She lay back on her tiny, uncomfortable cot, desperate for a cigarette. Reluctantly, she dragged herself out of bed. The heavy habit she wore and slept in rubbed against her sensitive skin like sandpaper. She thought of all the beautiful designer gowns hanging in her apartment in Rome and at her chalet in Gstaad. The Valentinos and Armanis and Giannis.

From outside her cell Sister Lucia could hear the soft, swishing movement of the nuns as they gathered in the passage. Carelessly, she made up her bed and stepped out into the long corridor, where the nuns were lining up, eyes downcast. Slowly, they all began to move towards the chapel.

They look like a bunch of penguins, Sister Lucia thought. It was beyond her comprehension why these women had deliberately thrown away their lives, giving up sex, pretty clothes and gourmet food. *Without those things, what reason is there to go on living? And the goddamned rules!*

When Sister Lucia had first entered the convent, the Reverend Mother had said to her, 'You must walk with your head bowed. Keep your hands folded under your habit. Take short steps. Walk slowly. You must never make eye contact with any of the other sisters, or even glance at them. You may not speak. Your ears are to hear only God's words.'

'Yes, Reverend Mother.'

For the next month Lucia took instruction.

'Those who come here come not to join others, but to dwell alone with God, *solam*. Solitude of spirit is essential to a union with God. It is safeguarded by the rules of silence.'

'Yes, Reverend Mother.'

31

'You must always obey the silence of the eyes. Looking into the eyes of others would distract you with useless images.'

'Yes, Reverend Mother.'

'The first lesson you will learn here will be to rectify the past, to purge out old habits and worldly inclinations, to blot out every image of the past. You will do purifying penance and mortification to strip yourself of self-will and self-love. It is not enough for us to be sorry for our past offences. Once we discover the infinite beauty and holiness of God, we want to make up not only for our own sins, but for every sin that has ever been committed.

'Yes, Reverend Mother.'

'You must struggle with sensuality, what John of the Cross called, "the night of the senses".'

'Yes, Reverend Mother.'

'Each nun lives in silence and in solitude, as though she were already in heaven. In this pure, precious silence for which she hungers, she is able to listen to the infinite silence and possess God.'

At the end of the first month, Lucia took her initial vows. On the day of the ceremony she had her hair shorn. It was a traumatic experience. The Reverend Mother Prioress performed the act herself. She summoned Lucia into her office and motioned for her to sit down. She stepped behind her, and before Lucia knew what was happening, she heard the snip of scissors and felt something tugging at her hair. She started to protest, but she suddenly realized that what was happening could only improve her disguise. *I can always let it grow back later*, Lucia thought. *Meanwhile, I'm going to look like a plucked chicken.*

When Lucia returned to the grim cubicle she had been assigned, she thought: *This place is a snake pit.* The floor consisted of bare boards. The pallet and the hard-backed chair took up most of the room. She was desperate to get hold of a newspaper. *Fat chance*, she thought. In this place they had never heard of newspapers, let alone radio or television. There were no links to the outside world at all.

But what got on Lucia's nerves most of all was the unnatural silence. The only communication was through hand signals, and learning those drove her crazy. When she needed a broom, she was taught to move her outstretched right hand from right to left, as though sweeping. When the Reverend Mother was displeased, she brought together the tips of her little fingers three times in front of her body, the other fingers pressing into her palm. When Lucia was slow in doing her work, the Reverend Mother pressed the palm of her right hand against her left shoulder. To reprimand Lucia, she scratched her own cheek near her right ear with all the fingers of her right hand in a downward motion.

For Christ's sake, Lucia thought, *it looks like she's scratching a flea bite.*

They had reached the chapel. The nuns said a silent mass, the sequence from the age-old Sanctus to the Pater Noster, but Sister Lucia's thoughts were on more important things than God.

In another month or two, when the police stop looking for me, I'll be out of this madhouse.

After morning prayers, Sister Lucia marched with the others to the dining room, surreptitiously breaking the rule, as she did every day, by studying their faces. It was her only entertainment. It was incredible to think that none of them knew what the other sisters looked like.

She was fascinated by the faces of the nuns. Some were old, some were young, some pretty, some ugly. She could not understand why they all seemed so happy. There were three faces that Lucia found particularly interesting. One was Sister Teresa, a woman who appeared to be in her sixties. She was far from beautiful, and yet there was a spirituality about her that gave her an almost unearthly loveliness. She seemed always to be smiling inwardly, as though she carried some wonderful secret within herself.

Another nun that Lucia found fascinating was Sister Graciela. She was a stunningly beautiful woman in her early thirties. She had olive skin, exquisite features, and eyes that were luminous black pools.

She could have been a film star, Lucia thought. *What's her story? Why would she bury herself in a place like this?*

The third nun who captured Lucia's interest was Sister Megan. Blue-eyed, blonde eyebrows and lashes. She was in her late twenties and had a fresh, open faced look.

What is she doing here? What are any of these women doing here? They're locked up behind these walls, given a tiny cell to sleep in, rotten food, eight hours of prayers, hard work and too little sleep. They must be pazzo – all of them.

She was better off than they were, because they were stuck here for the rest of their lives, while she would be out of here in a month or two. *Maybe three*, Lucia thought. *This is a perfect hiding place. I'd be a fool to rush away. In a few months, the police will decide that I'm dead. When I leave here and get my money out of Switzerland, maybe I'll write a book about this crazy place.*

A few days earlier Sister Lucia had been sent by the Reverend Mother to the office to retrieve a paper and while there she had taken the opportunity to start looking through the files. Unfortunately she had been caught in the act of snooping.

'You will do penance by using the Discipline,' the Mother Prioress Betina signalled her.

Sister Lucia bowed her head meekly and signalled, 'Yes, Reverend Mother.'

Lucia returned to her cell, and minutes later the nuns walking through the corridor heard the awful sound of the whip as it whistled through the air and fell again and again.

34

What they could not know was that Sister Lucia was whipping the bed.

These freaks may be into S & M, but not yours truly.

Now they were seated in the refectory, forty nuns at two long tables. The Cistercian diet was strictly vegetarian. Because the body craved meat, it was forbidden. Long before dawn, a cup of tea or coffee and a few ounces of dry bread were served. The principal meal was taken at 11.00 a.m., and consisted of a thin soup, a few vegetables and occasionally a piece of fruit.

We are not here to please our bodies, but to please God.

I wouldn't feed this breakfast to my cat, Sister Lucia thought. *I've been here two months, and I'll bet I've lost ten pounds. It's God's version of a health farm.*

When breakfast was ended, two nuns brought washing-up bowls to each end of the table and set them down. The sisters seated about the table sent their plates to the sister who had the bowl. She washed each plate, dried it on a towel and returned it to its owner. The water got darker and greasier.

And they're going to live like this for the rest of their lives, Sister Lucia thought disgustedly. *Oh, well. I can't complain. At least it's better than a life sentence in prison . . .*

She would have given her immortal soul for a cigarette.

Five hundred yards down the road, Colonel Ramón Acoca and two dozen carefully selected men from the GOE, the *Grupo de Operaciones Especiales*, were preparing to attack the convent.

Chapter Four

Colonel Ramón Acoca had the instincts of a hunter. He loved the chase, but it was the kill that gave him a deep visceral satisfaction. He had once confided to a friend, 'I have an orgasm when I kill. It doesn't matter whether it's a deer or a rabbit or a man – there's something about taking a life that makes you feel like God.'

Acoca had been in military intelligence, and he had quickly achieved a reputation for being brilliant. He was fearless, ruthless and intelligent, and the combination brought him to the attention of one of General Franco's aides.

Acoca had joined Franco's staff as a lieutenant, and in less than three years he had risen to the rank of colonel, an almost unheard-of feat. He was put in charge of the Falangists, the special group used to terrorize those who opposed Franco.

It was during the war that Acoca had been sent for by a member of the OPUS MUNDO.

'I want you to understand that we're speaking to you with the permission of General Franco.'

'Yes, sir.'

'We've been watching you, Colonel. We are pleased with what we see.'

'Thank you, sir.'

'From time to time we have certain assignments that are – shall we say – very confidential. And very dangerous.'

'I understand, sir.'

'We have many enemies. People who don't understand the importance of the work we're doing.'

'Yes, sir.'

'Sometimes they interfere with us. We can't permit that to happen.'

'No, sir.'

'I believe we could use a man like you, Colonel. I think we understand each other.'

'Yes, sir. I'd be honoured to be of service.'

'We would like you to remain in the army. That will be valuable to us. But from time to time, we will have you assigned to these special projects.'

'Thank you, sir.'

'You are never to speak of this.'

'No, sir.'

The man behind the desk had made Acoca nervous. There was something overpoweringly frightening about him.

In time, Colonel Acoca was called upon to handle half a dozen assignments for the OPUS MUNDO. As he had been told, they were all dangerous. And very confidential.

On one of the missions Acoca had met a lovely young girl from a fine family. Up to then, all of his women had been whores or camp followers, and Acoca had treated them with savage contempt. Some of the women had genuinely fallen in love with him, attracted by his strength. He reserved the worst treatment for them.

But Susana Cerredilla belonged to a different world. Her father was a professor at Madrid University, and Susana's mother was a lawyer. Susana was seventeen years old, and she had the body of a woman and the angelic face of a Madonna. Ramón Acoca had never met anyone like this woman-child. Her gentle vulnerability brought out in him a tenderness he had not known he was capable of. He fell madly in love with her, and for reasons which neither her parents nor Acoca understood, she fell in love with him.

On their honeymoon, it was as though Acoca had never known another woman. He had known lust, but the combination of love and passion was something he had never previously experienced.

Three months after they were married, Susana informed him that she was pregnant. Acoca was wildly excited. To add to their joy, he was assigned to the beautiful little village of Castilbanca, in the Basque country. It was in the autumn of 1936 when the fighting between the Republicans and Nationalists was at its fiercest.

On a peaceful Sunday morning, Ramón Acoca and his bride were having coffee in the village plaza when the square suddenly filled with Basque demonstrators.

'I want you to go home,' Acoca said. 'There's going to be trouble.'

'But you –?'

'Please. I'll be all right.'

The demonstrators were beginning to get out of hand.

With relief, Ramón Acoca watched his bride walk away from the crowd towards a convent at the far end of the square. And as she reached it, the door to the convent suddenly swung open and armed Basques who had been hiding inside, swarmed out with blazing guns. Acoca had watched helplessly as his wife went down in a hail of bullets, and it was on that day that he had sworn vengeance on the Basques. The Church had also been responsible.

And now he was in Ávila, outside another convent. *This time they'll die.*

Inside the convent, in the dark before dawn, Sister Teresa held the Discipline tightly in her right hand and whipped it hard across her body, feeling the knotted tails slashing into her as she silently recited the *Miserere*. She almost screamed aloud, but noise was not permitted, and she kept the screams inside her. *Forgive me, Jesus, for my sins. Bear witness that I punish myself, as you were punished, and I inflict wounds upon myself, as wounds were inflicted upon you. Let me suffer, as you suffered.*

She was near fainting from the pain. Three more times she flagellated herself and then sank, agonized, upon her cot. She had not drawn blood. That was forbidden. Wincing

38

against the agony that each movement brought, Sister Teresa returned the whip to its black case and rested it in a corner. It was always there, a constant reminder that the slightest sin had to be paid for with pain.

Sister Teresa's transgression had happened that morning as she was rounding the corner of a corridor, eyes down, and bumped into Sister Graciela. Startled, Sister Teresa had looked into Sister Graciela's face. Sister Teresa had immediately reported her infraction and the Reverend Mother Betina had frowned disapprovingly and made the sign of discipline, moving her right hand three times from shoulder to shoulder, her hand closed as though holding a whip, the tip of her thumb held against the inside of her forefinger.

Lying on her cot that night, Sister Teresa had been unable to get out of her mind the extraordinarily beautiful face of the young girl she had gazed at. Sister Teresa knew that as long as she lived she would never speak to her and would never even look at her again, for the slightest sign of intimacy between nuns was severely punished. In an atmosphere of rigid moral and physical austerity, no relationships of any kind were allowed to develop. If two sisters worked side by side and seemed to enjoy each other's silent company, the Reverend Mother would immediately have them separated. Nor were the sisters permitted to sit next to the same person at table twice in a row. The church delicately called the attraction of one nun to another 'a particular friendship', and the penalty was swift and severe. Sister Teresa had served her punishment for breaking the rule.

Now the tolling bell came to Sister Teresa as though from a great distance. It was the voice of God, reproving her.

In the next cell, the sound of the bell rang through the corridors of Sister Graciela's dreams, and the pealing of the bell was mingled with the lubricious creak of bedsprings. The Moor was moving towards her, naked, his manhood tumescent, his hands reaching out to grab her. Sister Graciela opened her eyes, instantly awake, her heart pounding frantically. She looked around, terrified, but she was alone in her tiny cell and the only sound was the reassuring tolling of the bell.

Sister Graciela knelt at the side of her cot. *Jesus, thank You for delivering me from the past. Thank You for the joy I have in being here in Your light. Let me glory only in the happiness of Your being. Help me, my Beloved, to be true to the call You have given me. Help me to ease the sorrow of Your sacred heart.*

Sister Graciela rose and carefully made her bed, then joined the procession of her sisters as they moved silently towards the chapel for Matins. She could smell the familiar scent of burning candles and feel the worn stones beneath her sandalled feet.

In the beginning when Sister Graciela had first entered the convent, she had not understood it when the Mother Prioress had told her that a nun was a woman who gave up everything in order to possess everything. Sister Graciela had been fourteen years old then. Now, seventeen years later, it was clear to her. In contemplation she possessed everything, for contemplation was the mind replying to the soul, the waters of Siloh that flowed in silence. Her days were filled with a wonderful peace.

Thank You for letting me forget the terrible past, Father. Thank You for standing beside me. I couldn't face my terrible past without you . . . Thank You . . . Thank You . . .

When Matins were over, the nuns returned to their cells to sleep until Lauds, the rising of the sun.

Outside, Colonel Ramon Acoca and his men moved swiftly in the darkness. When they reached the convent, Colonel Acoca said, 'Jaime Miró and his men will be armed. Take no chances.'

He looked at the front of the convent, and for an instant,

he saw that other convent with Basque partisans rushing out of it, and Susana going down in a hail of bullets.

'Don't bother taking Jaime Miró alive,' he said.

Sister Megan was awakened by the silence. It was a different silence, a moving silence, a hurried rush of air, a whisper of bodies. There were sounds she had never heard in her fifteen years in the convent. She was suddenly filled with a premonition that something was terribly wrong.

She rose quietly in the darkness and opened the door to her cell. Unbelievably, the long stone corridor was filled with men. A giant with a scarred face was coming out of the Reverend Mother's cell, pulling her by the arm. Megan stared in shock. *I'm having a nightmare*, Megan thought. *These men can't be here.*

'Where are you hiding him?' Colonel Acoca demanded.

The Reverend Mother Betina had a look of stunned horror on her face. 'Ssh! This is God's temple. You are desecrating it.' Her voice was trembling. 'You must leave at once.'

The Colonel's grip tightened on her arm and he shook her. 'I want Miró, Sister.'

The nightmare was real.

Other cell doors were beginning to open, and nuns were appearing, looks of total confusion on their faces. There had never been anything in their experience to prepare them for this extraordinary happening.

Colonel Acoca pushed Sister Betina away and turned to Patricio Arrieta, one of his lieutenants. 'Search the place. Top to bottom.'

Acoca's men began to spread out, invading the chapel, the refectory and the cells, waking those nuns who were still asleep, and forcing them roughly to their feet through the corridors and into the chapel. The nuns obeyed wordlessly, keeping even now their vows of silence. To Megan the scene was like a film with the sound turned off.

Acoca's men were filled with a sense of vengeance. They were all Falangists, and they remembered only too well how the Church had turned against them during the Civil War and supported the Loyalists against their beloved leader, Generalissimo Franco. This was their chance to get their own back. The nuns' strength and silence made the men more furious than ever.

As Acoca passed one of the cells, a scream echoed from it. Acoca looked in and saw one of his men ripping the habit from a nun. Acoca moved on.

Sister Lucia was awakened by the sounds of men's voices yelling. She sat up in a panic. *The police have found me*, was her first thought. *I've got to get out of here*. There was no way out of the convent except through the front door.

She hurriedly rose and peered out into the corridor. The sight that met her eyes was astonishing. The corridor was filled not with policemen, but with men in civilian clothes, carrying weapons, smashing lamps and tables. There was confusion everywhere as they raced around.

The Reverend Mother Betina was standing in the centre of the chaos, praying silently, watching them desecrate her beloved convent. Sister Megan moved to her side, and Lucia joined them.

'What the h – what's happening? Who are they?' Lucia asked. They were the first words she had spoken aloud since entering the convent.

The Reverend Mother put her right hand under her left armpit three times, the sign for *hide*.

Lucia stared at her unbelievingly. 'You can talk now. Let's get out of here, for Christ's sake. And I mean for Christ's sake.'

Patricio Arrieta, the Colonel's key aide, hurried up to Acoca. 'We've searched everywhere, Colonel. There's no sign of Jaime Miró or his men.'

'Search again,' Acoca said stubbornly.

It was then that the Reverend Mother remembered the one treasure that the convent had. She hurried over to Sister Teresa and whispered, 'I have a task for you. Remove the

gold cross from the chapel and take it to the convent at
Mendavia. You must get it away from here. Hurry!'

Sister Teresa was shaking so hard that her wimple fluttered
in waves. She stared at the Reverend Mother, paralyzed.
Sister Teresa had spent the last thirty years of her life in the
convent. The thought of leaving it was beyond imagining.
She raised her hand and signed, *I can't*.

The Reverend Mother was frantic. 'The cross must not
fall into the hands of these men of Satan. Now do this for
Jesus.'

A light came into Sister Teresa's eyes. She stood very tall.
She signed, *for Jesus*. She turned and hurried towards the
chapel.

Sister Graciela approached the group, staring in wonder
at the wild confusion around her.

The men were getting more and more violent, smashing everything in sight. Colonal Acoca watched them, approvingly.

Lucia turned to Megan and Graciela. 'I don't know about
you two, but I'm getting out of here. Are you coming?'

They stared at her, too dazed to respond.

Sister Teresa was hurrying towards them, carrying something wrapped in a piece of canvas. Some of the men were
herding more nuns into the refectory.

'Come on,' Lucia said.

Sisters Teresa, Megan and Graciela hesitated for a moment, then followed Lucia towards the front door. As they
turned at the end of the long corridor, they could see that
the huge door had been smashed in.

A man suddenly appeared in front of them. 'Going somewhere, ladies? Get back. My friends have plans for you.'

Lucia said, 'We have a gift for you.' She picked up one of
the heavy metal candlesticks that lined the hallway tables
and smiled.

The man was looking at it, puzzled. 'What can you do
with that?'

'This.' Lucia swung the candelabra against his head, and
he fell to the ground, unconscious.

The three nuns stared in horror.

'Move!' Lucia said.

A moment later Lucia, Megan, Graciela and Teresa were outside in the front courtyard, hurrying through the gate into the starry night.

Lucia stopped. 'I'm leaving you. They're going to be searching for you, so you'd better get away from here.'

She turned and started towards the mountains that rose in the distance, high above the convent. *I'll hide out up there until the search cools off and then I'll head for Switzerland. Of all the rotten luck. Those bastards blew a perfect cover.*

As Lucia made her way towards higher ground, she glanced down. From her vantage point she could see the three sisters. Incredibly, they were still standing in front of the convent gate, like three black-clad statues. *For God's sake*, she thought. *Get going before they catch you. Move!*

They could not move. It was as though all their senses had been paralyzed for so long that they were unable to take in what was happening to them. The nuns stared down at their feet. They were so dazed they could not think. They had been cloistered for so long behind the gates of God, secluded from the world, that now that they were outside the protective gates, they were filled with feelings of confusion and panic. They had no idea where to go or what to do. Inside, their lives had been organized for them. They had been fed, clothed, told what to do and when to do it. They had lived by the Rule. Suddenly there was no Rule. What did God want from them? What was His plan? They stood huddled together, afraid to speak, afraid to look at one another.

Hesitantly, Sister Teresa pointed to the lights of Ávila in the distance and signed, *that way*. Uncertainly, they began to move towards the town.

Watching them from the hills above, Lucia thought: *No, you idiots! That's the first place they'll look for you. Well, that's your problem. I have my own problems.* She stood there for a moment, watching them walk towards their doom, going to their slaughter. *Shit.*

Lucia scrambled down the hill, stumbling over the loose scree, and ran after them, her cumbersome habit slowing her down.

'Wait a minute,' she called. 'Stop!'

The sisters stopped and turned.

Lucia hurried up to them, out of breath. 'You're going the wrong way. The first place they'll search for you is in town. You've got to hide out somewhere.'

The three sisters stared at her in silence.

Lucia said impatiently, 'The mountains. Get up to the mountains. Follow me.'

She turned and started back towards the mountains. The others watched, and after a moment, they began to trail after her, one by one.

From time to time Lucia looked back to make sure they were following. *Why can't I mind my own business?* she thought. *They're not my responsibility. It's more dangerous if we're all together.* She kept climbing, making sure they stayed in sight.

The others were having a difficult time of it, and every time they slowed down, Lucia stopped to let them catch up with her. *I'll get rid of them in the morning.*

'Let's move faster,' Lucia called.

At the Abbey, the raid had come to an end. The dazed nuns, their habits wrinkled and bloodstained, were being rounded up and put into unmarked, closed trucks.

'Take them back to my headquarters in Madrid,' Colonel Acoca ordered. 'Keep them in isolation.'

'What charge –?'

'Harbouring terrorists.'

'Yes, Colonel,' Patricio Arrieta said. He hesitated. 'Four of the nuns are missing.'

Colonel Acoca's eyes turned cold. 'Find them.'

Colonel Acoca flew back to Madrid to report to the Prime Minister. 'Jaime Miró escaped before we reached the convent.'

45

Prime Minister Martinez nodded. 'Yes, I heard.' And he wondered whether Jaime Miró had ever been in the convent to begin with. There was no doubt about it. Colonel Acoca was getting dangerously out of control. There had been angry protests about the brutal attack on the convent. The Prime Minister chose his words carefully, 'The newspapers have been hounding me about what happened.'

'The newspapers are making a hero of this terrorist,' Acoca said, stone faced. 'We must not let them pressure us.'

'He's causing the government a great deal of embarrassment, Colonel. And those four nuns – if they talk –'

'Don't worry. They can't get far. I'll catch them and I'll find Miró.'

The Prime Minister had already decided that he could not afford to take any more chances. 'Colonel, I want you to be sure the thirty-six nuns you have are well-treated, and I'm ordering the army to join the search for Miró and the others. You'll work with Colonel Sostelo.'

There was a long, dangerous pause. 'Which one of us will be in charge of the operation?' Acoca's eyes were icy.

The Prime Minister swallowed. 'You will be, of course.'

Lucia and the three sisters travelled through the early dawn, moving north-east into the mountains, heading away from Ávila and the convent. The nuns, used to moving in silence, made little noise. The only sounds were the rustle of their robes, the clicking of their rosaries, an occasional snapping twig, and their gasps for breath as they climbed higher and higher.

They reached a plateau of the Guardarrama mountains and walked along a rutted road bordered by stone walls. They passed fields with sheep and goats. By sunrise they had covered several miles and found themselves in a wooded area outside the small village of Villacastin.

I'll leave them here, Lucia decided. *Their God can take care of them now. He certainly took great care of me*, she thought bitterly. *Switzerland is farther away than ever. I have no money and no passport, and I'm dressed like an undertaker. By now those men know we've escaped. They'll keep looking until they find us. The sooner I get away by myself, the better.*

But at that instant, something happened that made her change her plans.

Sister Teresa was moving through the trees when she stumbled and the package she had been so carefully guarding fell to the ground. It spilled out of its canvas wrapping and Lucia found herself staring at a large, exquisitely wrought gold cross glowing in the rays of the rising sun.

That's real gold, Lucia thought. *Someone up there is looking after me. That cross is manna. Sheer manna. It's my ticket to Switzerland.*

Lucia watched as Sister Teresa picked up the cross and carefully put it back in its wrapping. Lucia smiled to herself. It was going to be easy to take it. These nuns would do anything she told them.

The town of Ávila was in an uproar. News of the attack on the convent had spread quickly, and Father Berrendo was elected to confront Colonel Acoca. The priest was in his seventies, with an outward frailty that belied his inner strength. He was a warm and understanding shepherd to his parishioners. But at the moment he was filled with a cold fury.

Colonel Acoca kept him waiting for an hour, then allowed the priest to be shown into his office.

Father Berrendo said without preamble, 'You and your men attacked a convent without provocation. It was an act of madness.'

'We were simply doing our duty,' the Colonel said curtly. 'The Abbey was sheltering Jaime Miró and his band of murderers, so the sisters brought this on themselves. We're holding them for questioning.'

'Did you find Jaime Miró in the Abbey?' the priest demanded angrily.

Colonel Acoca said smoothly, 'No. He and his men escaped before we got there. But we'll find them, and justice will be done.'

My justice, Colonel Acoca thought savagely.

Chapter 5

The nuns travelled slowly. Their garb was ill-designed for the rugged terrain. Their sandals were too thin to protect their feet against the stony ground, and their habits caught on everything. Sister Teresa found she could not even say her rosary. She needed both hands to keep the branches from snapping in her face.

In the light of day, freedom seemed even more terrifying than before. God had cast the sisters out of Eden into a strange, frightening world, and His guidance that they had leaned on for so long was gone. They found themselves in an uncharted country with no map and no compass The walls that had protected them from harm for so long had vanished and they felt naked and exposed. Danger was everywhere, and they no longer had a place of refuge. They were aliens. The unaccustomed sights and sounds of the country were dazzling. There were insects and bird songs and hot, blue skies assaulting the senses. And there was something else that was disturbing.

When they first fled the convent, Teresa, Graciela and Megan had carefully avoided looking at one another, instinctively keeping to the rules. But now, each found herself avidly studying the faces of the others. Also, after all the years of silence, they found it difficult to speak, and when they did speak, their words were halting, as though they were learning a strange new skill. Their voices sounded strange in their ears. Only Lucia seemed uninhibited and sure of herself, and the others automatically turned to her for leadership.

'We might as well introduce ourselves,' Lucia said. 'I'm Sister Lucia.'

There was an awkward pause, and Graciela said shyly, 'I'm Sister Graciela.'

The dark-haired, arrestingly beautiful one.

'I'm Sister Megan.'

The young blonde with the striking blue eyes.

'I'm Sister Teresa.'

The eldest of the group. Fifty? Sixty?

As they lay in the woods resting outside of the village, Lucia thought: *They're like newborn birds fallen out of their nests. They won't last five minutes on their own. Well, too bad for them. I'll be on my way to Switzerland with the cross.*

Lucia walked to the edge of the clearing they were in and peered through the trees towards the little village below. A few people were walking along the street, but there was no sign of the men who had raided the convent. *Now*, Lucia thought. *Here's my chance.*

She turned to the others. 'I'm going down to the village to try to get us some food. You wait here.' She nodded towards Sister Teresa. 'You come with me.'

Sister Teresa was confused. For thirty years she had obeyed only the orders of Reverend Mother Betina and now suddenly this sister had taken charge. *But what is happening is God's will*, Sister Teresa thought. *He has appointed her to help us, so she speaks with His voice.* 'I must get this cross to the convent at Mendavia as soon as possible.'

'Right. When we get down there, we'll ask for directions.'

The two of them started down the hill towards the town, Lucia keeping a careful lookout for trouble. There was none.

This is going to be easy, Lucia thought.

They reached the outskirts of the little town. A sign said, 'Villacastin'. Ahead of them was the main street. To the left was a small, deserted street.

Good, Lucia thought. There would be no one to witness what was about to happen.

Lucia turned into the side street. 'Let's go this way. There's less chance of being seen.'

50

Sister Teresa nodded and obediently followed Lucia. The question now was how to get the cross away from her.

I could grab it and run, Lucia thought, *but she'd probably scream and attract a lot of attention. No, I'll have to make sure she stays quiet.*

The small limb of a tree had fallen to the ground in front of her, and Lucia paused, then stooped to pick it up. It was heavy. *Perfect.* She waited for Sister Teresa to catch up to her.

'Sister Teresa . . .'

The nun turned to look at her, and as Lucia started to raise the club, a male voice from out of nowhere said, 'God be with you, Sisters.'

Lucia spun around, ready to run. A man was standing there, dressed in the long brown robe and cowl of a friar. He was tall and thin, with an aquiline face and the saintliest expression Lucia had ever seen. His eyes seemed to glow with a warm inner light, and his voice was soft and gentle.

'I'm Friar Miguel Carrillo.'

Lucia's mind was racing. Her first plan had been interrupted. But now, suddenly, she had a better one. 'Thank God you found us,' Lucia said.

This man was going to be her escape. He would know the easiest way for her to get out of Spain.

'We come from the Cistercian convent near Ávila,' Lucia explained. 'Last night some men raided it. All the nuns were taken. Four of us managed to escape.'

When the friar replied, his voice was filled with anger. 'I come from the monastery at Saint Generro, where I have been for the past twenty years. We were attacked the night before last.' He sighed. 'I know that God has some plan for all His children, but I must confess that at this moment I don't understand what it might be.'

'These men are searching for us,' Lucia said. 'It is important that we get out of Spain as fast as possible. Do you know how that can be done?'

Friar Carrillo smiled gently. 'I think I can help you, Sister. God has brought us together. Take me to the others.'

51

Lucia brought the friar to the group.

'This is Friar Carrillo,' she said. 'He's been in a monastery for the last twenty years. He's come to help us.'

Their reactions to the friar were mixed. Graciela dared not look directly at him. Megan studied him with quick, interested glances, and Sister Teresa regarded him as a messenger sent by God, who would lead them to the convent at Mendavia.

Friar Carrillo said, 'The men who attacked the convent will undoubtedly keep searching for you. But they will be looking for four nuns. The first thing we must do is get you a change of clothing.'

Megan reminded him, 'We have no clothes to change into.'

Friar Carrillo gave her a beatific smile. 'Our Lord has a very large wardrobe. Do not worry, my child. He will provide. Let us go into town.'

It was two o'clock in the afternoon, siesta time, and Friar Carrillo and the four sisters walked down the main street of the village, alert for any signs of their pursuers. The shops were closed, but the restaurants and bars were open and from them they could hear strange music issuing, hard, dissonant and raucous sounding.

Friar Carrillo saw the look on Sister Teresa's face. 'That's rock and roll,' he said. 'Very popular with the young these days.'

A pair of young women standing in front of one of the bars stared at the nuns as they passed. The nuns stared back, wide-eyed, at the strange clothing the pair wore. One wore a skirt so short it barely covered her thighs, the other wore a longer skirt that was split up to the sides of her thighs. Both wore tight knitted bodices with no sleeves.

They might as well be naked, Sister Teresa thought, horrified.

In the doorway stood a man who wore a turtleneck sweater, a strange-looking jacket without a collar, and a jewelled pendant.

Unfamiliar odours greeted the nuns as they passed a bodega. Nicotine and whisky.

Megan was staring at something across the street. She stopped.

Friar Carrillo said, 'What is it? What's the matter?' He turned to look.

Megan was watching a woman carrying a baby. How many years had it been since she had seen a baby, or even a small child? Not since the orphanage, fourteen years ago. The sudden shock made Megan realize how far her life had been removed from the outside world.

Sister Teresa was staring at the baby, too, but she was thinking of something else. *It's Monique's baby.* The baby across the street was screaming. *It's screaming because I deserted it. But no, that's impossible. That was thirty years ago.* Sister Teresa turned away, the baby's cries ringing in her ears. They moved on.

They passed a cinema. The poster read, *Three Lovers*, and the photographs displayed showed skimpily-clad women embracing a bare-chested man.

'Why, they're – they're almost naked!' Sister Teresa exclaimed.

Friar Carrillo frowned. 'Yes. It's disgraceful what the cinema is permitted to show these days. That film is pure pornography. The most personal and private acts are there for everyone to see. They turn God's children into animals.'

They passed a hardware store, a hairdressing salon, a flower shop, a sweet shop, all closed for the siesta, and at each shop the sisters stopped and stared at the windows, filled with once familiar, faintly remembered goods.

When they came to a women's dress shop, Friar Carrillo said, 'Stop.'

The blinds were pulled down over the front windows and a sign on the front door said, 'Closed'.

'Wait here for me, please.'

The four women watched as he walked to the corner and turned out of sight. They looked at one another blankly. Where was he going, and what if he did not return?

A few minutes later, they heard the sound of the front

door of the shop opening, and Friar Carrillo stood in the doorway, beaming. He motioned them inside. 'Hurry.'

When they were all in the shop and the friar had locked the door, Lucia asked, 'How did you –?'

'God provides a back door as well as a front door,' the friar said gravely. But there was an impish edge to his voice that made Megan smile.

The sisters looked around the shop in awe. The store was a multi-coloured cornucopia of dresses and sweaters and bras and stockings, high-heeled shoes and boleros. Objects they had not seen in years. And the styles seemed so strange. There were handbags and scarves and compacts and blouses. It was all too much to absorb. The women stood there, gaping.

'We must move quickly,' Friar Carrillo warned them, 'and leave before siesta is over and the shop reopens. Help yourselves. Choose whatever fits you.'

Lucia thought: *Thank God I can finally dress like a woman again.* She walked over to a rack of dresses and began to sort through them. She found a beige skirt and tan silk blouse to go with it. *It's not Balenciaga, but it will do for now.* She picked out panties and a bra and a pair of soft boots. She stepped behind a clothes rack, stripped and in a matter of minutes was dressed and ready to go.

The others were slowly selecting their outfits.

Graciela chose a white cotton dress that set off her black hair and dark complexion, and a pair of sandals.

Megan chose a patterned blue cotton dress that fell below the knees and low-heeled shoes.

Sister Teresa had the most difficult time choosing something to wear. The array of choices was too dazzling. There were silks and flannels and tweeds and leather. There were cottons and twills and corduroys, and there were plaids and checks and stripes of every colour. And they all seemed – *skimpy,* was the word that came to Sister Teresa's mind. For the past thirty years she had been decently covered by the heavy robes of her calling. And now she was being asked to shed them and put on these indecent creations. She finally

54

selected the longest skirt she could find, and a long-sleeved, high-collared cotton blouse.

Friar Carrillo urged, 'Hurry, Sisters. Get undressed and change.'

They looked at one another in embarrassment.

He smiled. 'I'll wait in the office, of course.'

He walked to the back of the shop and entered the office.

The sisters began to undress, painfully self-conscious in front of one another.

In the office, Friar Carrillo had pulled a chair up to the transom and was looking out through it, watching the sisters strip. He was thinking: *Which one am I going to screw first?*

Miguel Carrillo had begun his career as a thief when he was only ten years old. He was born with curly blond hair and an angelic face, and they had proved to be of inestimable value in his chosen profession. He started at the bottom, snatching handbags and shoplifting, and as he got older, his career expanded and he began robbing drunks and preying on wealthy women. Because of his enormous appeal, he was very successful. He devised several original swindles, each more ingenious than the last. Unfortunately, his latest swindle had proved to be his undoing.

Posing as a friar from a distant monastery, Carrillo travelled from church to church begging sanctuary for the night. It was always granted, and in the morning when the priest came to open the church doors, all the valuable artefacts would be missing, along with the good friar. Unfortunately, fate had double-crossed him and two nights earlier in Benjar, a small town near Ávila, the priest had returned unexpectedly and Miguel Carrillo had been caught in the act of pilfering the church treasury. The priest was a beefy, heavy-set man, and he had wrestled Carrillo to the floor and announced that he was going to turn him over to the police. A heavy silver chalice had fallen to the floor, and Carrillo had picked it up and hit the priest with it. Either the chalice

55

was too heavy, or the priest's skull was too thin, but in any case the priest lay dead on the floor. Miguel Carrillo had fled, panicky, anxious to put himself as far away from the scene of the crime as possible. He had passed through Ávila and heard the story of the attack on the convent by Colonel Acoca and the secret GOE. It was fate that Carrillo had chanced upon the four escaped nuns.

Now, eager with anticipation, he studied their naked bodies, and thought: *There's another interesting possibility. Since Colonel Acoca and his men are looking for the sisters, there is probably a nice, fat reward on their heads. I'll lay them first, and then turn them over to Acoca.*

The women, except for Lucia, who was already dressed, were totally naked. Carrillo watched as they awkwardly put on the new underclothes. Then they finished dressing, clumsily buttoning unaccustomed buttons and fastening zips, hurrying to get away before they were caught.

Time to get to work, Carrillo thought happily. He got down from the chair and walked out into the shop. He approached the women, studied them approvingly, and said, 'Excellent. No one in the world would ever take you for nuns. I might suggest scarves for your heads.' He selected one for each of them and watched them put them on.

Miguel Carrillo had made his decision. Graciela was going to be the first. She was undoubtedly one of the most beautiful women he had ever seen. And that body! *How could she have wasted it on God? I'll show her what to do with it.*

He said to Lucia, Teresa and Megan, 'You must all be hungry. I want you to go to the café we passed and wait for us there. I'll go to the church and borrow some money from the priest so we can eat.' He turned to Graciela. 'I want you to come with me, Sister, to explain to the priest what happened at the convent.'

'I – very well.'

Carrillo said to the others, 'We'll be along in a little while. I would suggest you use the back door.'

He watched as Lucia, Teresa and Megan left. When he heard the door close behind them, he turned to Graciela.

She's fantastic, he thought. *Maybe I'll keep her with me, break her in to some cons. She could be a big help.*

Graciela was watching him. 'I'm ready.'

'Not yet.' Carrillo pretended to study her for a moment. 'No, I'm afraid it won't do. That dress is all wrong for you. Take it off.'

'But – why?'

'It doesn't fit properly,' Carrillo said glibly. 'People will notice, and you don't want to attract attention.'

She hesitated, then moved behind a rack.

'Hurry, now. We have very little time.'

Awkwardly, Graciela slipped the dress over her head. She was in her panties and brassiere when Carrillo suddenly appeared.

'Take everything off.' His voice was husky.

Graciela stared at him. 'What? No!' she cried. 'I – I can't. Please – I –'

Carrillo moved closer to her. 'I'll help you, Sister.'

His hands reached out and he ripped off her brassiere and tore at her panties.

'No!' she screamed. 'You mustn't! Stop it!'

Carrillo grinned. '*Carita*, we're just getting started. You're going to love this.'

His strong arms were around her. He forced her to the floor and lifted his robe.

It was as though a curtain in Graciela's mind suddenly descended. It was the Moor trying to thrust himself inside her, tearing into the depths of her, and her mother's shrill voice was screaming.

And Graciela thought, terrified, *No, not again. No, please – not again* . . .

She was struggling fiercely now, fighting Carrillo off, trying to get up.

'Goddamn you,' he cried.

He slammed his fist into her face, and Graciela fell back, stunned and dizzy.

She found herself spinning back in time.

Back . . . Back . . .

57

Chapter 6

Las Navas del Marqués, Spain 1950

She was five years old. Her earliest memories were of a procession of naked strangers climbing in and out of her mother's bed.

Her mother explained, 'They are your uncles. You must show them respect.'

The men were gross and crude and lacked affection. They stayed for a night, a week, a month, and then vanished. When they left, Dolores Pinero would immediately look for a new man.

In her youth, Dolores Pinero had been a beauty, and Graciela had inherited her mother's looks. Even as a child, Graciela was stunning to look at, with high cheekbones, an olive complexion, shiny black hair and thick, long eyelashes. Her young body was nubile with promise. With the passage of years, Dolores Pinero's body had turned to fat and her wonderfully boned face had become bruised with the bitter blows of time.

Although Dolores Pinero was no longer beautiful, she was accessible, and she had the reputation of being a passionate bed partner. Making love was her one talent, and she employed it to try to please men into bondage, hoping to keep them by buying their love with her body. She made a meagre living as a seamstress because she was an indifferent one, and was hired only by the women of the village who could not afford the better ones.

Graciela's mother despised her daughter, for she was a constant reminder of the one man whom Dolores. Pinero had ever loved. Graciela's father was a handsome young mechanic who had proposed to the beautiful young Dolores, and she had eagerly let him seduce her. When she had broken the news that she was pregnant, he had disappeared, leaving Dolores with the curse of his seed.

Dolores Pinero had a vicious temper, and she took her vengeance out on the child. Any time Graciela did something to displease her, her mother would hit her and scream, 'You're as stupid as your father!'

There was no way for the child to escape the rain of blows or the constant screaming. Graciela would wake up every morning and pray: 'Please, God, don't let Mama beat me today.

'Please, God, make Mama happy today.

'Please, God, let Mama say she loves me today.'

When she was not attacking Graciela, her mother ignored her. Graciela prepared her own meals and took care of her clothes. She made her lunch to take to school, and she would say to her teacher, 'My mother made me *empanadas* today. She knows how much I like *empanadas*.'

Or: 'I tore my dress, but my mother sewed it up for me. She loves doing things for me.'

Or: 'My mother and I are going to the pictures tomorrow.'

And it would break her teacher's heart. Las Navas del Marqués is a small village an hour from Ávila, and like all villages everywhere, everyone knew everyone else's business. The lifestyle of Dolores Pinero was a disgrace, and it reflected on Graciela. Mothers refused to let their children play with the little girl, lest their morals be contaminated. Graciela went to the school on Plazoleta del Cristo, but she had no friends and no playmates. She was one of the brightest students in the school, but her exam results were poor. It was difficult for her to concentrate, for she was always tired.

Her teacher would admonish her, 'You must get to bed

earlier, Graciela, so that you are rested enough to do your work properly.'

But her exhaustion had nothing to do with getting to bed late. Graciela and her mother shared a small, two-room *casa*. The girl slept on a couch in the tiny room, with only a thin, worn curtain separating it from the bedroom. How could Graciela tell her teacher about the obscene sounds in the night that awakened her and kept her awake, as she listened to her mother making love to whichever stranger happened to be in her bed?

When Graciela brought home her report card, her mother would scream, 'These are the cursed marks I expected you to get, and do you know why you got these terrible marks? Because you're stupid. Stupid!'

And Graciela would believe it and try hard not to cry.

In the afternoons when school was over, Graciela would wander around by herself, walking through the narrow, winding streets lined with acacia and sycamore trees, past the whitewashed stone houses, where loving fathers lived with their families. Graciela had many playmates, but they were all in her mind. There were beautiful girls and handsome boys, and they invited her to all their parties, where they served wonderful cakes and ice cream. Her imaginary friends were kind and loving, and they all thought she was very smart. When her mother was not around, Graciela would carry on long conversations with them.

Would you help me with my homework, Graciela? I don't know how to do sums, and you're so good at them.

What shall we do tonight, Graciela? We could go to the pictures, or walk into town and have a lemonade.

Will your mother let you come to dinner tonight, Graciela? We're having paella.

No, I'm afraid not. Mother gets lonely if I'm not with her. I'm all she has, you know.

On Sundays, Graciela rose early and dressed quietly, careful not to awaken her mother and whichever uncle was in her bed, and walked to the San Juan Bautista Church, where Father Perez talked of the joys of life after death, a fairytale life with Jesus; and Graciela could not wait to die and meet Jesus.

Father Perez was an attractive priest in his early forties. He had ministered to the rich and the poor, and the sick and the vital, since he had come to Las Navas del Marqués several years earlier, and there were no secrets in the little village to which he was not privy. Father Perez knew Graciela as a regular church-goer, and he, too, was aware of the stories of the constant stream of strangers who shared Dolores Pinero's bed. It was not a fit home for a young girl, but there was nothing anyone could do about it. It amazed the priest that Graciela had turned out as well as she had. She was kind and gentle and never complained or talked about her home life.

Graciela would appear at church every Sunday morning wearing a clean, neat outfit that he was sure she had washed herself. Father Perez knew she was shunned by the other children in town, and his heart went out to her. He made it a point to spend a few moments with her after mass each Sunday, and when he had time, he would take her to a little café for a treat of *helado*.

In the winter Graciela's life was a dreary landscape, monotonous and gloomy. Las Navas del Marqués was in a valley surrounded by the Cruz Verde mountains and, because of that, the winters were six months long. The summers were easier to bear, for then the tourists arrived and filled the town with laughter and dancing and the streets came alive. The tourists would gather at the Plaza de Manuel Delgado Barredo, with its little bandstand built on stone, and listen to the orchestra and watch the natives dance the Sardana, the centuries-old traditional folk dance, barefoot, their hands linked, as they moved gracefully around in a colourful circle. Graciela watched the visitors as they sat at the pavement cafés drinking *aperitivos* or shopping at the *pescaderia* – the

61

fish market, or the *farmacia*. At one o'clock in the afternoon the *bodega* was always filled with tourists drinking *chateo* and picking at *tapas*, seafood and olives and chips.

The most exciting thing for Graciela was to watch the *paseo* each evening. Boys and girls would walk up and down the Plaza Mayor in segregated groups, the boys eyeing the girls, while parents and grandparents and friends watched, hawk-eyed, from sidewalk cafés. It was the traditional mating ritual, observed for centuries. Graciela longed to join in it, but her mother forbade her.

'Do you want to be a *puta*?' she would scream at Graciela. 'Stay away from boys. They want only one thing from you. I know from experience,' she added bitterly.

If the days were bearable, the nights were an agony. Through the thin curtain that separated their beds, Graciela could hear the sounds of savage moaning and writhings and heavy breathing, and always the obscenities.

'Faster . . . harder!'

'*¡Cogeme!*'

'*¡Mamame la verga!*'

'*¡Metela en el culo!*'

Before she was ten years old. Graciela had heard every obscene word in the Spanish vocabulary. They were whispered and shouted and shuddered and moaned. The cries of passion repelled Graciela, and at the same time awakened strange longings in her.

When Graciela was fourteen years old, the Moor moved in. He was the biggest man Graciela had ever seen. His skin was shiny black, and his head was shaved. He had enormous shoulders, a barrel chest and huge arms. The Moor had arrived in the middle of the night when Graciela was asleep, and she got her first sight of him in the morning when he pushed the curtain aside and walked stark naked past Graciela's bed to go outside to the outhouse in the yard.

Graciela looked at him and almost gasped aloud. He was enormous, in every part. *That will kill my mother*, Graciela thought.

The Moor was staring at her. 'Well, well. And who do we have here?'

Dolores Pinero hurried out of her bed and moved to his side. 'My daughter,' she said curtly.

A wave of embarrassment swept over Graciela, as she saw her mother's naked body next to the man.

The Moor smiled, showing beautiful white, even teeth. 'What's your name, *guapa*?'

Graciela was too shamed by his nakedness to speak.

'Her name's Graciela. She's retarded.'

'She's beautiful. I'll bet you looked like that when you were young.'

'I'm still young,' Dolores Pinero snapped. She turned to her daughter. 'Get dressed. You'll be late for school.'

'Yes, Mama.'

The Moor stood there, eyeing her.

The older woman took his arm and said cajolingly, 'Come back to bed, *querida*. We're not finished yet.'

'Later,' the Moor said. He was still looking at Graciela.

The Moor stayed. Every day when Graciela came home from school she prayed that he would be gone. For reasons she did not understand, he terrified her. He was always polite to her and never made any advances, yet the mere thought of him sent shivers through her body.

His treatment of her mother was something different. The Moor stayed in the small house most of the day, drinking heavily. He took whatever money Dolores Pinero earned. Sometimes at night in the middle of lovemaking, Graciela would hear him beating her mother, and in the morning Dolores Pinero would appear with a blackened eye or split lip.

'Mama, why do you put up with him?' Graciela asked.

'You wouldn't understand,' she said sullenly. 'He's a real

63

man, not a midget like the others. He knows how to satisfy a woman.' She ran her hand through her hair coquettishly. 'Besides, he's madly in love with me.'

Graciela did not believe it. She knew that the Moor was using her mother, but she did not dare protest again. She was too terrified of her mother's temper, for when Dolores Pinero was really angry, a kind of insanity took possession of her. She had once chased Graciela with a kitchen knife because she had dared make a pot of tea for one of the 'uncles'.

Early one Sunday morning Graciela rose to get ready for church. Her mother had left early to deliver some dresses. As Graciela pulled off her nightgown, the curtain was pushed aside and the Moor appeared. He was naked.

'Where's your mother, *guapa*?'

'Mama went out early. She had some errands to do.'

The Moor was studying Graciela's nude body. 'You really are a beauty,' he said softly.

Graciela felt her face flush. She knew what she should do. She should cover her nakedness, put on her skirt and blouse and leave. Instead, she stood there, unable to move. She watched his manhood begin to swell and grow before her eyes. She could hear the voices ringing in her ears:

'Faster . . . Harder!'

She felt faint.

The Moor said huskily, 'You're a child. Get your clothes on and get out of here.'

And Graciela found herself moving. Moving towards him. She reached up and slid her arms around his waist and felt his male hardness against her body.

'No,' she moaned. 'I'm not a child.'

The pain that followed was like nothing Graciela had ever known. It was excruciating, unbearable. It was wonderful, exhilarating, beautiful. She held the Moor tightly in her arms, screaming with ecstasy. He brought her to orgasm after orgasm, and Graciela thought: *So this is what the mystery is all about*. And it was so wonderful to finally know the secret of all creation, to be a part of life at last, to know what joy was for now and for ever.

'*What the fuck are you doing?*'

It was Dolores Pinero's voice screaming, and for an instant everything stopped, frozen in time. Dolores Pinero was standing at the side of the bed, staring down at her daughter and the Moor.

Graciela looked up at her mother, too terrified to speak. Dolores Pinero's eyes were filled with an insane rage.

'You bitch!' she yelled. 'You rotten bitch.'

'Mama – please –'

Dolores Pinero picked up a heavy iron ashtray at the bedside and slammed it against her daughter's head.

That was the last thing Graciela remembered.

She awoke in a large, white hospital ward with two dozen beds in it, all of them occupied. Harried nurses scurried back and forth, trying to attend to the needs of the patients.

Graciela's head was racked with excruciating pain. Each time she moved, rivers of fire flowed through her. She lay there, listening to the cries and moans of the other patients.

Late in the afternoon, a young doctor stopped by the side of her bed. He was in his early thirties, but he looked old and tired.

'Well,' he said. 'You're finally awake.'

'Where am I?' It hurt her to speak.

'You're in the charity ward of the Hospital Provincial in Ávila. You were brought in yesterday. You were in terrible shape. We had to stitch up your forehead.' The doctor went on: 'Our chief surgeon decided to sew you up himself. He said you were too beautiful to have scars.'

He's wrong, Graciela thought. *I'll be scarred for the rest of my life.*

On the second day Father Perez came to see Graciela. A nurse moved a chair to the bedside. The priest looked at the beautiful, pale young girl lying there and his heart melted. The terrible thing that had happened to her was the scandal of Las Navas del Marqués, but there was nothing anyone could do about it. Dolores Pinero had told the *policia* that her daughter had injured her head in a fall.

Now, Father Perez asked, 'Are you feeling better, child?'

Graciela nodded, and the movement made her head pound.

'The *policia* have been asking questions. Is there anything you would like me to tell them?'

There was a long silence. Finally she said, 'It was an accident.'

He could not bear the look in her eyes. 'I see.'

What he had to say was painful beyond words. 'Graciela, I spoke with your mother . . .'

And Graciela knew. 'I – I can't go home again, can I?'

'No, I'm afraid not. We'll talk about it.' Father Perez took Graciela's hand. 'I'll come back to see you tomorrow.'

'Thank you, Father.'

When he left, Graciela lay there, and she prayed: *Dear God, please let me die. I don't want to live.*

She had nowhere to go and no one to go to. Never again would she see her home. She would never see her school again, or the familiar faces of her teachers. There was nothing in the world left for her.

A nurse stopped at her bedside. 'You need anything?'

Graciela looked up at her in despair. What was there to say?

The following day the doctor appeared again.

'I have good news,' he said awkwardly. 'You're well enough to leave now.' That was a lie, but the rest of his speech was true. 'We need the bed.'

She was free to go – but go where?

When Father Perez arrived an hour later, he was accompanied by another priest.

66

'This is Father Berrendo, an old friend of mine.'

Graciela glanced up at the frail-looking priest. 'Father.'

He was right, Father Berrendo thought. *She is beautiful*.

Father Perez had told him the story of what had happened to Graciela. The priest had expected to see some visible signs of the kind of environment the child had lived in, a hardness, a defiance, or self-pity. There were none of those things in the young girl's face.

'I'm sorry you've had such a bad time,' Father Berrendo told her. The sentence carried a deeper meaning.

Father Perez said, 'Graciela, I must return to Las Navas del Marqués. I am leaving you in Father Berrendo's hands.'

Graciela was filled with a sudden sense of panic. She felt as though her last link with home was being cut. 'Don't go,' she pleaded.

Father Perez took her hand in his. 'I know you feel alone,' he said warmly, 'but you're not. Believe me, child, you're not.'

A nurse approached the bed carrying a bundle. She handed it to Graciela. 'Here are your clothes. I'm afraid you're going to have to leave now.'

An even greater panic seized her. '*Now?*'

The two priests exchanged a look.

'Why don't you get dressed and come with me?' Father Berrendo suggested. 'We can talk.'

Fifteen minutes later Father Berrendo was helping Graciela out of the hospital door into the warm sunlight. There was a garden in front of the hospital with brightly coloured flowers, but Graciela was too dazed even to notice them.

When they were seated in his office, Father Berrendo said, 'Father Perez told me that you have no place to go.'

Graciela nodded.

'No relatives?'

'Only –' It was difficult to say it. 'Only – my mother.'

'Father Perez said that you were a regular churchgoer in your village.'

A village she would never see again. 'Yes.'

Graciela thought of those Sunday mornings, and the beauty of the church services and how she had longed to be with Jesus and escape from the pain of the life she lived.

'Graciela, have you ever thought of entering a convent?'

'No.' She was startled by the idea.

'There is a convent here in Ávila – the Cistercian convent. They would take care of you there.'

'I – I don't know.' The idea was frightening.

'It is not for everyone,' Father Berrendo told her. 'And I must warn you, it is the strictest order of them all. Once you walk through the gates and take the vows, you have made a promise to God never to leave.'

Graciela sat there, her mind filled with conflicting thoughts, staring out the window. The idea of shutting herself away from the world was terrifying. *It would be like going to prison.* But on the other hand, what did the world have to offer her? Pain and despair beyond bearing. She had often thought of suicide. This might offer a way out of her misery.

Father Berrendo said, 'It's up to you, my child. If you like, I will take you to meet the Reverend Mother Prioress.'

Graciela nodded. 'All right.'

The Reverend Mother studied the face of the young girl before her. Last night for the first time in many, many years she had heard the voice. *A young child will come to you. Protect her.* 'How old are you, my dear?'

'Fourteen.'

She's old enough. In the fourth century the Pope decreed that girls could be permitted to become nuns at the age of twelve.

'I'm afraid,' Graciela said to the Reverend Mother Betina.

I'm afraid. The words rang in Betina's mind: *I'm afraid* . . .

That had been so many long years ago. She was speaking

68

to her priest. 'I don't know if I have a calling for this, Father. I'm afraid.'

'Betina, the first contact with God can be very disturbing, and the decision to dedicate your life to Him is a difficult one.'

How did I find my calling? Betina had wondered.

She had never been even faintly interested in religion. As a young girl she had avoided church and Sunday school. In her teens she was more interested in parties and clothes and boys. If her friends in Madrid had been asked to select possible candidates to become a nun, Betina would have been at the bottom of the list. More accurately, she would not even have been on their list. But when she was nineteen, events started to happen that changed her life.

She was in her bed, asleep, when a voice said, 'Betina, get up and go outside.'

She opened her eyes and sat up, frightened. She turned on the bedside lamp. She was alone. *What a strange dream.*

But the voice had been so real. She lay down again, but it was impossible to go back to sleep.

Betina, get up and go outside.

It's my subconscious, she thought. *Why would I want to go outside in the middle of the night?*

She turned out the light and a moment later turned it on again. *This is crazy.*

But she put on a dressing-gown and slippers and went downstairs. The household was asleep.

She opened the kitchen door, and as she did a wave of fear swept over her, because somehow she knew that she was supposed to go out the back into the yard. She looked around in the darkness, and her eye caught a glint of moonlight shining on an old refrigerator that had been abandoned and was used to store tools.

Betina suddenly knew why she was there. She walked over to the refrigerator as though hypnotized, and opened it. Her three-year-old brother was inside, unconscious.

That was the first incident. In time, Betina rationalized it as a perfectly normal experience. *I must have heard my*

69

brother get up and go out into the yard, and I knew the refrigerator was there, and I was worried about him so I went outside to check.

The next experience was not so easy to explain. It happened a month later.

In her sleep, Betina heard a voice say, 'You must put out the fire.'

She sat up, wide awake, her pulse racing. Again, it was impossible to go back to sleep. She put on a dressing-gown and slippers and went into the landing. No smoke. No fire. She opened her parents' bedroom door. Everything was normal there. There was no fire in her brother's bedroom. She went downstairs and looked through every room. There was no sign of a fire

I'm an idiot, Betina thought. *It was only a dream.*

She went back to bed, just as the house was rocked by an explosion. She and her family escaped, and the firemen managed to put out the fire.

'It started in the basement,' a fireman explained. 'And a boiler exploded.'

The next incident happened three weeks later. This time it was no dream.

Betina was on the patio, reading, when she saw a stranger walking across the yard. He looked at her and in that instant she felt a malevolence coming from him that was almost palpable. He turned away and was gone.

Betina was unable to get him out of her mind.

Three days later, she was in an office building, waiting for the lift. The lift door opened, and she was about to step into it when she looked at the lift operator. It was the man she had seen in her garden. Betina backed away, frightened. The lift door closed and the lift went up. Moments later, it crashed, killing everyone in it.

The following Sunday, Betina went to church.

Dear Lord, I don't know what's happening to me, and I'm scared. Please guide me and tell me what you want me to do.

The answer came that night as Betina slept. The voice said one word. *Devotion.*

She thought about it all night, and in the morning she went to talk to the priest.

He listened intently to what she had to say.

'Ah. You are one of the fortunate ones. You have been chosen.'

'Chosen for what?'

'Are you willing to devote your life to God, my child?'

'I – I don't know. I'm afraid.'

But in the end, she had joined the convent.

I chose the right path, the Reverend Mother Betina thought, *because I have never known so much happiness . . .*

And now there was this battered child saying, 'I'm afraid.'

The Reverend Mother took Graciela's hand. 'Take your time, Graciela. God won't go away. Think about it and come back and we can discuss it.'

But what was there to think about? *I've got nowhere else in the world to go*, Graciela thought. And the silence would be welcome. *I have heard too many terrible sounds.* She looked at the Reverend Mother and said, 'I will welcome the silence.'

That had been seventeen years earlier, and in that time Graciela had found peace for the first time in her life. Her life was dedicated to God. The past no longer belonged to her. She was forgiven the horrors she had grown up with. She was Christ's bride, and at the end of her life, she would join Him.

As the years passed in deep silence, despite the occasional nightmares, the terrible sounds in her mind gradually faded away.

Sister Graciela was assigned to work in the garden, tending the tiny rainbows of God's miracle, never tiring of their splendour. The walls of the convent rose high above her on

71

all sides like a stone mountain, but Graciela never felt that they were shutting her in; they were shutting the terrible world out, a world she never wanted to see again.

Life in the convent was serene and peaceful. But now, suddenly her terrible nightmares had turned into a reality. Her world had been invaded by barbarians. They had forced her out of her sanctuary, into the world she had renounced for ever. And her sins came flooding back, filling her with horror. The Moor had returned. She could feel his hot breath on her face. As she fought him, Graciela opened her eyes, and it was the friar on top of her trying to penetrate her. He was saying, 'Stop fighting me, Sister. You're going to enjoy this!'

'Mama,' Graciela cried aloud. 'Mama! Help me!'

Chapter 7

Lucia Carmine felt wonderful as she walked down the street with Megan and Teresa. It was marvellous to wear feminine clothes again and hear the whisper of silk against her skin. She glanced at the others. They were walking nervously, unaccustomed to their new clothes, looking self-conscious and embarrassed in their skirts and stockings. *They look as though they've been dropped from another planet. They certainly don't belong on this one*, Lucia thought. *They might as well be wearing signs that say: 'Catch Me.'*

Sister Teresa was the most uncomfortable of the women. Thirty years in the convent had deeply ingrained a sense of modesty in her, and it was being violated by the events that had been thrust upon her. This world to which she had once belonged now seemed unreal. It was the convent that was real, and she longed to hurry back to the sanctuary of its protective walls.

Megan was aware that men were eyeing her as she walked down the street, and she blushed. She had lived in a world of women for so long that she had forgotten what it was like to see a man, let alone have one smile at her. It was embarrassing, indecent . . . exciting. The men aroused feelings in Megan that had been long since buried. For the first time in years, she was conscious of her femaleness.

They were passing the bar they had gone by before and the music was blaring out into the street. What had Friar Carrillo called it? *Rock and roll. Very popular with the young.* Something bothered her. And suddenly Megan realized what it was. When they had passed the cinema, the friar had said:

It's disgraceful what the cinema is permitted to show these days. That film is pure pornography. The most personal and private acts are there for everyone to see.

Megan's heart began to beat faster. If Friar Carrillo had been locked up in a monastery for the past twenty years, how could he possibly have known about rock music or what was in the film? Something was terribly wrong.

She turned to Lucia and Teresa and said urgently, 'We've got to return to the shop.'

They watched as Megan turned and ran back, and they quickly began to follow her.

Graciela was on the floor, desperately fighting to get free, scratching and clawing at Carrillo.

'God damn you! Hold still!' He was getting winded.

He heard a sound and glanced up. He saw the heel of a shoe swinging towards his head, and that was the last thing he remembered.

Megan picked up the trembling Graciela and held her in her arms. 'Shh. It's all right. He won't bother you any more.'

It was several minutes before Graciela could speak. 'He – he – it wasn't my fault this time,' she said pleadingly.

Lucia and Teresa had come into the shop. Lucia sized up the situation at a glance.

'The bastard!'

She looked down at the unconscious, half-naked figure on the floor. As the others watched, Lucia grabbed some belts from a counter and tied Miguel Carrillo's hands tightly behind his back. 'Tie his feet,' she told Megan.

Megan went to work.

Finally, Lucia stood up, satisfied. 'There. When they open up the shop this afternoon, he can explain to them what he was doing here.' She looked at Graciela closely. 'Are you all right?'

'I – I – yes.' She tried to smile.

'We'd better get out of here,' Megan said. 'Get dressed. Quickly.'

74

When they were ready to leave, Lucia said, 'Wait a minute.'

She went over to the cash register and pressed a key. There were a few hundred peseta notes inside. She scooped them up, picked up a purse from a counter and put the money inside. She saw the disapproving expression on Teresa's face.

Lucia said, 'Look at it this way, Sister. If God didn't want us to have this money, He wouldn't have put it there for us.'

They were seated in the café, having a conference. Sister Teresa was speaking. 'We must get the cross to the convent at Mendavia as quickly as possible. There will be safety there for all of us.'

Not for me, Lucia thought. *My safety is that Swiss bank. But first things first. I've got to get hold of that cross.*

'The convent at Mendavia is north of here, isn't it?'

'Yes.'

'The men will be looking for us in every town. So we'll sleep in the hills tonight.'

Nobody will hear her even if she does scream.

A waitress brought menus to the table and handed them out. The sisters examined them, their expressions confused. Suddenly Lucia understood. It had been so many years since they had been given choices of any kind. At the convent they had automatically eaten the simple food placed before them. Now they were confronted with a cornucopia of unfamiliar delicacies.

Sister Teresa was the first to speak. 'I – I will have some coffee and bread, please.'

Sister Graciela said, 'I, too.'

Megan said, 'We have a long, hard journey ahead of us. I suggest that we order something more nourishing, like eggs.'

Lucia looked at her with new eyes. *She's the one to keep an eye on*, Lucia thought. Aloud she said, 'Sister Megan is right. Let me order for you, Sisters.'

75

She ordered sliced oranges, *Tortillas de Patatas*, bacon, hot rolls, jam and coffee.

'We're in a hurry,' she told the waitress.

Siesta ended at 4.30, and the town would be waking up. She wanted to be out of there before that happened, before they discovered Miguel Carrillo in the dress shop.

When the food arrived, the sisters sat there staring at it.

'Help yourselves,' Lucia urged them.

They began to eat, hesitatingly at first, and then with gusto, overcoming their feelings of guilt.

Sister Teresa was the only one having a problem. She took one bite of food and said, 'I – I can't. It's – it's surrendering.'

Megan said, 'Sister, you want to get to the convent, don't you? Then you must eat to keep up your strength.'

Sister Teresa said primly, 'Very well. I'll eat. But I promise you, I won't enjoy it.'

It was all Lucia could do to keep a straight face. 'Good, Sister. Eat.'

When they had finished, Lucia paid the bill with some of the money she had taken from the cash register and they walked out into the hot sunshine. The streets were beginning to come alive, and the shops were starting to open. *By now they have probably caught Miguel Carrillo*, Lucia thought.

Lucia and Teresa were impatient to get out of town, but Graciela and Megan were walking slowly, fascinated by the sights and sounds and the smells of the town.

Not until they had reached the outskirts and headed towards the mountains did Lucia begin to relax. They moved steadily north, climbing upwards, making slow progress in the hilly terrain. Lucia was tempted to ask Sister Teresa if she would like her to carry the package, but she did not want to say anything that might make the older woman suspicious.

When they reached a small glade in the highland, surrounded by trees, Lucia said, 'We can spend the night here. In the morning we'll head for the convent at Mendavia.'

The others nodded, believing her.

*

The sun moved slowly across the blue sky, and the glade was silent, except for the soothing sounds of summer. Finally, night fell.

One by one the women stretched out on the green grass.

Lucia lay there, breathing lightly, listening for a deeper silence, waiting for them to fall asleep so that she could make her move.

Sister Teresa was finding it difficult to sleep. It was a strange experience sleeping out under the stars, surrounded by her sisters. They had names now, and faces and voices, and she was afraid that God was going to punish her for this forbidden knowledge. She felt terribly lost.

Sister Megan, too, was having difficulty getting to sleep. She was filled with the excitement of the day's events. *How did I know that the friar was a fraud?* she wondered. *And where did I get the courage to save Sister Graciela?* She smiled, unable to keep from being a tiny bit pleased with herself, even though she knew such a feeling was a sin.

Graciela was asleep, emotionally drained by what she had gone through. She tossed and turned in her sleep, haunted by dreams of being chased down dark, long, endless corridors.

Lucia Carmine lay still, waiting. She lay there for almost two hours and then quietly sat up and moved through the darkness towards Sister Teresa. She would take the package and disappear.

As she neared Sister Teresa, Lucia saw that the nun was awake on her knees, praying. Damn! Lucia hurriedly retreated.

Lucia lay down again, forcing herself to be patient. Sister Teresa could not pray all night. She had to get some sleep.

Lucia planned. The money taken from the cash register would be enough for her to take a bus or a train to Madrid. Once there, it would be simple to find a pawnbroker. She saw herself walking in and handing him the golden cross. The pawnbroker would suspect that it was stolen, but that would not matter. He would have plenty of customers eager to buy it.

I will give you one hundred thousand pesetas for it.

She would pick it up from the counter. *I would rather sell my body first.*

One hundred and fifty thousand pesetas.

I would prefer to melt it down and let the gold run in the gutter.

Two hundred thousand pesetas. That is my last offer.

You are robbing me blind, but I will accept it.

The pawnbroker would eagerly reach for it.

On one condition.

A condition?

Yes. I misplaced my passport. Do you know someone who can arrange a passport for me? Her hands would still be on the golden cross.

He would hesitate, then say, *I happen to have a friend who does things like that.*

And the deal would be done. She would be on her way to Switzerland and freedom. She remembered her father's words: *There is more money there than you could spend in ten lifetimes.*

Her eyes began to close. It had been a long day.

In her half-sleep, Lucia heard the sound of a church bell from the distant village. It sent memories flooding through her, of another place, another time . . .

Chapter 8

Taormina, Sicily 1968

She was awakened every morning by the distant sound of the bells of the Church of San Domenico, high in the Peloritani mountains surrounding Taormna. She enjoyed waking up slowly, languorously stretching like a cat. She kept her eyes closed, knowing that there was something wonderful to remember. *What was it?* The question teased at her mind, and she pushed it back, not wanting to know just yet, wanting to savour the surprise. And suddenly her mind was joyously flooded with it. She was Lucia Maria Carmine, the daughter of Angelo Carmine, and that was enough to make anyone in the world happy.

They lived in a large, storybook villa filled with more servants than the fifteen-year-old Lucia could count. A bodyguard drove her to school each morning in an armoured limousine. She grew up with the prettiest dresses and the most expensive toys in all of Sicily, and was the envy of her schoolmates.

But it was her father around whom Lucia's life centred. In her eyes, he was the most handsome man in the world. He was short and heavyset with a strong face and stormy brown eyes that radiated power. He had two sons, Arnaldo and Victor, but it was his daughter whom Angelo Carmine adored. And Lucia worshipped him. In church when the priest spoke of God, Lucia always thought of her father.

He would come to her bedside in the morning and say, 'Time to get up for school, *faccia del angelo*.' Angel face.

It was not true, of course. Lucia knew she was not really beautiful. *I'm attractive*, she thought, studying herself objectively in the mirror. Yes. Striking, rather than beautiful. Her reflection showed a young girl with an oval face, creamy skin, even, white teeth, a strong chin – too strong? – voluptuous, full lips – too full? – and dark, knowing eyes. But if her face fell just short of being beautiful, her body more than made up for it. At fifteen, Lucia had the body of a woman, with round, firm breasts, a narrow waist and hips that moved with sensuous promise.

'We're going to have to marry you off early,' her father would tease her. 'Soon you will drive the young men *pazzo*, my little virgin.'

'I want to marry someone like you, Papa, but there is no one like you.'

He laughed. 'Never mind. We'll find you a prince. You were born under a lucky star, and one day you will know what it is like to have a man hold you in his arms and make love to you.'

Lucia blushed. 'Yes, Papa.'

It was true that no one had made love to her – not for the past twelve hours. Benito Patas, one of her bodyguards, always came to her bed when her father was out of town. Having Benito make love to her in her house added to the thrill because Lucia knew that her father would kill them both if he ever discovered what was going on.

Benito was in his thirties, and it flattered him that the beautiful young virgin daughter of the great Angelo Carmine had chosen him to deflower her.

'Was it as you expected?' he asked the first time he bedded her.

'Oh, yes,' Lucia breathed. 'Better.'

She thought: *While he's not as good as Mario, Tony or Enrico, he's certainly better than Roberto and Leo.* She could not remember the names of all the others.

At thirteen, Lucia had felt that she had been a virgin long

enough. She had looked around and decided that the lucky boy would be Paolo Costello, the son of Angelo Carmine's doctor. Paolo was seventeen, tall and husky, and the star soccer player at his school. Lucia had fallen madly in love with Paolo the first time she had seen him. She managed to run into him as often as possible. It never occurred to Paolo that their constant meetings had been carefully contrived. He regarded the attractive young daughter of Angelo Carmine as a child. But on a hot summer day in August, Lucia decided she could wait no longer. She telephone Paolo.

'Paolo – this is Lucia Carmine. My father has something he would like to discuss with you, and he wondered whether you could meet him this afternoon at our pool house?'

Paolo was both surprised and flattered. He was in awe of Angelo Carmine, but he had not known that the powerful Mafioso was even aware of his existence. 'I would be delighted,' Paolo said. 'What time would he like me to be there?'

'Three o'clock.'

Siesta time, when the world would be asleep. The pool house was isolated, at the far end of their widespread property, and her father was out of town. There would be no chance of their being interrupted.

Paolo arrived promptly at the appointed hour. The gate leading to the garden was open, and he walked directly to the pool house. He stopped at the closed door and knocked. 'Signore Carmine? *Pronto* . . .?'

There was no response. Paolo checked his watch. Cautiously, he opened the door and stepped inside. The room was dark.

'Signore Carmine?'

A figure moved towards him. 'Paolo . . .'

He recognized Lucia's voice. 'Lucia, I'm looking for your father. Is he here?'

She was closer to him now, close enough for Paolo to see that she was stark naked.

'My God!' Paolo gasped. 'What –?'

'I want you to make love to me.'

81

'You're *pazzo*! You're only a child. I'm getting out of here.' He started towards the door.

'Go ahead. I'll tell my father you raped me.'

'No, you wouldn't.'

'Leave, and you'll find out.'

He stopped. If Lucia carried out her threat, there was not the slightest doubt in Paolo's mind as to what his fate would be. Castration would be only the beginning.

He walked back to Lucia to reason with her. 'Lucia, dear –'

'I like it when you call me dear.'

'No – listen to me, Lucia. This is very serious. Your father will kill me if you tell him I raped you.'

'I know.'

He made another stab at it. 'My father would be disgraced. My whole family would be disgraced.'

'I know.'

It was hopeless. 'What do you want from me?'

'I want you to do it to me.'

'No. It is impossible. If your father found out, he would kill me.'

'And if you leave here, he will kill you. You haven't got much choice, have you?'

He stared at her, panicky. 'Why me, Lucia?'

'Because I'm in love with you, Paolo!' She took his hands and pressed them gently between her legs. 'I'm a woman. Make me feel like one.'

In the dim light Paolo could see the twin mounds of her breasts, her hard nipples, and the soft, dark hair between her legs.

Jesus, Paolo thought. *What can a man do?*

She was leading him to a couch, helping him out of his trousers and his shorts. She knelt and put his male hardness in her mouth, sucking it gently, and Paolo thought: *She's done this before.* And when he was on top of her, plunging deep inside her, and she had her hands tightly wrapped around his backside, her hips thrusting hungrily against his, Paolo thought: *My God, she's marvellous.*

82

Lucia was in heaven. It was as though she had been born for this. Instinctively she knew exactly what to do to please him and to please herself. Her whole body was on fire. She felt herself building to a climax, higher and higher, and when it finally happened, she screamed aloud in sheer joy. They both lay there, spent, breathing hard.

Lucia finally spoke. She said, 'Same time tomorrow.'

When Lucia was sixteen, Angelo Carmine decided that it was time for his daughter to see something of the world. With an elderly Aunt Rosa as chaperone, Lucia spent her school holidays in Capri and Ischia, Venice and Rome, and a dozen other places.

'You must be cultured – not a peasant, like your Papa. Travel will round out your education. In Capri Aunt Rosa will take you to see the Carthusian Monastery of St James and the Chapel of San Michele and the Palazzo a Mare . . .'

'Yes, Papa.'

'In Venice there is St Mark's Basilica, the Doges' Palace, the church of San Gregorio, and the Accademia Museum.'

'Yes, Papa.'

'Rome is the treasure house of the world. There you must visit the Citta Vaticano, and the Basilica of Santa Maria Maggiore, and the Galleria Borghese, of course.'

'Of course.'

'And Milano! You must go to the Conservatorio for a concert recital. I will arrange tickets for La Scala for you and Aunt Rosa. You will see the Municipal Museum of Art, and there are dozens of churches and museums.'

'Yes, Papa.'

With very careful planning, Lucia managed to see none of those places. Aunt Rosa insisted on taking a siesta every afternoon and retiring early each evening.

'You must get your rest too, child.'

'Certainly, Aunt Rosa.'

And so while Aunt Rosa slept, Lucia danced at the Quisisana in Capri, rode in a *carrozza* with a beplumed and behatted horse pulling it, joined a group of college boys at the Marina Piccola, went on picnics at Bagni di Tiberio, and took the *Funicolare* up to Anacapri, where she joined a group of French students for drinks at the Piazza Umertol.

In Venice a handsome gondolier took her to a disco, and a fisherman took her fishing at Chioggia. And Aunt Rosa slept.

In Rome Lucia drank wine from Apulia and discovered all the off-beat fun restaurants like Marte and Ranieri and Giggi Fazi.

Wherever she went, Lucia found hidden little bars and nightclubs and romantic, good-looking men, and she thought: *Dear Papa was so right. Travel has rounded out my education.*

In bed, she learned to speak several different languages, and she thought: *This is so much more fun than my language classes at school.*

When Lucia returned home to Taormina, she confided to her closest girl-friends: 'I was naked in Naples, stoned in Salermo, felt up in Florence, and laid in Lucca.'

Sicily itself was a wonder to explore, an island of Grecian temples, Roman Byzantine amphitheatres, chapels, Arab baths and Swabian castles.

Lucia found Palermo raucous and lively, and she enjoyed wandering around the Kalsa, the old Arab quarter, and visiting the Opera dei Pupi, the puppet theatre. But Taormina, where she was born, was her favourite. It was a picture postcard of a city on the Ionian Sea on a mountain overlooking the world. It was a city of dress shops and jewellery stores, bars and beautiful old squares, *trattorias* and colourful hotels like the Excelsior Palace and the San Domenico.

The winding road leading up from the seaport of Nachos is steep and narrow and dangerous, and when Lucia Carmine was given a car on her fifteenth birthday, she broke every traffic law in the book but was never once stopped by the *Carabiniere*. After all, she was the daughter of Angelo Carmine.

To those who were brave enough or stupid enough to inquire, Angelo Carmine was in the property business. And it was partially true, for the Carmine family owned the villa at Taormina, a house on Lake Como at Cernobbio, a lodge at Gstaad, an apartment in Rome, and a large farm outside Rome. But it happened that Angelo Carmine was also in more colourful businesses. He owned a dozen whorehouses, two gambling casinos, six ships that brought in cocaine from his plantations in Colombia, and an assortment of other very lucrative enterprises, including loan sharking. Angelo Carmine was the Capo of the Sicilian Mafiosi, so it was only appropriate that he lived well. His life was an inspiration to others, heartwarming proof that a poor Sicilian peasant who was ambitious and worked hard could become rich and successful.

Angelo Carmine had started out as an errand boy for the Mafiosi when he was twelve. By fifteen he had become an enforcer for the loan sharks, and at sixteen he had killed his first man and made his bones. Shortly after that, he married Lucia's mother, Anna. In the years that followed, Angelo Carmine had climbed the treacherous corporate ladder to the top, leaving a string of dead enemies behind him. He had grown, but Anna had remained the simple peasant girl he married. She bore him three fine children, but after that her contribution to Angelo's life came to a halt. As though knowing she no longer had a place in her family's life, she obligingly died and was considerate enough to manage it with a minimum of fuss.

Arnaldo and Victor were in business with their father, and from the time Lucia was a small girl, she eavesdropped on the exciting conversations between her father and her brothers, and listened to the tales of how they had outwitted or overpowered their enemies. To Lucia, her father was a knight in shining armour. She saw nothing wrong in what her father and brothers were doing. On the contrary, they were helping people. If people wanted to gamble, why let stupid laws stand in their way? If men took pleasure in buying sex, why not assist them? And how generous of her father and brothers to loan money to people who were turned away by the hard-hearted bankers. To Lucia, her father and brothers were model citizens. The proof of it lay in her father's friends. Once a week Angelo Carmine gave an enormous dinner party at the villa, and oh, the people who would be seated at the Carmine table! The mayor would be there, and a few aldermen, and judges, and seated next to them were film stars and opera singers and often the chief of police and a monsignor. Several times a year the governor himself would appear.

Lucia lived an idyllic life, filled with parties and beautiful clothes and jewels, cars and servants, and powerful friends. And then one February, on her twenty-third birthday, it all came to an abrupt end.

It began innocuously enough. Two men came to the villa to see her father. One of the men was their friend, the chief of police, and the other was his lieutenant.

'Forgive me, *Padrone*,' the police chief apologized, 'but this is a stupid formality which the Commissioner is forcing me to go through with. A thousand pardons, *Padrone*, but if you will be kind enough to accompany me to the police station, I will see to it that you are home in time to enjoy your daughter's birthday party.'

'No problem,' Angelo Carmine said genially. 'A man must do his duty.' He grinned. 'This new Commissioner who's been appointed by the President is – in the American phrase – "an eager beaver", eh?'

'I'm afraid that is so,' the police chief sighed. 'But don't worry You and I have seen these pains-in-the-asses come and go very quickly, eh, *Padrone*?'

They laughed and left.

*

86

Angelo Carmine was not home for the party that day, nor the next. In fact, he never saw any of his homes again. The State entered a one-hundred-count indictment against him that included murder, drug trafficking, prostitution, arson, and scores of other crimes. Bail was denied. A police dragnet went out that swept up Carmine's crime organization. He had counted on his powerful connections in Sicily to have the charges against him dismissed, but instead he was taken to Rome in the middle of the night and held at the Regina Coeli, the notorious Queen of Heaven prison. He was put in a small cell that contained barred windows, a radiator, a narrow bed and a toilet with no seat. It was outrageous! It was an indignity beyond imagining.

In the beginning Angelo Carmine was sure that Tommaso Contorno, his lawyer, would have him released immediately.

When Contorno came to the visiting room of the prison, Carmine stormed at him, 'They've closed down my whorehouses and drug operation and they know everything about my money laundering operation. Somebody is talking. Find out who it is and bring me his tongue.'

'Do not worry, *Padrone*,' Contorno assured him. 'We will find him.'

His optimism turned out to be unfounded. In order to protect their witnesses, the State adamantly refused to reveal their names until the trial began.

Two days before the trial, Angelo Carmine and the other members of the Mafia were transferred to Rebibbia Prigione, a top-security prison twelve miles outside of Rome. A nearby courtroom had been fortified like a bunker. A hundred and sixty accused Mafia members were brought in through an underground tunnel wearing handcuffs and chains and put in thirty cages made of steel and bullet-proof glass. Armed guards surrounded the inside and outside of the courtroom and spectators were searched before they were allowed to enter.

When Angelo Carmine was marched into the courtroom, his heart leaped for joy, for the judge on the bench was Giovanni Buscetta, a man who had been on the Carmine payroll for the last fifteen years and who was a frequent guest at the Carmine house. Angelo Carmine knew at last that justice was going to be served.

The trial began. Angelo Carmine looked to *Omerta*, the Sicilian code of silence, to protect him. But to his astonishment, the chief witness for the State turned out to be none other than Benito Patas, the bodyguard. Benito Patas had been with the Carmine family so long and had been so trusted that he had been allowed to be in the room at meetings where confidential matters of business were discussed, and since that business consisted of every illegal activity on the police statutes, Patas was privy to a great deal of information. When the police had apprehended Patas minutes after he had cold-bloodedly murdered and mutilated the new boyfriend of his mistress, they had threatened him with life imprisonment, and Patas had reluctantly agreed to help the police build their case against Carmine in exchange for a lighter sentence. Now, to Angelo Carmine's horrified disbelief, he sat in the courtroom and listened to Patas reveal the innermost secrets of the Carmine fiefdom.

Lucia was also in the courtroom every day listening to the man who had been her lover destroying her father and her brothers.

Benito Patas' testimony opened the floodgates. Once the Commissioner's investigation began, dozens of victims came forward to tell their stories of what Angelo Carmine and his hoodlums had done to them. The Mafia had muscled into their businesses, blackmailed them, forced them into prostitution, murdered or crippled their loved ones, sold drugs to their children. The list of horrors was endless.

Even more damaging was the testimony of the *Pentiti*, the repentant members of the Mafia who decided to talk.

Lucia was allowed to visit her father in prison.

He greeted her cheerfully. He hugged her and whispered,

'Do not worry, *faccia del angelo*. Judge Giovanni Buscetta is my secret ace in the hole. He knows all the tricks of the law. He will use them to see that your brothers and I are acquitted.'

Angelo Carmine proved to be a poor prophet.

The public had been outraged by the excesses of the Mafia, and when the trial finally ended, Judge Giovanni Buscetta, an astute political animal, sentenced the Mafia members to long prison terms and sentenced Angelo Carmine and his two sons to the maximum permitted by Italian law, life imprisonment, a mandatory sentence of twenty-eight years.

For Angelo Carmine it was a death sentence.

All of Italy cheered. Justice had finally triumphed. But to Lucia, it was a nightmare beyond imagining. The three men she loved most in the world were being sent to hell.

Once again, Lucia was allowed to visit her father in his cell. The overnight change in him was heartbreaking. In the space of a few days, he had become an old man. His figure had shrunk and his healthy, ruddy complexion had turned sallow.

'They have betrayed me,' he moaned. 'They have all betrayed me. Judge Giovanni Buscetta – I owned him, Lucia! I made him a wealthy man, and he did this terrible thing to me. And Patas. I was like a father to him. What has the world come to? Whatever happened to honour? They are Sicilians, like me.'

Lucia took her father's hand in hers and said in a low voice, 'I am Sicilian, too, Papa. You shall have your vengeance. I swear it to you, on my life.'

'My life is over,' her father told her. 'But yours is still ahead of you. I have a numbered account in Zurich. The Bank Leu. There is more money there than you could spend in ten lifetimes.' He whispered a number in her ear. 'Leave cursed Italy. Take the money and enjoy yourself.'

Lucia held him close. 'Papa –'

'If you ever need a friend, you can trust Dominic Durell. We are like brothers. He has a home in France at Béziers, near the Spanish border.'

'I'll remember.'

'Promise me you'll leave Italy.'

'Yes, Papa. But there is something I have to do first.'

Having a burning desire for revenge was one thing. Figuring out a way to get it was another. She was alone, and it was not going to be easy. Lucia thought of the Italian expression, '*Rubare il mestiere.*' *You steal their profession. I must think the way they do.*

A few weeks after her father and brothers had started serving their prison sentences, Lucia Carmine appeared at the home of Judge Giovanni Buscetta. The judge himself opened the door.

He stared at Lucia in surprise. He had seen her often when he was a guest at the Carmine home, but they had never had much to say to each other.

'Lucia Carmine? What are you doing here? You shouldn't have –'

'I have come to thank you, Your Honour.'

He studied her suspiciously 'Thank me for what?'

Lucia looked deep into his eyes. 'For exposing my father and brothers for what they were. I was an innocent, living in that house of horrors. I had no idea what monsters –' She broke down and began to sob.

The judge stood there uncertainly, then patted her shoulder. 'There, there. Come in and have some tea.'

'Th – thank you.'

When they were seated in the living room, Judge Buscetta said, 'I had no idea that you felt that way about your father. I had the impression that you were very close.'

'Only because I had no idea what he and my brothers were really like. When I found out –' She shuddered. 'You don't know what it was like,' Lucia said. 'I wanted to get away, but there was no escape for me.'

'I didn't understand.' He patted her hand. 'I'm afraid I misjudged you, my dear.'

'I was terrified of him.' Her voice was filled with passion.

Judge Buscetta noticed, not for the first time, what a beautiful young girl Lucia was. She was wearing a simple black dress that revealed the outlines of her lush body. He looked at her rounded breasts and could not help observing how grown up she had become.

It would be amusing, Buscetta thought, *to sleep with the daughter of Angelo Carmine. He's powerless to hurt me now. The old bastard thought he owned me, but I was too smart for him. Lucia is probably a virgin. I could teach her a few things in bed.*

An elderly housekeeper brought in a tray of tea and a plate of biscuits. She put them on a table. 'Shall I pour?'

'Let me,' Lucia said. Her voice was warm and filled with promise.

Judge Buscetta smiled at Lucia. 'You can go,' he told the housekeeper.

'Yes, sir.'

The judge watched as Lucia walked over to the small table where the tray had been set down and carefully poured out tea for the judge and herself.

'I have a feeling you and I could become very good friends, Lucia,' Giovanni Buscetta said, probing.

Lucia gave him a seductive smile. 'I would like that very much, Your Honour.'

'Please – Giovanni.'

'Giovanni.' Lucia handed him his cup. She raised her cup in a toast. 'To the death of villains.'

Smiling, Buscetta lifted his cup. 'To the death of villains.' He took a swallow and grimaced. The tea tasted bitter.

'Is it too –?'

'No, no. It is fine, my dear.'

Lucia raised her cup again. 'To our friendship.'

She took another sip, and he joined her.

'To –'

Buscetta never finished his toast. He was seized by a sudden spasm, and he felt a red-hot poker stabbing at his heart. He grabbed his chest. 'Oh, my God! Call a doctor . . .'

Lucia sat there, calmly sipping her tea, watching him stumble to his feet and fall to the floor. He lay there, his body twitching, and then he was still.

'That's one, Papa,' Lucia said.

Benito Patas was in his cell playing solitaire when the jailer announced, 'You have a conjugal visitor.'

Benito beamed. He had been given special status as an informer, with many privileges, and conjugal visits was one of them. Patas had half a dozen girl-friends, and they alternated their visits. He wondered which one had come today.

He studied himself in the little mirror hanging on the wall of his cell, put some pomade on his hair, slicked it back, then followed the guard through the prison corridor to the section where there were private rooms.

The guard motioned him inside. Patas strutted into the room, filled with anticipation. He stopped and stared in surprise.

'Lucia! My God, what the hell are you doing here? How did you get in?'

Lucia said softly, 'I told them we were engaged, Benito.'

She was wearing a stunning red, low-cut silk dress that clung to the curves of her body.

Benito Patas backed away from her. 'Get out.'

'If you wish. But there is something you should hear first. When I saw you get up on the stand and testify against my father and brothers, I hated you. I wanted to kill you.' She moved closer to him. 'But then I realized that what you were doing was an act of bravery. You dared to stand up and tell the truth. My father and my brothers were not evil men, but they did evil things, and you were the only one strong enough to stand up against them.'

'Believe me, Lucia,' he said, 'the police forced me to –'

'You don't have to explain,' she said softly. 'Not to me. Remember the first time we made love? I knew then that I was in love with you and that I always would be.'

'Lucia, I would never have done what I –'

'*Caro*, I want us to forget what happened. It's done. What's important now is you and me.'

She was close to him now, and he could smell her heady perfume. His mind was in a state of confusion. 'Do – do you mean that?'

'More than I've ever meant anything in my life. That's why I came here today, to prove it to you. To show you that I'm yours. And not with just words.'

Her fingers went to her shoulder straps, and an instant later her dress shimmered to the floor. She was naked. 'Do you believe me now?'

By God, she was beautiful. 'Yes, I believe you.' His voice was husky.

Lucia moved close to him, and her body brushed against his. 'Get undressed,' she whispered. 'Hurry!'

She watched Patas as he undressed. When he was naked, he took her hand and led her to the little bed in the corner of the room. He did not bother with foreplay. In a moment he was on top of her, spreading her legs, plunging deep inside her, an arrogant smile on his face.

'It's like old times,' he said smugly. 'You couldn't forget me, could you?'

'No,' Lucia whispered in his ear. 'And do you know why I couldn't forget you?'

'No, *mi amore*. Tell me.'

'Because I'm Sicilian, like my father.'

She reached behind her head and removed the long, ornate pin that held her hair in place.

Benito Patas felt something stab him under his rib cage, and the sudden pain made him open his mouth to scream, but Lucia's mouth was on his, kissing him, and as Benito's body bucked and writhed on top of her, Lucia had an orgasm.

A few minutes later she was clothed again, and the pin had been replaced in her hair. Benito was under the blanket, his eyes closed. Lucia knocked at the cell door and smiled at the guard who opened it to let her out. 'He's asleep,' she whispered.

The guard looked at the beautiful young woman and smiled. 'You probably wore him out.'

'I hope so,' Lucia said.

The sheer daring of the two murders took Italy by storm. The beautiful young daughter of a Mafioso had avenged her father and brothers, and the excitable Italian public cheered her, rooting for her to escape. The police, quite naturally, took a rather different point of view. Lucia Carmine had murdered a respected judge and had then committed a second murder within the very walls of a prison. In their eyes, equal to her crimes was the fact that she had made fools of them. The newspapers were having a wonderful time at their expense.

'I want her neck,' the police commissioner roared to the deputy commissioner. 'And I want it *today*.'

The manhunt intensified. The object of all this attention was hiding in the home of Salvatore Giuseppe, one of her father's men who had managed to escape the firestorm.

In the beginning, Lucia's only thought had been to avenge the honour of her father and brothers. She had fully expected to be caught and was prepared to sacrifice herself. When she had managed to walk out of the prison and make her escape, however, her thoughts changed from vengeance to survival. Now that she had accomplished what she had set out to do, life suddenly became precious again. *I'm not going to let them capture me*, she vowed to herself. *Never*.

Salvatore Giuseppe and his wife had done what they could to disguise Lucia. They had lightened her hair, stained her teeth, and bought her glasses and some ill-fitting clothes. Salvatore examined their handiwork critically.

'It is not bad,' he said. 'But it is not enough. We must get you out of Italy. You have to go somewhere where your picture is not on the front page of every newspaper. Somewhere you can hide out for a few months.'

And Lucia remembered:

If you ever need a friend, you can trust Dominic Durell. We are like brothers. He has a home in France at Béziers, near the Spanish border.

'I know where I can go,' Lucia said. 'I'll need a passport.'

'I will arrange it.'

Twenty-four hours later Lucia was looking at a passport in the name of Lucia Roma, with a photograph taken in her new persona.

'Where will you go?'

'My father has a friend in France who will help me.'

Salvatore said, 'If you wish me to accompany you to the border –?'

Both of them knew how dangerous that could be.

'No, Salvatore,' Lucia said. 'You have done enough for me. I must do this alone.'

The following morning Salvatore Giuseppe rented a Fiat in the name of Lucia Roma and handed her the keys.

'Be careful,' he pleaded.

'Don't worry. I was born under a lucky star.'

Had not her father told her so?

At the Italian–French border the cars waiting to get into France were advancing slowly in a long line. As Lucia moved closer to the immigration booth, she became more and more nervous. They would be looking for her at all exit points. If they caught her, she knew she would be sentenced to prison for life. *I'll kill myself first*, Lucia thought.

She had reached the immigration officer.

'Passport, signorina.'

Lucia handed him her black passport through the car window. As the officer took it, he glanced at Lucia, and she saw a puzzled look come into his eyes. He looked from the passport to her face and back again, this time more carefully. Lucia felt her body tense.

'You're Lucia Carmine,' he said.

Chapter 9

'Lucia Carmine.'

'No!' Lucia cried. The blood drained from her face. She looked around for a way to escape. There was none. And suddenly, to her disbelief, the guard was smiling. He leaned towards her and whispered, 'Your father was good to my family, signorina. You may pass through. Good luck.'

Lucia felt dizzy with relief. '*Grazie.*'

She stepped on the accelerator and drove the twenty-five yards towards the French border. The French immigration officer prided himself on being a connoisseur of beautiful women, and the woman who pulled up before him was certainly no beauty. She had mousy hair, thick glasses, stained teeth and was dowdily dressed.

Why can't Italian women look as beautiful as French women? he thought disgustedly. He stamped Lucia's passport and waved her through.

She arrived in Béziers many hours later.

The phone was answered on the first ring, and a smooth male voice said, 'Hello.'

'Dominic Durell, please.'

'This is Dominic Durell. Who is this speaking?'

'Lucia Carmine. My father told me –'

'Lucia!' His voice was warm with welcome. 'I was hoping to hear from you.'

'I need help.'

'You can count on me.'

Lucia's heart lightened. It was the first good news she had heard in a long time. She suddenly realized how drained she was.

'I need a place where I can hide out from the police.'

'No problem. My wife and I have a perfect place for you to use for as long as you like.'

It was almost too good to be true.

'Thank you.'

'Where are you, Lucia?'

'I'm –'

At that moment the blare of a police shortwave radio crackled over the phone. It was instantly shut off.

'Lucia –'

A loud alarm rang in her head.

'Lucia – where are you? I'll come and get you.'

Why would he have a police radio in his house? And he had answered the telephone on the first ring. Almost as though he had been expecting her call.

'Lucia – can you hear me?'

She knew, with an absolute certainty, that the man on the other end of the line was a policeman. So the dragnet was out for her This call was being traced.

'Lucia –'

She replaced the receiver and walked quickly away from the telephone booth.

I've got to get out of France, she thought.

She returned to her car and took a map from the glove compartment. The Spanish border was only a short distance away. She replaced the map and started off. She turned a corner and headed south towards San Sebastian.

It was at the Spanish border that things started to go wrong.

'Passport, please.'

Lucia handed the Spanish immigration officer her passport. He gave it a cursory glance and started to hand it back, but something made him hesitate. He took a closer look at Lucia, and his expression changed.

'Just a moment, please. I will have to have this stamped inside.'

He recognized me, Lucia thought desperately. She watched him walk into the little office kiosk and show the passport to another officer. The two of them were talking excitedly. She had to escape. She opened the door on the driver's side and stepped out. A group of German tourists who had just cleared customs was noisily boarding an excursion coach next to Lucia's car. The sign on the front of the coach read 'Madrid'.

'*Achtung!*' their guide was calling out. '*Schnell.*'

Lucia glanced towards the hut. The guard who had taken her passport was yelling into the telephone.

'All aboard, *bitte.*'

Without a second thought, Lucia moved towards the laughing, chattering tour group and stepped on to the coach, averting her face from the guide. She took a seat in the rear of the coach, keeping her head down. *Move!* she prayed. *Now.*

Through the window Lucia saw that another guard had joined the first two and the three of them were examining her passport. As though in answer to Lucia's prayer, the coach door closed and the engine sprang into life. A short time later the coach was rolling out of San Sebastian towards Madrid. What would happen when the border guards found that she had left her car? Their first thought would be that she had gone to the ladies' room. They would wait and finally send someone in to get her. Their next step would be to search the area to see if she had hidden somewhere. By then dozens of cars and buses would have passed through. The police would have no idea where she had gone, nor in which direction she was travelling.

The tour group on the coach was obviously having a happy holiday. *Why not?* Lucia thought bitterly. *They haven't got the police snapping at their heels. Was it worth risking the rest of my life for?* She thought about it, reliving the scenes with Judge Buscetta and Benito in her mind.

I have a feeling you and I could become very good friends, Lucia . . . To the death of villains.

And Benito Patas: *It's like old times. You couldn't forget me, could you?*

And she had made the two traitors pay for their sins against her family. *Was it worth it?* They were dead, but her father and brothers would suffer for the rest of their lives. *Oh, yes*, Lucia thought. *It was worth it.*

Someone on the coach started a German song, and the others joined in:

'*In München ist ein Hofbrau Haus, ein, zwei, drei . . .*'

I'll be safe with this group for a while, Lucia thought. *I'll decide what to do next when I get to Madrid.*

She never reached Madrid.

At the walled city of Ávila, the tour coach made a scheduled stop for refreshments and what the guide delicately referred to as a 'comfort station'.

'*Alle raus aus dem Bus*,' he called.

Lucia stayed in her seat, watching the passengers rise and scramble for the front door of the coach. *I'll be safer if I stay here.* But the guide noticed her.

'Out, *Fräulein*,' he said. 'We have only fifteen minutes.'

Lucia hesitated, then reluctantly rose and moved towards the door.

As she passed the guide, he said, '*Warten Sie, bitte!* You are not of this tour.'

Lucia gave him a warm smile. 'No,' she said. 'You see, my car broke down in San Sebastian and it is very important that I get to Madrid, so I –'

'*Nein!*' the guide bellowed. 'This is not possible. This is a private tour.'

'I know,' Lucia told him, 'but you see, I need –'

'You must arrange this with the company headquarters in Munich.'

'I can't. I'm in a terrible hurry and –'

'*Nein, nein.* You will get me in trouble. Go away or I will call the police.'

'But –'

Nothing she said could sway him. Twenty minutes later Lucia watched the coach pull away and roar down the highway towards Madrid. She was stranded with no passport and almost no money, and by now the police of half a dozen countries would be looking for her to arrest her for murder.

She turned to examine her surroundings. The coach had stopped in front of a circular building with a sign in front that read '*Estación de Autobúses*'.

I can get another bus here, Lucia thought.

She walked into the station. It was a large building with marble walls, and scattered around the room were a dozen ticket windows with a sign over each one: *Segovia . . . Muñogalindo . . . Valladolid . . . Salamanca . . . Madrid.* Stairs and an escalator led to the downstairs level where the buses departed. There was a *pastelería* where they sold doughnuts and sweets and sandwiches wrapped in wax paper, and Lucia suddenly realized that she was starved.

I'd better not buy anything, she thought, *until I find out how much a bus ticket costs.*

As she started towards the window marked Madrid, two uniformed policemen hurried into the station. One of them was carrying a photograph. They moved from window to window showing the picture to the clerks.

They're looking for me. That damned bus driver reported me.

A family of newly arrived passengers was coming up the escalator. As they moved towards the door, Lucia stepped up beside them, mingling with them, and went outside.

She walked down the cobblestoned streets of Ávila, trying not to rush, afraid of drawing attention to herself. She turned into the Calle de la Madre Soledad, with its granite buildings and black wrought-iron balconies, and when she reached the

101

Plaza de la Santa, she sat down on a park bench to try to figure out her next move. A hundred yards away, several women and some couples were seated in the park, enjoying the afternoon sunshine.

As Lucia sat there, a police car appeared. It pulled up at the far end of the square and two policemen got out. They moved over to one of the women seated alone and began questioning her. Lucia's heart began to beat faster.

She forced herself to get to her feet slowly, her heart pounding, and turned away from the policemen and kept walking. The next street was called, unbelievably, 'The Street of Life and Death'. *I wonder if it's an omen.*

There were realistic-looking stone lions in the plaza, their tongues out, and in Lucia's fevered imagination, they seemed to be snapping at her. Ahead of her was a large cathedral, and on its façade was a carved medallion of a young girl and a grinning skull. The very air seemed to be filled with death.

Lucia heard the sound of a church bell and looked up through the open city gate. In the distance, high on a hill, rose the walls of an abbey. She stood there, staring at it.

'Why have you come to us, my daughter?' the Reverend Mother Betina asked softly.

'I need a place of refuge.'

'And you have decided to seek the refuge of God?'

Exactly. 'Yes.' Lucia began to improvise. 'This is what I have always wanted – to devote myself to the life of the spirit.'

'In our souls it is what we all wish for, is it not, daughter?'

Jesus, she's really falling for it, Lucia thought happily.

The Reverend Mother went on: 'You must understand that the Cistercian Order is the strictest of all the orders, my child. We are completely isolated from the outside world.'

Her words were music to Lucia's ears.

'Those who enter these walls have vowed never to leave.'

'I never want to leave,' Lucia assured her. *Not for the next few months, anyway.*

The Reverend Mother rose. 'It is an important decision. I suggest that you go and think about it carefully before you make up your mind.'

Lucia felt the situation slipping away from her and she began to panic. She had nowhere to go. Her only hope was to stay behind these walls.

'I have thought about it,' Lucia said quickly. 'Believe me, Reverend Mother, I've thought about nothing else. I want to renounce the world.' She looked the Mother Prioress in the eye. 'I want to be here more than I want to be anywhere else in the world.' Lucia's voice rang with truth.

The Reverend Mother was puzzled. There was something unsettled and frantic about this woman that was disturbing. And yet what better reason for anyone to come to this place where their spirit would be calmed by meditation and prayer?

'Are you Catholic?'

'Yes.'

The Reverend Mother picked up an old-fashioned quill pen. 'Tell me your name, child.'

'My name is Lucia Car – *Roma.*

'Are your parents alive?'

'My father is.'

'What does he do?'

'He was a businessman. He's retired.' She thought of how pale and wasted he looked the last time she had seen him, and a pang went through her.

'Do you have any brothers or sisters?'

'Two brothers.'

'And what do they do?'

Lucia decided she needed all the help she could get. 'They're priests.'

'Lovely.'

The catechism went on for three hours. At the end of that time, the Reverend Mother Betina said, 'I will find you a bed for the night. In the morning you will begin instructions and when they are finished, if you still feel the same, you

103

may join the order. But I warn you, it is a very difficult path you have chosen.'

'Believe me,' Lucia said earnestly. 'I have no choice.'

The night wind was soft and warm, whispering its way across the wooded glade, and Lucia slept. She was at a party in a beautiful villa, and her father and brothers were there, and everyone was having a wonderful time, and a stranger walked into the room and said, 'Who the hell are these people?' And the lights went out and a bright flashlight shone in her face and she came awake and sat up, the light blinding her.

There were half a dozen men surrounding the nuns in the clearing. With the light in her eyes, Lucia could only dimly make out their shapes.

'Who are you?' the man demanded again. His voice was deep and rough.

Lucia was instantly awake, her mind alert. She was trapped. But if these men were from the police, they would have known who the nuns were. And what were they doing in the woods at night?

Lucia took a chance. 'We are sisters from the convent at Ávila,' she said. 'Some government men came and –'

'We heard about it,' the man interrupted.

The other sisters were all sitting up now, awake and terrified.

'Who – who are you?' Megan asked.

'My name is Jaime Miró.'

There were six of them, dressed in rough trousers, leather jackets, turtleneck sweaters and canvas rope-soled shoes, and the traditional Basque berets. They were heavily armed, and in the dim moonlight they had a demonic look. Two of the men looked as though they had been badly beaten.

The man who called himself Jaime Miro was tall and lean, with fierce black eyes. 'They could have been followed here.'

He turned to one of the members of his band. 'Have a look around.'

'*Si.*'

Lucia realized that it was a woman who answered. Lucia watched her move silently into the trees.

'What are we going to do with them?' Ricardo Mellado asked.

Jaime Miró said, '*Nada*. We leave them and move on.'

One of the men protested, 'Jaime – these are little sisters of Jesus.'

'Then let Jesus take care of them,' Jaime Miró said curtly. 'We have work to do.'

The nuns were all standing now, waiting. The men were gathered around Jaime, arguing with him.

'We can't let them get caught. Acoca and his men are searching for them.'

'They're searching for us, too, *amigo*.'

'The sisters will never make it without our help.'

Jaime Miró said firmly, 'No. We're not risking our lives for them. We have problems of our own.'

Felix Carpio, one of his lieutenants, said, 'We could escort them part of the way, Jaime. Just until they get away from here.' He turned to the nuns. 'Where are you sisters headed?'

Teresa spoke up, the light of God in her eyes. 'I have a holy mission. There is a convent at Mendavia that will shelter us.'

Felix Carpio said to Jaime Miró, 'We could escort them there. Mendavia's on our way to San Sebastian.'

Jaime Miró turned on him, furious. 'You damned fool! Why don't you put up a signpost telling everyone where we're going?'

'I only meant –'

'*Mierda!*' His voice was filled with disgust. 'Now we have no choice. We'll have to take them with us. If Acoca finds them, he'll make them talk. They're going to slow us down and make it that much easier for Acoca and his butchers to track us.'

Lucia was only half listening. The gold cross lay within

tempting reach. *But these damned men! You have lousy timing, God, and a weird sense of humour.*

'All right,' Jaime Miró was saying. 'We'll have to make the best of it. We'll take them as far as the convent and drop them, but we can't all travel together like some bloody circus.' He turned to the nuns. He could not keep the anger out of his voice. 'Do any of you even know where Mendavia is?'

The sisters looked at one another.

Graciela said, 'Not exactly.'

'Then how the hell did you ever expect to get there?'

'God will lead us,' Sister Teresa said firmly.

Another one of the men, Rubio Arzano, grinned. 'You're in luck.' He nodded towards Jaime. 'He came down to guide you in person, sister.'

Jaime silenced him with a look. 'We'll split up. We'll take three different routes.'

He pulled a map out of a backpack and the men squatted down on the ground, shining flashlights on the map.

'The convent at Mendavia is here, south-east of Logroño. I'll head north through Valladolid, then up to Burgos.' He ran his fingers along the map and turned to Rubio, a tall, pleasant-looking man. 'You take the route to Olmedo up to Peñafiel and Aranda de Duero.'

'Right, *amigo*.'

Jaime Miró was concentrating on the map again. He looked up at Ricardo Mellado, one of the men whose face was bruised. 'Ricardo, head for Segovia, then take the mountain route to Carezo de Abono, then to Soria. We'll all meet at Logroño.' He put the map away. 'Logroño is two hundred and ten kilometres from here.' He calculated silently. 'We'll meet there in seven days. Keep away from the main roads.'

Felix asked, 'Where in Logroño shall we meet?'

Ricardo said, 'The Cirque Japon will be playing in Logroño next week.'

'Good. We'll meet there. The matinee performance.'

Felix Carpio, the bearded one, spoke up. 'Who are the nuns going to travel with?'

106

'We'll split them up.'

It was time to put a stop to this, Lucia decided. 'If the soldiers are searching for you, signore, then we'd be safer travelling on our own.'

'But *we* wouldn't be, Sister,' Jaime said. 'You know too much about our plans now.'

'Besides,' the man called Rubio added, 'you wouldn't have a chance. We know the country. We're Basques, and the people up north are our friends. They'll help us and hide us from the nationalist soldiers. You'd never get to Mendavia by yourselves.'

I don't want to get to Mendavia, you idiot.

Jaime Miró was saying, grudgingly, 'All right, then, let's get moving. I want us far away from here by dawn.'

Sister Megan stood quietly listening to the man who was giving orders. He was rude and arrogant, but somehow he seemed to radiate a reassuring sense of power.

Jaime Miró looked over at Teresa and pointed to Tomas Sanjuro and Rubio Arzano. 'They will be responsible for you.'

Sister Teresa said, 'God is responsible for me.'

'Sure,' Jaime replied drily. 'I suppose that's how you got here in the first place.'

Rubio walked over to Teresa. 'Rubio Arzano at your service, Sister. How are you called?'

'I am Sister Teresa.'

Lucia spoke up quickly. 'I will travel with Sister Teresa.' There was no way she was going to let them separate her from the gold cross.

Jaime Miró nodded. 'All right.' He pointed to Graciela. 'Ricardo, you'll take this one.'

Ricardo Mellado nodded. '*Bueno.*'

The woman, whom Jaime had sent to reconnoitre, had returned to the group. 'It's all clear,' she said.

'Good.' Jaime Miró looked at Megan. 'You come with us, Sister.'

Megan nodded. Jaime Miró fascinated her. And there was something intriguing about the woman. She was dark and

107

fierce-looking, with the hawk-like features of a predator. Her mouth was a red wound. There was something intensely sexual about her.

The woman walked up to Megan. 'I'm Amparo Jiron. Keep your mouth shut, Sister, and there will be no trouble.'

Jaime said to the others, 'Let's get moving. We'll meet in Logroño in seven days. Don't let the sisters out of your sight.'

Sister Teresa and the man called Rubio Arzano had already started to move down the path. Lucia hurried after them. She had seen the map that Rubio Arzano had put in his backpack. *I'll take it*, Lucia decided, *when he's asleep*.

Their flight across Spain began.

Chapter 10

Miguel Carrillo was nervous. In fact, Miguel Carrillo was *very* nervous. It had not been a wonderful day for him. What had started so well in the morning when he had encountered the four nuns and convinced them that he was a friar, had ended up with him being knocked unconscious and tied hand and foot and left on the floor of the dress shop.

It was the owner's wife who had discovered him. She was a heavyset, elderly woman with a moustache and a foul temper. She had looked down at him, trussed up on the floor and said, *'¡Madre de Dios!* Who are you? What are you doing here?'

Carrillo had turned on all his charm. 'Thank heavens you've come, *señorita*.' He had never met anyone who was more obviously a *señora*. 'I've been trying to get out of these straps so I could use your phone to call the police.'

'You haven't answered my question.'

He tried to struggle into a more comfortable position. 'The explanation is simple, *señorita*. I am Friar Gonzales. I come from a monastery near Madrid. I was passing by your beautiful shop when I saw two young men breaking into it. I felt it was my duty as a man of God to stop them. I followed them inside hoping to persuade them of the errors of their ways, but they overpowered me and tied me up. Now, if you would be good enough to untie me –'

'¡Mierda!'

He stared at her. 'I beg your pardon?'

'Who are you?'

'I told you, I'm –'

'What you are is the worst liar I've ever heard.'

She walked over to the robes that the nuns had discarded.

'What are those?'

'Ah. Those, yes. The two young men were wearing them as disguises, you see, and –'

'There are four outfits here. You said there were two men.'

'Right. The other two joined them later, and –'

She walked over to the phone.

'What are you doing?'

'Cailing the police.'

'That's not necessary, I assure you. As soon as you release me, I'm going right to the police station to make a full report.'

The woman looked down at him.

'Your robe is open, Friar.'

The police were even less sympathetic than the woman had been. Carrillo was being questioned by four members of the *guardia civil*. Their green uniforms and eighteenth-century black patent leather hats were enough to inspire fear throughout Spain, and they certainly worked their magic on Carrillo.

'Are you aware that you answer to the exact description of a man who murdered a priest up north?'

Carrillo sighed. 'I am not surprised. I have a twin brother, may heaven punish him. It is because of him that I joined the monastery. Our poor mother –'

'Spare us.'

A giant with a scarred face walked into the room.

'Good afternoon, Colonel Acoca.'

'Is this the man?'

'Yes, Colonel. Because of the nuns' robes that we found with him in the shop, we thought you might be interested in questioning him yourself.'

Colonel Ramon Acoca walked up to the hapless Carrillo.

'Yes. I'm very interested.'

Carrillo gave the Colonel his most ingratiating smile. 'I'm glad you're here, Colonel. I'm on a mission for my church, and it's very important that I get to Barcelona as quickly as possible. As I tried to explain to these nice gentlemen, I am a victim of circumstances simply because I tried to be a good samaritan.'

Colonel Acoca nodded pleasantly. 'Since you are in a hurry, I will try not to waste your time.'

Carrillo beamed at him. 'Thank you, Colonel.'

'I'm going to ask you a few simple questions. If you answer truthfully, everything will be fine. If you lie to me, it will be very painful for you.' He slipped something into his hand.

Carrillo said righteously, 'Men of God do not lie.'

'I'm very happy to hear that. Tell me about the four nuns.'

'I don't know anything about four nuns, Col –'

The fist that hit him in the mouth had brass knuckles on it, and blood spurted across the room.

'My God! What are you doing?' Carrillo gasped.

Colonel Acoca repeated his question. 'Tell me about the four nuns.'

'I don't –'

The fist slammed into Carrillo's mouth again, breaking teeth.

Carrillo was choking on his blood. 'Don't. I –'

'Tell me about the four nuns.' Acoca's voice was soft and reasonable.

'I –' He saw the fist being raised. 'Yes! I – I –'

The words came tumbling out. 'They were in Villacastin, running away from their convent. Please don't hit me again.'

'Go on.'

'I – I told them I would help them. They needed to change clothes.'

'So you broke into the shop . . .

'No. I – yes. I – they stole some clothes and then they knocked me out and left me.'

'Did they say where they were headed?'

A peculiar sense of dignity suddenly took possession of Carrillo. 'No.' His not mentioning Mendavia had nothing to

111

do with protecting the nuns. Carrillo did not give a damn about them. It was because the Colonel had ruined his face. It was going to be very difficult to make a living after he was released from prison.

Colonel Acoca turned to the members of the *guardia civil*.

'See what a little friendly persuasion can do? Send him to Madrid and hold him for murder.'

Lucia, Sister Teresa, Rubio Arzano and Tomas Sanjuro walked north-east, heading towards Olmeda, staying away from the main roads and walking through fields of grain. They passed flocks of sheep and goats, and the innocence of the pastoral countryside was in ironic contrast to the grave danger they were all in. They walked through the night, and at dawn they headed for a secluded spot in the hills.

Rubio Arzano said, 'The town of Olmeda is just ahead. We'll stop here until nightfall. You both look as though you could do with some sleep.'

Sister Teresa was physically exhausted. But something was happening to her emotionally that was far more disturbing. She felt she was losing touch with reality. It had begun with the disappearance of her precious rosary. Had she lost it – or had someone stolen it? She was not sure. It had been her solace for more years than she could remember. How many thousands of Hail Marys and how many Our Fathers and how many Hail, Holy Queens? It had become a part of her, her security, and now it was missing.

Had she lost it in the convent during the attack? And had there really been an attack? It seemed so unreal now. She was no longer sure what was real and what was imaginary. The baby she had seen. Was it Monique's baby? Or was God playing tricks on her? It was all so confusing. When she was young, everything had been so simple. When she was young . . .

112

Chapter 11

Èze, France 1924

When she was only eight years old, most of the happiness in Teresa DeFosse's life came from the church. It was like a sacred flame drawing her to its warmth. She visited the Chapelle des Penitents Blancs, and prayed at the cathedral in Monaco and Notre Dame Bon Voyage in Cannes, but most frequently she attended services at the church in Èze.

Teresa lived in a château on a mountain above the medieval village of Èze, near Monte Carlo, overlooking the Côte d'Azur. The village was perched high on a rock and it seemed to Teresa that she could look down upon the whole world. There was a monastery at the top, with rows of houses cascading down the side of the mountain to the blue Mediterranean below.

Monique, a year younger than Teresa, was the beauty in the family. Even when she was a child, one could see that she would grow up to be an exquisite woman. She had fine-boned features, sparkling blue eyes, and an easy self-assurance that suited her looks.

Teresa was the ugly duckling. The truth was that the DeFosses were embarrassed by their elder daughter. If Teresa had been conventionally ugly, they might have sent her to a plastic surgeon and had her nose shortened, or her chin brought forward, or her eyes fixed. But the problem was that all Teresa's features were just slightly askew. Everything seemed out of place, as though she were a comedienne who had donned her face for laughter.

113

But if God had cheated her in the matter of looks, He had compensated for it by blessing her with a remarkable gift. Teresa had the voice of an angel. It had been noticed the first time she sang in the church choir. The parishioners listened in astonishment to the pure, clear tones that came from the young child. And as Teresa grew older, her voice grew even more beautiful. She was given all the solos to sing in church. There, she felt as though she belonged. But away from church, Teresa was inordinately shy, painfully aware of her appearance.

At school it was Monique who had all the friends. Boys and girls alike flocked to her side. They wanted to play with her, be seen with her. Monique was invited to all the parties. Teresa was invited also, but it was an after-thought, the fulfilling of a social obligation, and Teresa was painfully aware of it.

'Now, Renée. You can't invite one of the DeFosse children without the other. It would be bad manners.'

Monique was ashamed to have an ugly sister. She felt that it was somehow a reflection on her.

Teresa's parents behaved properly towards their elder daughter. They fulfilled their parental duty punctiliously, but it was obvious that it was Monique they adored. The one ingredient that Teresa longed for was missing: love.

She was an obedient child, willing and eager to please, a good student who loved music, history and foreign languages and worked hard in school. Her teachers and the servants and the townspeople felt sorry for her. As a tradesman said one day when Teresa left his shop, 'God wasn't paying attention when he made her.'

Where Teresa found love was in the church. The priest loved her, and Jesus loved her. She went to mass every morning and made the fourteen stations of the cross. Kneeling in the cool, vaulted church, she felt God's presence. When she sang there, Teresa was filled with a sense of hope, of expectation. She felt as though something wonderful were about to happen to her. It was the only thing that made her life bearable.

Teresa never confided her unhappiness to her parents or to her sister, for she did not want to burden them, and she hugged to herself the secret of how much God loved her and how much she loved God.

Teresa adored her sister. They played together in the estate grounds surrounding their château, and she let Monique win the games they played. They went exploring together, down the steep stone steps cut into the mountain to Èze Village below, and wandered down the narrow streets of artists' shops to watch the artists in front selling their wares.

As the girls grew into their teens, the predictions of the villagers came true. Monique grew more beautiful. The boys came flocking around Monique, while Teresa stayed in her room sewing or reading or went shopping in the village.

As Teresa passed the drawing room one day, she heard her mother and father in a discussion.

'She's going to be an old maid. We're going to have her on our hands all our lives.'

'Teresa will find someone. She has a very sweet disposition.'

'That's not what the young men of today are after. They want someone they can enjoy having in their bed.'

Teresa fled.

Teresa still sang in church on Sundays; and because of that an event occurred that almost changed her life. In the congregation was a Madame Neff, the aunt of a radio station director in Nice.

She stopped to speak to Teresa one Sunday morning. 'You're wasting your life here, my dear. You have an extraordinary voice. You should be using it.'

'I am using it. I –'

'I'm not talking about –' She looked around the church. – *this*. I'm talking about your using your voice professionally. I pride myself on knowing talent when I hear it. I want

115

you to sing for my nephew. He can put you on the radio. Are you interested?'

'I – I don't know.' The very thought of it terrified Teresa.

'Talk it over with your family.'

'I think it's a wonderful idea,' Teresa's mother said.

'It could be a good thing for you,' her father agreed.

It was Monique who had reservations about it. 'You're not a professional,' she said. 'You could make a fool of yourself.' Which had nothing to do with Monique's reasons for trying to discourage her sister. What Monique was afraid of was that Teresa would *succeed*. Monique was the one who had always been in the limelight. *It's not fair*, she thought, *that God should have given Teresa a voice like that. What if she should become famous? I would be left out, ignored.*

And so Monique tried to persuade her sister not to audition.

But the following Sunday at church, Madame Neff stopped Teresa and said, 'I've talked to my nephew. He is willing to give you an audition. He's expecting you on Wednesday at three o'clock.'

And so it was that the following Wednesday a very nervous Teresa appeared at the radio station in Nice and met the director.

'I'm Louis Bonnet,' he said curtly. 'I can give you five minutes.'

Teresa's physical appearance only confirmed his worst fears. His aunt had sent him talent before.

I should tell her to stick to her kitchen. But he knew that he would not. The problem was that his aunt was very rich, and he was her only heir.

Teresa followed Louis Bonnet down a narrow corridor into a small broadcasting studio.

'Have you ever sung professionally?'

'No, sir.' Her blouse was soaked with perspiration. *Why did I ever let myself get talked into this?* Teresa wondered. She was in a panic, ready to flee.

Bonnet placed her in front of a microphone. 'I don't have a piano player around today, so you're going to have to sing *a capella*. Do you know what *a capella* means?'

'Yes, sir.'

'Wonderful.' He wondered, not for the first time, if his aunt was rich enough to make all these stupid auditions worthwhile.

'I'll be in the control booth. You'll have time for one song.'

'Sir – what shall I –?'

He was gone. Teresa was alone in the room staring at the microphone in front of her. She had no idea what she was going to sing. 'Just go and meet him,' his aunt had said. 'The station has a musical programme every Saturday evening, and . . .'

I've got to get out of here.

Louis' voice came out of nowhere. 'I haven't got all day.'

'I'm sorry. I can't –'

But the director was determined to punish her for wasting his time.

'Just a few notes,' he insisted. Enough so he could report to his aunt what a fool the girl had made of herself. Perhaps that would persuade her to stop sending him her protégées.

'I'm waiting,' he said.

He leaned back in his chair and lit a Gitane. Four more hours to go. Yvette would be waiting for him. He would have time to call at her apartment before he went home to his wife. Maybe there would even be time to –

He heard it then, and he could not believe it. It was a voice so pure and so sweet that it sent chills down his spine. It was a voice filled with longing and desire, a voice that sang of loneliness and despair, of lost loves and dead dreams, and it brought tears to his eyes. It stirred emotions in him that he had thought long since dead. All he could say to himself was, 'Jesus Christ! Where has she been?'

An engineer had wandered into the control booth, and he stood there listening, mesmerized. The door was open and others began to come in, drawn by the voice. They stood there silently listening to the poignant sound of a heart

117

desperately crying out for love, and there was not another sound in the room.

When the song ended, there was a long silence, and one of the women said, 'Whoever she is, don't let her get away.'

Louis Bonnet hurried out of the room into the broadcasting studio. Teresa was getting ready to leave.

'I'm sorry I took too long. You see, I've never –

'Sit down, Maria.'

'Teresa.'

'Sorry.' He took a deep breath. 'We do a musical radio broadcast every Saturday night.'

'I know. I listen to it.'

'How would you like to be on it?'

She stared at him, unable to believe what she was hearing. 'You mean – you want to *employ* me?'

'Beginning this week. We'll start you at the minimum. It will be a great showcase for you.'

It was almost too good to be true. *They're* going to pay me to sing.

'Pay you? How much?' Monique asked.

'I don't know. I don't care.' *The important thing is that somebody wants me*, she almost said, but she stopped herself.

'That's wonderful news. So you're going to be on the radio!' her father said.

Her mother was already making plans.

'We'll see that all our friends listen, and we'll have them send in letters saying how good you are.'

Teresa looked at Monique, waiting for her to say, *You don't have to do that. Teresa is good.*

But Monique said nothing. *It will blow over quickly*, she thought.

She was wrong.

That Saturday night at the broadcasting station, Teresa was in a panic.

118

'Believe me,' Louis Bonnet assured her, 'it's perfectly natural. All artists go through this.'

They were seated in the small green-room used by performers.

'You're going to be a sensation.'

'I'm going to be sick.'

'There's no time. You're on in two minutes.'

Teresa had rehearsed that afternoon with the small orchestra that was going to accompany her. The rehearsal had been extraordinary. The stage from which they broadcast was crowded with station personnel who had heard about the young girl with the incredible voice. They listened in awed silence as Teresa rehearsed the songs she was going to sing. There was no question in any of their minds but that they were witnessing the birth of an important star.

'It's too bad she's not better looking,' a stage manager commented, 'but in radio who can tell the difference?'

Teresa's performance that evening was superb. She was aware that she had never sung better. And who knew where this could lead? She might become famous and have men at her feet, begging her to marry them. As they begged Monique.

As though reading her thoughts, Monique said, 'I'm really happy for you, Sis, but don't let yourself get carried away by all this. These things never last.'

This will, Teresa thought happily. *I'm finally a person. I'm somebody*.

On Monday morning, there was a long-distance telephone call for Teresa.

'It's probably somebody's idea of a joke,' her father warned her. 'He says he's Jacques Raimu.' *The most important stage director in France*.

Teresa picked up the telephone, wary. 'Hello?'

'Miss DeFosse?'

'Yes.'

'Teresa DeFosse?'

'Yes.'

'This is Jacques Raimu. I heard your radio programme on Saturday night. You're exactly what I'm looking for.'

'I – I don't understand.'

'I'm staging a play at the Comédie Française, a musical. I start rehearsals next week. I've been searching for someone with a voice like yours. To tell you the truth, there *is* no one with a voice like yours. Who is your agent?'

'Agent? I – I have no agent.'

'Then I'll come up there and we'll work out a deal between us.'

'Monsieur Raimu – I – I'm not very pretty.' It was painful for her to say the words, but she knew that it was necessary. *He mustn't have any false expectations.*

He laughed. 'You will be when I get through with you. Theatre is make-believe. Stage makeup can do all kinds of incredible magic.'

'But –'

'I'll drive up to see you tomorrow.'

It was a dream on top of a fantasy. To be starring in a play by Raimu!

'I'll work out the contract with him,' Teresa's father said. 'You must be careful when you deal with theatre people.'

'We must get you a new dress,' her mother said. 'And I'll invite him to dinner.'

Monique said nothing. What was happening was unbearable. It was unthinkable that her sister was going to become a star. Perhaps there was a way . . .

Monique saw to it that she was the first one downstairs when Jacques Raimu arrived at the DeFosse château that afternoon. He was greeted by a young girl so beautiful

120

that his heart jumped. She was dressed in a simple white afternoon frock that set off her figure to perfection.

My God, he thought. *Those looks and that voice! She's perfect. She's going to be an enormous star.*

'I can't tell you how happy I am to meet you,' Raimu said.

Monique smiled warmly. 'I'm very happy to meet you. I'm a big admirer of yours, Monsieur Raimu.'

'Good. Then we'll work well together. I brought a script with me. It's a beautiful love story, and I think –'

Teresa came into the room. She was wearing a new dress, but she looked awkward in it. She stopped as she saw Jacques Raimu.

'Oh – hello. I didn't know you were here. I mean – you're early.'

He looked at Monique inquiringly.

'This is my sister,' Monique said. 'Teresa.'

They both watched the expression on his face change. It went from shock to disappointment to disgust.

'You're the singer?'

'Yes.'

He turned to Monique. 'And you're –'

Monique smiled innocently. 'I'm Teresa's sister.'

Raimu turned to examine Teresa again, then shook his head. 'I'm sorry,' he said to Teresa. 'You're too –' he fumbled for a word. '– You're too young. If you'll excuse me, I must get back to Paris.'

And they stood there watching him walk out the door.

It worked, Monique thought jubilantly. *It worked.*

That was the last broadcast Teresa ever made. Louis Bonnet pleaded with her to come back, but the hurt was too deep.

After looking at my sister, Teresa thought, *how could anyone want me? I'm so ugly.*

As long as she lived, she would never forget the look on Jacques Raimu's face.

It's my fault for having silly dreams, Teresa told herself. *It's God's way of punishing me.*

After that, Teresa would only sing in church, and she became more of a recluse than ever.

During the next ten years the beautiful Monique turned down more than a dozen marriage proposals. She was proposed to by the sons of the mayor, the banker, the doctor, the merchants in the village. Her suitors ranged from young men fresh out of school to established and successful men in their forties and fifties. They were rich and poor, handsome and ugly, educated and uneducated. And to all of the Monique said *non*.

'What are you looking for?' her father asked, baffled.

'Papa, everyone here is boring. Èze is such an unsophisticated place My dream prince is in Paris.'

And so her father dutifully sent her to Paris. As an afterthought, he sent Teresa with her. The two girls stayed at a small hotel near the Bois de Boulogne.

Each sister saw a different Paris. Monique attended charity balls and glamorous dinner parties and had tea with titled young men. Teresa visited Les Invalides and the Louvre. Monique went to the races at Longchamps and to galas at Malmaison. Teresa went to the Cathedral of Notre Dame to pray, and walked along the tree-shaded path of the Canal St Martin. Monique went to Maxim's and the Moulin Rouge, while Teresa strolled along the Quays, browsing at the book stalls and the flower vendors and stopping at the Basilica St Denis. Teresa enjoyed Paris, but as far as Monique was concerned, the trip was a failure.

When she returned home, she said, 'I can't find any man I want to marry.'

'You met no one who interested you?' her father asked.

'Not really. There was a young man who took me to dinner at Maxim's. His father owns coal mines.'

'What was he like?' her mother asked eagerly.

'Oh, he was rich, handsome, polite, and he adored me.'

'Did he ask you to marry him?'

'Every ten minutes. Finally I simply refused to see him again.'

Her mother stared at Monique in amazement. 'Why?'

'Because all he could talk about was coal: bituminous coal, lump coal, black coal, grey coal. Boring, boring, boring.'

The following year Monique decided she wanted to return to Paris again.

'I'll pack my things,' Teresa said.

Monique shook her head. 'No. This time I think I'll go alone.'

So while Monique went to Paris, Teresa stayed at home and went to church every morning and prayed that her sister would find a handsome prince. And one day the miracle occurred. A miracle because it was to Teresa that it happened. His name was Raoul Giradot.

He had gone to church on Sunday and heard Teresa sing. He had never heard anything like it. *I must meet her*, he vowed.

Early on Monday morning, Teresa called at the village general store to buy fabric for a dress she was making. Raoul Giradot was working behind the counter.

He looked up as Teresa walked in, and his face lit up. 'The voice!'

She stared at him, flustered. 'I – I beg your pardon?'

'I heard you sing in church yesterday. You are magnificent.'

He was handsome and tall, with intelligent, flashing dark eyes and lovely, sensual lips. He was in his early thirties, a year or two older than Teresa.

Teresa was so taken aback by his appearance that she could only stammer. She stared at him, her heart pounding. 'T – thank you,' Teresa said. 'I – I – I would like three yards of muslin, please.'

Raoul smiled. 'It will be my pleasure. This way.'

It was suddenly difficult for Teresa to concentrate on her errand. She was overpoweringly aware of the young man's presence, his good looks and charm, the masculine aura surrounding him.

When Teresa had decided on her purchase and Raoul was wrapping it for her, she dared to say, 'You're – you're new here, aren't you?'

He looked at her and smiled, and it sent shivers through Teresa.

'*Oui*. I arrived in Èze a few days ago. My aunt owns this shop and she needed help, so I thought I would work here for a while.'

How long is a while? Teresa found herself wondering.

'You should be singing professionally,' Raoul told her.

She remembered the expression on Raimu's face when he had seen her. No, she would never risk exposing herself publicly again. 'Thank you,' Teresa mumbled.

He was touched by her embarrassment and shyness. He tried to draw her into conversation.

'I haven't been to Èze before. It's a beautiful little town.'

'Yes,' Teresa mumbled.

'Were you born here?'

'Yes.'

'Do you like it?'

'Yes.'

Teresa picked up her parcel and fled.

The following day Teresa found an excuse to go back to the shop again. She had stayed up half the night preparing what she was going to say to Raoul.

I'm glad you like Èze . . .

The monastery was built in the fourteenth century, you know . . .

Have you ever visited Saint-Paul-de-Vence? There's a lovely chapel there . . .

I enjoy Monte Carlo, don't you? It's wonderful to have it so close to here. Sometimes my sister and I drive down the Grand Corniche and go to the Fort Antoine Theatre. Do you know it? It's the big, open-air theatre . . .

Did you know that Nice was once called Nkaia? Oh, you

didn't? Yes, it was. The Greeks were there a long time ago. There's a museum in Nice with the remains of cavemen who lived there thousands of years ago. Isn't that interesting?

Teresa was prepared with dozens of such verbal gambits. Unfortunately, the moment she walked into the shop and saw Raoul everything flew out of her head. She simply stared at him, unable to speak.

'*Bonjour*,' Raoul said cheerfully. 'It's nice to see you again, Mademoiselle DeFosse.'

'M – *merci*.' She felt like an idiot. *I'm thirty years old*, she told herself, *and I'm acting like a silly schoolgirl. Stop it.*

But she could not stop it.

'And what may I do for you today?'

'I – I need more muslin.'

Which was the last thing she needed.

Teresa watched Raoul as he went to get the bolt of fabric. He set it on the counter and started to measure it out.

'How many yards would you like?'

She started to say two, but what came out was, 'Are you married?'

He looked up at her with a warm smile on his face. 'No,' he said. 'I haven't been that fortunate yet.'

You are going to be, Teresa thought. *As soon as Monique returns from Paris.*

Monique was going to adore this man. They were perfect for each other. The thought of Monique's reaction when she met Raoul filled Teresa with happiness. It would be lovely to have Raoul Giradot as her brother-in-law.

The following day as Teresa was passing the shop, Raoul caught sight of her and hurried outside.

'Good afternoon, Mademoiselle. I was about to take a break. If you're free, would you care to join me for tea?'

'I – I – yes, thank you.'

She was tongue-tied in his presence, and yet Raoul could not have been more pleasant. He did everything he could to put her at ease, and soon Teresa found herself telling this stranger things she had never told anyone before. They talked of loneliness.

'Crowds can make one lonely,' Teresa said. 'I always feel like an island in a sea of people.'

He smiled. 'I understand.'

'Oh, but you must have so many friends.'

'Acquaintances. In the end, does anyone really have many friends?'

It was as though she were speaking to a mirror image. The hour melted away so quickly, and soon it was time for him to go back to work.

As they rose, Raoul asked, 'Will you join me for lunch tomorrow?'

He was being kind, of course. Teresa knew that no man could ever be attracted to her. Especially someone as wonderful as Raoul Giradot. She was sure that he was kind to everyone.

'I would enjoy that,' Teresa said.

When she went to meet Raoul the following day, he said boyishly, 'I've been given the afternoon off. If you're not too busy, why don't we drive down to Nice?'

They drove along the Moyen Corniche, with his car top down, and the city was spread out like a magic carpet below. Teresa leaned back in her seat and thought: *I've never been so happy.* And then, filled with guilt: *I'm being happy for Monique.*

Monique was returning from Paris the following day. Raoul would be Teresa's gift to her sister. Teresa was realistic enough to know that the Raouls of the world were not for her. She had had enough pain in her life. She had long since learned what was real and what was impossible. The handsome man seated beside her driving the car was an impossible dream she dared not even let herself think about.

They had lunch at Le Chantecler in the Negrecso Hotel in Nice. It was a superb meal, but afterwards Teresa had no recollection of what she had eaten. It seemed to her that she and Raoul had not stopped talking. They had so much to say to each other. He was witty and charming, and he appeared to find Teresa interesting – really interesting. He asked her opinion about many things and listened attentively to her answers. They agreed on almost everything. It was as though they were soul mates. If Teresa had any regrets about what was about to happen, she resolutely forced them out of her mind.

'Would you like to come to dinner at the château tomorrow night? My sister is returning from Paris. I would like you to meet her.'

'I'd be delighted, Teresa.'

When Monique returned home the following day, Teresa hurried to greet her at the door.

In spite of her resolve, Teresa could not help asking, 'Did you meet anyone interesting in Paris?' And she held her breath, waiting for her sister's answer.

'The same boring men,' Monique replied.

So God had made the final decision.

'I've invited someone to dinner tonight,' Teresa said. 'I think you're going to like him.'

I must never let anyone know how much I care for him, Teresa thought.

That evening at half seven promptly, the butler ushered Raoul Giradot into the drawing room where Teresa, Monique and their parents were waiting.

'This is my mother and father. Monsieur Raoul Giradot.'

'How do you do?'

Teresa took a deep breath. 'And my sister, Monique.'

'How do you do?' Monique's expression was polite, nothing more.

Teresa looked at Raoul, expecting him to be stunned by Monique's beauty.

'Enchanted.' Merely courteous.

Teresa stood there, holding her breath, waiting for the sparks that she knew would start flying between them. But Raoul was looking at Teresa.

'You look lovely tonight, Teresa.

She blushed and stammered, 'Th – thank you.'

Everything about that evening was topsy-turvy. Teresa's plan to bring Monique and Raoul together, to watch them get married, to have Raoul as a brother-in-law – none of it even began to happen. Incredibly, Raoul's attention was focused entirely on Teresa. It was like some impossible dream come true. She felt like Cinderella, only she was the ugly sister and the prince had chosen her. It was unreal, but it was happening, and Teresa found herself struggling to resist Raoul and his charm because she knew that it was too good to be true, and she dreaded being hurt again. All these years she had hidden her emotions, guarding against the pain that came with rejection. Now, instinctively, she tried to do the same. But Raoul was irresistible.

'I heard your daughter sing,' Raoul said. 'She is a miracle!'

Teresa found herself blushing.

'Everyone loves Teresa's voice,' Monique said sweetly.

It was a heady evening. But the best was yet to come.

When dinner was finished, Raoul said, 'Your grounds look lovely.' He turned to Teresa. 'Would you show me the gardens?'

Teresa looked over at Monique, trying to read her sister's emotions, but Monique seemed completely indifferent.

She must be deaf, dumb and blind, Teresa thought.

And then she recalled all the times Monique had gone to Paris and Cannes and St Tropez looking for her perfect prince but had never found him.

So it's not the fault of the men. It's the fault of my sister. She has no idea what she wants.

Teresa turned to Raoul. 'I would love to.'

Outside, Teresa could not let the subject drop.

'How did you like Monique?'

'She seems very nice,' Raoul replied. 'Ask me how I like her sister.'

And he took Teresa in his arms and kissed her.

It was like nothing Teresa had ever experienced before.

She trembled in his arms, and she thought: *Thank you, God. Oh, thank you.*

'Will you have dinner with me tomorrow night?' Raoul asked.

'Yes,' Teresa breathed. 'Oh, yes.'

When the two sisters were alone, Monique said, 'He really seems to like you.'

'I think so,' Teresa said shyly.

'Do you like him?'

'Yes.'

'Well, be careful, big sister,' Monique laughed. 'Don't get in over your head.'

Too late, Teresa thought helplessly. *Too late.*

Teresa and Raoul were together every day after that. Monique usually chaperoned them. The three of them walked along the promenades and beaches at Nice and laughed at the wedding-cake hotels. They lunched at a charming bistro at Cap d'Antibes, and visited the Matisse Chapel in Vence. They dined at the Château de la Chèvre d'Or, and at the fabulous La Ferme St Michel. One morning at 5.00 a.m. the three of them went to the open farmers' market that filled the streets of Monte Carlo and bought fresh breads and vegetables and fruit.

On Sundays, when Teresa sang in church, Raoul and Monique were there to listen, and afterwards Raoul would hug Teresa and say, 'You really are a miracle. I could listen to you sing for the rest of my life.'

Four weeks after Teresa met him, Raoul proposed.

'I'm sure you could have any man you want, Teresa,' Raoul said, 'but I would be honoured if you chose me.'

For one terrible moment Teresa thought he was ridiculing her, but before she could speak, he went on.

'My darling, I must tell you that I have known many

women, but you are the most sensitive, the most talented, the warmest –'

Each word was music to Teresa's ears. She wanted to laugh; she wanted to cry. *How blessed I am*, she thought, *to love and be loved*.

'Will you marry me?'

And her look was answer enough.

When Raoul left, Teresa went flying into the library where her sister, mother and father were having coffee.

'Raoul asked me to marry him.' Her face was glowing, and there was almost a beauty about her.

Her parents stared at her, stunned. It was Monique who spoke.

'Teresa, are you sure he's not after the family money?'

It was like a slap in the face.

'I don't mean that unkindly,' Monique went on, 'but it all seems to be happening so fast.'

Teresa was determined not to let anything spoil her happiness. 'I know you want to protect me,' she told her sister, 'but Raoul has money. His father left him a small inheritance, and he's not afraid to work for a living.' She took her sister's hand in hers and begged, 'Please be glad for me, Monique. I never thought I'd know this feeling. I'm so happy I could die.'

And then the three of them embraced her and told her how pleased they were for her and they began to talk excitedly about plans for the wedding.

Very early the next morning Teresa went to church and knelt to pray.

'Thank you, Father. Thank You for giving me such happiness. I will do everything to make myself worthy of your love and of Raoul's. Amen.'

Teresa walked into the general store, her feet above the ground, and said, 'If you please, sir, I would like to order some material for a wedding gown.'

130

Raoul laughed and took her in his arms. 'You're going to make a beautiful bride.'

And Teresa knew he meant it. That was the miracle.

The wedding was set to take place a month later in the village church. Monique, of course, was to be the maid of honour.

At five o'clock on Friday afternoon, Teresa spoke to Raoul for the last time. At 12.30 on Saturday, standing in the church vestry waiting for Raoul, who was thirty minutes late, Teresa was approached by the priest. He took her arm and led her aside, and she wondered at his agitation. Her heart began to pound.

'What is it? Is something wrong? Has anything happened to Raoul?'

'Oh, my dear,' her father said. 'My poor, dear Teresa.'

She was beginning to panic. 'What is it, Father? Tell me!'

'We – we just received word a moment ago. Raoul –'

'Is it an accident? Was he hurt?'

'Giradot left town a half an hour ago.'

'*He what?* Then some emergency must have come up to make him –'

'He left with your sister. They were seen taking the train to Paris.'

The room began to whirl. *No*, Teresa thought. *I mustn't faint. I mustn't embarrass God.*

She had only a hazy memory of the events that followed. Teresa's mother put her arms around her daughter and said, 'My poor Teresa. That your own sister could be so cruel. I'm so sorry.'

But Teresa was suddenly calm. She knew how to make everything all right.

'Don't worry, Mama. I don't blame Raoul for falling in love with Monique. Any man would. I should have known that no man could ever love me.'

'You're wrong,' her father cried. 'You're worth ten of Monique.'

But his compassion came years too late.

131

'I would like to go home now, please.'

They made their way through the crowd. The guests at the church moved aside to let them pass, staring silently after them.

When they returned to the château, Teresa said again, 'Please don't worry about me. I promise you that everything is going to be fine.'

Then she went up to her father's room, took out his razor and slashed her wrists.

Chapter 12

When Teresa opened her eyes, the family doctor and the village priest were standing beside her bed.

'No!' she screamed. 'I don't want to come back. Let me die. Let me die!'

The priest said, 'Suicide is a mortal sin. God gave you life, Teresa. Only He may decide when it is finished. You are young. You have a whole lifetime ahead of you.'

'To do what?' Teresa sobbed. 'Suffer more? I can't stand the pain I'm in. I can't stand it!'

He said gently, 'Jesus stood the pain and died for the rest of us. Don't turn your back on Him.'

The doctor finished examining Teresa. 'You need to rest. I've told your mother to put you on a light diet for a while.' He wagged a finger at her. 'That does not include razor blades.'

The following morning Teresa dragged herself out of bed. When she walked into the drawing room, her mother said in alarm, 'What are you doing up? The doctor told you –'

Teresa said hoarsely, 'I have to go to church. I have to talk to God.'

Her mother hesitated. 'I'll go with you.'

'No. I must go alone.'

'But –'

Her father nodded. 'Let her go.'

They watched the dispirited figure walk out of the house.

'What's going to happen to her?' Teresa's mother moaned.

'God only knows.'

*

She entered the familiar church, walked up to the altar and knelt.

'I've come to Your house to tell You something, God. I despise You. I despise You for letting me be born ugly. I despise You for letting my sister be born beautiful. I despise You for letting her take away the only man I ever loved. I spit on You.'

Her last words were so loud that the people inside turned to stare at her as she rose and stumbled out of the church.

Teresa had never believed there could be such pain. It was unbearable. It was impossible to think of anything else. She was unable to eat or sleep. The world seemed muffled and far away. Memories kept flashing into her mind, like scenes from a film.

She remembered the day she and Raoul and Monique had walked along the beach at Nice.

'It's a beautiful day for a swim,' Raoul said.

'I'd love to go, but we can't. Teresa doesn't swim.'

'I don't mind if you two go ahead. I'll wait for you at the hotel.'

And she had been so pleased that Raoul and Monique were getting along so well together.

They were lunching at a small inn near Cagnes. The maître d' said, 'The lobster is particularly good today.'

'I'll have it,' Monique said. 'Poor Teresa can't. Shellfish makes her break out in hives.'

St Tropez. 'I miss horseback riding. I used to ride every morning at home. Do you want to ride with me, Teresa?'

'I – I'm afraid I don't ride, Raoul.'

'I wouldn't mind going with you,' Monique said. 'I love to ride.'

And they had been gone all morning.

There were a hundred clues, and she had missed all of them. She had been blind because she wanted to be

134

blind. The looks that Raoul and Monique had exchanged, the innocent touching of hands, the whispers and the laughter.

How could I have been so stupid?

At night when Teresa finally managed to doze off, she had dreams. It was always a different dream. It was always the same dream.

Raoul and Monique were on a train, naked, making love and the train was crossing a trestle high over a canyon, and the trestle collapsed and everyone on the train plunged to their deaths.

Raoul and Monique were in a hotel room, naked in bed, and Raoul laid down a cigarette and the room exploded in flames and the two of them were burned to death, and their screams awakened Teresa.

Raoul and Monique fell from a mountain, drowned in a river, died in an airplane crash.

It was always a different dream.

It was always the same dream.

Teresa's mother and father were frantic. They watched their daughter wasting away, and there was nothing they could do to help her. And then suddenly Teresa began to eat. She ate constantly. She could not seem to get enough food. She gained her weight back, and then kept gaining and gaining until her body was gross.

When her mother and father tried to talk to her about her pain, Teresa said, 'I'm fine now. Don't worry about me.'

Teresa carried on her life as though nothing were wrong. She continued to go into town and shop and do all the errands she had always done. She joined her mother and father for dinner each evening and read or sewed. She had built an emotional fortress around herself, and she was determined that no one would ever breach it. *No man will ever want to look at me. Never again.*

Outwardly, Teresa seemed fine. Inside, she was sunk in an abyss of deep, desperate loneliness. Even when she was surrounded by people, she sat in a lonely chair in a lonely room, in a lonely house, in a lonely world.

A little over a year after Raoul had left Teresa, her father was packing to leave for Ávila.

'I have some business to transact there,' he told Teresa. 'But after that, I'll be free. Why don't you come with me? Ávila is a fascinating town. It will do you good to get away from here for a while.'

'No, thank you, Father.'

He looked at his wife and sighed. 'Very well.'

The butler walked into the drawing room.

'Excuse me, Miss DeFosse. This letter just arrived for you.'

Even before Teresa opened it, she was filled with a prescience of something terrible looming before her.

The letter read:

Teresa, my darling Teresa:

God knows I do not have a right to call you darling, after the terrible thing I have done, but I promise to make it up to you if it takes me a lifetime. I don't know where to begin.

Monique has run off and left me with our two-month-old daughter. Frankly, I am relieved. I must confess that I have been in hell ever since the day I left you. I will never understand why I did what I did. I seem to have been caught up in some kind of magic spell of Monique's, but I knew from the beginning that my marriage to her was a terrible mistake. It was you I always loved. I know now that the only place I can find my happiness is at your side. By the time you receive this letter, I will be on my way back to you.

I love you, and I have always loved you, Teresa.

136

> For the sake of the rest of our lives together, I beg
> your forgiveness. I want . . .

She could not finish reading the letter. The thought of seeing
Raoul again and his and Monique's baby was unthinkable,
obscene.

She threw the letter down, hysterical.

'I must get out of here,' Teresa screamed. 'Tonight. Now.
Please . . . please!'

It was impossible for them to calm her.

'If Raoul is coming here,' her father said, 'you should at
least talk to him.'

'No! If I see him, I'll kill him.' She grabbed her father's
arms, tears streaming down her face. 'Take me with you,'
Teresa pleaded.

She would go anywhere, as long as she escaped from this
place.

And so that evening Teresa and her father set out for Ávila.

Teresa's father was distraught over his daughter's unhappiness. He was not by nature a compassionate man, but in the
last year Teresa had won his admiration by her courageous
behaviour. She had faced the townspeople with her head
held high and had never complained. He felt helpless, unable
to console her.

He remembered how much solace she had once found in
the church, and when they arrived in Ávila he said to Teresa,
'Father Berrendo, the priest here, is an old friend of mine.
Perhaps he can help you. Will you speak to him?'

'No.' She would have nothing to do with God.

Teresa stayed in the hotel room alone while her father
conducted his business. When he returned, Teresa was
seated in the same chair, staring at the walls.

'Teresa, please see Father Berrendo.'

'No.'

He was at a loss. Teresa refused to leave the hotel room
and she refused to return to Èze.

137

In the end, the priest came to see Teresa.

'Your father tells me that you once attended church regularly.'

Teresa looked into the eyes of the frail-looking priest and said coldly, 'I'm no longer interested. The Church has nothing to offer me.'

Father Berrendo smiled. 'The Church has something to offer everyone, my child. The Church gives us hope and dreams . . .'

'I've had my fill of dreams. Never again.'

He took her hands in his thin hands and saw the white scars of razor slashes on her wrists, as faint as a long ago memory.

'God doesn't believe that. Talk to Him and He will tell you.'

Teresa sat there, staring at the wall, and when the priest finally made his way out, she was not even aware of it.

The following morning Teresa walked into the cool, vaulted church, and almost immediately the old, familiar feeling of peace stole over her. The last time she had been in a church was to curse God. A feeling of deep shame filled her. It was her own weakness that had betrayed her, not God.

'Forgive me,' she whispered. 'I have sinned. I have lived in hate. Help me. Please help me.'

She looked up, and Father Berrendo was standing there. When she finished, he led her into his office behind the vestry.

'I don't know what to do, Father. I don't believe in anything any more. I've lost faith.' Her voice was filled with despair.

'Did you have faith when you were a young girl?'

'Yes. Very much.'

'Then you still have it, my child. Faith is real and permanent. It is everything else that is transient.'

They talked that day for hours.

When Teresa returned to the hotel late in the afternoon,

her father said, 'I must get back to Èze. Are you ready to leave?'

'No, Papa. Let me stay here for a while.'

He hesitated. 'Will you be all right?'

'Yes, Father. I promise.'

Teresa and Father Berrendo met every day after that. Father Berrendo's heart went out to Teresa. He saw in her not a fat, unattractive woman, but a beautiful, unhappy spirit. They spoke of God and creation and the meaning of life, and slowly, almost in spite of herself, Teresa began to find comfort again. Something that Father Berrendo said one day triggered a deep response.

'My child, if you do not believe in this world, then believe in the next world. Believe in the world where Jesus is waiting to receive you.'

And for the first time since the terrible thing that had happened to her, Teresa began to feel at peace again. The church had become her haven, just as it had once been. But there was her future to think about.

'I have no place to go.'

'You could return home.'

'No. I could never go back there. I could never face Raoul again. I don't know what to do. I want to hide, and there is no place to hide.'

Father Berrendo was silent for a long time. Finally he spoke. 'You could stay here.'

She looked around the office, puzzled. 'Here?'

'The Cistercian convent is nearby.' He leaned forward. 'Let me tell you about it. It is a world inside a world, where everyone is dedicated to God. It is a place of peace and serenity.'

And Teresa's heart began to lift. 'It sounds wonderful.'

'I must caution you. It is one of the strictest orders in the world. Those who are admitted take a vow of chastity, silence and obedience. No one who enters there ever leaves.'

The words sent a thrill through Teresa. 'I will never want

139

to leave. It is what I have been searching for, Father. I despise the world I live in.'

But Father Berrendo was still concerned. He knew that Teresa would be facing a life totally different from anything she had ever experienced.

'There can be no turning back.'

'I won't turn back.'

Early the next day, Father Berrendo took Teresa to the convent to meet the Reverend Mother Betina. He left the two of them there to talk.

The moment Teresa entered the convent, she knew. *At last*, she thought exultantly. *At last*.

Teresa telephoned her mother and father.

'I've been so worried,' her mother said. 'When are you coming home?'

'I am home.'

The Bishop of Ávila performed the rite:

'Creator, Lord, send thy benediction upon thy handmaid that she shall be fortified with celestial virtue, that she may maintain complete faith and unbroken fidelity.'

Teresa responded, 'The kingdom of this world and all secular adornings, I have despised for the love of our Lord, Jesus Christ.'

The bishop made the sign of the cross over her.

'*De largitatis tuae fonte defluxit ut cum honorem nupiarum nulla interdicta minuissent ac super sanctum conjugium nuptialis benedictio permaneret existerent connubium, concupiscerent sacramentum, nec imitarentur quod nuptiis agitur, sed diligerent quod nuptiis prae notatur. Amen.*'

'Amen.'

'I espouse thee to Jesus Christ, the son of the Supreme Father. Therefore receive the seal of the Holy Ghost, so that thou be called the spouse of God, and if thou serve him faithfully, be crowned everlastingly.' The bishop rose. 'God, the Father Almighty, Creator of heaven and earth, who hath vouchsafed to choose you to an espousalship like that of the blessed Mary, mother of our Lord, Jesus Christ – *ad beatae Mariae matris Domini nostri* Jesus Christ consortium – hallow you, that in the presence of God and of His angels, you may persevere, untouched and undefiled, and hold to your purpose, love, chastity, and keep patience that you may merit to receive the crown of His blessing, through the same Christ our Lord. God make you strong when frail, strengthen you when weak, relieve and govern your mind with piety and direct your ways. Amen.'

Now, thirty years later, lying in the woods watching the sun come up over the horizon, Sister Teresa thought: *I came to the convent for all the wrong reasons. I was not running to God. I was running away from the world. But God read my heart.*

She was sixty years old, and the last thirty years of her life had been the happiest she had ever known. And now she had suddenly been flung back into the world she had run away from. And her mind was playing strange tricks on her.

She was no longer sure what was real and what was unreal. The past and the present seemed to be blending together in a strange dizzying blur. *Why is this happening to me? What does God have planned for me?*

Chapter 13

For Sister Megan, the journey was an adventure. She had become used to the new sights and sounds that surrounded her, and the speed with which she had adapted surprised her.

She found her companions fascinating. Amparo Jiron was a powerful woman, easily able to keep up with the two men, and yet at the same time she was very feminine.

Felix Carpio, the husky man with a reddish beard and a scar, seemed amiable and pleasant.

But to Megan, the most compelling of the group was Jaime Miró. There was a relentless strength about him, an unshakable faith in his beliefs that reminded Megan of the nuns in the convent.

When they began the journey, Jaime and Amparo and Felix were carrying sleeping-bags and rifles on their shoulders.

'Let me carry one of the sleeping-bags,' Megan suggested.

Jaime Miró had looked at her in surprise, then shrugged. 'All right, Sister.'

He handed her the bag. It was heavier than Megan had expected, but she did not complain. *As long as I'm with them, I'm going to do my share.*

It seemed to Megan that they had been walking for ever, stumbling through the darkness, hit by branches, scratched by underbrush, attacked by insects, guided only by the light of the moon.

Who are these people? Megan wondered. *And why are they being hunted?* Because Megan and the other nuns were also being pursued, Megan felt a strong rapport with her new companions.

There was little talking, but from time to time they held cryptic conversations.

'Is everything set at Valladolid?'

'Right, Jaime. Rubio and Tomas will meet us at the bank during the bullfight.'

'Good. Send word to Largo Cortez to expect us. But don't give him a date.'

'*Comprendo.*'

Who are Largo Cortez and Rubio and Tomas? Megan wondered. *And what was going to happen at the bullfight and the bank?* She almost started to ask, but thought better of it. *I have the feeling they wouldn't welcome a lot of questions.*

Near dawn they smelled smoke from the valley below them.

'Wait here,' Jaime whispered. 'Be quiet.'

They watched as Jaime made his way towards the edge of the forest and disappeared from sight.

Megan said, 'What is it –?'

'Shut up!' Amparo Jiron hissed.

Fifteen minutes later Jaime Miró returned.

'Soldiers. We'll circle around them.'

They back-tracked for half a mile, then moved cautiously through the woods until they reached a side road. The countryside stretched out ahead of them, redolent with the odours of mown hay and ripe fruit.

Megan's curiosity got the better of her. 'Why are the soldiers looking for you?' she asked.

Jaime Miró said, 'Let's say we don't see eye to eye.'

And she had to be satisfied with that. *For now*, she thought. She was determined to know more about this man.

Half an hour later when they reached a sheltered clearing, Jaime said, 'The sun's up. We'll stay here until nightfall.' He looked at Megan. 'Tonight we're going to have to travel faster.'

She nodded. 'Very well.'

Jaime took the sleeping-bags and rolled them out.

Felix Carpio said to Megan, 'You take mine, Sister. I'm used to sleeping on the ground.'

'It's yours,' Megan said. 'I couldn't –'

'For Christ's sake,' Amparo snapped. 'Get into the bag. We don't want you to keep us awake screaming about god-damned spiders.' There was an animosity in her tone that Megan did not understand.

Without another word, Megan climbed into the sleeping-bag. *What's bothering her?* Megan wondered.

Megan watched as Jaime unrolled his sleeping-bag a few feet away from where she lay. He crawled into the bag. Amparo Jiron crawled in beside him. *I see*, Megan thought.

Jaime looked over at Megan. 'You'd better get some sleep,' he said. 'We have a long way ahead of us.'

Megan was awakened by a moaning. It sounded as though someone were in terrible pain. Megan sat up, concerned. The sounds were coming from Jaime's sleeping-bag. *He must be terribly ill*, was her first thought.

The moaning was getting louder, and then Megan heard Amparo Jiron's voice saying, 'Oh, yes, yes. Give it to me, *Querida*. Harder! Yes! Now! Now!'

And Megan's face flushed. She tried to close her ears to the sounds she was hearing, but it was impossible. And she wondered what it would be like to have Jaime Miró make love to her.

Instantly Megan crossed herself and began to pray: *Forgive me, Father. Let my thoughts be filled only with You. Let my spirit seek You that it may find its source and good in You.*

And the sounds went on. Finally, when Megan thought she would be unable to bear it an instant longer, they stopped. But there were other noises to keep her awake. The sounds of the forest ricocheted around her. There was a cacophony of mating birds and crickets and the chattering of small animals and the guttural growlings of larger ones.

Megan had forgotten how noisy the outside world could be. She missed the wonderful silence of the convent. To her own astonishment, she even missed the orphanage. The terrible, wonderful orphanage . . .

Chapter 14

Ávila 1957

They called her 'Megan the Terror'.

They called her 'Megan the Blue-eyed Devil'.

They called her 'Megan the Impossible'.

She was ten years old.

She had been brought to the orphanage when she was an infant, left on the doorstep of a farmer and his wife who were unable to care for her.

The orphanage was an austere, two-storey, white-washed building on the outskirts of Avila, in the poorer section of the city, off the Plaza de Saint Vicente, run by Mercedes Angeles, an Amazon of a woman with a fierce manner that belied the warmth she felt for her wards.

Megan was different from the other children, an alien with blonde hair and bright blue eyes, standing out in stark contrast to the dark-eyed, dark-haired children. But from the beginning, Megan was different in other ways. She was a fiercely independent child, a leader, a mischief-maker. Whenever there was trouble at the orphanage, Mercedes Angeles could be certain that Megan was at the bottom of it.

Over the years, Megan led riots protesting about the food, she tried to form the children into a union, and she found inventive ways of tormenting the supervisors, including half a dozen escape attempts. Needless to say, Megan was immensely popular with the other children. She was younger than many of them, but they all turned to her for guidance.

She was a natural leader. And the younger children loved to have Megan tell them stories. She had a wild imagination.

'Who were my parents, Megan?'

'Ah. Your father was a clever jewel thief. He climbed over the roof of a hotel in the middle of the night to steal a diamond belonging to a famous actress. Well, just as he was putting the diamond in his pocket, the actress woke up. She turned on the light and saw him.'

'Did she have him arrested?'

'No. He was very handsome.'

'What happened then?'

'They fell in love and got married. Then you were born.'

'But why did they send me to an orphanage? Didn't they love me?'

That was always the difficult part. 'Of course they loved you. But – well – they were skiing in Switzerland and they were killed in a terrible avalanche –'

'What's a terrible avalanche?'

'That's when a bunch of snow comes down all at once and buries you.'

'And my mother and father both died?'

'Yes. And their last words were that they loved you. But there was no one to take care of you, so you were sent here.'

Megan was as anxious as the others to know who her parents were, and at night she would put herself to sleep by making up stories to herself: 'My father was a soldier in the Civil War,' she would think. 'He was a captain and very brave. He was wounded in battle, and my mother was the nurse who took care of him. They married, and he went back to the front and was killed. My mother was too poor to keep me, so she had to leave me at the farmhouse, and it broke her heart.' And she would weep with pity for her courageous, dead father and her bereaved mother.

Or: 'My father was a bullfighter. He was one of the great Matadors. He was the toast of Spain. Everyone adored him. My mother was a beautiful flamenco dancer. They were married, but he was killed one day by a huge, dangerous bull. My mother was forced to give me up.'

Or: 'My father was a clever spy from another country . . .'
The fantasies were endless.

There were thirty children in the orphanage, ranging from
abandoned newborn infants to fourteen-year-olds. Most of
them were Spanish, but there were children there from half
a dozen countries, and Megan became fluent in several
languages. She slept in a dormitory with a dozen other girls.
There were late-night whispered conversations about dolls
and clothes, and as the girls grew older, about sex. It soon
became the primary topic of conversation.

'I hear it hurts a lot.'

'I don't care. I can't wait to do it.'

'I'm going to get married, but I'm never going to let my
husband do it to me. I think it's dirty.'

One night, when everyone was asleep, Primo Conde, one
of the young boys at the orphanage, crept into the girls'
dormitory. He moved to the side of Megan's bed.

'Megan . . .' His voice was a whisper.

She was instantly awake. 'Primo? What's the matter?'

He was sobbing, frightened. 'Can I get into bed with you?'

'Yes. Be quiet.'

Primo was thirteen, the same age as Megan, but he was
small for his age, and had been an abused child. He suffered
from terrible nightmares and would wake up in the middle
of the night screaming. The other children tormented him,
and Megan was the one who always protected him.

Primo climbed into bed beside her, and Megan felt the
tears running down his cheeks. She held him close in her
arms.

'It's all right,' Megan whispered. 'It's all right.'

She rocked him gently and his sobs subsided. His body
was pressed against hers, and she could feel his growing
excitement.

'Primo . . .'

'I'm sorry. I – I can't help it.'

His erection was pressing into her.

'I love you, Megan. You're the only one I care about in the whole world.'

'You haven't been out in the world yet.'

'Please don't laugh at me.'

'I'm not.'

'I have no one but you.'

'I know.'

'I love you.'

'I love you, too, Primo.'

'Megan – would you – let me make love to you? Please.'

'No.'

There was silence. 'I'm sorry I bothered you. I'll go back to my bed.' His voice was filled with pain. He started to move away.

'Wait.' Megan held him close to her, wanting to ease his suffering, feeling aroused herself. 'Primo, I – I can't let you make love to me, but I can do something to make you feel better. Will that be all right?'

'Yes.' His voice was a murmur.

He was wearing pyjamas. Megan pulled the cord that held his pyjama bottom up and reached inside. *He's a man*, Megan thought. She held him gently in her hand and began to stroke him. Primo groaned and said, 'Oh, that feels wonderful,' and a moment later, 'God, I love you, Megan.'

Her body was on fire, and if at that moment he had said, 'I want to make love to you,' she would have said yes.

But he lay there, silent, and in a few minutes he returned to his own bed.

There was no sleep for Megan that night. And she had never allowed him to come into her bed again.

The temptation was too great.

From time to time the children would be called into the supervisor's office to meet a prospective foster parent. It was always a moment of great excitement for the children, for it would mean a chance to escape from the dreary routine of

149

the orphanage, a chance to have a real home, to belong to someone.

Over the years Megan watched as other orphans were chosen. They went to the homes of merchants, farmers, bankers, shopkeepers. But it was always the other children, never Megan. Her reputation proceeded her. She would hear the prospective parents talk among themselves.

'She's a very pretty child, but I hear she's difficult.'

'Isn't she the one who smuggled twelve dogs into the orphanage last month?'

'They say she's a ringleader. I'm afraid she wouldn't get along with our children.'

They had no idea how much the other children adored Megan.

Father Berrendo came to the orphanage once a week to visit the wards, and Megan looked forward to his visits. Megan was an omnivorous reader, and the priest and Mercedes Angeles saw to it that she was well supplied with books. She could discuss things with the priest that she dared not talk about with anyone else. It was Father Berrendo to whom the farm couple had turned over the infant Megan

'Why didn't they want to keep me?' Megan asked.

The old priest said gently, 'They wanted to very much, Megan, but they were old and ill.'

'Why do you suppose my real parents left me at that farm?'

'I'm sure it was because they were poor and couldn't afford to keep you.'

As Megan grew up, she became more and more devout. She was stirred by the intellectual aspects of the Catholic Church. She read St Augustine's Confessions, the writings of St Francis of Assisi, Thomas Merton, Thomas More, and a dozen others. Megan went to church regularly, and she enjoyed the solemn rituals, the Gloria Patri, receiving the Eucharist, the doxology, the benediction. Perhaps most of all, she loved the wonderful feeling of serenity that always stole over her in church.

'I want to become a Catholic,' Megan told Father Berrendo one day.

He took her hand in his and said with a twinkle, 'Perhaps you are already, Megan, but we'll hedge our bets.' He gave her the Catholic cathechism:

'*Quid petis ab Ecclesia dei?*'

'*Fidem!*'

'*Fides quid tibi praestat?*'

'*Vitam Aeternam.*'

'*Abrenuntias Satanae?*'

'*Sic.*'

'Dost thou believe in God the Father Almighty, creator of heaven and earth?'

'*Credo!*'

'Dost thou believe in Jesus Christ, His only son, who was born and suffered?'

'*Credo!*'

'Dost thou believe in the Holy Spirit in the Holy Catholic Church, the communion of saints, the remission of sins, the resurrection of the body and eternal life?'

'*Credo!*'

The priest blew gently into her face. '*Exi ab eo spiritus immunde.* Depart from her, thou impure spirit and give place to the Holy Spirit, the paraclete.' He breathed again into her face. 'Megan, receive the good Spirit through this breathing and receive the blessing of God. Peace be with thee.'

At fifteen Megan had become a beautiful young woman, with long blonde hair and a milky complexion that set her off even more from most of her companions.

One day she was summoned to the office of Mercedes Angeles. Father Berrendo was there.

'Hello, Father.'

'Hello, my dear Megan.'

Mercedes Angeles said, 'I'm afraid we have a problem, Megan.'

151

'Oh?' She wracked her brain, trying to remember her latest misdeed.

The head mistress went on: 'There is an age limit here of fifteen, and you've reached your fifteenth birthday.'

Megan had long known of the rule, of course. But she had put it in the back of her mind, because she did not want to face the fact that she had nowhere in the world to go, that no one wanted her, and that she was going to be abandoned once again.

'Do I – do I have to leave?'

The kindly Amazon was upset, but she had no choice. 'I'm afraid we must abide by the rules. We can find a position for you as a maid.'

Megan had no words.

Father Berrendo spoke. 'Where would you like to go?'

As she thought about it, an idea came to Megan. There *was* somewhere for her to go.

From the time Megan was twelve years old, she had helped earn her keep at the orphanage by making outside deliveries in town, and many of them were made to the Cistercian convent. They were always delivered to the Reverend Mother Betina. Megan had sneaked glimpses of the nuns praying, or walking through the corridors, and she had sensed an almost overpowering feeling of serenity. She envied the joy that the nuns seemed to radiate. To Megan, the convent seemed a house of love.

The Reverend Mother had taken a liking to the bright young girl, and they had had long talks over the years.

'Why do people join convents?' Megan had asked.

'People come to us for many reasons. Most come to dedicate themselves to God. But some come because they have no hope. We give them hope. Some come because they feel they have no reason to live. We show them that God is the reason. Some come because they are running away. Others come here because they are alienated and they want to belong.'

That was what had struck a responsive chord in the young girl. *I've never really belonged to anyone*, Megan thought. *This is my chance.*

'I think I would like to join the convent.'

Six weeks later, Megan took her vows.

And finally Megan had found what she had been searching for so long. She belonged. These were her sisters, the family she had never had, and they were all one under their Father.

Megan worked in the convent as a bookkeeper, keeping the records. She was fascinated by the ancient sign language that the sisters used when they needed to communicate with the Reverend Mother. There were 472 signs, enough to convey among themselves everything they needed to express.

When it was a sister's turn to dust the long corridors, Prioress Betina held out her right hand with the heel forward and blew on the back of it. If a nun had a fever, she went to the Reverend Mother and pressed the tip of her right forefinger and middle finger on the outside of her left wrist. If a request was to be delayed, Prioress Betina held her right fist before her right shoulder and pushed it slightly forward and down. *Tomorrow*.

One November morning Megan was introduced to the rites of death. A nun was dying, and a wooden rattle was rung in the cloister, the signal for the beginning of a ritual unchanged since the year 1030. All those who could answer the call hurried to kneel in the infirmary for the anointing and the psalms. They silently prayed for the saints to intercede for the departing sister's soul. To signify that it was time for the last sacraments to be given, the Mother Prioress held out her left hand with the palm up and drew a cross on it with the tip of her right thumb.

And finally, there was the sign of death itself, a sister placing the tip of her right thumb under her chin and raising it slightly.

When the last prayers had been said, the body was left alone for an hour so that the soul could go in peace. At the foot of the bed the great Paschal candle, the Christian symbol of eternal light, burned in its wooden holder.

The infirmarian washed the body and clothed the dead

nun in her habit, black scapular over white cowl, rough stockings and handmade sandals. From the garden one of the nuns brought fresh flowers, woven into a crown. When the dead woman was dressed, six of the nuns in a procession carried her to the church and placed her on the white-sheeted bier facing the altar. She would not be left alone before her God, and in their stalls by her side, two nuns stayed through the rest of the day and on through the night praying, while the Paschal candle flickered at her side.

The next afternoon, after the requiem mass, she was carried through the cloister by the nuns to the private, walled cemetery where even in death the nuns kept their enclosure. The sisters, three and three, lowered her carefully into the grave, supported on white bands of linen. It was the Cistercian custom for their dead to lie uncovered in the earth, buried without a coffin. And the last service they performed for their sister was for two nuns to start to drop soil softly on to her still body before they all returned to the church to say the psalms of penance. Three times they begged that God have mercy on her soul:

Domine miserere super peccatrice
Domine miserere super peccatrice
Domine miserere super peccatrice

There were often times when young Megan was filled with melancholy. The convent gave her serenity, and yet she was not completely at peace. It was as though a part of her was missing. She felt longings that she should have long ago forgotten. She found herself thinking about the friends she had left behind in the orphanage, and wondering what had happened to them. And she wondered what was happening in the outside world, the world that she had renounced, a world where there was music and dancing and laughter.

Megan went to Reverend Mother Betina.

'It happens to all of us from time to time,' she assured Megan. 'The church calls it "acedia". It is a spiritual malaise, an instrument of Satan. Do not worry about it, child. It will pass.'

154

And it did.

But what did not pass was the bone-deep longing to know who her parents were. *I'll never know*, Megan thought despairingly. *Not as long as I live.*

Chapter 15

New York City 1976

The reporters gathered outside the grey façade of New York's Waldorf Astoria Hotel watched the parade of celebrities in evening dress alight from their limousines, enter the revolving doors and head for the Grand Ballroom on the third floor. The guests had come from around the world.

Cameras flashed as reporters called out, 'Mr Vice President, would you look this way, please?'

'Governor Adams, could I have one more picture, please?'

There were senators and representatives from several foreign countries, business tycoons and celebrities. And they were all there to celebrate Ellen Scott's sixtieth birthday. In truth, it was not so much Ellen Scott that they were honouring as the philanthropy of Scott Industries, one of the most powerful conglomerates in the world. The huge, sprawling empire included oil companies and steel mills, communications systems and banks. All the money raised this evening would go to international charities.

Scott Industries had interests in every part of the world. Twenty-five years earlier, its President, Milo Scott, had died unexpectedly of a heart attack, and his wife, Ellen, had taken over the management of the huge conglomerate and in the ensuing years had proved to be a brilliant executive, more than tripling the assets of the company.

The Grand Ballroom of the Waldorf Astoria is an enormous room, decorated in beige and gold, with a red-carpeted stage at one end and a balcony curving around the entire

156

room, holding thirty-three boxes with a chandelier over each one. In the centre balcony sat the guest of honour. There were at least 600 men and women present, dining at tables gleaming with silver.

When dinner was finished, the Governor of New York strode on to the stage.

'Mr Vice President, ladies and gentlemen, honoured guests, we are all here tonight for one purpose: to pay tribute to a remarkable woman and to her unselfish generosity over the years. Ellen Scott is the kind of person who could have made a success in any field. She would have been a great scientist or doctor. She would also have made a great politician, and I must tell you that if Ellen Scott decides to run for President of the United States, I'll be the first one to vote for her. Not in the next election, of course, but the one after that.'

There was laughter and applause.

'But Ellen Scott is much more than just a brilliant woman. She is a charitable, compassionate human being who never hesitates to get involved in the problems that face the world today –'

The speech went on for ten more minutes, but Ellen Scott was no longer listening. *How wrong he is*, she thought wryly. *How wrong they all are. Scott Industries isn't even my company. Milo and I stole it. And I'm guilty of a far greater crime than that. It doesn't matter any longer. Not now. Because I'll be dead soon.*

She remembered the doctor's exact words as he read the lab report that was her death sentence.

'I'm dreadfully sorry, Mrs Scott, but I'm afraid there's no way to break this to you gently. The cancer has spread throughout your lymphatic system. It's inoperable.'

She had felt the sudden leaden weight in her stomach.

'How . . . how long do I have?'

He hesitated. 'A year – maybe.'

Not enough time. Not with so much still to do. 'You will say nothing of this, of course.' Her voice was steady.

'Certainly not.'

'Thank you, doctor.'

She had no recollection of leaving the Presbyterian Medical Center or of the drive downtown. Her only thought was: *I must find her before I die.*

Now the Governor's speech was over.

'Ladies and gentlemen, it is my honour and privilege to introduce Mrs Ellen Scott.'

Ellen Scott rose to a standing ovation. She walked towards the stage, a thin, grey-haired, straight-backed woman, smartly dressed and projecting a vitality she no longer felt.

Looking at me is like seeing the distant light of a long dead star, she thought bitterly. *I'm not really here any more.*

On the stage she waited for the applause to die down. *They're applauding a monster. What would they do if they knew?* When she spoke, her voice was firm.

'Mr Vice President, Senators, Governor Adams . . .'

A year, she was thinking. *I wonder where she is and if she is still alive. I must find out.*

She talked on, automatically saying all the things her audience expected to hear. 'I gladly accept this tribute not for myself, but for all those who have worked so hard to lighten the burden of those who are less fortunate than we are . . .'

Her mind was drifting back forty-two years to Gary, Indiana . . .

At eighteen, Ellen Dudash was employed at the Scott Industries automotive parts plant in Gary, Indiana. She was an attractive, outgoing girl, popular with her fellow workers. On the day Milo Scott came to inspect the plant, Ellen was selected to escort him around.

'Hey! How about you, Ellie? Maybe you'll marry the boss's brother and we'll all be working for you.'

Ellen Dudash laughed. 'Right. And that's when pigs will grow wings.'

Milo Scott was not at all what Ellen had expected. He was

in his early thirties, tall and slim. *Not bad looking*, Ellen thought. He was shy and almost deferential.

'It's very kind of you to take the time to show me around, Miss Dudash. I hope I'm not taking you away from your work.'

She grinned. 'I hope you are.'

He was so easy to talk to.

I can't believe I'm kidding around with the big boss's brother. Wait till I tell Mom and Pop about this.

Milo Scott seemed genuinely interested in the workers and their problems. Ellen took him through the department where the round drive gears and the long driven gears were made. She showed him through the annealing room, where the soft gears were put through a hardening process, and the packing section and the shipping department, and he seemed properly impressed.

'It's certainly a large operation, isn't it, Miss Dudash?'

He owns all of this, and he acts like an awed kid. I guess it takes all kinds.

It was in the assembly section where the accident happened. An overhead cable car carrying metal bars to the machine shop snapped and a load of iron came tumbling down. Milo Scott was directly beneath it. Ellen saw it coming a fraction of a second before it hit, and without thinking, shoved Milo Scott out of harm's way. Two of the heavy iron bars hit her before she could escape, and she was knocked unconscious.

She awakened in a private suite in a hospital. The room was literally filled with flowers. When Ellen opened her eyes and looked around, she thought: *I've died and gone to heaven.*

There were orchids and roses and lilies and chrysanthemums and rare blooms she could not even begin to identify.

Her right arm was in a cast and her ribs were taped and felt bruised.

A nurse came in. 'Ah, you're awake, Miss Dudash. I'll inform the doctor.'

'Where – where am I?'

'Blake Center – it's a private hospital.'

Ellen looked around the large suite. *I can never afford to pay for all this.*

'We've been screening your calls.'

'What calls?'

'The press has been trying to get in to interview you. Your friends have been calling. Mr Scott has telephoned several times . . .'

Milo Scott! 'Is he all right?'

'I beg your pardon?'

'Was he hurt in the accident?'

'No. He was here again early this morning, but you were asleep.'

'He came to see *me*?'

'Yes.' She looked around the room. 'Most of these flowers are from him.'

Unbelievable.

'Your mother and father are in the waiting room. Do you feel up to seeing them now?'

'Of course.'

'Thank you. I'll send them in.'

Boy, I've never been treated like this in a hospital before, Ellen thought.

Her mother and father walked in and came up to the bed. Ellen's parents had been born in Poland and their English was tentative. Ellen's father was a mechanic, a burly, rough-hewn man in his fifties, and Ellen's mother was a bluff, northern European peasant.

'I brought you some soup, Ellen.'

'Mom – they feed people in hospitals.'

'Not my soup, they don't feed you in the hospital. Eat it and you'll get well faster.'

Her father said, 'Have you see the papers? I brung you copy.'

He handed the newspaper to her. The headline read:

FACTORY WORKER RISKS LIFE TO SAVE BOSS.

She read the story twice.

'That was brave thing you done to save him.'

Brave? It was stupid. If I had had time to think, I would have saved myself. That was the dumbest thing I ever did. Why, I could have been killed!

Milo Scott came to see Ellen later that morning. He was carrying another bouquet of flowers.

'These are for you,' he said awkwardly. 'The doctor tells me you're going to be fine. I – I can't tell you how grateful I am to you.'

'It was nothing.'

'It was the most courageous act I've ever seen. You saved my life.'

She tried to move, but it sent a sharp pain through her arm.

'Are you all right?'

'Sure.' Her side was beginning to throb. 'What did the doc say was wrong with me?'

'You have a broken arm and three broken ribs.'

He couldn't have given her worse news. Her eyes filled with tears.

'What's the matter?'

How could she tell him? He would only laugh at her. She had been saving up for a long-awaited vacation to New York, on a tour with some of the girls from the factory. It had been her dream. *Now I'll be out of work for a month or more. There goes Manhattan.*

Ellen had worked since she was fifteen. She had always been fiercely independent and self-sufficient, but now she thought: *Maybe if he's so grateful he'll pay part of my hospital bills. But I'll be damned if I'll ask him.* She was beginning to feel drowsy. *It must be the medication.*

She said sleepily, 'Thank you for all the flowers, Mr Scott. And it was nice meeting you.' *I'll worry about the hospital bills later.*

Ellen Dudash slept.

*

161

The following morning, a tall, distinguished-looking man came into Ellen's suite.

'Good morning, Miss Dudash. How are you feeling this morning?'

'Better, thank you.'

'I'm Sam Norton. I'm chief public relations officer for Scott Industries.'

'Oh.' She had never seen him before. 'Do you live here?'

'No. I flew in from Washington.'

'To see me?'

'To assist you.'

'To assist me *what*?'

'The press is outside, Miss Dudash. Since I don't believe you've ever held a press conference, I thought perhaps you could use some help.'

'What do they want?'

'Mainly, they're going to ask you to tell them about how and why you saved Mr Scott.'

'Oh. That's easy. If I had stopped to think, I'd have run like hell.'

Norton stared at her. 'Miss Dudash – I don't think I would say that, if I were you.'

'Why not? It's the truth.'

This was not at all what he had expected. The girl seemed to have no idea of her situation.

There was something worrying Ellen, and she decided to get it out in the open. 'Are you going to see Mr Scott?'

'Yes.'

'Would you do me a favour?'

'If I can, certainly.'

'I know the accident's not his fault, and he didn't ask me to push him out of the way, but –' The strong, independent streak in her made her hesitate. 'Oh, never mind.'

Ah, here it comes, Norton thought. How much reward was she going to try to extort? Would it be cash? A better job? What? 'Please, go on, Miss Dudash.'

She blurted it out. 'The truth is, I don't have a lot of money, and I'm going to lose some pay because of this, and

162

I don't think I can afford all these hospital bills. I don't want to bother Mr Scott, but if he could arrange a loan for me, I'd pay it back.' She saw the expression on Norton's face, and misread it 'I'm sorry. I guess I sound mercenary. It's just that I've been saving up for a trip, and – well, this screws everything up.' She took a deep breath. 'It's not his problem. I'll manage.'

He almost kissed her. *How long has it been since I've come across real innocence? It's enough to restore my faith in womankind.*

He sat down at the side of her bed, and his professional manner disappeared. He took her hand. 'Ellen, I have a feeling you and I are going to be great friends. I promise you, you're not going to have to worry about money. The first thing we have to do is get you through this press conference. We want you to come out of this looking good, so that –' He stopped himself. 'I'm going to be honest. My job is to see that Scott Industries comes out of this looking good. Do you understand?'

'I guess so. You mean it wouldn't sound so good if I said I wasn't really interested in saving Milo Scott? It would sound better if I said something like, "I like working for Scott Industries so much that when I saw Milo Scott was in danger, I knew I had to try to save him, even at the risk of my own life?"'

'Yes.'

She laughed. 'Okay. If it'll help you. But I don't want to kid you, Mr Norton. I don't know what made me do it.'

He smiled. 'That will be our secret. I'll let the lions in.'

There were more than two dozen reporters and photographers from radio, newspapers and magazines. It was a man-bites-dog story, and the press intended to make the most of it. It was not every day that a pretty young employee risked her life to save her boss. And the fact that her employer happened to be Milo Scott did not hurt the story one bit.

'Miss Dudash – when you saw all that iron hurtling down at you, what was your first thought?'

Ellen looked over at Sam Norton with a straight face and

said, 'I thought, "I must save Mr Scott. I'd never forgive myself if I let him be killed."'

The press conference proceeded smoothly, and when Sam Norton saw that Ellen was beginning to tire, he said, 'That's it, ladies and gentlemen. Thank you very much.'

'Did I do all right?'

'You were great. Now get some sleep.'

She slept fitfully. She dreamed that she was in the lobby of the Empire State Building, and they would not let her in because she did not have enough money to buy a ticket.

Milo Scott came to visit Ellen Dudash that afternoon. She was surprised to see him. She had heard that his home was in New York.

'I heard the press conference went very well. You're quite a heroine.'

'Mr Scott – I have to tell you something. I'm not a heroine. I didn't stop to think about saving you. I – I just did it.'

'I know. Sam Norton told me.'

'Well, then –'

'Ellen, there are all kinds of heroism. You didn't think about saving me, but you did it instinctively, instead of saving yourself.'

'I – I just wanted you to know.'

'Sam also told me that you're worried about the hospital bills.'

'Well –'

'They're all taken care of. And as for your losing some wages –' He smiled. 'Miss Dudash, I – I don't think you know how much I owe you.'

'You don't owe me anything.'

'The doctor told me that you'll be leaving the hospital tomorrow. Will you let me buy you dinner?'

He doesn't understand, Ellen thought. *I don't want his charity. Or his pity.* 'I meant it when I said you don't owe

164

me anything. Thanks for taking care of the hospital bills. We're even.'

'Good. Now may I buy you dinner?'

That was how it began. Milo Scott stayed in Gary for a week, and he saw Ellen every night.

Ellen's mother and father warned, 'Be careful. Big bosses don't go out with factory girls unless they want something.'

That had been Ellen Dudash's attitude at the beginning. Milo Scott changed her mind. He was a perfect gentleman at all times, and the truth finally dawned on Ellen: *He really enjoys being with me.* Where Milo was shy and reserved, Ellen was forthright and open. All his life, Milo had been surrounded by women whose burning ambition was to become a part of the powerful Scott dynasty. They had played their calculating games. Ellen Dudash was the first totally honest woman Milo had ever met. She said exactly what was on her mind. She was bright, she was attractive, and most of all, she was fun to be with. By the end of the week, they were both falling in love.

'I want to marry you,' Milo Scott said. 'I can't think about anything else. Will you marry me?'

'No.'

Nor had Ellen been able to think about anything else. The truth was that she was terrified. The Scotts were as close as America could come to royalty. They were famous, rich and powerful. *I don't belong in their circle. I would only make a fool of myself. And of Milo.* But she knew she was fighting a losing battle.

They were married by a justice of the peace in Greenwich, and returned to Manhattan so that Ellen Dudash could meet her in-laws.

Byron Scott greeted his brother with, 'What the fuck have you done – marry a Polish hooker? Are you out of your mind?'

Susan Scott was just as ungiving. 'Of course she married Milo for his money. When she finds out he doesn't have any, we'll arrange an annulment. This marriage will never last.'

They badly underestimated Ellen Dudash.

'Your brother and sister-in-law hate me, but I didn't marry them. I married you. I don't want to come between you and Byron. If this is making you too unhappy, Milo, say so, and I'll leave.'

He took his bride in his arms and whispered, 'I adore you, and when Byron and Susan really get to know you, they'll adore you.'

She held him closely and thought: *How naïve he is. And how I love him.*

Byron and Susan were not unpleasant to their new sister-in-law. They were patronizing. To them, she would always be the little Polish girl who worked in one of the Scott factories.

Ellen studied, and read, and learned. She watched how the wives of Milo's friends dressed and copied them. She was determined to become a fit wife to Milo Scott, and in time she succeeded. But not in the eyes of her in-laws. And slowly her naïveté turned to cynicism. *The rich and powerful aren't all that wonderful*, she thought. *All they want is to be richer and more powerful.*

Ellen was fiercely protective of Milo, but there was little she could do to help him. Scott Industries was one of the few privately held conglomerates in the world, and all the stock belonged to Byron. Byron's younger brother was a salaried employee, and he never let him forget it. Byron treated his brother shabbily. Milo was given all the dirty jobs to do, and never given credit.

'Why do you put up with it, Milo? You don't need him. We could move away from here. You could start your own business.'

'I couldn't leave Scott Industries. Byron needs me.'

166

But in time, Ellen came to understand the real reason. Milo was weak. He needed someone strong to lean on. Ellen knew then that he would never have the courage to leave the company.

All right, she thought fiercely. *One day the company will be his. Byron can't live for ever. Milo is his only heir.*

When Susan Scott announced that she was pregnant, it was a blow to Ellen. *The baby's going to inherit everything.*

When the baby was born, Byron Scott said, 'It's a girl, but I'll teach her how to run the company.'

The bastard, Ellen Scott thought. Her heart ached for Milo.

All Milo said was, 'Isn't she a beautiful baby?'

Chapter 16

The pilot of the Lockheed Lodestar was worried.

'A front is closing in. I don't like the look of it.' He nodded to the co-pilot. 'Take over.' He left the cockpit to go back to the cabin.

There were five passengers on board besides the pilot and co-pilot: Byron Scott, the brilliant, dynamic founder and chief executive officer of Scott Industries, his attractive wife, Susan; their year-old daughter, Patricia; Milo Scott, Byron Scott's younger brother; and Milo's wife, Ellen Scott. They were flying in one of the company planes from Paris to Madrid. Bringing the baby had been a last-minute impulse on Susan Scott's part.

'I hate to be away from her for so long,' she told her husband.

'Afraid she'll forget us?' he teased. 'All right. We'll take her with us.'

Now that World War II was over, Scott Industries was rapidly expanding into the European market. In Madrid, Byron Scott would investigate the possibilities of opening a new steel mill

The pilot approached him.

'Excuse me, sir. We're heading into some thunder clouds. It doesn't look very good ahead. Do you want to turn back?'

Byron Scott looked out of the small window. They were flying through a grey mass of cumulus clouds, and every few seconds distant lightning illuminated them. 'I have a meeting in Madrid tonight. Can you go around the storm?'

'I'll try. If I can't, then I'm going to have to turn us around.'

Byron Scott nodded. 'All right.'

'Would you all fasten your seat belts, please?'

The pilot hurried back to the cockpit.

Susan Scott had heard the conversation. She picked up the baby and held her in her arms, suddenly wishing she had not brought her along. *I've got to tell Byron to have the pilot turn back*, she thought.

'Byron –'

They were suddenly caught in the eye of the storm, and the plane began bucking up and down, caught in the gusting winds. The motion began to grow more violent. Rain was smashing against the windows. The storm had closed off all visibility. The passengers felt as though they were riding on a rolling cotton sea.

Byron Scott flicked down the intercom switch. 'Where are we, Blake?'

'We're a hundred kilometres northwest of Madrid, over the town of Ávila.'

Byron Scott looked out of the window again. 'We'll forget Madrid tonight. Let's turn around and get the hell out of here.'

'Roger.'

He was a fraction too late. As the pilot started to bank the plane, a mountain peak looked suddenly in front of him. There was no time to avoid the crash. There was a rending tear, and the sky exploded as the plane tore into the side of the mountain, ripping apart, scattering chunks of fuselage and wings along a high plateau.

There was an unnatural silence that lasted for what seemed an eternity. It was broken by the crackle of flames starting to lick at the undercarriage.

'Ellen –'

Ellen Scott opened her eyes. She was lying under a tree. Her husband was bending over her, lightly slapping her face.

When he saw that she was alive, he said, 'Thank God.'

Ellen Scott sat up, dizzy, her head throbbing, every muscle in her body aching. She looked around at the obscene pieces of wreckage that had once been an airplane filled with human bodies, and shuddered.

'The others?' she asked hoarsely.

'They're dead.'

She stared at her husband. 'Oh, my God! No!'

He nodded, his face tight with grief. 'Byron, Susan, the baby, the pilots, everyone.'

Ellen Scott closed her eyes again and said a silent prayer *Why were Milo and I spared?* she wondered. It was hard to think clearly. *We have to go down and get help. But it's too late. They're all dead.* It was impossible to believe. They had been so full of life just a few minutes before.

'Can you stand up?'

'I – I think so.'

Milo Scott helped his wife to her feet. There was a surge of sickening dizziness, and she stood there, waiting for it to pass.

Milo turned to look at the plane. Flames were beginning to get higher. 'Let's get out of here,' he said. 'The damned thing is going to blow up any second.'

They quietly moved away and watched it burn. A moment later, there was an explosion as the gas tanks blew apart and the plane was engulfed in flames.

'It's a miracle we're alive,' Milo Scott said.

It was a miracle. But not for the others.

Ellen Scott looked at the burning plane. Something was nagging at the edges of her mind, but she was having trouble thinking clearly. Something about Scott Industries. And then suddenly she knew.

'Milo?'

'Yes?' He was not really listening.

'It's fate.'

The fervour in her voice made him turn. 'What?'

'Scott Industries – it belongs to you, now.'

'I don't –'

170

'Milo, God left it to you.' Her voice was filled with a burning intensity. 'All your life you've lived in the shadow of your big brother.' She was thinking clearly now, coherently, and she forgot her headache and the pain. The words came tumbling out now in a spate that shook her whole body. 'You worked for Byron for twenty years building up the company. You're as responsible for its success as he is, but did he – did he ever give you credit for it? No. It was always *his* company, his success, his profits. Well now you – you finally have a chance to come into your own.'

He looked at her, horrified. 'Ellen – their bodies are – how can you even think about –?'

'I know. But we didn't kill them. It's our turn, Milo. We've finally come into our own. There's no one alive to claim the company but us. It's ours! Yours!'

And at that moment they heard the cry of a baby. Ellen and Milo Scott stared at each other unbelievingly.

'It's Patricia! She's *alive*. Oh, my God!'

They found the baby near a clump of bushes. By some miracle she was unhurt.

Milo Scott picked her up gently and held her close. 'Ssh! It's all right, darling,' he whispered. 'Everything's going to be all right.'

Ellen was standing at his side, a look of shock on her face. 'You – you said she was dead.'

'She must have been knocked unconscious.'

Ellen Scott stared at the baby for a long time. 'She should have been killed with the others,' she said in a strangled voice.

He looked up at her, shocked. 'What are you saying?'

'Byron's will leaves everything to Patricia. You can look forward to spending the next twenty years being her guardian so that when she grows up she can treat you as shabbily as her father did. Is that what you want?'

He was silent.

'We'll never have a chance like this again.' She was staring at the baby, and there was a wild look in her eyes that Milo

171

had never seen before. It was almost as though she wanted to –

She's not herself. She's suffering from a concussion. 'For God's sake, Ellen, what are you thinking?'

She looked at her husband for a long moment, and the wild light faded from her eyes. 'I don't know,' she said calmly. After a pause she said, 'There's something we can do. We can leave her somewhere, Milo. The pilot said we were near Ávila. There should be plenty of tourists there. There's no reason for anyone to connect the baby with the plane crash.'

He shook his head. 'Their friends know that Byron and Susan took Patricia with them.'

Ellen Scott looked at the burning plane. 'That's no problem. They all burned up in the crash. We'll have a private memorial service here.'

'Ellen,' he protested. 'We can't do this. We'd never get away with it.'

'God did it for us. We *have* gotten away with it.'

Milo Scott looked at the baby. 'But she's so –'

'She'll be fine,' Ellen said soothingly. 'We'll drop her off at a nice farmhouse outside of town. They'll adopt her and she'll grow up to have a lovely life here.'

He shook his head. 'I can't do it. No.'

'If you love me you'll do this for us. You have to choose, Milo. You can either have me, or you can spend the rest of your life working for your brother's child.'

'Please, I –'

'Do you love me?'

'More than my life,' he said simply.

'Then prove it.'

They made their way carefully down the mountainside in the dark, whipped by the wind. Because the plane had crashed in a high wooded area, the sound was muffled, so the townspeople would be unaware of what had happened.

Three hours later, on the outskirts of Ávila, Ellen and

172

Milo reached a small farmhouse. It was not yet dawn.

'We'll leave her here,' Ellen whispered.

He made one last try. 'Ellen, couldn't we –?'

'Do it!' she said fiercely.

Without another word, he turned and carried the baby to the door of the farmhouse. She was wearing only a torn pink nightgown and had a blanket wrapped around her.

Milo Scott looked at Patricia for a long moment, his eyes filled with tears, then laid her gently down.

He whispered, 'Have a good life, darling.'

The crying awakened Anuncion Moras. For a sleepy moment, she thought it was the bleating of a goat or a lamb. How had it got out of its pen?

Grumbling, she rose from her warm bed, put on an old faded dressing-gown, and walked to the door.

When she saw the infant lying on the ground screaming and kicking, she said, '*¡Madre de Dios!*' and yelled for her husband.

They brought the child inside and stared at it. It would not stop crying, and it seemed to be turning blue.

'We've got to get her to the hospital.'

They hurriedly wrapped another blanket around the baby, carried her to their pick-up truck and drove her to the hospital. They sat on a bench in the long corridor waiting for someone to attend to them, and thirty minutes later a doctor came and took the baby away to examine her.

When he returned, he said, 'She's got pneumonia.'

'Is she going to live?'

The doctor shrugged.

Milo and Ellen Scott stumbled into the police station at Ávila.

The desk sergeant looked up at the two bedraggled tourists. '*Buenos dias*. Can I help you?'

'There's been a terrible accident,' Milo Scott said. 'Our plane crashed up in the mountains and . . .'

One hour later a rescue party was on its way to the mountainside. When they arrived, there was nothing to see but the smouldering, charred remains of an aircraft and its passengers.

The investigation of the airplane accident conducted by the Spanish authorities was cursory.

'The pilot should not have attempted to fly into such a bad storm. We must attribute the accident to pilot error.'

There was no reason for anyone in Ávila to associate the airplane crash with a small child left on the doorstep of a farmhouse.

It was over.

It was just beginning.

Milo and Ellen Scott held a private memorial service for Byron Scott, his wife Susan, and their daughter, Patricia. When they returned to New York, they held a second memorial service, attended by the shocked friends of the Scotts.

'What a terrible tragedy. And poor little Patricia.'

'Yes,' Ellen Scott said sadly. 'The only blessing is that it happened so quickly that none of them suffered.'

The financial community was shaken by the death of Byron Scott. The stock of Scott Industries plummeted. Ellen Scott was not disturbed.

She reassured her husband, 'Don't worry. It will go back up. You're better than Byron ever was. He held the company back, Milo. You're going to make it go forward.'

Milo took her in his arms. 'I don't know what I'd do without you.'

She smiled. 'You'll never have to. From now on we're

going to have everything in the world we've ever dreamed of.'

She held him close and thought: *Who would have believed that Ellen Dudash, from a poor Polish family in Gary, Indiana, would have one day said, 'From now on, we're going to have everything in the world we ever dreamed of?'*

And meant it.

For ten days the baby remained in the hospital, fighting for her life, and when the crisis was past, Father Berrendo went to see the farmer and his wife.

'I have joyous news for you,' he said happily. 'The child is going to be all right.'

The Morases exchanged an uncomfortable look.

'I'm glad for her sake,' the farmer said evasively.

Father Berrendo beamed. 'She is a gift from God.'

'Certainly, Father. But my wife and I have talked it over and decided that God is too generous to us. His gift requires feeding. We can't afford to keep it.'

'But she's such a beautiful baby,' Father Berrendo pointed out. 'And –'

'Agreed. But my wife and I are old and sick, and we can't take on the responsibility of bringing up a baby. God will have to take back his gift.'

And so it was that with nowhere else to go the baby was sent to the orphanage in Ávila.

They were seated in the law offices of Byron Scott's attorney for the reading of the will. Besides the lawyer, only Milo and Ellen Scott were present. Ellen Scott was filled with a sense of almost unbearable excitement. A few words on a piece of paper were going to make her and Milo rich beyond imagining.

We'll buy old masters and a place in Southampton, and a castle in France. And that's only the beginning.

The lawyer started to speak, and Ellen turned her attention

175

to him. Months before she had seen a copy of Byron Scott's will and knew exactly what it said:

In the event that my wife and I should both be deceased, I bequeath all my stock in Scott Industries to my only child, Patricia, and I appoint my brother, Milo, as executor of my estate until she reaches the legal age and is able to take over, etc., etc.

Well, all that is changed now, Ellen thought excitedly.

The lawyer, Lawrence Gray, said solemnly, 'This has been a terrible shock to all of us. I know how much you loved your brother, Milo, and as for that darling little baby . . .' He shook his head. 'Well, life must go on. You may not be aware that your brother had changed his will. I won't bother you with the legalese. I will just read you the gist of it.' He thumbed through the will and came to the paragraph he was looking for. 'I amend this will so that my daughter, Patricia, will receive the sum of five million dollars plus a distribution of one million dollars a year for the rest of her life. All the stock in Scott Industries held in my name will go to my brother, Milo, as a reward for the faithful and valuable services he has provided the company through the years '

Milo Scott felt the room begin to sway.

Mr Gray looked up. 'Are you all right?'

Milo was finding it difficult to breathe. *Good God, what have we done? We've taken away her birthright, and it wasn't necessary at all. Now we can give it back to her.*

He turned to say something to Ellen, but the look in her eyes stopped him.

'There has to be *something* we can do, Ellen. We can't just leave Patricia there. Not now.'

They were in their Fifth Avenue apartment getting dressed to go to a charity dinner.

'That's exactly what we're going to do,' Ellen told him. 'Unless you'd like to bring her back here and try to explain why we said she was burned to death in the airplane crash.'

He had no answer to that. He thought for a moment. 'All

right, then. We'll send her money every month so she –'

'Don't be a fool, Milo.' Her voice was curt. 'Send her money? And have the police start checking on why someone is sending her money and trace it back to us? No. If your conscience bothers you, we'll have the company give money to charity. Forget about the child, Milo. She's dead. Remember?'

Remember . . . remember . . . remember . . .

The words echoed in Ellen Scott's mind as she looked out at the audience in the Waldorf Astoria ballroom and finished her speech. There was another standing ovation.

You're standing up for a dead woman, she thought.

That night the ghosts came again. She had thought she had exorcised them long ago. In the beginning, after the memorial services for her brother-in-law and sister-in-law, and Patricia, the night visitors had come frequently. Pale mists had hovered over her bed and voices had whispered in her ear. She would awaken, her pulse racing, but there was nothing to see. She told none of this to Milo. He was weak, and it might have terrified him into doing something foolish, something that would jeopardize the company. If the truth got out, the scandal would destroy Scott Industries, and Ellen Scott was determined that that must never happen. And so she suffered the ghosts in silence, until finally they went away and left her in peace.

Now, the night of the banquet, they returned. She awakened and sat up in her bed and looked around. The room was empty and quiet, but she knew they had been there. What were they trying to tell her? Did they know she would be joining them soon?

Ellen Scott rose and walked into the spacious, antique-filled drawing room of the beautiful townhouse she had bought after Milo had passed away. She looked around the lovely room and thought: *Poor Milo*. He had had so little time to enjoy any of the benefits of his brother's death. He had died of a heart attack a few years after the plane crash, and Ellen Scott had taken over the company, running it with an efficiency and expertise that had catapulted Scott Industries into greater international prominence.

The company belongs to the Scott family, she thought. *I'm not going to turn it over to faceless strangers.*

And that led her thoughts to Byron's and Susan's daughter. The rightful heiress to the throne that had been stolen from her. Was there fear in her thoughts? Was it a wish to make an atonement before her own death?

Ellen Scott sat in her drawing room all night staring into nothingness, thinking and planning. How long ago had it been? Twenty-eight years. Patricia would be a grown woman now, assuming that she was still alive. What had her life become? Had she married a farmer or a merchant in the village? Did she have children? Was she still living in Ávila, or had she gone away to some other place?

I must find her, Ellen Scott thought. *And quickly. If Patricia is still alive, I've got to see her, talk to her. I have to finally set the account straight. Money can turn lies into truth. I'll find a way to solve the situation without ever letting her know what really happened.*

The following morning Ellen Scott sent for Alan Tucker, chief of security for Scott Industries. He was a former detective, in his forties, a thin, balding, sallow-looking man, hard-working and brilliant.

'I want you to go on a mission for me.'

'Yes, Mrs Scott.'

She studied him for a moment, wondering how much she could tell him. *I can tell him nothing*, she decided. *As long as I am alive, I refuse to put myself or the company in jeopardy. Let him find Patricia first, and then I'll decide how to handle her.*

She leaned forward. 'Twenty-eight years ago, an orphan was left on the doorstep of a farmhouse outside of Ávila,

Spain. I want you to find out where she is today and bring her back here to me as quickly as possible.'

Alan Tucker's face remained impassive. Mrs Scott did not like her employees to show emotion.

'Yes, ma'am. I'll leave tomorrow.'

Chapter 17

Colonel Ramón Acoca was in an expansive mood. All the pieces were finally falling into place.

An orderly came into the office. 'Colonel Sostelo has arrived.'

'Show him in.'

I won't be needing him any more, Acoca thought. *He can go back to his tin soldiers.*

Colonel Fal Sostelo walked in. 'Colonel.'

'Colonel.'

It's ironic, Sostelo thought. *We hold the same rank, but the scarred giant has the power to break me. Because he's connected to the OPUS MUNDO.*

It was an indignity for Sostelo to have to answer Acoca's summons, as though he were some unimportant subordinate. But he managed to show none of his feelings. 'You wanted to see me?'

'Yes.' Acoca waved him to a chair. 'Sit down. I have some news for you. Jaime Miró has the nuns.'

'*What?*'

'Yes. They're travelling with Miró and his men. He's split them up into three groups.'

'How – how do you know that?'

Ramón Acoca leaned back in his chair. 'Do you play chess?'

'No.'

'Pity. It's a very educational game. In order to be a good player, it's necessary to get into the mind of your opponent. Jaime Miró and I play chess with each other.'

Fal Sostelo was staring at him. 'I don't understand how –

'Not literally, Colonel. We don't use a chess board. We use our minds. I probably understand Jaime Miró better than anyone in the world. I know how his mind works. I knew that he would try to blow up the dam at Puenta la Reina. We captured two of his lieutenants there, and it was only by luck that Miró himself got away. I knew that he would try to rescue them, and Miró knew that I knew it.' Ramón Acoca shrugged. 'I didn't anticipate that he would use the bulls to effect their escape.' There was a note of admiration in his voice.

'You sound as though you –'

'Admire him? I admire his mind. I despise the man.'

'Do you know where Miró is headed?'

'He is travelling north. I will catch him within the next three days.'

Colonel Sostelo was gaping at him, stunned.

'It will finally be checkmate.'

It was true that Colonel Acoca understood Jaime Miró, and the way his mind worked, but it was not enough for him. The Colonel wanted an edge, to ensure victory, and he had found it.

'How –?'

'One of Miró's terrorists,' Colonel Acoca said, 'is an informer.'

Rubio, Tomas and the two sisters avoided the large cities and took side roads, passing old stone villages with grazing sheep and goats, and shepherds listening to music and soccer games on their transistor radios. It was a colourful juxtaposition of the past and the present, but Lucia had other things on her mind.

She stayed close to Sister Teresa, watching for the first opportunity to get the cross and leave. The two men were always at their side. Rubio Arzano was the more considerate of the two, a tall, pleasant-looking, cheerful man. *A simple-minded peasant*, Lucia decided.

181

Tomas Sanjuro was slight and balding. *He looks more like a shop assistant than a terrorist. It will be easy to outwit them both.*

They walked across the plains north of Ávila by night, cooled by the winds blowing down from the Guarrama Steppe. There was a haunting emptiness about the plains by moonlight. They passed *granjas* of wheat and olive trees and vines and maize, and they foraged for potatoes and lettuce, fruit from the trees and eggs and chickens from the hen coops.

'The whole countryside of Spain is a huge market,' said Rubio Arzano.

Tomas Sanjuro grinned. 'And it's all for free.'

Sister Teresa was totally oblivious to her surroundings. Her only thought was to reach the convent at Mendavia. The cross was getting heavy, but she was determined not to let it out of her hands. *Soon*, she thought. *We'll be there soon. We're fleeing from Gethsemane and our enemies to the new mansion He has prepared for us.*

Lucia said, 'What?'

Sister Teresa was unaware that she had spoken aloud.

'I – nothing,' she mumbled.

Lucia took a closer look at her. The older woman seemed distracted and vaguely disoriented, unaware of what was happening around her.

Lucia nodded towards the canvas package that Sister Teresa carried. 'That must be heavy,' Lucia said sympathetically. 'Wouldn't you like me to carry it for a while?'

Sister Teresa clutched it to her body more tightly. 'Jesus carried a heavier burden. I can carry this for Him.' Did it not say in Luke: *If any man would come after me, let him deny himself and take up his cross daily and follow me.*

'I'll carry it,' Teresa said stubbornly.

There was something odd in her tone.

'Are you all right, Sister?'

'Of course.'

*

Sister Teresa was far from all right. She had not been able to sleep. She felt dizzy and feverish. Her mind was playing tricks again. *I mustn't let myself become ill*, she thought. *Sister Betina will scold me.* But Sister Betina was not there. It was so confusing. And who were these men? *I don't trust them. What do they want with me?*

Rubio Arzano had attempted to strike up a conversation with Sister Teresa, trying to make her feel at ease.

'It must seem strange to you, being out in the world again, Sister. How long were you in the convent?'

Why did he want to know? 'Thirty years.'

'My, that's a long time. Where are you from?'

It was painful for her even to say the word. 'Èze.'

His face brightened. 'Èze? I spent a summer there once on holiday. It's a lovely town. I know it well. I remember –'

I know it well. How well? Did he know Raoul? Had Raoul sent him? And the truth hit her like a bolt of lightning. These strangers had been sent to bring her back to Èze, to Raoul Giradot. They were kidnapping her. God was punishing her for deserting Monique's baby. She was certain now that the baby she had seen in the village square in Villacastin was her sister Monique's. *But it couldn't have been, could it? That was thirty years ago*, Teresa muttered to herself. *They're lying to me.*

Rubio Arzano was watching her, listening to her mumbling.

'Is something wrong, Sister?'

Sister Teresa shrank away from him. 'No.'

She was on to them now. She was not going to let them take her back to Raoul and the baby. She had to get to the convent at Mendavia and hand over the gold crucifix, and then God would forgive her for the terrible sin she had committed. *I must be clever. I must not let them know I am on to their secret.*

She looked up at Rubio Arzano. 'I am fine,' Sister Teresa said.

They moved on across the dry, sunbaked plains. They came to a small village where peasant women dressed in black were doing their wash at a spring covered by a roof resting on four ancient beams. The water poured into a long wooden trough and out again, so that it was always fresh, and the women scrubbed their wash on stone slabs and rinsed it clean in the running water.

It's such a peaceful scene, Rubio thought. It reminded him of the farm he had left behind. *It's what Spain used to be like. No bombs, no killing. Will we ever know peace again?*

'Buenos dias.'

'Buenos dias.'

'I wonder if we might have a drink? Travelling is thirsty work.'

'Certainly. Please help yourselves.'

The water was cold and refreshing.

'Gracias. Adiós.'

'Adiós.'

Rubio hated to leave.

The two women and their escorts moved on, past cork and olive trees, the summer air filled with the smell of ripe grapes and oranges. They went by orchards of apples and cherry and plum trees, and farms noisy with the sound of chickens and pigs and goats.

Rubio and Tomas walked ahead, talking quietly together.

They are talking about me. They think I do not know their plan. Sister Teresa moved nearer to them so she could hear what they were saying.

'. . . A reward of five hundred thousand pesetas on our heads. Of course Colonel Acoca would pay more for Jaime, but he doesn't want his head. He wants his *cojones*.'

The men laughed.

As Sister Teresa listened to them talk, her conviction grew stronger. *These men are killers doing Satan's work, messengers of the devil sent to damn me to everlasting hell. But God is stronger than they are. He will not let them take me back home.*

Raoul Giradot was at her side, smiling the smile that she knew so well.

The voice!

I beg your pardon?

I heard you sing yesterday. You are magnificent.

May I help you?

I would like three yards of muslin, please.

Certainly. This way . . . My aunt owns this shop and she needed help, so I thought I'd work for her for a while.

I'm sure you could have any man you want, Teresa, but I hope you will choose me.

He looked so handsome.

I have never known anyone like you, my darling.

Raoul was taking her in his arms and kissing her.

You're going to make a beautiful bride.

But now I'm Christ's bride. I can't return to Raoul.

Lucia was watching her closely. Sister Teresa was talking to herself, but Lucia could not make out the words.

She's cracking up, Lucia thought. *She's not going to make it. I've got to get hold of that cross soon.*

It was dusk when they saw the town of Olmedo in the distance.

Rubio stopped. 'There will be soldiers there. Let's move up to the hills and skirt the city.'

They moved off the road and left the plains, headed for the hills above Olmedo. The sun was skipping across the mountain tops and the sky was beginning to darken.

'We've only a few more miles to go,' Rubio Arzano said reassuringly. 'Then we can rest.'

They had reached the top of a high ridge when Tomas Sanjuro suddenly held up a hand. 'Hold it,' he whispered.

Rubio Arzano walked to his side and they moved to the edge of the ridge and looked down into the valley below. There was an encampment of soldiers there.

'¡*Mierda!*' Rubio whispered. 'There must be a whole platoon. We'll stay up here for the rest of the night. They'll probably pull out in the morning and we can move on.' He turned to Lucia and Sister Teresa, trying not to show how worried he was. 'We'll spend the night here, Sisters. We must be very quiet. There are soldiers down there and we don't want them to find us.'

It was the best news Lucia could have heard. *It's perfect*, she thought. *I'll disappear with the cross during the night. They won't dare try to follow me because of the soldiers.*

To Sister Teresa, the news had a different meaning. She had heard the men say that someone named Colonel Acoca was searching for them. *They called Colonel Acoca the enemy. But these men are the enemy, so Colonel Acoca must be my friend. Thank you, dear God, for sending me Colonel Acoca.*

The tall man called Rubio was speaking to her.

'Do you understand, Sister? We must all be very, very quiet.'

'Yes, I understand.' *I understand more than you think.* They had no idea that God permitted her to see into their evil hearts.

Tomas Sanjuro said kindly, 'I know how difficult this must be for both of you, but don't worry. We'll see that you get safely to the convent.'

To Èze, he means. Oh, but he is cunning. He speaks the honeyed words of the devil. But God is within me, and He is guiding me. She knew what she must do. But she had to be careful.

The two men arranged the sleeping-bags for the women, next to each other.

'Both of you get some sleep now.'

The women got into the unfamiliar sleeping-bags. The night was incredibly clear and the sky was spangled with glimmering stars. Lucia looked up at them and thought happily: *In just a few hours now, I'll be on my way to freedom. As soon as they're all asleep.*

She yawned. She had not realized how tired she was. The long, hard journey and the emotional strain had taken their toll. Her eyes felt heavy. *I'll just rest for a little while*, Lucia thought.

She slept.

Sister Teresa lay near Lucia, wide awake, fighting the

demons trying to possess her, trying to send her soul to hell. *I must be strong. The Lord is testing me. I have been exiled, so that I can find my way back to Him. And these men are trying to stop me. I must not let them.*

At four o'clock in the morning, Sister Teresa silently sat up and looked around. Tomas Sanjuro was asleep only a few feet from her. The tall, dark man called Rubio was keeping watch at the edge of the clearing, his back to her. She could see his silhouette against the trees.

Very quietly, Sister Teresa rose. She hesitated, thinking about the cross. *Should I carry it with me? But I'll be coming back here very soon. I must find a place where it will be safe until I return.* She looked over to where Sister Lucia lay sleeping. *Yes. It will be safe with my sister in God*, Sister Teresa decided.

Silently she moved over to the sleeping-bag and gently slipped the wrapped cross inside. Lucia did not stir. Sister Teresa turned and moved into the woods, out of Rubio Arzano's sight, and carefully began to make her way downhill towards the soldiers' camp. The hill was steep and slippery with dew, but God gave her wings and she sped downhill without stumbling or falling, hurrying towards her salvation.

In the darkness ahead the figure of a man suddenly materialized.

A voice called out, 'Who goes there?'

'Sister Teresa.'

She approached the sentry. He wore an army uniform and was carrying a rifle, pointed at her.

'Where did you come from, old woman?' he demanded

She looked at him with golden eyes. 'God sent me.'

The sentry stared at her. 'Did He, now?'

'Yes. He sent me to see Colonel Acoca.'

The guard shook his head. 'You'd better tell Him you're not the Colonel's type. *Adiós, señora.*'

'You don't understand. I am Sister Teresa from the Abbey Cistercian. I have been taken prisoner by Jaime Miró and his men.' She watched the stunned expression that came over his face.

'You're – you're from the convent?'

'Yes.'

'The one at Ávila?'

'Yes,' Teresa said impatiently. What was the matter with the man? Didn't he realize how important it was that she be rescued from those evil men?

The soldier said carefully, 'The Colonel isn't here just now, Sister –'

It was an unexpected blow.

'– But Colonel Sostelo is in charge. I can take you to him.'

'Will he be able to help me?'

'Oh, I'm sure he will. Follow me, please.'

The sentry was scarcely able to believe his good fortune. Colonel Fal Sostelo had sent squadrons of soldiers scouring the entire countryside searching for the four nuns, and they had had no success. Now one of the sisters had stumbled into the camp and given herself up to him. The Colonel was going to be pleased. The Colonel was going to be very pleased

They reached the tent where Colonel Fal Sostelo and his second in command were poring over a map. The men looked up as the sentry and a woman entered.

'Excuse me, Colonel. This is Sister Teresa from the Cistercian convent.'

Colonel Sostelo stared at her, unbelievingly. All of his energies for the last three days had been focused on finding Jaime Miró and the nuns, and now, here in front of him was one of them. There *was* a God.

'Sit down, Sister.'

There is no time for that, Sister Teresa thought. She had to make him realize how urgent this was. 'We must hurry. They are trying to take me back to Èze.'

The Colonel was puzzled. 'Who's trying to take you back to Èze?'

'The men of Jaime Miró.'

188

He got to his feet. 'Sister – do you by any chance happen to know where these men are?'

Sister Teresa said impatiently, 'Of course.' She turned and pointed. 'They're up in those hills hiding from you.'

Chapter 18

Alan Tucker arrived in Ávila the day after his conversation with Ellen Scott. It had been a long flight, and Tucker should have been exhausted, but he was exhilarated. Ellen Scott was not a woman given to whims. *There's something strange going on behind all this*, Alan Tucker thought, *and if I play my cards right, I have a hunch it could be very profitable for me.*

He checked into the Cuatro Postes Hotel and said to the clerk behind the desk, 'Is there a newspaper office around here?'

'Down the street, *señor*. To your left, two blocks. You can't miss it.'

'Thank you.'

'*De nada.*'

Walking down the main street, watching the town come alive after its afternoon siesta, Tucker thought about the mysterious girl he had been sent to bring back. This had to be something important. But important *why*? He could hear Ellen Scott's voice.

If she's alive, bring her back to me. You are not to discuss this with anyone.

No, ma'am. What shall I tell her?

Simply tell her that a friend of her father's wishes to meet her. She'll come.

Tucker found the newspaper office. Inside, he approached one of the half a dozen people working behind desks. '*Perdon*, I would like to see the managing editor.'

The man pointed to an office. 'In there, *señor*.'

'*Gracias.*'

Tucker walked over to the open door and looked inside. A man in his mid-thirties was seated behind a desk, busily editing copy.

'Excuse me,' Tucker said. 'Could I speak to you for a moment?'

The man looked up. 'What can I do for you?'

'I'm looking for a *señorita*.'

The editor smiled. 'Aren't we all, *señor*?'

'She was left at a farmhouse around here when she was an infant.'

The smile faded. 'Oh. She was abandoned?'

'Yes.'

'And you are trying to find her?'

'Yes.'

'How many years ago would that be, *senor?*'

'Twenty-eight.'

The young man shrugged. 'It was before my time.'

Perhaps it's not going to be so easy. 'Would you happen to know anything about the woman or could you suggest someone who might be able to help me?'

The editor leaned back in his chair, thinking. 'As a matter of fact, I can. I would suggest you speak with Father Berrendo.'

Father Berrendo sat in his study, a rug over his thin legs, listening to the stranger.

When Alan Tucker had finished talking, Father Berrendo said, 'Why do you wish to know about this matter, *señor*? It happened so long ago. What is your interest in it?'

Tucker hesitated, choosing his words carefully. 'I am not at liberty to say. I can only assure you that I mean the woman no harm. If you could just tell me where the farmhouse is where she was left –?'

The farmhouse. Memories came flooding back of the day the Morases had come to him after they had taken the little girl to hospital.

I think she's dying, Father. What shall we do?

Father Berrendo had talked to his friend, Don Morago, the chief of police.

'I think the baby was abandoned by tourists visiting Avila. Could you check the hotels and inns and see if anyone arrived with a baby and left without one?'

The police had gone through the registration cards that all hotels were required to fill out, but they were of no help.

'It is as if the baby just dropped out of the sky,' Don Morago said.

And he had no idea of how close he had come to solving the mystery.

When Father Berrendo had taken the infant to the orphanage, Mercedes Angeles had asked, 'Has the baby got a name?'

'I don't know.'

'Wasn't there a blanket or something with the name on it?'

'No.'

Mercedes Angeles looked at the infant in the priest's arms. 'Well, we'll just have to give her a name, won't we?'

She had recently finished reading a romantic novel, and she liked the name of the heroine in it.

'Megan,' she said. 'We'll call her Megan.'

And fourteen years later, Father Berrendo had taken Megan to the Abbey Cistercian.

So many years after that, this stranger was looking for her. *Life always comes full circle*, Father Berrendo thought. *In some mysterious way, it has come full circle for Megan.* No, not Megan. That was the name given her by the orphanage.

'Sit down, *señor*,' Father Berrendo said. 'There is much to tell you.'

And he told him.

When the priest had finished, Alan Tucker sat there quietly, his mind racing. There had to be a strong reason for Ellen Scott's interest in a baby abandoned at a farmhouse in Spain twenty-eight years earlier. A woman now called Megan, according to the priest.

Tell her that a friend of her father's wishes to meet her.

If he remembered correctly, Byron Scott and his wife and daughter had died in an airplane crash many years ago somewhere in Spain. Could there be a connection? Alan Tucker felt a growing sense of excitement.

'Father – I'd like to get into the convent to see her. It's very important.'

The priest shook his head. 'I'm afraid you are too late. The convent was attacked two days ago by agents of the government.'

Alan Tucker stared at him. 'Attacked? What happened to the nuns?'

'They were arrested and taken to Madrid.'

Alan Tucker got to his feet. 'Thank you, Father.' He would catch the first plane to Madrid.

Father Berrendo went on: 'Four of the nuns escaped. Sister Megan was one of them.'

Things were becoming complicated. 'Where is she now?'

'No one knows. The police and the army are searching for her and the other sisters.'

'I see.' Under ordinary circumstances, Alan Tucker would have telephoned Ellen Scott and informed her that he had reached a dead end. But all his instincts as a detective told him that there was something here that warranted further investigation.

He placed a call to Ellen Scott.

'There's a complication, Mrs Scott.' He repeated his conversation with the priest.

There was a long silence. 'No one knows where she is?'

'She and the others are on the run, but they can't hide out

193

much longer. The police and half the Spanish army are looking for them. When they surface, I'll be there.'

Another silence. 'This is very important to me, Tucker.'

'Yes, Mrs Scott.'

Alan Tucker returned to the newspaper office. He was in luck. It was still open.

He said to the editor, 'I would like to look through your files, if I may.'

'Are you looking for something in particular?'

'Yes. There was an airplane crash here.'

'How long ago, *señor*?'

If I'm right – 'Twenty-eight years ago. Nineteen forty-eight.'

It took Alan Tucker fifteen minutes to find the item he was looking for. The headline leaped out at him.

PLANE CRASH KILLS EXECUTIVE FAMILY
1 October 1948. Byron Scott, President of Scott Industries, his wife, Susan, and their one-year-old daughter, Patricia, were burned to death in an airplane crash . . .

I've hit the jackpot! He could feel his pulse begin to race. *If this is what I think it is, I'm going to be a rich man . . . a* very *rich man.*

Chapter 19

She was naked in her bed, and she could feel the male hardness of Benito Patas pressing into her groin. His body felt wonderful, and she moved closer to him, grinding her hips against him, feeling the heat growing in her loins. She started to stroke him, to excite him. But something was wrong. *I killed Patas*, she thought. *He's dead.*

Lucia opened her eyes and sat up, trembling, looking around wildly. Benito was not there. She was in the forest, in a sleeping-bag. Something was pressing against her thigh. Lucia reached down inside the sleeping-bag and pulled out the canvas-wrapped cross. She stared at it, unbelievingly. *God has just performed a miracle for me*, Lucia thought.

She had no idea how the cross had got there, nor did she care. She had it in her hands at last. All she had to do now was to slip away from the others.

She crept out of the sleeping-bag and looked over to where Sister Teresa had slept. She was gone. Lucia looked around in the darkness, and she could barely make out the figure of Tomas Sanjuro at the edge of the clearing, facing away from her. She was not sure where Rubio was. *It doesn't matter. It's time to get out of here*, Lucia thought.

She started to move to the edge of the clearing, away from Sanjuro, bending low so she would not be seen.

At that instant all hell broke loose.

Colonel Fal Sostelo had had a command decision to make. He had been given orders by the Prime Minister himself to work closely with Colonel Ramón Acoca to help capture Jaime Miró and the nuns. But fate had blessed him by delivering one of the nuns into his hands. Why share the credit with Colonel Acoca when he could catch the terrorists and keep all the glory? *Fuck Colonel Acoca*, Fal Sostelo thought. *This one is mine. Maybe the OPUS MUNDO will use me instead of Acoca, with all his bullshit about chess games and getting into the minds of people. No, it's time to teach the scarred giant a lesson.*

Colonel Sostelo gave specific orders to his men.

'Don't take any prisoners. You're dealing with terrorists. Shoot to kill.'

Major Ponte hesitated. 'Colonel, there are nuns up there with Miró's men. Shouldn't we –?'

'Let the terrorists hide behind the nuns? No. We'll take no chances.'

Fal Sostelo selected a dozen men to accompany him on the raid and he saw to it that they were heavily armed. They moved noiselessly in the dark, up the slope of the mountain. The moon had disappeared behind clouds. There was almost no visibility. *Good. They won't be able to see us coming.*

When his men were in position, Colonel Sostelo shouted, for the sake of the record, 'Put down your arms. You're surrounded.' And in the same breath he called out the command, 'Fire! Keep firing!'

A dozen automatic weapons began spraying the clearing.

Tomas Sanjuro never had a chance. A hail of machine gun bullets caught him in the chest and he was dead before he hit the ground. Rubio Arzano was at the far edge of the clearing when the firing started. He saw Sanjuro fall, and he whirled and started to raise his gun to return the fire but stopped. It was pitch black in the clearing and the soldiers were firing blindly. If he returned their fire, he would give his position away.

To his amazement, he saw Lucia crouched two feet away from him.

'Where's Sister Teresa?' he whispered.

'She's – she's gone.'

'Stay low,' Rubio told her.

He grabbed Lucia's hand and zigzagged towards the forest, away from the enemy fire. Shots whizzed dangerously close as they ran, but moments later, Lucia and Rubio were among the trees. They continued running.

'Hold on to me, Sister,' he said.

They heard the sound of their attackers behind them, but gradually it died away. It was impossible to pursue anyone through the inky blackness of the woods.

Rubio stopped to let Lucia catch her breath.

'We've lost them for now,' Rubio told her. 'But we have to keep moving.'

Lucia was breathing hard.

'If you want to rest for a minute –?'

'No,' she said. She was exhausted, but she had no intention of letting them catch her. Not now when she had the cross. 'I'm fine,' she said. 'Let's get out of here.'

Colonel Fal Sostelo was facing disaster. One terrorist dead, but God alone knew how many had escaped. He did not have Jaime Miró and he had only one of the nuns. He knew he would have to inform Colonel Acoca of what had happened. He was not looking forward to it.

The second call from Alan Tucker to Ellen Scott was even more disturbing than the previous call.

'I've come across some rather interesting information, Mrs Scott,' he said cautiously.

'Yes?'

'I went through some old newspaper files here, hoping to get more information on the girl.'

'And?' She braced herself for what she knew was coming.

Tucker kept his voice casual. 'It seems that the girl was abandoned about the time of your plane crash.'

Silence.

He went on: 'The one that killed your brother-in-law and his wife and their daughter, Patricia.'

Blackmail. There was no other explanation. So he had found out.

'That's right,' Ellen Scott said casually. 'I should have mentioned that. I'll explain everything when you get back. Have you any more news of the girl?'

'No, but she can't hide out for very long. The whole country's looking for her.'

'Let me hear from you as soon as she's found.'

The line went dead.

Alan Tucker sat there, staring at the dead telephone in his hand. *She's a cool lady*, he thought admiringly. *I wonder how she's going to feel about having a partner?*

I made a mistake in sending him, Ellen Scott thought. *Now I'll have to stop him.* And what was she going to do about the girl? *A nun! I won't judge her until I see her.*

Her secretary buzzed her on the intercom.

'They're ready for you in the board room, Mrs Scott.'

'I'm coming.'

Lucia and Rubio Arzano kept moving through the woods, stumbling and slipping, attacked by tree limbs and bushes and insects, but each step took them farther away from their pursuers.

Finally, Rubio Arzano said, 'We can stop here. They won't find us.'

They were high in the mountains in the middle of a dense forest.

Lucia lay down on the ground, fighting to catch her breath. In her mind, she replayed the terrible scene she had witnessed earlier. Tomas shot down without warning. *And the bastards intended to murder us all*, Lucia thought. The only reason she was still alive was because of the man sitting beside her.

Lucia watched Rubio as he got to his feet and scouted the area around them.

'We can spend the rest of the night here, Sister.'

'All right.' She was impatient to get moving, but she knew she needed to rest.

As though reading her mind, Rubio Arzano said, 'We'll move on again at dawn.'

Lucia felt a gnawing in her stomach. Even as she was thinking about it, Rubio Arzano said, 'You must be hungry. I'll go and find some food for us. Will you be all right here by yourself?'

'Yes. I'll be fine.'

The big man crouched down beside her.

'Please try not to be frightened. I know how difficult it must be for you to be out in the world again after all those years in the convent. Everything must seem very strange to you.'

Lucia looked up at him and said tonelessly, 'I'll try to get used to it.'

'You're very brave, Sister.' Rubio rose. 'I'll be back soon.'

She watched Rubio disappear into the trees. It was time to make a decision, and she had two choices: she could escape now, try to reach a nearby town and trade the gold cross for a passport and enough money to get to Switzerland, or she could stay with this man until they got farther away from the soldiers. *That will be safer*, Lucia decided.

Lucia heard a noise in the woods and swung around. It was Rubio Arzano. He moved towards her, smiling. In his hand he held his beret, bulging with tomatoes, grapes and apples.

He sat down on the ground next to her. 'Supper. A nice, plump poulet was available but the fire we would have needed to cook it would have given us away.'

Lucia stared at the contents of the beret. 'It looks like manna from heaven. I'm starving.'

*

They had finished eating and were sitting against a tree. Rubio Arzano was talking, but Lucia was paying no attention, absorbed in her own thoughts.

'Ten years, you said you were in the convent, Sister?'

Lucia was startled out of her reverie. 'What?'

'You've been in the convent for ten years?'

'Oh. Yes.'

He shook his head. 'Then you have no idea what's been happening in all that time.'

'Uh – no.'

'In the last ten years the world has changed a great deal, Sister.'

'Has it?'

'*Si.*' Rubio said earnestly, 'Franco has died.'

'No!'

'Oh, yes. Last year.'

And named Don Juan Carlos, his heir.

'You may find this very hard to believe, but a man has walked on the moon. That is the truth.'

'Really?' *Actually, two men*, Lucia thought. *What were their names? Neil Armstrong and Buzz Something.*

'Oh, yes. North Americans. And there is now a plane for passengers that travels faster than sound '

'Incredible.' *I can't wait to travel in Concorde*, Lucia thought.

Rubio was childlike, so pleased to be bringing her up to date on world events.

'There has been a revolution in Portugal, and in the United States of America, their President Nixon was involved in a big scandal and had to resign.'

Rubio is really sweet, Lucia decided.

He took out a pack of Ducados cigarettes, the heavy black tobacco of Spain. 'I hope it won't offend you if I smoke, Sister?'

'No,' Lucia said. 'Please go ahead.'

She watched him light up, and the moment the smoke reached her nostrils she was desperate to have a cigarette.

'Do you mind if I try one?'

He looked at her in surprise. 'You wish to try a cigarette?'

'Just to see what it's like,' Lucia said quickly.

'Oh. Of course.'

He held the pack towards her. She took out a cigarette, put it between her lips and he lit the end of it for her. Lucia inhaled deeply, and as the smoke filled her lungs, she felt wonderful.

Rubio was watching her, puzzled.

Lucia coughed. 'So that's what a cigarette tastes like.'

'Do you like it?'

'Not really, but –'

She took another deep, satisfying puff. God, how she had missed this. But she knew she had to be careful. She did not want to make him suspicious. She put out the cigarette she had held clumsily in her fingers. She had been in the convent for only a few months, and yet Rubio was right. It did seem strange to be out in the world again. She wondered how Megan and Graciela were doing. And what had happened to Sister Teresa? Had she been captured by the soldiers?

Lucia's eyes were beginning to sting. It had been a long, tension-filled night. 'I think I may take a little nap.'

'Don't worry. I will watch over you, Sister.'

'Thank you,' she smiled. Within moments, she was asleep.

Rubio Arzano looked down at her and thought: *I have never seen a woman like this one.* She was so spiritual that she had dedicated her life to God, and yet at the same time there was an earthiness about her. And she had behaved this night as bravely as any man. *You are a very special woman,* Rubio Arzano thought as he watched her sleep. *Little sister of Jesus.*

Chapter 20

Colonel Fal Sostelo was on his tenth cigarette. *I can't put it off any longer*, he decided. *Bad news is best got out of the way quickly.*

He took several deep breaths to calm himself and then he dialled a number. When he had Ramón Acoca on the telephone, he said, 'Colonel, we raided a terrorist camp last night, where I was informed Jaime Miró was, and I thought you should know about it.'

There was a dangerous silence.

'Did you catch him?'

'No.'

'You undertook this operation without consulting me?'

'There was no time to –'

'But there was time to let Miró escape.' Ramón Acoca's voice was filled with fury. 'What led you to undertake this magnificently executed operation?'

Colonel Sostelo swallowed. 'We caught one of the nuns from the convent. She led us to Miró and his men. We killed one of them in the attack.'

'But the others all escaped?'

'Yes, Colonel.'

'Where is the nun now? Or did you let her get away, too?' His tone was scathing.

'No, Colonel,' Sostelo said quickly. 'She is here at the camp. We have been questioning her and –'

'Don't. I'll question her myself. I'll be there in one hour.

See if you can manage to hang on to her until I get there.'
He slammed down the receiver.

Exactly one hour later, Colonel Ramón Acoca arrived at the
camp where they were holding Sister Teresa. With him were
a dozen of his men from the GOE.

'Bring the nun to me,' Colonel Acoca ordered.

Sister Teresa was brought to the headquarters tent where
Colonel Acoca was waiting for her. He stood up politely
when she entered the tent and smiled.

'I am Colonel Acoca.'

At last! 'I knew you would come. God told me.'

He nodded pleasantly. 'Did he? Good. Please sit down,
Sister.'

Sister Teresa was too nervous to sit. 'You must help me.'

'We're going to help each other,' the Colonel assured her.
'You escaped from the Abbey Cistercian at Ávila, is that
correct?'

'Yes. It was terrible. All those men. They did godless
things and –'

And stupid things. We let you and the others escape. 'How
did you get here, Sister?'

'God brought me here. He's testing me as He once
tested –'

Colonel Acoca said patiently, 'As well as God, did some
men also bring you here, Sister?'

'Yes. They kidnapped me. I had to escape from them.'

'You told Colonel Sostelo where he could find those men?'

'Yes. The evil ones. Raoul is behind it all, you see. He
sent me a letter and said –'

'Sister, the man we're looking for in particular is Jaime
Miró. Have you seen him?'

She shivered. 'Yes. Oh, yes. He –'

The Colonel leaned forward. 'Excellent. Now you must
tell me where I can find him.'

'He and the others are on their way to Èze.'

He frowned, puzzled. 'To Èze? To France?'

Her words were a wild babble. 'Yes. Monique deserted Raoul, and he sent the men to kidnap me because of the baby so –'

He tried to control his growing impatience. 'Miró and his men are headed north. Èze is to the east.'

'– You must not let them take me back to Raoul. I don't want to see him ever again. You can understand that. I couldn't face him –'

Colonel Acoca said curtly, 'I don't give a damn about this Raoul. I want to know where I can find Jaime Miró.'

'I told you. He is in Èze waiting for me. He wants to –'

'You're lying. I think you're trying to protect Miró. Now I don't want to hurt you, so I'm going to ask you once more. Where is Jaime Miró?'

Sister Teresa stared at him helplessly. 'I don't know,' she whispered. She looked around wildly. 'I don't know.'

'A moment ago you said he was in Èze.' His voice was like a whiplash.

'Yes. God told me.'

Colonel Acoca had had enough. The woman was either demented or a brilliant actress. Either way, she sickened him with all her talk of God.

He turned to Patricio Arrieta, his lieutenant. 'The sister's memory needs prodding. Take her to the quartermaster's tent. Perhaps you and your men can help her remember where Jaime Miró is.'

'Yes, Colonel.'

Patricio Arrieta and the men with him had been part of the group that had attacked the convent at Ávila. They felt responsible for letting the four nuns escape. *Well, we can make up for that now*, Arrieta thought.

Arrieta turned to Sister Teresa. 'Come along with me, Sister.'

'Yes.' *Dear blessed Jesus, thank You.* She babbled on. 'Are we leaving now? You won't let them take me to Eze, will you?'

'No,' Arrieta assured her. 'You're not going to Èze.'

The Colonel is right, he thought. *She is playing games with*

204

us. Well, we'll show her some new games. I wonder if she'll lie quietly, or if she'll scream?

When they reached the quartermaster's tent, Arrieta said, 'Sister, we've going to give you one last chance. Where is Jaime Miró?'

Haven't they asked me that before? Or was that someone else? Was it here or – it's all terribly confusing. 'He kidnapped me for Raoul because Monique deserted him and he thought –'

'*Bueno*. If that's the way you want it,' Arrieta said, 'we'll see if we can't refresh your memory for you.'

'Yes. Please. Everything is so puzzling.'

Half a dozen of Acoca's men had entered the tent, along with some of Sostelo's uniformed soldiers.

Sister Teresa looked up. She blinked dazedly. 'Are these men going to take me to the convent now?'

'They're going to do better than that,' Patricio Arrieta grinned. 'They're going to take you to heaven, Sister.'

The men moved closer to her, surrounding her.

'That's a pretty dress you're wearing,' a soldier said. 'Are you sure you're a nun, darling?'

'Oh, yes,' she said *Raoul had called her darling. Was this Raoul?* 'You see, we had to change clothes to escape from the soldiers.' *But these were soldiers. Everything was muddled.*

One of the men pushed Teresa down on the cot. 'You're no beauty, but let's see what you look like underneath all those clothes.'

'What are you doing?'

He reached down and ripped off the top of her dress while another man tore at her skirt.

'That's not a bad body for an old lady, is it, fellows?'

Teresa screamed.

She looked up at the circle of men surrounding her. *God will strike them all dead. He will not let them touch me, for I am His vessel. I am one with the Lord, drinking from His fountain of purity.*

One of the soldiers unfastened his belt. An instant later she felt rough hands pushing her legs apart, and as the soldier

205

sprawled on top of her, she felt his hard flesh penetrate her and again she screamed.

'Now, God! Punish them now.'

She waited for the clap of thunder, the bright flash of lightning that would destroy them all.

Nothing happened.

Another soldier climbed on top of her. A red haze came over her eyes. Teresa lay there waiting for God to strike, almost unaware of the men who were ravaging her. She no longer felt the pain.

Lieutenant Arrieta was standing next to the cot. After each man finished with Teresa, he said, 'Have you had enough, Sister? You can stop this at any time. All you have to do is tell me where Jaime Miró is.'

Sister Teresa did not hear him. She screamed in her mind: *Smite them down with Your power, Lord. Wipe them out as You wiped out the other wicked ones at Sodom and Gomorrah.*

Incredibly, He did not answer. It was not possible, for God was everywhere. And then she knew. As the sixth man entered her body, the epiphany suddenly came to her.

God was not listening to her because there was no God. All these years she had deceived herself into worshipping a Supreme power and had served Him faithfully. But there was no Supreme Power. *If God exists, He would have saved me.*

The red haze lifted from Sister Teresa's eyes and she got a clear look at her surroundings for the first time. There were at least a dozen soldiers in the tent waiting their turn to rape her. Lieutenant Arrieta was standing at one side of the bed watching. The soldiers in line were in full uniform, not bothering to undress.

As one soldier lifted himself from Teresa, the next soldier opened his fly and took out his penis. He squatted down over her and a moment later penetrated her.

There is no God, but there is a Satan, and these are his helpers, Sister Teresa thought. *And they must die. All of them.*

As the soldier plunged into her, Sister Teresa grabbed the pistol from his holster and before anyone could react, she turned the pistol on Arrieta. The bullet hit him in the throat.

Sister Teresa pointed the gun at the other soldiers and kept firing. Four of them fell to the floor dead before the others came to their senses and began shooting at her. Because of the soldier on top of her, they had difficulty aiming.

Sister Teresa and her last ravisher died at the same moment.

Chapter 21

Jaime Miró came awake instantly, aroused by a movement
at the edge of the clearing. He slipped out of the sleeping-bag
and rose, gun in hand. He saw Megan on her knees, praying.
He stood there, studying her. There was an unearthly beauty
about the image of this lovely woman praying in the forest
in the middle of the night, and Jaime found himself resenting
it. *If Felix Carpio hadn't blurted out that we were headed for
San Sebastian, I wouldn't have been burdened with the sister
in the first place.*

It was imperative that he get to San Sebastian as quickly
as possible. Colonel Acoca and his men and the army were
all around them, and it would have been difficult enough
slipping through their net alone. With the added burden of
this woman to slow him down, the danger was increased
tenfold.

He walked over to Megan, angry, and his voice was harsher
than he had intended.

'I told you to get some sleep. I don't want you slowing us
down tomorrow.'

Megan looked up and said quietly, 'I'm sorry if I've
angered you.'

'Sister, I save my anger for more important things. Your
kind just bore me. You spend your lives hiding behind stone
walls waiting for a free trip to the next world. You make me
sick, all of you.'

'Because we believe in the next world?'

'No, Sister. Because you don't believe in this one. You
ran away from it.'

208

'To pray for you. We spend our lives praying for you.'

'And you think that will solve the problems of the world?'

'In time, yes.'

'There is no time. Your God can't hear your prayers because of the noise of the cannons and the screams of children being torn apart by bombs.'

'When you have faith –'

'Oh, I have lots of faith, Sister. I have faith in what I'm fighting for. I have faith in my men, and in my guns. What I don't have faith in are people who walk on water. If you think your God is listening now, tell him to get us to the convent at Mendavia so I can be rid of you.'

He was angry with himself for losing his temper. It wasn't her fault that the church had stood idly by while Franco's Falangists tortured and raped and murdered Basques and Catalans. *It wasn't her fault*, Jaime told himself, *that my family was among the victims.*

Jaime had been a young boy then, but it was a memory that would be etched for ever in his brain . . .

He had been awakened in the middle of the night by the noise of bombs falling. They fell from the sky like deadly flowers of sound planting their seeds of destruction everywhere.

'Get up, Jaime. Hurry!'

The fear in his father's voice was more frightening to the boy than the terrible roar of the aerial bombardment.

Guernica was a stronghold of the Basques and General Franco had decided to make it an object lesson.

'Destroy it.'

The dreaded Nazi Condor Legion and half a dozen Italian planes had mounted a concentrated attack, and they showed no mercy. The townspeople tried to flee from the rain of death pouring down from the skies, but there was no escape.

Jaime, his mother and father and two older sisters fled with the others.

209

'To the church,' Jaime's father said. 'They won't bomb the church.'

He was right. Everyone knew that the church was on the side of the Caudillo, turning a blind eye to the savage treatment of his enemies.

The Miró family headed for the church, fighting their way through the panicky crowds trying to flee.

The young boy held his father's hand in a fierce grip and tried not to hear the terrible noises around him. He remembered a time when his father was not frightened, was not running away.

'Are we going to have a war, Papa?'

'No, Jaime. That's just newspaper talk. All we're asking is that the government give us a reasonable amount of independence. The Basques and the Catalans are entitled to have their own language and flag and holidays. We're still one nation. And Spaniards will never fight against Spaniards.'

Jaime was too young then to understand it, but of course it was more than the issue of the Catalans and Basques that was at stake. It was a deep ideological conflict between the Republican government and the right-wing Nationalists, and what started out as a spark of dissension quickly became an uncontrollable conflagration that drew in a dozen foreign powers.

When Franco's superior forces had defeated the Republicans and the Nationalists were firmly in control of Spain, Franco turned his attention to the intransigent Basques.

'Punish them.'

And the blood continued to flow.

A hard core of Basque leaders had formed ETA, a movement for a Basque Free State, and Jaime's father was asked to join.

'No. It is wrong. We must gain what is rightfully ours by peaceful means. War accomplishes nothing.'

But the hawks proved stronger than the doves, and ETA quickly became a prime target.

Jaime had friends whose fathers were members of ETA, and he listened to the stories of their heroic exploits.

210

'My father and a group of his friends bombed the head-quarters of the *guardia civil*,' they would say.

Or, 'Did you hear about the bank robbery in Barcelona? My father did that. Now they can buy weapons to fight the fascists.'

And Jaime's father was saying, 'Violence is wrong. We must negotiate.'

'We blew up one of their factories in Madrid. Why isn't your father on our side? Is he a coward?'

'Don't listen to your friends, Jaime,' his father told him. 'What they are doing is criminal.'

'Franco ordered a dozen Basques executed without even a trial. We're staging a nationwide strike. Is your father going to join us?'

'Papa –?'

'We are all Spaniards, Jaime. We must not let anyone divide us.'

And the boy was torn. *Are my friends right? Is my father a coward?* Jaime believed his father.

And now – armageddon. The world was collapsing around him. The streets of Guernica were crowded with a screaming mob trying to escape from the falling bombs. All around them buildings and statues and pavements were exploding in showers of concrete and blood.

Jaime and his mother and father and sisters had reached the large church, the only building in the square still standing. A dozen people were pounding at the door.

'Let us in! In the name of Jesus, open up!'

'What's going on?' cried Jaime's father.

'The priests have locked the church. They won't let us in.'

'Let's break the door in!'

'No!'

Jaime looked at his father in surprise.

'We don't break into God's house,' his father said. 'He will protect us wherever we are.'

Too late, they saw the squad of Falangists that appeared from around the corner and opened machine-gun fire on them, mowing down the unarmed crowd of men, women and children in the square. Even as Jaime's father felt the bullets tearing into him, he grabbed his son and pushed him down to safety, his own body shielding Jaime from the deadly hail of bullets.

An eerie silence seemed to blanket the world. The sounds of guns and running feet and screams vanished, a trick of magic. Jaime opened his eyes and lay there for a long time, feeling the weight of his father's body on him, like a loving blanket. His father and mother and sisters were dead, along with hundreds of others. And in front of their bodies were the locked doors of the church.

Late that night, Jaime made his way out of the city and two days later when he reached Bilbao, he joined ETA.

The recruiting officer had looked at him and said, 'You're too young to join, son. You should be in school.'

'You're going to be my school,' Jaime Miró said quietly. 'You're going to teach me how to fight to avenge the murder of my family.'

He never looked back. He was battling for himself and for his family, and his exploits became legendary. Jaime planned and executed daring raids against factories and banks and carried out the executions of the oppressors. When any of Jaime's men were captured, he conducted daredevil missions to rescue them.

When Jaime heard about the GOE being formed to pursue Basques, he smiled and said, 'Good. They've noticed.'

Jaime never asked himself if the risks he took had anything to do with the cries of, 'Your father is a coward,' or if he was trying to prove anything to himself and to others. It was enough that he proved his bravery again and again, that he was not afraid to risk his life for what he believed in.

Now, because one of his men had talked too freely, Jaime found himself saddled with a nun.

It's ironic that her Church is on our side now. But it's much

212

too late, unless they can arrange a Second Coming and include my mother and father and sisters, he thought bitterly.

They walked through the woods at night, the white moonlight dappling the forest around them. They avoided the towns and main roads, alert for any sign of danger. Jaime ignored Megan. He walked with Felix, talking about past adventures, and Megan found herself intrigued. She had never known anyone like Jaime Miró. He was filled with such self-assurance.

If anyone can get me to Mendavia, Megan thought, *this man can.*

There had been moments when Jaime had felt pity for the sister, and even a reluctant admiration for the way she coped on the arduous journey. He wondered how his other men were getting along with their charges from God.

At least he had Amparo Jiron. At night Jaime found her a great comfort.

She's as dedicated as I am, Jaime thought. *She has even more reason than I do to hate the government.*

Amparo's entire family had been wiped out by the Nationalist army. She was fiercely independent, and filled with a deep passion.

At dawn they were nearing Salamanca, on the banks of the Rio Tormes.

'Students come here from all over Spain,' Felix explained to Megan, 'to attend the university here. It's probably the best in all of Spain.'

Jaime was not listening. He was concentrating on his next move. *If I were the hunter, where would I set my trap?*

He turned to Felix. 'We'll skip Salamanca. There's a *parador* just outside town. We will stop there.'

*

The *parador* was a small inn away from the mainstream of tourist traffic. Stone steps led to the lobby, which was guarded by an ancient knight in armour.

As the group approached the entrance, Jaime said to the two women, 'Wait here.'

He nodded to Felix Carpio and the two men disappeared.

'Where are they going?' Megan asked.

Amparo Jiron gave her a contemptuous look. 'Maybe they went looking for your God.'

'I hope they find him,' Megan said evenly.

Ten minutes later the men were back.

'All clear,' Jaime told Amparo. 'You and the sister will share a room. Felix will stay with me.' He handed her a key.

Amparo said petulantly, '*Querida*, I want to stay with you, not –'

'Do as I say. Keep an eye on her.'

Amparo turned to Megan. '*Bueno*. Come along, Sister.'

Megan followed Amparo up the stairs.

The room was one of a dozen set in a row along the grey, bare corridor. Amparo unlocked the door and the two women entered. The room was small and drab and sparsely furnished, with wooden floors, stucco walls, a bed, a small cot, a battered dressing-table and two chairs.

Megan looked around the room and exclaimed, 'It's lovely.'

Amparo Jiron swung around in anger, thinking that Megan was being sarcastic. 'Who the hell are you to complain about –?'

'It's so large,' Megan went on.

Amparo looked at her for a moment, then laughed. Of course it would seem large compared to the cells that the sisters lived in.

Amparo started to get undressed.

Megan could not help staring at her. It was the first time she had really looked at Amparo Jiron in the daylight. The woman was beautiful, in an earthy way. She had red hair, white skin, and was full-breasted, with a small waist and hips that swayed as she moved.

214

Amparo saw her watching. 'Sister – would you tell me something? Why would anyone join a convent?'

It was a simple question to answer. 'What could be more wonderful than to devote oneself to the glory of God?'

'Offhand, I could think of a thousand things.' Amparo walked over to the bed and sat down. 'You can sleep on the cot. From what I've heard about convents, your God doesn't want you to be too comfortable.'

Megan smiled. 'It doesn't matter. I'm comfortable inside.'

In their room across the corridor, Jaime Miró was stretching out on the bed. Felix Carpio was trying to get settled on the small cot. Both men were fully dressed. Jaime's gun was under his pillow. Felix's gun was on the small, battered table next to him.

'What do you think makes them do it?' Felix wondered aloud.

'Do what, *amigo*?'

'Lock themselves up in a convent all their lives like prisoners.'

Jaime Miró shrugged. 'Ask the sister. I wish to hell we were travelling alone. I have a bad feeling about this.'

'Jaime, God will thank us for this good deed.'

'Do you really believe that? Don't make me laugh.'

Felix did not pursue the subject. It was not tactful to discuss the Catholic Church with Jaime. The two men were silent, each preoccupied with his own thoughts.

Felix Carpio was thinking: *God put the sisters in our hands. We must get them to a convent safely.*

Jaime was thinking about Amparo. He wanted her badly now. *That damned nun.* He started to pull up the covers when he realized there was something he still had to do.

In the small, dark lobby downstairs, the manager sat quietly, waiting until he was sure that the new guests were asleep.

His heart was pounding as he picked up the telephone and dialled a number.

A lazy voice answered, 'Police Headquarters.'

The manager whispered into the telephone to his nephew, 'Florian, I have Jaime Miró and three of his people here. How would you like the honour of capturing them?'

Chapter 22

Many miles to the east, in a wooded area along the way to Peñafiel, Lucia Carmine was asleep.

Rubio Arzano sat watching her, reluctant to awaken her. *She sleeps like an angel*, he thought.

But it was almost dawn, time to be moving on.

Rubio leaned over and whispered gently in her ear, 'Sister Lucia . . .'

Lucia opened her eyes.

'It is time for us to go.'

She yawned and stretched lazily. The blouse she was wearing had become unbuttoned and part of her breast was showing. Rubio hastily looked away.

I must guard my thoughts. She is the bride of Jesus.

'Sister . . .'

'Yes?'

'I – I wonder if I could ask a favour of you.' He was almost blushing.

'Yes?'

'I – it's been a long time since I prayed. But I was brought up a Catholic. Would you mind saying a prayer?'

That was the last thing Lucia had expected.

How long has it been since I said a prayer? she wondered.

The convent did not count. While the others were praying, her mind had been busy with plans to escape.

'I – I don't –'

'I'm sure it would make us both feel better.'

How could she explain that she did not remember any prayers? 'I – er –' *Yes.* There was one she remembered. She

217

had been a little girl kneeling at her bedside and her father had stood beside her, ready to tuck her into bed. Slowly, the words of the twenty-third Psalm started coming.

'The Lord is my shepherd. I shall not want. He maketh me to lie down in green pastures. He leadeth me beside the still waters. He restoreth my soul. He leadeth me in the paths of righteousness, for His name's sake . . .'

Memories came flooding back.

She and her father had owned the world. And he had been so proud of her.

You were born under a lucky star, faccia del angelo.

And hearing that, Lucia had felt lucky and beautiful. Nothing could ever hurt her. Was she not the beautiful daughter of the great Angelo Carmine?

'. . . Yea, though I walk through the valley of the shadow of death, I will fear no evil . . .'

The evil ones were the enemies of her father and brothers. And she had made them pay.

'. . . For Thou art with me; Thy rod and Thy staff they comfort me . . .'

Where was God when I needed comforting?

'Thou preparest a table before me in the presence of mine enemies; Thou anointest my head with oil, my cup runneth over. . .'

She was speaking more slowly now, her voice a whisper. What had happened, she wondered, to the little girl in the white communion dress? The future had been so golden. Somehow it had all gone wrong. Everything. *I've lost my father and my brothers and myself.*

In the convent she had not thought about God. But now, out here with this simple peasant . . .

Would you mind saying a prayer for us?

Lucia went on. 'Surely goodness and mercy shall follow me all the days of my life; And I will dwell in the house of the Lord for ever.'

Rubio was watching her, moved.

'Thank you, Sister.'

Lucia nodded, unable to speak. *What's the matter with me?* Lucia asked herself.

'Are you ready, Sister?'

She looked at Rubio Arzano and said, 'Yes. I'm ready.'

Five minutes later they were on their way.

They were caught in a sudden downpour and took shelter in a deserted cabin. The rain beat against the roof and sides of the cabin like angry fists.

'Do you think the storm will ever let up?'

Rubio smiled. 'It's not a real storm, Sister. It's what we Basques call a *sirimiri*. It will stop as quickly as it started. The earth is dry right now. It needs this rain.'

'Really?'

'Yes. I'm a farmer.'

It shows, Lucia thought.

'Forgive me for saying this, Sister, but you and I have a lot in common.'

Lucia looked over at the country bumpkin and thought: *That will be the day*. 'We do?'

'Yes. I truly believe that in many ways being on a farm must be much like being in a convent.'

The connection eluded her. 'I don't understand.'

'Well, Sister, in a convent you think a lot about God and His miracles. Is that not true?'

'Yes.'

'In a sense a farm is God. One is surrounded by creation – all the things that grow from God's earth, whether it's wheat or olives or grapes – everything comes from God, does it not? These are all miracles, and you watch them happen every day, and because you help them grow, you are part of the miracle.'

Lucia had to smile at the enthusiasm in his voice.

Suddenly the rain stopped.

'We can move on now, Sister.'

*

219

'We will be coming to Rio Duero soon,' Rubio said. 'The Peñafiel Falls is just ahead of us. We will go on to Aranda de Duero and then Logroño, where we will meet the others.'

You'll be going to those places, Lucia thought. *And good luck to you. I'll be in Switzerland, my friend.*

They heard the sound of the Falls half an hour before they reached them. The Peñafiel Falls was a beautiful sight cascading down into the swift-moving river. The roar of it was almost deafening.

'I want to bathe,' Lucia said. It seemed years since she had last had a bath.

Rubio Arzano stared at her. 'Here?'

No, you idiot, in Rome. 'Yes.'

'Be careful. The river is swollen because of the rain.'

'Don't worry.' She stood there, patiently waiting.

'Oh. I will go away while you undress.'

'Stay nearby,' Lucia said quickly. There were probably wild animals in the woods.

As Lucia started to undress, Rubio hastily walked a few yards away and turned his back.

'Don't go in too far, Sister,' he called. 'The river is treacherous.'

Lucia put down the wrapped cross where she could keep an eye on it. The cool morning air felt wonderful on her naked body. When she had stripped completely, she stepped into the water. It was cold and invigorating. She turned and saw that Rubio was steadfastly looking in the other direction, his back turned to her. She smiled to herself. All the other men she had known would be feasting their eyes.

She stepped in deeper, avoiding the rocks that were all around, and splashed the water over herself, feeling the rushing river tugging hard at her legs.

A few feet away a small tree was being swept downstream. As Lucia turned to watch it, she suddenly lost her balance and slipped, screaming. She fell hard, slamming her head against a boulder.

Rubio turned and watched in horror as Lucia disappeared downstream in the raging waters.

Chapter 23

At the police station in Salamanca, when Sergeant Florian Santiago replaced the receiver, his hands were trembling.

I have Jaime Miró and three of his people here. How would you like the honour of capturing them?

The government had offered a large reward for the head of Jaime Miró, and now the Basque outlaw was in his hands. The reward money would change his whole life. He could afford to send his children to a better school, he could buy a washing machine for his wife and jewellery for his mistress. Of course he would have to share some of the reward money with his uncle. *I'll give him twenty per cent*, Santiago thought. *Or maybe ten per cent.*

He was well aware of Jaime Miró's reputation, and he had no intention of risking his life trying to capture the terrorist. *Let others face the danger and give me the reward.*

He sat at his desk deciding the best way to handle the situation. Colonel Acoca's name immediately sprang to his mind. Everybody knew there was a blood vendetta between the Colonel and the outlaw. Besides, the Colonel had the whole GOE at his command. Yes, that was definitely the way to proceed.

He picked up a telephone, and ten minutes later he was speaking to the Colonel himself.

'This is Sergeant Florian Santiago calling from the police station at Salamanca. I have tracked down Jaime Miró.'

Colonel Ramón Acoca fought to keep his voice even. 'Are you certain of this?'

'Yes, Colonel. He is at the Parador Nacional Raimundo

de Borgon, just outside of town. He is spending the night. My uncle is the manager. He telephoned me himself. There is another man and two women with Miró.'

'Your uncle is positive it is Miró?'

'Yes, Colonel. He and the others are sleeping in the two back rooms on the second floor of the inn.'

Colonel Acoca said, 'Listen to me very carefully, Sergeant. I want you to go to the *parador* immediately and stand watch outside to make certain none of them leaves. I should be able to reach there in an hour. You are not to go inside. And stay out of sight. Is that clear?'

'Yes, sir. I will leave immediately.' He hesitated. 'Colonel, about the reward money –'

'When we catch Miró, it's yours.'

'Thank you, Colonel. I am most –'

'Go.'

'Yes, sir.'

Florian Santiago replaced the receiver. He was tempted to call his mistress to tell her the exciting news, but that could wait. He would surprise her later. Meanwhile, he had a job to do.

He summoned one of the policemen on duty upstairs.

'Take over the desk. I have an errand to do. I'll be back in a few hours.' *And I'll come back a rich man*, he thought. *The first thing I'll buy will be a new car – a Seat. A blue one. No, maybe it will be white.*

Colonel Ramón Acoca replaced the receiver and sat still, letting his brain go to work. This time there would be no slip-up. It was the final move in the chess game between them. He would have to proceed very carefully. Miro would have sentries alert for trouble.

Acoca called in his aide-de-camp.

'Yes, Colonel?'

'Pick out two dozen of your best marksmen. See that they're armed with automatic weapons. We're leaving for Salamanca in fifteen minutes.'

223

'Yes, sir.'

There would be no escape for Miró. The Colonel was already planning the raid in his mind. The *parador* would be completely surrounded by a cordon that would move in quickly and quietly. *A sneak attack before the butcher has a chance to murder any more of my men. We'll kill them all in their sleep.*

Fifteen minutes later, his aide returned.

'We're ready to move, Colonel.'

Sergeant Santiago lost no time in getting to the *parador*. Even without the Colonel's warning, he would have had no intention of going after the terrorists. But now, in obedience to Acoca's orders, he stood in the shadows, twenty yards away from the inn, where he had a good view of the front door. There was a chill in the night air, but the thought of the reward money kept Santiago warm. He wondered whether the two women inside were pretty and whether they were in bed with the men. Of one thing Santiago was certain: in a few hours, they would all be dead.

The army truck moved into town quietly and drove towards the *parador*.

Colonel Acoca flicked on a flashlight and looked at his map, and when they were a mile from the inn, he said, 'Stop here. We'll walk the rest of the way. Maintain silence.'

Florian Santiago was unaware of their approach until a voice in his ear startled him with, 'Who are you?'

He turned and found himself facing Colonel Ramón Acoca. *My God, he's frightening-looking*, Santiago thought.

'I am Sergeant Santiago, sir.'

'Has anyone left the inn?'

'No, sir. They're all inside, probably asleep by now.'

The Colonel turned to his aide. 'I want half our men to

224

form a perimeter around the hotel. If anyone tries to escape, they are to shoot to kill. The others will come with me. The fugitives are in the two back bedrooms upstairs. Let's go.'

Santiago watched as the Colonel and his men entered the front door of the *parador*, moving quietly. Santiago wondered if there would be a lot of shooting. And if there was, he wondered if his uncle might be killed in the cross-fire. That would be a pity. But on the other hand, there would be no one he would have to share the reward money with.

When Colonel Acoca and his men reached the top of the stairs, he whispered, 'Take no chances. Open fire as soon as you see them.'

His aide asked, 'Colonel, would you like me to go ahead of you?'

'No.' He intended to have the pleasure of killing Jaime Miró himself.

At the end of the corridor were the two rooms where Miró and his group were staying. Colonel Acoca silently motioned six of his men to cover one door and the other six to cover the other door.

'Now!' he screamed.

It was the moment he had been burning for. At his signal, the soldiers kicked in both doors simultaneously and rushed into the rooms, weapons ready. They stood there in the middle of the empty rooms staring at the rumpled beds.

'Spread out. Hurry! Downstairs!' Acoca shrieked.

The soldiers raced through every room in the hotel, smashing doors open, waking up startled guests. Jaime Miró and the others were nowhere to be found. The Colonel stormed downstairs to confront the hotel manager. There was no one in the lobby.

'Hello,' he called out. 'Hello.' There was no response. The coward was hiding.

One of the soldiers was staring at the floor behind the desk. 'Colonel . . .'

Acoca strode over to his side and stared down at the floor.

The bound and gagged body of the manager was slumped against the wall. A sign had been hung around his neck. It read:

PLEASE DO NOT DISTURB.

Chapter 24

Rubio Arzano watched in horror as Lucia disappeared under the rushing waters and was swept downstream. In a split second, he turned to race along the river bank, leaping over small logs and bushes. At the first bend of the river, he caught a glimpse of Lucia's body coming towards him. Diving in, he swam frantically to reach her, struggling against the powerful current. It was almost impossible. He felt himself being pulled away. Lucia was ten feet from him, but it seemed like miles. He made one last heroic effort and grabbed her arm, his fingers almost slipping away. He held her in a death grip, as he began grappling his way to the safety of the shore.

When Rubio finally reached the river bank, he pulled Lucia up on to the grass and he lay there, fighting for breath. Lucia was unconscious and not breathing Rubio turned her over on her stomach, straddled her and began applying pressure against her lungs. A minute went by, then two, and just as he was beginning to despair, a stream of water gushed out of her mouth and she groaned. Rubio uttered a prayer of thanks.

He kept up the pressure, gentler now, until her heartbeat was steady. She began to shiver from the cold. Rubio hurried over to a clump of trees and pulled down handfuls of leaves. He carried them over to her and started to dry her body with them. He was wet and cold, and his clothes were soaked, but he paid no attention. He had been panicky with fear that Sister Lucia would die. Now, as he gently rubbed her naked body with the dry leaves, unworthy thoughts came into his mind.

She has the body of a goddess. Forgive me, Lord, she belongs to You, and I must not think these wicked thoughts . . .

Lucia was gradually awakened by the gentle stroking of her body. She was on the beach with Ivo, and his soft tongue was moving down her body. *Oh, yes,* she thought. *Oh, yes. Don't stop, caro.* She was aroused before she even opened her eyes.

When Lucia had fallen into the river, her last thought had been that she was going to die. But she was alive, and she found herself looking up at the man who had saved her. Without even thinking, Lucia reached up and pulled Rubio down to her. There was a look of shocked surprise on his face.

'Sister –' he protested. 'We can't –'

'Sh!'

Her lips were on his, fierce and hungry and demanding, and her tongue was exploring his mouth. It was too much for Rubio.

'Hurry,' Lucia whispered. 'Hurry.'

She watched as Rubio nervously stripped off his wet clothes. *He deserves a reward,* she thought. *So do I.*

As Rubio moved hesitantly towards her, he said, 'Sister, we shouldn't –'

Lucia was in no mood for conversation. She felt him joining his body to hers in a timeless, mindless ritual, and she gave herself up to the glorious sensations that flooded her. It was all the sweeter because of her close brush with death.

Rubio was a surprisingly good lover, both gentle and fierce at the same time. He had a vulnerability that took Lucia completely by surprise. And there was a look of such tenderness in his eyes that Lucia felt a sudden lump in her throat.

I hope the big oaf isn't falling in love with me. He's so eager to please me. When was the last time a man cared about pleasing me? Lucia wondered. And she thought of her father. And she wondered how he would have liked Rubio Arzano. And then she wondered why she wondered whether her

228

father would have liked Rubio Arzano. *I must be crazy. This man is a farmer. I'm Lucia Carmine, the daughter of Angelo Carmine. Rubio's life has nothing to do with my life. We were thrown together by a stupid accident of fate.*

Rubio was holding her and saying over and over, 'Lucia. My Lucia.'

And the shining in his eyes told her everything he felt. *He's so dear*, she thought. And then: *What is the matter with me? Why am I even thinking about him like this? I'm running away from the police and* – She suddenly remembered the gold cross and gasped. *Oh, my God! How could I have forgotten it even for a moment?*

She sat up quickly. 'Rubio, I left a – a package on the bank of the river back there. Would you bring it to me, please? And my clothes?'

'Of course. I'll be right back.

Lucia sat there waiting, frantic that something might have happened to the cross. What if it was gone? What if someone had come along and picked it up?

It was with an enormous feeling of relief that Lucia saw Rubio returning with the wrapped cross under his arm. *I mustn't let it out of my sight again*, she thought. 'Thank you.'

Rubio handed Lucia her clothes. She looked up at him and said softly, 'I won't need these right away.'

The sun on her naked skin made her feel lazy and warm, and there was a wonderful comfort in Rubio's arms. It was as though they had found a peaceful oasis and the dangers they had been running away from seemed light years away.

'Tell me about your farm,' Lucia said idly.

His face lit up, and there was pride in his voice. 'It was a small farm outside a little village near Bilbao. It was in my family for generations.'

'What happened to it?'

His expression darkened. 'Because I am Basque, the government in Madrid punished me with extra taxes. When I refused to pay, they confiscated the farm. That was when

229

I met Jaime Miró. I joined him to fight against the government for what is right. I have a mother and two sisters, and one day we will have our farm back, and I will run it again.'

Lucia thought of her father and two brothers locked away in a prison for ever. 'Are you close to your family?'

Rubio smiled warmly. 'Of course. Families are our first love, are they not?'

Yes, Lucia thought. *But I will never see mine again.*

'Tell me about your family, Lucia,' Rubio said. 'Before you joined the convent, were you close to them?'

The conversation was taking a dangerous turn. *What can I tell him? My father is a mafioso. He and my two brothers are in prison for murder.* 'Yes – we are very close.'

'What does your father do?'

'He – he's a businessman.'

'Have you got brothers and sisters?'

'I have two brothers. They work for him.'

'Lucia, why did you enter the convent?'

Because the police are looking for me for murdering two men. I've got to stop this conversation, Lucia thought. Aloud, she said, 'I needed to get away.' *That's close enough to the truth*

'You felt the world was – was too much for you?'

'Something like that.'

'I have no right to say this, Lucia, but I am in love with you.'

'Rubio –'

'I want to marry you. In all my life, I have never said that to another woman.'

There was something so touching and earnest about him. *He doesn't know how to play games*, she thought. *I must be careful not to hurt him. But the idea of Angelo Carmine's daughter being a farmer's wife!* Lucia almost laughed aloud.

Rubio misunderstood the smile on Lucia's face. 'I will not live in hiding for ever. The government will have to make peace with us. Then I will return to my farm. *Querida* – I want to spend the rest of my life making you happy. We will have many children and the girls will all look like you . . .'

I can't let him go on like this, Lucia decided. *I should stop him now.* But somehow she could not bring herself to do it. She listened to Rubio paint romantic pictures of their life together, and she found herself almost wishing it could happen. She was so tired of running away. It would be wonderful to find a haven where she could be safe, taken care of by someone who loved her . . . *I must be losing my mind.*

'Let's not talk about it now,' Lucia said. 'We should be moving on.'

They travelled northeast, following the winding banks of the Duero River, with its hilly countryside and lush green trees. They stopped at the picturesque village of Villalba de Duero at the foot of the mountains, and stopped to buy bread and cheese and wine and had an idyllic picnic in a grassy meadow.

Lucia felt content at Rubio's side. There was a quiet strength about him that seemed to give her strength. *He's not for me, but he's going to make some lucky woman very happy*, she thought.

When they had finished eating, Rubio said, 'The next town is Aranda de Duero. It's a fairly large town. It would be best if we skirted around it to avoid the GOE and the soldiers.'

It was the moment of truth, time to leave him. She had been waiting for them to reach a large town. Rubio Arzano and his farm were a dream, escaping to Switzerland was the reality. Lucia knew how much she was going to hurt him, and she could not bear to look into his eyes when she said, 'Rubio – I'd like us to go into town '

He frowned. 'That could be dangerous, *querida*. The soldiers –'

'They won't be looking for us there.' She thought quickly. 'Besides, I – I need a change of clothes. I can't keep going on in this.'

The idea of entering the town disturbed Rubio, but all he said was, 'If that is what you wish.'

In the distance the walls and buildings of Aranda de Duero

loomed before them, like a man-made mountain hewn out of the earth.

Rubio tried one more time. 'Lucia – you're sure you must go into the town?'

'Yes. I'm sure.

The two of them crossed the long bridge that led to the main street, Avenida Castilla, and headed for the centre of town. They passed a sugar factory and churches and poultry shops, and the air was thick with their smells. Shops and blocks of flats lined the avenue. They walked slowly, careful not to draw attention to themselves. Finally, to her relief, Lucia saw what she had been looking for – a sign that read: '*Casa de Empeños*' – a pawnshop. She said nothing.

They reached the village square, with its shops and markets and bars, and they passed the *Taverna Cueva*, with its long bar and wooden tables. There was a juke box inside, and hanging from the oak beam ceiling were hams and strings of garlic.

Lucia saw her opportunity. 'I'm thirsty, Rubio,' she said. Can we go in there?'

'Of course.'

Rubio took Lucia's arm and led her inside.

There were half a dozen men crowded around the bar. Lucia and Rubio took a table in the corner.

'What would you like, *querida*?'

'Order a glass of wine for me, please. I'll be right back. There's something I have to do.'

She rose and walked out into the street, leaving Rubio staring after her, puzzled.

Outside, Lucia turned and hurried back to the *Casa de Empeños*, clutching her tightly wrapped package. Across the street she saw a door with a black sign in white lettering that read, '*Policia*'. She stared at it a moment, her heart skipping a beat, then skirted it and entered the pawnshop.

A shrunken man with a large head stood behind the counter, barely visible.

'*Buenos días, señorita.*'

'*Buenos días, señor.* I have something I would like to sell.'
She was so nervous that she had to press her knees together
to keep them from shaking.

'*Sí?*'

Lucia unwrapped the gold cross and held it out. 'Would –
would you be interested in buying this?'

The pawnbroker took it in his hands, and Lucia watched
the light that came into his eyes.

'May I ask where you acquired this?'

'It was left to me by an uncle who has just died.' Her
throat was so dry she could hardly speak.

The man fingered the cross, turning it over in his hands
slowly. 'How much are you asking for it?'

Her dream was coming to life. 'I want two hundred and
fifty thousand pesetas.'

He frowned and shook his head. 'No. It is worth only a
hundred thousand pesetas.'

'I would sell my body first.'

'Perhaps I could go as high as one hundred and fifty
thousand pesetas.'

'I would rather melt it down and let the gold run in the
streets.'

'Two hundred thousand pesetas. That is my last offer.'

Lucia took the gold cross from him. 'You are robbing me
blind, but I will accept it.'

She could see the excitement in his face. '*Bueno, señorita.*'
He reached for the cross.

Lucia pulled it back. 'There is a condition.'

'What condition would that be, *señorita*?'

'My passport was stolen. I need a new one in order to get
out of the country to visit my stricken aunt.'

He was studying her now, his eyes wise. He nodded. 'I
see.'

'If you can help me with my problem, then the cross is
yours.'

He sighed. 'Passports are difficult to come by, *señorita*.
The authorities are very strict.'

233

Lucia watched him, saying nothing.

'I don't see how I can help you.'

'Thank you, anyway, *señor*.' She started towards the door. He let her reach it before he said, '*Momentito*.'

Lucia stopped.

'Something has just occurred to me. I have a cousin who is sometimes involved in delicate matters like this. He is a *distant* cousin, you understand.'

'I understand.'

'I could speak to him. When do you require this passport?'

'Today.'

The large head nodded slowly. 'And if I can do this thing, we have a deal?'

'When I get my passport.'

'Agreed. Come back after eight o'clock and my cousin will be here. He will arrange to take the necessary photograph and insert it in the passport.'

Lucia could feel her heart pounding. 'Thank you, *señor*.'

'Would you like to leave the cross here for safekeeping?'

'It will be safe with me.'

'Eight o'clock, then. *Hasta luego*.'

She left the shop. Outside she carefully avoided the police station and headed back to the *taverna*, where Rubio was waiting. Her footsteps slowed. She had finally succeeded. With the money from the cross, she would be able to get to Switzerland and freedom. She should have been happy. Instead she felt strangely depressed.

What's wrong with me? I'm on my way. Rubio will get over me soon enough. He'll find someone else.

She remembered the look in his eyes when he said, *I want to marry you. In all my life, I have never said that to another woman.*

Damn the man, she thought. *Well, he's not my problem.*

Outside the *taverna* she paused and took a deep breath. She forced a smile and walked inside to join him.

Chapter 25

The news media were in a feeding frenzy. The headlines tumbled over one another. There was the attack on the convent; the wholesale arrest of the nuns for sheltering terrorists; the escape of four nuns; the murder of half a dozen soldiers by one of the nuns before she was shot and killed. The international news wires were on fire.

Reporters had arrived in Madrid from all parts of the world and Prime Minister Martinez, in an effort to cool things down, had agreed to a press conference. They were gathered in his office, almost four dozen reporters, from all over the world. Colonel Ramón Acoca and Colonel Fal Sostelo were at the Prime Minister's side. The Prime Minister had seen that afternoon's headline in the London *Times*: TERRORISTS AND NUNS EVADE SPAIN'S ARMY AND POLICE.

A reporter from *Paris Match* was asking, 'Mr Prime Minister, do you have any idea where the missing nuns are now?'

Prime Minister Leopoldo Martinez replied, 'Colonel Acoca is in charge of the search operation. I will let him answer that.'

Colonel Acoca said, 'We have reason to believe that they are in the hands of the Basque terrorists. I'm also sorry to say there is evidence to indicate that the nuns are collaborating with the terrorists.'

The reporters were scribbling feverishly.

'What about the shooting of Sister Teresa and the soldiers?'

'We have information that Sister Teresa was working with

235

Jaime Miró. Under the pretext of helping us find Miró, she went into an army camp and murdered half a dozen soldiers before she could be stopped. I can assure you that the army and the GOE are bending every effort to bring the criminals to justice.'

'And the nuns who were arrested and taken to Madrid?'

'They are being interrogated,' Colonel Acoca said.

The Prime Minister was anxious to end the meeting. It was difficult for him to keep his temper in check. The failure to locate the nuns or capture the terrorists made his government – and himself – look inept and foolish, and the press was taking full advantage of the situation.

'Can you tell us anything about the backgrounds of the four nuns who escaped, Prime Minister?' asked a reporter from OGGI.

'I'm sorry. I can give you no further information. I repeat, ladies and gentlemen, the government is doing everything in its power to find the nuns.'

'Prime Minister, there have been reports about the brutality of the attack on the convent at Ávila. Would you respond to that?'

It was a sore point with Martinez because it was true. Colonel Acoca had grossly exceeded his authority. But he would deal with the Colonel later. This was the time for a show of unity.

He turned to the Colonel and said smoothly, 'Colonel Acoca can respond to that.'

Colonel Acoca said, 'I, too, have heard those unfounded reports. The facts are simple. We received reliable information that the terrorist Jaime Miró and a dozen of his men were hiding in the Abbey Cistercian and that they were heavily armed. By the time we raided the abbey, they had fled.'

'Colonel, we heard that some of your men molested –'

'That is an outrageous accusation.'

Prime Minister Martinez said, 'Thank you, ladies and gentlemen. That will be all. You will be informed of any further developments.'

The press conference was over. When the reporters left, the Prime Minister turned to Colonel Acoca and Colonel Sostelo. 'They're making us look like savages in the eyes of the world.'

Colonel Acoca had not the slightest interest in the Prime Minister's opinion. What concerned him was a telephone call he had received in the middle of the night.

'Colonel Acoca?'

It was a voice he was all too familiar with. He was instantly wide awake.

'Yes, sir.'

'We're disappointed in you. We had hoped to see some results before this.'

'Sir, I'm closing in on them.' He found that he was perspiring heavily. 'I ask that you be a little more patient. I won't disappoint you.'

He held his breath, waiting for a response.

'You're running out of time.'

The line went dead.

Colonel Acoca replaced the receiver and sat there, frustrated. *Where is that bastard Miró?*

Chapter 26

I'm going to kill her, Ricardo Mellado thought. *I could strangle her with my bare hands, throw her off the mountain, or simply shoot her. No, I think strangling her would give me the greatest pleasure.*

Sister Graciela was the most exasperating human being he had ever encountered. She was impossible. In the beginning when Jaime Miró had assigned him to escort her, Ricardo Mellado had been pleased. True, she was a nun, but she was also the most ravishing beauty he had ever laid eyes on. He was determined to get to know her, to find out why she had decided to lock up all that exquisite beauty behind convent walls for the rest of her life. Under the skirt and blouse she was wearing, he could discern the rich, nubile curves of a woman. *It's going to be a very interesting trip*, Ricardo decided.

But things had taken a totally unexpected turn. The problem was that Sister Graciela refused to speak to him. She had not said one word since their journey began, and what completely baffled Ricardo was that she did not appear to be angry or frightened or upset. Not at all. She simply retreated into some remote part of herself and appeared totally uninterested in him and in what was going on around her. They had travelled at a good pace, walking along hot, dusty side roads, past fields of wheat, rippling golden in the sunlight, and fields of barley, oats and grapevines. They skirted the little villages along the way and went by fields of sunflowers with their wide yellow faces following the sun.

When they crossed the Moros River, Ricardo asked, 'Would you like to rest awhile, Sister?'

Silence.

They were approaching Segovia before heading north-east to the snow-capped Guadarrama mountains. Ricardo kept trying to make polite conversation, but it was completely hopeless.

'We will be at Segovia soon, Sister.'

No reaction.

What could I have done to offend her? 'Are you hungry, Sister?'

Nothing.

It was as though he were not there. He had never felt so frustrated in his life. *Perhaps the woman is retarded*, he thought. *That must be the answer. God gave her an unearthly beauty and then cursed her with a feeble mind.* But he did not believe it.

When they reached the outskirts of Segovia, Ricardo noted that the town was crowded, which meant that the *guardia civil* would be even more alert than usual.

As they approached the Plaza del Conde de Cheste, Ricardo saw soldiers of the *guardia civil* strolling in their direction. He whispered, 'Hold my hand, Sister. We must look like two lovers out for a stroll.'

She ignored him.

Jesus, Ricardo thought. *Maybe she's deaf and dumb.*

He reached over and took her hand in his, and her sudden fierce resistance surprised him. She pulled away as if she had been stung.

The guards were getting closer.

Ricardo leaned towards Graciela. 'You mustn't be angry,' he said loudly. 'My sister feels the same way. After dinner last night when she put the children to bed she was saying that it would be much better if we men didn't sit around together smoking smelly cigars and telling stories while you women went off by yourselves. I'll bet –'

The guards had passed. Ricardo turned to look at Graciela Her face was expressionless. Mentally, Ricardo began to curse Jaime, wishing he had given him one of the other nuns. This one was made of stone, with no chisel hard enough to penetrate that cold exterior.

In all modesty, Ricardo Mellado knew that he was attractive to women. Enough of them had told him so. He was light complexioned, tall and well-built, with a patrician nose, an intelligent face and perfect white teeth. He came from one of the most prominent Basque families. His father was a banker from the Basque country in the north and had seen to it that Ricardo was well educated. He had gone to the University of Salamanca, and his father had looked forward to his son joining him in the family business.

When Ricardo returned home, he dutifully went to work at the bank, but within a short period of time he became involved with the problems of his people. He began attending meetings and rallies and protests against the government and he soon became one of the leaders of ETA. His father learned about his son's activities and called him into his huge, panelled office and lectured him.

'I am a Basque, too, Ricardo, but I am also a businessman. We cannot foul our own nest by encouraging a revolution in the country where we make our living.'

'None of us is trying to overthrow the government, Father. All we're demanding is freedom. The government's oppression of the Basques and the Catalans is intolerable.'

The senior Mellado leaned back in his chair and studied his son. 'My good friend the Mayor had a quiet word with me yesterday. He suggested it would be to your benefit not to attend any more rallies. It would be better if you expended your energy on bank business.'

'Father –'

'Listen to me, Ricardo. When I was young, my blood ran hot, too. But there are other ways to cool it off. You're engaged to a lovely girl. I hope you will have many children.' He waved his hand at their surroundings. 'And you have much to look forward to in your future.'

'But don't you see –?'

'I see more clearly than you, my son. Your prospective father-in-law is also unhappy with your activities. I would not want anything to happen that would prevent the wedding. Do I make myself clear?'

'Yes, Father.'

The following Saturday Ricardo Mellado was arrested leading a Basque rally in an auditorium in Barcelona. He refused to let his father bail him out unless he would also bail out the other demonstrators who had been arrested. His father refused. Ricardo's career was ended and so was his engagement. That had been five years earlier. Five years of danger and narrow escapes. Five years filled with the excitement of fighting for a cause he passionately believed in. Now he was on the run, a fugitive from the police. escorting a retarded and mute nun across Spain.

'We'll go this way,' he said to Sister Graciela. He was careful not to touch her arm.

They turned off the main street on to St Valentin. On the corner was a shop that sold musical instruments.

Ricardo said, 'I have an idea. Wait here, Sister. I'll be right back.'

He entered the shop and walked up to a young clerk standing behind the counter.

'*Buenos días.* May I help you?'

'Yes. I would like to buy two guitars.'

The clerk smiled. 'Ah, you are in luck. We've just got in some Ramirezes. They are the best.'

'Perhaps something of not such a high quality. My friend and I are only amateurs.'

'As you wish, *señor.* What about these?' The clerk walked over to a section of the store where a dozen guitars were on display. 'I can let you have two Konos for five thousand pesetas apiece.'

'I think not.' Ricardo selected two inexpensive guitars. 'These will do nicely,' he said.

A few moments later Ricardo walked back out to the street, carrying the two guitars. He had half hoped Sister

Graciela would be gone. She was standing there, patiently waiting.

Ricardo opened the strap on one of the guitars and held out the instrument to her. 'Here, Sister. Put this over your shoulder.'

She stared at him.

'It isn't necessary for you to play it,' Ricardo said patiently. 'It is only for effect.'

He shoved the guitar at her, and she reluctantly took it. They walked along the winding streets of Segovia under the enormous viaduct built by the Romans centuries ago.

Ricardo decided to try again. 'You see this viaduct, Sister? There is no cement between the stones. Legend has it that it was built by the devil two thousand years ago, stone piled on stone, with nothing but the devil's magic to hold it together.' He looked at her for some reaction.

Nothing.

To hell with her, Ricardo Mellado thought. *I give up*.

The members of the *guardia civil* were everywhere, and whenever they passed them, Ricardo would pretend to be in earnest conversation with Graciela, always careful to avoid body contact.

The numbers of police and soldiers seemed to be increasing, but Ricardo felt reasonably safe. They would be looking for a nun in robes and a group of Jaime Miró's men, but they would have no reason to suspect two young tourists alone, carrying guitars.

Ricardo was feeling hungry, and even though Sister Graciela had said nothing, he was sure that she must be hungry also. They passed a small *bodega*.

'We'll stop in here and have a bite to eat, Sister.'

She stood there, watching him.

He sighed. 'Right. Suit yourself.'

He walked inside the small café. A moment later Graciela followed him.

When they were seated, Ricardo asked, 'What would you like to order, Sister?'

There was no response. She was infuriating.

Ricardo said to the waitress, 'Two *gazpachos* and two helpings of *chorizos*.'

When the soup and sausages came, Graciela ate what was put in front of her. He noticed that she ate automatically, without enjoyment, as though fulfilling some duty. The men seated at other tables were staring at her, and Ricardo could not blame them. *It would take the young Goya to capture her beauty*, he thought.

In spite of Graciela's sullen behaviour, Ricardo felt a lump in his throat every time he looked at her, and he cursed himself for a romantic fool. She was an enigma, buried behind some kind of impenetrable wall. Ricardo Mellado had known dozens of beautiful women, but none of them had ever affected him this way. There was something almost mystical about her beauty. The irony was that he had absolutely no idea what lay behind the breath-taking facade. Was she intelligent or stupid? Interesting or dull? Cold-blooded or passionate? *I hope she's stupid, dull, and cold-blooded*, Ricardo thought, *or I won't be able to stand losing her. As though I could ever have her. She belongs to God.* He looked away, afraid that she might sense what he was thinking.

When it was time to leave, Ricardo paid the bill and they rose. During the journey he had noticed that Sister Graciela was limping slightly. *I'll have to get us some kind of transportation*, he thought. *We still have a long way to go.*

They started down the street, and at the far end of town, in the Manzanares el Real, they came upon a gypsy caravan. There were four colourfully decorated wagons in the caravan, pulled by horses. In the back of the wagons were women and children, all dressed in gypsy costumes.

Ricardo said, 'Wait here, Sister. I'm going to try to get us a lift.'

He approached the driver of the front wagon, a burly man in full gypsy regalia, including wearing earrings.

'*Buenos tardes*, señor. I would consider it a great kindness if you could give my fiancée and me a lift.'

The gypsy looked over to where Graciela was standing. 'It is possible. Where are you headed?'

'To the Guadarrama mountains.'

'I can take you as far as Cerezo.'

'That would be of great value. Thank you.'

He shook the gypsy's hand and put money in it.

'Get in the last wagon.'

'*Gracias.*'

Ricardo returned to where Graciela was waiting. 'The gypsies are going to take us as far as Cerezo de Abajo,' he told her. 'We'll go in the last wagon.'

For an instant, he was sure she was going to refuse. She hesitated, then started towards the wagon.

There were half a dozen gypsies inside the wagon and they made room for Ricardo and Graciela. As they climbed aboard, Ricardo started to help the sister up, but the moment he touched her arm, she pushed him away with a fierceness that took him by surprise. *All right, to hell with you.* He caught a glimpse of Graciela's bare leg as she lifted herself on to the wagon, and he could not help thinking: *She has the most beautiful legs I've ever seen.*

They made themselves as comfortable as possible on the hard wooden floor of the wagon and the long journey began. Graciela sat in a corner, her eyes closed and her lips moving in prayer. Ricardo could not take his eyes off her.

As the day wore on, the sun became a hot furnace, beating down on them, baking the earth, and the sky was a deep, cloudless blue. From time to time as the wagon crossed the plains, huge birds soared overhead. *Buitre leonado*, Ricardo thought. The lion-coloured griffon vultures.

Late in the afternoon the gypsy caravan came to a stop. The leader approached their wagon.

'This is as far as we can take you. We're headed for Vinuelas.'

Wrong direction. 'This is fine,' Ricardo assured him. 'Thank you.'

He started to reach out a hand for Graciela and quickly thought better of it.

Ricardo turned to the leader of the gypsies. 'I would

244

consider it a kindness if you would sell some food to my fiancee and me.'

The chief turned to one of the women and said something in a foreign tongue, and a few moments later two packages of food were handed to Ricardo.

'*Muchas gracias*.' He pulled out some money.

The gypsy chief studied him for a moment. 'You and the sister have already paid for the food.'

You and the sister. So he knew. Yet Ricardo felt no sense of danger. The gypsies were as oppressed by the government as were the Basques and Catalans.

'*Vayan con dios*.'

Ricardo stood there watching the caravan move out of sight. He turned to Graciela. She was watching him, silent, impassive.

'You won't have to put up with my company much longer,' Ricardo assured her. 'In two days we will be in Logroño. You'll meet your friends there and you'll be on your way to the convent at Mendavia.'

No reaction. He could have been talking to a stone wall. *I am talking to a stone wall.*

They had been dropped off in a peaceful valley rich with orchards of apple, pear and fig trees. A few feet away from them was the Tormes River, filled with fat trout. In the past, Ricardo had fished there often. It would have been an ideal place to stay and rest, but there was a long road to travel.

He turned to study the Guadarrama mountains, the range that lay ahead of them. Ricardo knew the area well. There were several trails that wound through the length of the mountains. *Cabras*, wild mountain goats, and wolves roamed the passes, and Ricardo would have chosen that if he had been travelling alone. But with Sister Graciela at his side, he decided on the safest.

'Well, we'd better get started,' Ricardo said. 'We have a long climb ahead of us.'

He had no intention of missing the rendezvous with the

others in Logroño. Let the silent sister become someone else's headache.

Sister Graciela stood there waiting for Ricardo to lead the way. He turned and began to climb. As they started up the steep mountain path, Graciela slipped on some loose pebbles and Ricardo instinctively reached out to help her. She jerked away from his hand and righted herself. *Fine*, he thought angrily. *Break your neck.*

They kept moving upwards, heading towards the majestic peak high above. The trail started to get steeper and narrower and the chilled air became thinner. They were heading east, passing through a forest of pine trees. Ahead of them lay a village that was a haven for skiers and mountain climbers. There would be hot food and warmth and rest there, Ricardo knew. It was tempting. *Too dangerous*, he decided. It would be a perfect place for Acoca to set a trap.

He turned to Sister Graciela. 'We'll skirt the village. Can you go on a little farther before we rest?'

She looked at him and, as her answer turned and began to walk.

The unnecessary rudeness offended him, and he thought: *Thank heavens at Logroño I will be rid of her. Why in the name of God do I have mixed feelings about that?*

They skirted the village, walking along the edge of the forest, and soon they were on the path again, climbing upwards. It was getting more difficult to breathe, and the path grew steeper. As they rounded a bend, they came upon an empty eagle's nest. They skirted another mountain village, quiet and peaceful in the afternoon sun, and rested outside it, stopping at a mountain stream where they drank the icy water.

By dusk they had reached a rugged area that was famous for its caves. After that the trail would start downwards.

From now on, Ricardo thought, *it will be easy. The worst is over.*

He heard a faint buzzing sound overhead. He looked up,

searching for the source of it. An army plane appeared suddenly over the top of the mountain, flying towards them.

'Down!' Ricardo shouted. 'Down!'

Graciela kept walking. The plane circled and began to swoop lower.

'Get down!' Ricardo yelled again.

He jumped on her and pushed her down to the ground, his body on top of hers. What happened next took him completely by surprise. Without any warning, Graciela began yelling hysterically, fighting him. She was kicking him in the groin, clawing at his face, trying to rip at his eyes. But the most astonishing thing was what she was saying. She was screaming out a string of obscenities that sent Ricardo into shock, a verbal torrent of filth that assailed him. He could not believe that these words were coming from that beautiful, innocent mouth.

He tried to grab her hands to protect himself from her raking nails. She was like a wildcat under him.

'Stop it!' he shouted. 'I'm not going to hurt you. It's an army scout plane. They've seen us. We've got to get out of here.'

He held her down until her frantic struggling finally ceased. Strange, strangled sounds were coming from her, and he realized that she was sobbing. Ricardo, with all his experience with women, was completely baffled. He was straddled atop a hysterical nun who had the vocabulary of a truck driver, and he had no notion of what to do next.

He made his voice as calm and as reasonable as possible. 'Sister, we have to find a place to hide quickly. The plane will have reported us and in a few hours there'll be soldiers swarming all over the place. If you ever want to reach the convent, you'll get up and come with me.'

He waited a moment, then carefully raised himself off her and sat alongside her until the sobs subsided. Finally Graciela sat up. Her face was smudged from the dirt, her hair was tousled, her eyes were red from crying, and yet her beauty made Ricardo ache.

He said quietly, 'I'm sorry I frightened you. I don't seem

247

to know how to behave with you. I promise to try to be more careful in the future.'

She looked up at him with her luminous black eyes filled with tears, and Ricardo had no idea what she was thinking. He sighed and rose. She followed suit.

'There are dozens of caves around here,' Ricardo told her. 'We'll hide in one of them for the night. By dawn we can be on our way again.'

His face was raw and bleeding where she had clawed at him, but in spite of what had happened, he felt a defencelessness about her, a fragility that touched him, that made him want to say something to reassure her. But now he was the one who was silent.

He could not think of a single thing to say.

The Cuevas del Aguila have been carved out by aeons of winds and floods and earthquakes, and they come in an infinite variety. Some of the caves are mere indentations in the mountain rocks, others are endless tunnels never explored by man.

A mile from where they had spotted the plane, Ricardo found a cave that was to his satisfaction. The low entrance was almost covered by underbrush.

'Stay here,' he said.

He ducked into the entrance and walked into the cave. It was dark inside, with only faint light spilling through the opening. There was no telling what the length of the cave was, but it did not matter, for there was no reason to explore it.

He went back outside to Graciela.

'It looks safe,' Ricardo said. 'Wait inside, please. I'll gather some branches to cover up the mouth of the cave. I'll be back in a few minutes.'

He watched Graciela as she went silently into the cave, and Ricardo wondered whether she would be there when he returned. He realized that he desperately wanted her to be.

*

Inside the cave, Graciela watched him leave. She sank to the cold ground in despair.

I can't stand any more, she thought. *Where are you, Jesus? Please release me from this hell.*

And it had been hell. From the beginning Graciela had been fighting the attraction she felt towards Ricardo. She thought of the Moor. *I'm afraid of myself. Of the evil in me. I want this man, and I must not.*

And so she had built a barrier of silence between them, the silence she had lived with in the convent. But now, without the discipline of the convent, without the Instrument and prayers, without the crutch of the rigid routine, Graciela found herself unable to banish her inner darkness. She had spent years fighting the satanic urges of her body, fighting the remembered sounds, the moans and sighs that came from her mother's bed.

The Moor was looking at her naked body.

You're just a child. Get your clothes on and get out of here . . .

I'm a woman.

She had spent so many years trying to forget the feel of the Moor inside her, trying to push out of her mind the rhythm of their bodies moving together, filling her, giving her a feeling of being alive at last.

Her mother screaming, *You bitch!*

And the doctor saying: *Our chief surgeon decided to sew you up himself. He said you were too beautiful to have scars.*

All the years of praying had been to purge herself of guilt. And they had failed.

The first time Graciela looked at Ricardo Mellado, the past had come flooding back. He was handsome and gentle and kind. When Graciela was a little girl, she had dreamed of someone like Ricardo. And when he was near her, when he touched her, her body was instantly aflame and she was filled with a deep shame. *I am the bride of Christ, and my thoughts are a betrayal of God. I belong to You, Jesus. Please help me now. Cleanse my mind of impure thoughts.*

Graciela had tried desperately to keep the wall of silence

between them, a wall that no one but God could penetrate, a wall to keep out the devil. But did she want to keep the devil out? When Ricardo had jumped on her and pushed her to the ground, it was the Moor making love to her, and the friar trying to rape her, and in her surging panic, it was them she was fighting off. *No*, she admitted to herself, *that's not the truth*. It was her own deep desire she was fighting. She was torn between her spirit and the cravings of her flesh. *I must not give in. I must get back to the convent. He'll be back any minute. What should I do?*

Graciela heard a low mewing from the back of the cave and quickly turned. There were four green eyes staring at her in the dark, moving towards her. Graciela's heart began to beat faster.

Two baby wolf cubs trotted up to her on soft, padded feet, rubbing their heads against her. She smiled and began to stroke them gently. There was a sudden rustle from the entrance of the cave. *Ricardo is back*, she thought.

The next instant, an enormous grey wolf was flying at her throat.

Chapter 27

Lucia Carmine paused outside the *taverna* in Aranda de Duero and took a deep breath. Through the window she could see Rubio Arzano seated inside, waiting for her.

I must not let him suspect, she thought. *At eight o'clock I'll have a new passport and be on my way to Switzerland.*

She forced a smile and entered the *taverna*. Rubio grinned in relief when he saw her, and as he rose, the look in his eyes gave Lucia a pang.

'I was very worried, *querida*. When you were gone for so long, I was afraid something terrible had happened to you.'

Lucia put her hand over his. 'Nothing happened.' *Except that I've bought my way to freedom. I'll be out of the country tomorrow.*

Rubio sat there looking into her eyes, holding her hand, and there was such an intense feeling of love coming from him that Lucia felt uneasy. *Doesn't he know it could never work? No. Because I haven't the courage to tell him. He's not in love with me. He's in love with the woman he thinks I am. He'll be much better off without me.*

She turned away and looked around the room for the first time. It was filled with locals. Most of them seemed to be staring at the two strangers.

One of the young men in the café started to sing and others joined in. A man walked over to the table where Lucia and Rubio were sitting.

'You're not singing, *señor*. Join us.'

Rubio shook his head. 'No.'

'What's the problem, *amigo*?'

251

'It's your song.' Rubio saw the puzzled expression on Lucia's face, and explained. 'It is one of the old songs praising Franco.'

Other men began to gather around the table. It was obvious that they had been drinking.

'You were against Franco, *señor*?'

Lucia saw Rubio's fists clench. *Oh, God, not now. He mustn't start anything that will attract attention.*

She said to him warningly, 'Rubio . . .'

And, thank God, he understood.

He looked up at the young men and said pleasantly, 'I have nothing against Franco. I just don't know the words.'

'Ah. Then we'll all hum the song together.'

They stood there waiting for Rubio to refuse.

Rubio glanced at Lucia. '*Bueno.*'

The men began to sing again, and Rubio hummed loudly. Lucia could feel the tension in him as he held himself under control. *He's doing this for me.*

When the song ended, a man slapped Rubio on the back. 'Not bad, old man. Not bad at all.'

Rubio sat there silently willing them to go away.

One of the men saw the package in Lucia's lap.

'What are you hiding there, *querida*?'

His companion said, 'I'll bet she's got something better than that up her skirt.'

The men laughed.

'Why don't you pull your panties down and show us what you've got there?'

Rubio sprang to his feet and grabbed one of the men by the throat. He punched him so hard that he flew across the room, breaking a table.

'No!' Lucia screamed. 'Don't!'

But it was too late. In an instant it became a free-for-all, with everybody eagerly joining in. A wine bottle shattered the glass behind the bar. Chairs and tables were knocked over as men went flying through the air, screaming curses. Rubio knocked down two men and a third ran towards him and hit him in the stomach. He gave a grunt of pain.

252

'Rubio! Let's get out of here!' Lucia screamed.

He nodded. He was clutching his stomach. They pushed their way through the mêlée and found themselves outside on the street.

'We've got to get away,' Lucia said.

You will have your passport tonight. Come back after eight o'clock.

She had to find a place to hide until then. *Damn him! Why couldn't he have controlled himself?*

They turned down Calle Santa Maria, and the noises of the fight behind them gradually diminished. Two streets away they came to a large church, the Iglesia Santa Maria. Lucia ran up the steps, opened the door and peered inside. The church was deserted.

'We'll be safe in here,' she said.

They walked into the dimness of the church. Rubio was still holding his stomach.

'We can rest for a while.'

'Yes.'

Rubio let his hand fall away from his stomach, and blood came gushing out.

Lucia felt sick. 'My God! What happened?'

'A knife,' Rubio whispered. 'He used a knife.' He slumped to the floor.

Lucia knelt at his side, panicky. 'Don't move.'

She removed his shirt and pressed it against his stomach, trying to stem the flow of blood. Rubio's face was chalk white.

'You shouldn't have fought them, you idiot,' Lucia said angrily.

His voice was a slurred whisper. 'I could not let them speak to you that way.'

I could not let them speak to you that way.

Lucia was touched as she had never been touched before. She stood there staring at him and thought: *How many times has this man risked his life for me?*

'I won't let you die,' she said fiercely. 'I'm not going to let you die.' She stood up abruptly. 'I'll be right back.'

253

She found water and towels in the priest's changing room in the rear of the church and she bathed Rubio's wound. His face was hot to the touch, and his body was soaked in perspiration. Lucia put cold towels on his forehead. Rubio's eyes were closed and he seemed to be asleep. Lucia cradled his head in her arms and talked to him. It did not matter what she said. She was talking to keep him alive, forcing him to hold on to the thin thread of his existence. She babbled on, afraid to stop for even a second.

'We'll work your farm together, Rubio. I want to meet your mother and sisters. Do you think they'll like me? I want them to, so much. And I'm a good worker, *caro*. You'll see. I've never worked on a farm, but I'll learn. We'll make it the best farm in all of Spain.'

She spent the afternoon talking to him, bathing his fevered body, changing the dressing. The bleeding had almost stopped.

'You see, *caro*? You're getting better. You're going to be well. I told you. You and I will have such a wonderful life together, Rubio. Only please don't die. Please!'

She found that she was weeping.

She watched the afternoon shadows paint the church walls through the stained-glass windows and slowly fade away. The setting sun dimmed the sky and finally it was dark. Lucia changed Rubio's bandage again, and so close that it startled her, the church bell began to ring. She held her breath and counted. One . . . three . . . five . . . seven . . . eight. Eight o'clock. It was calling her, telling her it was time to return to the *Casa de Empeños*. Time to escape from this nightmare and save herself.

She knelt down beside Rubio and felt his forehead again. He was burning with fever. His body was soaked with perspiration and his breathing was shallow and rasping. She could see no sign of bleeding, but that could mean that he was bleeding internally. *God damn it. Save yourself, Lucia.*

'Rubio . . . darling . . .'

He opened his eyes, only half conscious.

'I have to leave for a little while,' Lucia said.

He gripped her hand. 'P!ease . . .'

'It's all right,' she whispered. 'I'll be back.'

She rose and took a long last look at him. *I can't help him*, she thought.

Lucia picked up the gold cross and turned and hurried out the church door, her eyes filled with tears. She stumbled out on to the street and began to walk rapidly, heading towards the pawnshop. The man and his cousin would be there waiting for her with her passport to freedom. *In the morning when church services begin, they'll find Rubio and get him to a doctor. They'll treat him and he'll get well. Except that he will not live through the night*, Lucia thought. *Well, that's not my problem.*

The *Casa de Empeños* was just ahead. She was only a few minutes late. She could see that the lights were on in the shop. The men were waiting for her.

She began walking faster, then running. She crossed the street and burst through the open door.

Inside the police station, a uniformed officer was behind the desk. He looked up as Lucia appeared.

'I need you,' Lucia cried. 'A man has been stabbed. He may be dying.'

The policeman did not ask questions. He picked up a telephone and spoke into it. When he put the phone down, he said, 'Someone will be with you in a moment.'

Two detectives appeared almost immediately.

'Someone has been stabbed, *señorita*?'

'Yes. Please follow me. Hurry!'

'We'll pick up the doctor on the way,' one of the detectives said. 'Then you can take us to your friend.'

They picked up the doctor at his home and Lucia hurried the group to the church.

When they entered the church the doctor walked over to the still figure on the floor and knelt beside him.

A moment later he looked up. 'He's alive, but barely. I'll call for an ambulance.'

Lucia sank to her knees and said silently, *Thank you, God. I've done all I can. Now let me get away safely and I'll never bother you again.*

One of the detectives had been staring at Lucia all the way to the church. She looked so familiar. And then he suddenly realized why. She bore an uncanny resemblance to the picture in the Red, Top Priority Circulation from Interpol.

The detective whispered something to his companion and now they both turned to study her. The two of them walked over to Lucia.

'Excuse me, *señorita*. Would you be good enough to come back to the station with us? We have a few questions we wish to ask you.'

Chapter 28

Ricardo Mellado was a short distance away from the mountain cave when suddenly he saw a large grey wolf trotting towards the entrance. He froze for a single instant, then moved as he had never moved in his life. He raced towards the mouth of the cave, and burst through the entrance.

'Sister!'

In the dim light he saw the huge, grey shape leaping towards Graciela. Instinctively, he reached for his pistol and fired. The wolf let out a yelp of pain and turned towards Ricardo. He felt the sharp fangs of the wounded beast tearing at his clothing and smelled the animal's fetid breath. The wolf was stronger than he had expected, heavily muscled and powerful. Ricardo tried to fight free, but it was impossible.

He felt himself beginning to lose consciousness. He was only dimly aware of Graciela coming towards him and he called, 'Get away!'

He saw Graciela's hand raised above his head, and as it started to descend towards him, he glimpsed a huge rock in it and he thought: *She's going to kill me.*

An instant later the rock swept past him and smashed into the wolf's skull. There was a last savage gasp and the animal lay still on the ground. Ricardo was huddled on the floor, fighting for breath. Graciela knelt at his side.

'Are you all right?' Her voice was trembling with concern.

He managed to nod. He heard a whimpering sound behind him and turned to see the cubs huddled in a corner.

He lay there, gathering his strength. Then he rose with difficulty.

They staggered out into the clean mountain air, shaken. Ricardo stood there, taking deep, lung-filling breaths until his head cleared. The physical and emotional shock of their close brush with death had taken a severe toll on both of them.

'Let's get away from this place. They may come looking for us here.'

Graciela shuddered at the reminder of how much danger they were still in.

They travelled along the steep mountain path for the next hour, and when they finally reached a small stream, Ricardo said, 'Let's stop here.'

With no bandages or antiseptic, they cleaned the scratches as best they could, bathing them in the clean, cold spring water. Ricardo's arm was so stiff that he had trouble moving it. To his surprise, Graciela said, 'Let me do it.'

He was even more surprised by the gentleness with which she did the task.

Without warning, Graciela began trembling violently in an aftermath of shock.

'It's all right,' Ricardo said. 'It's all over.'

She could not stop shaking.

Ricardo took her in his arms and said soothingly, 'Ssh. It's dead. There's nothing more to fear.'

He was holding her closely, and he could feel her thighs pressing against his body and her soft lips were on his and she was holding him close, whispering things he could not understand.

It was as though he had known Graciela always. And yet he knew nothing about her. *Except that she's God's miracle*, he thought.

Graciela was also thinking of God. *Thank you, God, for this joy. Thank you for finally letting me feel what love is.*

It had been an experience for which she had no words, beyond anything she had ever imagined.

Ricardo was watching her, and her beauty still took his breath away. *She belongs to me now*, Ricardo thought. *She doesn't have to go back to a convent. We'll get married and have beautiful children – strong sons.*

'I love you,' he said. 'I'll never let you go, Graciela.'

'Ricardo –'

'Darling, I want to marry you. Will you marry me?'

And without even thinking, Graciela said, 'Yes. Oh, yes.'

And she was in his arms again, and she thought: *This is what I wanted and thought I would never have.*

Ricardo was saying, 'We'll live in France for a while, where we'll be safe. This fight will be over soon, and we'll return to Spain.'

She knew that she would go anywhere with this man, and that if there was danger, she wanted to share it with him.

They talked of so many things. Ricardo told her how he had first become involved with Jaime Miró, and of the broken engagement and of his father's displeasure. But when Ricardo waited for Graciela to speak about her past, she was silent.

She looked at him and thought: *I can't tell him. He'll hate me.* 'Hold me,' Graciela begged.

They slept and woke up at dawn to watch the sun creeping over the ridge of the mountain, bathing the hills in a warm red glow.

Ricardo said, 'We'll be safer hiding out here today. We'll start travelling when it gets dark.'

They ate from the sack of food that the gypsies had given them, and planned their future.

'There are wonderful opportunities here in Spain,' Ricardo said. 'Or there will be when we have peace. I have dozens of ideas. We'll own our own business. We'll buy a beautiful home and raise handsome sons.'

'And beautiful daughters.'

'And beautiful daughters.' He smiled. 'I never knew I could be so happy.'

'Nor I, Ricardo.'

'We'll be in Logroño in two days and meet the others,' Ricardo said. He took her hand. 'We'll tell them you won't be returning to the convent.'

'I wonder if they'll understand.' Then she laughed. 'I don't really care. God understands. I loved my life in the convent,' she said softly, 'but –' She leaned over and kissed him.

Ricardo said, 'I have so much to make up to you.'

She was puzzled. 'I don't understand.'

'Those years you were in the convent, shut away from the world. Tell me, darling – does it bother you that you've lost all those years?'

How could she make him see? 'Ricardo – I didn't lose anything. Have I really missed so much?'

He thought about it, not knowing where to begin. He realized that events he thought of as important would not really have mattered to the nuns in their isolation. Wars, like the Arab–Israeli War? Assassinations of political leaders such as the American President John Kennedy and his brother Robert Kennedy? And of Martin Luther King, Jr., the great black leader of the non-violence movement for black equality? The Berlin Wall? Famines? Floods? Earthquakes? Strikes and demonstrations protesting at man's inhumanity to man?

In the end, how deeply would any of these things have affected her personal life? Or the personal lives of the majority of people on this earth?

Finally, Ricardo said, 'In one sense, you haven't missed much. But in another sense, yes. Something important has been going on. Life. While you were shut away all those years, babies have been born and have grown up; lovers have married; people have suffered and been happy; people have died, and all of us out here were a part of that, a part of the living.'

'And you think I never was?' Graciela asked. And the words came tumbling out before she could stop them. 'I was once a part of that life you are talking about, and it was a living hell. My mother was a whore, and every night I had

260

a different uncle. When I was fourteen years old I gave my body to a man because I was attracted to him and jealous of my mother and what she was doing.' The words were coming in a torrent now. 'I would have become a whore, too, if I had stayed there to be part of the life you think is so precious. No, I don't believe I ran away from anything. I ran *to* something. I found a safe world that is peaceful and good.'

Ricardo was staring at her, horrified. 'I – I'm sorry,' he said. 'I didn't mean to –'

She was sobbing now, and he took her in his arms and said, 'Sh! It's all right. That's over. You were a child. I love you.'

And it was as though Ricardo had given her absolution. She had told him about the awful things she had done in the past, and still he forgave her. And – wonder of wonders – loved her.

He held her very close. 'There is a poem by Federico Garcia Lorca:

> The night does not wish to come
> so that you cannot come
> and I cannot go.
> But you will come
> with your tongue burned by the salt rain.
> The day does not wish to come
> so that you cannot come
> and I cannot come
> and I cannot go.
> But I will come
> through the muddy waters of darkness.
> Neither night nor day wishes to come
> so that I may die for you and you die
> for me.'

And suddenly she thought of the soldiers who were hunting them and she wondered if she and her beloved Ricardo were going to live long enough to have a future together.

Chapter 29

There was a link missing, a clue to the past, and Alan Tucker was determined to find it. There had been no mention in the newspaper of a baby being abandoned, but it should be easy enough to find out the date it was brought to the orphanage. If the date coincided with the time of the plane crash, Ellen Scott would have some interesting explaining to do. *She couldn't be that stupid*, Alan Tucker thought. *To risk pretending that the Scott heiress was dead, and then leave her on the doorstep of a farmhouse. Risky. Very risky. On the other hand, look at the reward: Scott Industries. Yes, she could have pulled it off. If it is a skeleton in her closet, it's a live one, and it's going to cost her plenty.*

Tucker knew that he had to be very careful. He had no illusion about whom he was dealing with. He was confronting raw power. He knew he had to have all the evidence in hand before he made his move.

His first stop was to return to Father Berrendo.

'Father – I would like to speak to the farmer and his wife, where Patricia – Megan was dropped off.'

The old priest smiled. 'I hope your conversation with them will not take place for a long time.'

Tucker stared at him. 'You mean –?'

'They died many years ago.'

Damn. But there had to be other avenues to explore. 'You said the baby was taken to a hospital with pneumonia?'

'Yes.'

There would be records there. 'Which hospital was it?'

'It burned down in nineteen sixty-one. There is a new

262

hospital now.' He saw the look of dismay on his visitor's face. 'You must remember, *señor*, that the information you are seeking goes back twenty-eight years. Many things have changed.'

Nothing's going to stop me, Alan Tucker thought. *Not when I've come this close. There must be a file on her somewhere.*

There was still one place left to investigate. The orphanage.

He was reporting daily now to Ellen Scott.

'Keep me informed of every development. I want to know the moment the girl is found.'

And Alan Tucker wondered about the urgency in her voice.

She seems in an awful big rush over something that happened all those years ago. Why? Well, that can wait. First I have to get the proof I'm looking for.

That morning Alan Tucker visited the orphanage. He looked around the dreary community room where a noisy, chattering group of children were playing, and he thought: *This is where the heiress to the Scott dynasty grew up, while that bitch in New York kept all the money and all the power. Well, she's going to share some of that with yours truly. Yes, sir, we'll make a great team, Ellen Scott and me.*

A young woman came up to him and said, 'May I help you, *señor*?'

He smiled. *Yeah. You can help me to about a billion dollars.* 'I'd like to talk to whoever's in charge here.'

'That would be Señora Angeles.'

'Is she here?'

'*Si, señor.* I will take you to her.'

He followed the woman through the main hall to a small office at the rear of the building.

'Go in, please.'

Alan Tucker entered the office. The woman seated at the desk was in her eighties. She had once been a very large woman, but her frame had shrunk, so she looked as though her body had at one time belonged to someone else. Her hair was grey and thin, but her eyes were bright and clear.

'Good morning, *señor*. May I help you? You have come to adopt one of our lovely children? We have so many delightful ones to choose from.'

'No, *señora*. I have come to inquire about a child who was left here many years ago.'

Mercedes Angeles frowned. 'I do not understand.'

'A baby girl was brought in here –' He pretended to consult a piece of paper – 'in October of nineteen forty-seven.'

'That is so long ago. She would not be here now. You see, we have a rule, *señor*, that at the age of fifteen –'

'No, *señora*. I know she's not here. What I wish to know is the exact date she was brought here.'

'I'm afraid I cannot help you, *señor*.'

His heart sank.

'You see, so many children are brought in here. Unless you know her name –'

Patricia Scott, he thought. Aloud, he said, 'Megan. Her name is Megan.'

Mercedes Angeles' face lit up. 'No one could forget that child. She was a devil, and everyone adored her. Do you know that one day she –'

Alan Tucker had no time for anecdotes. His instincts told him how close he was to getting hold of a piece of the Scott fortune. And this gabby old woman was the key to it. *I must be patient with her.* 'Señora Angeles – I don't have much time. Would you have that date in your files?'

'Of course, *señor*. We are commanded by the state to keep very accurate records.'

Tucker's heart lifted. *I should have brought a camera to take a picture of the file. Never mind. I'll have it photocopied.* 'Could I see that file, *señora*?'

She frowned. 'I don't know. Our records are confidential and –'

'Of course,' Tucker said smoothly, 'and I certainly respect that. You said you were fond of little Megan, and I know you'd want to do anything you could to help her. Well, that's why I'm here. I have some good news for her.'

'And for this you need the date she was brought in here?'

He said glibly, 'That's just so I'll have the proof that she's the person I think she is. Her father died and left her a small inheritance, and I want to make sure she gets it.'

The woman nodded wisely. 'I see.'

Tucker pulled a roll of bills from his pocket. 'And to show my appreciation for the trouble I've put you to, I'd like to contribute a hundred dollars to your orphanage.'

She was looking at the roll of bills, an uncertain expression on her face.

He peeled off another bill. 'Two hundred.'

She frowned.

'All right. Five hundred.'

Mercedes Angeles beamed. 'That is very generous of you, *señor*. I will go and get the file.'

I've done it, he thought jubilantly. *Jesus Christ, I've done it! She stole Scott Industries for herself. If it hadn't been for me, she would have gotten away with it.*

When he confronted Ellen Scott with his evidence there was no way she could deny it. The plane crash happened on 1 October. Megan was in the hospital for ten days. So she would have been brought into the orphanage around 11 October.

Mercedes Angeles returned to the office, holding a file in her hands. 'I found it,' she said proudly.

It was all Alan Tucker could do to keep from grabbing it out of her hands. 'May I look at it?' he asked politely.

'Certainly. You have been so generous.' She frowned. 'I hope you will not mention this to anyone. I should not be doing this at all.'

'It will be our secret, *señora*.'

She handed him the file.

He took a deep breath and opened it. At the top it said: 'Megan. Baby Girl. Parents unknown.' And then the date. But there was some mistake.

'It says here that Megan was brought in here on 14 June 1947.'

'*Si*, señor.'

'That's impossible!' He was almost screaming. *The plane crash happened on 1 October.*

There was a puzzled expression on her face. 'Impossible, *señor*? I do not understand.'

'Who – who keeps these records?'

'I do. When a child is left here, I put down the date and whatever information is given to me.'

His dream was collapsing. 'Couldn't you have made a mistake? About the date, I mean – couldn't it have been October the eleventh?'

'*Señor*,' she said indignantly. 'I know the difference between June the fourteenth and October the eleventh.'

It was over. He had built a dream on too flimsy a foundation. So Patricia Scott had really died in the plane crash. It was a coincidence that Ellen Scott was searching for a girl who had been born around the same time.

Alan Tucker rose heavily and said, 'Thank you, señora.'

'*De nada, señor*.'

She watched him leave. He was such a nice man. And so generous. His five hundred dollars would buy many things for the orphanage. So would the hundred thousand dollar cheque sent by the kind lady who had telephoned from New York. *October the eleventh was certainly a lucky day for our orphanage. Thank you, Lord.*

Alan Tucker was reporting.

'Still no hard news, Mrs Scott. They're rumoured to be heading north. As far as I know, the girl is safe.'

The tone of his voice has completely changed, Ellen Scott thought. *The threat is gone. So he's visited the orphanage.*

266

*He's back to being an employee. Well, after he finds Patricia,
that will change, too.*

'Report in tomorrow.'

'Yes, Mrs Scott.'

Chapter 30

'Preserve me, Oh God, for in Thee I take refuge. Thou art
my Lord; I have no good apart from Thee. I love Thee, O
Lord, my strength. The Lord is my rock and my fortress and
my deliverer . . .'

Sister Megan glanced up to see Felix Carpio watching her,
a concerned expression on his face.

She's really frightened, he thought.

Ever since they had started on their journey, he had seen
Sister Megan's deep anxiety. *Of course. It's only natural. She's
been locked up in a convent for God only knows how many
years, and now she's suddenly thrown out into a strange, terrifying world. We'll have to be very gentle with the poor girl.*

Sister Megan was indeed frightened. She had been praying
hard ever since leaving the convent.

*Forgive me, Lord, for I love the excitement of what is
happening to me, and I know that is wicked of me.*

But no matter how hard Sister Megan prayed, she could
not help thinking. *I don't remember when I've had such a
good time.* It was the most amazing adventure she had ever
had. In the orphanage she had often planned daring escapes,
but that was child's play. This was the real thing. She was in
the hands of terrorists, and they were being pursued by the
police and the army. But instead of being terrified, Sister
Megan felt strangely exhilarated.

After travelling all night they stopped at dawn. Megan and
Amparo Jiron stood by as Jaime Miró and Felix Carpio
huddled over a map.

'It's four miles to Medina del Campo,' Jaime said. 'Let's avoid it. There's a permanent army garrison stationed there. We'll keep heading north-east to Valladolid. We should reach it by early afternoon.'

Easily, Sister Megan thought happily.

It had been a long and gruelling night without rest, but Megan felt wonderful. Jaime was deliberately pushing the group, but Megan understood what he was doing. He was testing her, waiting for her to crack. *Well, he's in for a surprise*, she thought.

As a matter of fact, Jaime Miró found himself intrigued by Sister Megan. Her behaviour was not at all what he would have expected of a nun. She was miles away from her convent, travelling through strange territory, being hunted, and she seemed to be actually enjoying it. *What kind of nun is she?* Jaime Miró wondered.

Amparo Jiron was less impressed. *I'll be glad to be rid of her*, she thought. She stayed close to Jaime, letting the nun walk with Felix Carpio.

The countryside was wild and beautiful, caressed by the soft fragrance of the summer wind. They passed old villages, some of them deserted and forlorn, and saw an ancient abandoned castle high on a hill.

Amparo seemed to Megan like a wild animal – gliding effortlessly over hills and valleys, never seeming to tire.

When finally hours later Valladolid loomed up in the distance, Jaime called a halt.

Jaime turned to Felix. 'Everything is arranged?'

'Yes.'

Megan wondered exactly what had been arranged. She found out very quickly.

'Tomas is instructed to contact us at the bullring.'

'What time does the bank close?'

'Five o'clock. There will be plenty of time.'

Jaime nodded. 'And today there should be a fat pay-roll.'

Good Lord, they're going to rob a bank, Megan thought.

It was a little more excitement than she had bargained for.

'What about a car?' Amparo was asking.

'No problem,' Jaime assured her.

They're going to steal one, Megan thought. *God isn't going to like this.*

When the group reached the outskirts of Valladolid, Jaime warned, 'Stay with the crowds. Today is bullfight day and there will be thousands of people. Let's not get separated.'

Jaime Miró had been right about the crowds. Megan had never seen so many people. The streets were swarming with pedestrians and cars and motorcycles, for the bullfight had drawn not only tourists, but citizens from all the neighbouring towns. Even the children on the street were playing at bullfighting.

Megan was fascinated by the crowds and the noise and the bustle around her. She looked into the faces of passers-by and wondered what their lives were like. *Soon enough I'll be back in the convent where I won't be allowed to look at anyone's face again. I might as well take advantage of this while I can.*

The pavements were filled with vendors displaying trinkets, religious medals and crosses, and everywhere was the pungent smell of fritters frying in boiling oil.

Megan suddenly realized how hungry she was.

It was Felix who said, 'Jaime, we're all hungry. Let's try some of those fritters.'

Felix bought four of them and handed one to Megan. 'Try this, Sister. You'll like it.'

It was delicious. For so many of her years, food was not meant to be enjoyed, but to sustain the body for the glory of the Lord. *This one's for me*, Megan thought irreverently.

'The arena is this way,' Jaime said.

They followed the crowds past the park in the middle of town to the Plaza Poinente, which flowed into the Plaza de Toros. The arena itself was inside an enormous adobe structure, three storeys high. There were four ticket windows at the entrance. Signs on the left said, '*Sol*', and on the right,

'*Sombra*'. Sun or shade. There were hundreds of people standing in queues waiting to purchase tickets.

'Wait here,' Jaime ordered.

They watched him as he walked over to where half a dozen touts were hawking tickets.

Megan turned to Felix. 'Are we going to watch a bullfight?'

'Yes, but don't worry, Sister,' Felix reassured her. 'You will find it exciting.'

Worry? Megan was thrilled by the idea. At the orphanage, one of her fantasies had been that her father had been a great torero, and Megan had read every book on bullfighting that she could get her hands on.

Felix was saying, 'The real bullfights are held in Madrid and Barcelona. The bullfight here will be by *novilleros*, instead of professionals. They are amateurs. They have not been granted the *alternativa*.

Megan knew that the *alternativa* was the accolade given only to the top-ranked matadors.

'The ones we will see today fight in rented costumes instead of the gold-encrusted suit of lights, against bulls with filed, dangerous horns that the professionals refuse to fight.'

'Why do they do it?'

Felix Carpio shrugged. '*Mas cornadas da el hambre.* Hunger is more painful than horns.'

Jaime returned, holding four tickets. 'We're all set,' Jaime said. 'Let's go in.'

Megan felt a growing sense of excitement.

As they approached the entrance to the huge arena, they passed a poster plastered to the wall. Megan stopped and stared at it.

'Look!'

There was a picture of Jaime Miró, and under it:

> WANTED FOR MURDER
> JAIME MIRÓ
> ONE MILLION PESETAS REWARD
> FOR HIS CAPTURE
> DEAD OR ALIVE

And suddenly it brought back to Megan the sober realization of the kind of man she was travelling with, the terrorist who held her life in his hands.

Jaime was studying the picture. 'Not a bad likeness.' He ripped off the poster, folded it and put it in his pocket.

What good will that do? Amparo wondered. *They must have posted hundreds of them.*

Jaime grinned. 'This particular one is going to bring us a fortune, *querida.*'

What a strange remark, Megan thought. She could not help admiring his coolness. There was an air of solid competence about Jaime Miró that Megan found reassuring. *The soldiers will never catch him*, she thought.

'Let's go inside.'

There were twelve widely spaced entrances to the building. The red iron doors had been flung open, each one numbered. Inside the entrance there were *puestos* selling cola and beer, and next to them small toilet cubicles. In the stands, each section and seat were numbered. The tiers of stone benches made a complete circle, and in the centre was the large arena covered with sand. There were commercial signs everywhere: BANCO CENTRAL . . . BOUTIQUE CALZADOS . . . SCHWEPPES . . . RADIO POPULAR . . .

Jaime had purchased tickets on the shady side and as they sat down on the stone benches, Megan looked around in wonder. It was not at all as she had imagined it. When she was a young girl, she had seen romantic colour photographs of the bullring in Madrid, huge and elaborate. This was a makeshift ring. The arena was rapidly filling up with spectators.

A trumpet sounded. The bullfight began.

Megan leaned forward in her seat, her eyes wide. A huge bull charged into the ring and a matador stepped out from behind a small wooden barrier at the side of the ring and began teasing the animal.

'The picadors will be next,' Megan said excitedly.

Jaime Miro looked at her in wonder. He had been concerned that the bullfight would make her ill and that she would attract attention to them. Instead, she seemed to be having a wonderful time. *Strange.*

A picador was approaching the bull, riding a horse covered with a heavy blanket. The bull lowered its head and charged at the horse, and as it buried its horns in the blanket, the picador drove an eight foot *pica* into the bull's shoulder.

Megan was watching, fascinated. 'He's doing that to weaken the bull's neck muscles,' she explained, remembering the well-loved books she had read all those years ago.

Felix Carpio blinked in surprise. 'That's right, Sister.'

Megan watched as the pairs of colourfully decorated *banderillas* were slammed into the bull's shoulders.

Now it was the matador's turn. He stepped into the ring holding at his side a red cape with a sword inside it. The bull turned and began to charge.

Megan was getting more excited. 'He will make his passes now,' she said. 'First the *pase verónica*, then the *media verónica*, and last the *rebolera*.'

Jaime could contain his curiosity no longer. 'Sister – where did you learn all this?'

Without thinking, Megan said, 'My father was a bull-fighter. Watch!'

The action was so swift that Megan could barely follow it. The maddened bull kept charging at the matador, and each time he neared him, the matador swung his red cape to the side and the bull followed the cape. Megan was concerned.

'What happens if the bullfighter gets hurt?'

Jaime shrugged. 'In a place like this, the town barber will take him over to the barn and sew him up.'

The bull charged again, and this time the matador leapt out of the way. The crowd booed.

Felix Carpio said apologetically, 'I am sorry this is not a better fight, Sister. You should see the great ones. I have seen Manolete and el Cordobés and Ordonez. They made bullfighting a spectacle never to be forgotten.'

'I have read about them,' Megan said.

273

Felix asked, 'Have you ever heard the wonderful story about Manolete?'

'Which story?'

'At one time, the story goes, Manolete was just another bullfighter, no better and no worse than a hundred others. He was engaged to a beautiful young girl, but one day when Manolete was in the ring a bull gored him in the groin and the doctor patched him up and told him that he would no longer be able to have children. Manolete loved his fiancée so much that he didn't tell her, because he was afraid she wouldn't marry him. They married and a few months later she proudly told Manolete that she was going to have a baby. Well, of course he knew that it wasn't his baby, and he left her. The heartbroken girl killed herself. Manolete reacted like a madman. He had no more desire to live, so he went into the bullring and did things that no matador had ever done before. He kept risking his life, hoping to be killed, and he became the greatest matador in the world. Two years later he fell in love again and married the young lady. A few months after the wedding she came to him and proudly announced that she was going to have his baby. And that's when Manolete discovered that the doctor had been wrong.'

Megan said, 'How awful.'

Jaime laughed aloud. 'That's an interesting story. I wonder if there is any truth to it.'

'I would like to think so,' Felix said.

Amparo was listening, her face impassive. She had watched Jaime's growing interest in the nun with resentment. *The sister had better watch her step.*

Aproned food vendors were moving up and down the aisles calling out their wares. One of them approached the row where Jaime and the others were seated.

'*Empanadas*,' he called out. '*Empanadas caliente*.'

Jaime raised a hand. '*Aquí*.'

The vendor skilfully tossed a wrapped package across the crowd into Jaime's hands. Jaime handed ten pesetas to the man next to him to be passed to the vendor. Megan watched as Jaime lowered the wrapped *Empanada* to his lap and carefully opened it. Inside the wrapping was a piece of paper. Jaime read it, then read it again, and Megan saw his jaw tighten.

Jaime slipped the paper into his pocket. 'We're leaving,' he said curtly. 'One at a time.' He turned to Amparo. 'You first. We'll meet at the gate.'

Wordlessly, Amparo got up and made her way across to the aisle.

Jaime nodded to Felix, and Felix rose and followed Amparo.

'What is happening?' Megan asked. 'Is something wrong?'

'We're leaving for Logroño.' He rose. 'Watch me, Sister. If I'm not stopped, go to the gate.'

Megan watched, tense, as Jaime made his way to the aisle and started towards the exit. No one seemed to pay any attention to him. When Jaime had disappeared from sight, Megan rose and started to leave. There was a roar from the crowd and she turned to look back at the bullring. A young matador was lying on the ground being gored by the savage bull. Blood was pouring on to the sand. Megan closed her eyes and offered up a silent prayer: *Oh, blessed Jesus, have mercy on this man. He shall not die, but he shall live. The Lord has chastened him sorely, but he has not given him over to death. Amen.* She opened her eyes, turned and hurried out.

Jaime, Amparo and Felix were waiting for her at the entrance.

'Let's move,' Jaime said.

They started walking.

'What's wrong?' Felix asked Jaime.

'The soldiers shot Tomas,' Jaime said tersely. 'He's dead. And the police have Rubio. He was stabbed in a bar fight.'

Megan crossed herself. 'What's happened to Sister Teresa and Sister Lucia?' she asked anxiously.

'I don't know.' Jaime turned to the others. 'We must hurry.' He looked at his watch. 'The bank should be busy.'

'Jaime, maybe we should wait,' Felix suggested. 'It's going to be dangerous for just the two of us to hold up the bank now.'

Megan listened to what he was saying and thought: *That won't stop him.* She was right.

The three of them were headed for the huge car-park behind the arena. When Megan caught up with them, Felix was examining a blue Seat sedan.

'This should do.' Felix said.

He fumbled with the lock on the door for a moment, opened it and put his head inside. He crouched down under the wheel, and a moment later the engine started.

'Get in,' Jaime told them.

Megan stood there, uncertainly. 'You're stealing a car?'

'For Christ's sake,' Amparo hissed. 'Stop acting like a nun and get into the car.'

The two men were in the front seat, with Jaime at the wheel. Amparo scrambled into the back.

'Are you coming or not?' Jaime demanded.

Megan took a deep breath and got into the car next to Amparo. They started off. Megan closed her eyes. *Dear Lord, where are You leading me?*

'If it makes you feel any better, Sister,' Jaime said, 'we're not stealing this car. We're confiscating it in the name of the Basque army.'

Megan started to say something, then stopped. There was nothing she could say that would make him change his mind. She sat there in silence as Jaime drove towards the centre of town.

He's going to rob a bank, Megan thought, *and in the eyes of God, I'll be as guilty as he is.* She crossed herself and began silently to pray.

The Banco de Bilbao is on the ground floor of a nine-storey apartment building on the Calle de Cervantes at the Plaza de Circular.

When the car pulled up in front of the building, Jaime said

to Felix, 'Keep the engine running. If there's any trouble, take off and meet the others in Logroño.'

Felix stared at him in surprise. 'What are you talking about? You're not going in there *alone*? You can't. The odds are too great, Jaime. It's too dangerous.'

Jaime slapped him on the shoulder. 'If they get hurt, they get hurt,' he said with a grin. He stepped out of the car.

They watched as Jaime walked into a leather goods shop next door to the bank. A few minutes later he emerged carrying an attache case. He nodded to the group in the car and entered the bank.

Megan could hardly breathe. She began to pray:

> *Prayer is a calling.*
> *Prayer is a listening.*
> *Prayer is a dwelling.*
> *Prayer is a presence.*
> *Prayer is a lamp*
> *aflame with Jesus.*
> *I am calm and filled with peace.*

She was not calm and filled with peace.

Jaime Miró walked through two sets of doors that led to the marble lobby of the bank. Inside the entrance, mounted high on the wall, he noted a security camera. He gave it a casual glance, then looked the room over. Behind the counters a staircase led to a second floor, where bank officers were working at desks. It was near closing time and the bank was filled with customers eager to finish transacting their business. There were queues of people in front of the three tellers' cages, and Jaime noticed that several of the customers were carrying packages.

Jaime stepped into a queue and patiently waited his turn.

When he reached the teller's cage, he smiled pleasantly and said, '*Buenos tardes*.'

'*Buenos tardes, señor*. What can we do for you today?'

Jaime leaned against the window and pulled out the folded

277

wanted poster. He handed it to the teller. 'Would you take a look at this, please?'

The teller smiled. 'Certainly, *señor*.'

He unfolded it, and as he saw what it was, his eyes widened. He looked up at Jaime, and panic was in his eyes.

'It's a nice likeness, isn't it?' Jaime said softly. 'As you can tell from that, I have killed many people, so one more really won't make a difference to me. Do I make myself understood?'

'P-perfectly, *señor*. P-perfectly. I have a family. I beg of you –'

'I respect families, so I will tell you what I want you to do to save your children's father.' Jaime pushed the attache case towards the teller. 'I want you to fill this for me. I want you to do it quickly and quietly. If you truly believe that the money is more important than your life, then go ahead and raise the alarm.'

The teller shook his head. 'No, no, no.'

He began to pull money out of the cash drawer and stuff it into the attache case. His hands were trembling.

When the attache case was full, the cashier said, 'There you are, *señor*. I – I promise you I won't raise any alarm.'

'That's very wise of you,' Jaime said. 'I'll tell you why, *amigo*.' He turned around and pointed to a middle-aged woman standing near the end of the line, carrying a package wrapped in brown paper. 'Do you see that woman? She is one of us. There is a bomb in that package. If the alarm should sound, she will set off the bomb instantly.'

The cashier turned even paler. 'No, please!'

'You will wait until ten minutes after she leaves the bank before you make a move,' Jaime warned.

'On my children's life,' the teller whispered.

'*Buenos tardes*.'

Jaime took the attache case and moved towards the door. He felt the cashier's eyes riveted on him.

Jaime stopped at the side of the woman with the package.

'I must compliment you,' Jaime said. 'That is a most becoming dress you are wearing.'

278

She blushed. 'Why thank you, *señor – gracias.*'

'*De nada.*'

Jaime turned to nod to the cashier, then strolled out of the bank. It would be at least fifteen minutes before the woman finished her business and left. By that time, he and the others would be long gone.

As Jaime came out of the bank and walked towards the car, Megan almost fainted with relief.

Felix Carpio grinned. 'The bastard got away with it.' He turned to Megan. 'I beg your pardon, Sister.'

Megan had never been so glad to see anyone in her life. *He did it,* she thought. *And all by himself. Wait until I tell the sisters what happened.* And then she remembered. She could never tell this to anyone. When she went back to the convent, there would be only silence for the rest of her life. It gave her an odd feeling.

Jaime said to Felix, 'Move over, *amigo.* I'll drive. He tossed the briefcase into the back seat.

'Everything went well?' Amparo asked.

Jaime laughed. 'Couldn't have gone better. I must remember to thank Colonel Acoca for his calling card.'

The car started down the street. At the first corner, Calle de Tudela, Jaime made a left turn. Suddenly, appearing out of nowhere, a policeman moved in front of the car and held out a hand signalling him to stop. Jaime stepped on the brake. Megan's heart began to pound.

The policeman walked over to the car.

Jaime asked calmly, 'What's the problem, officer?'

'The problem, *señor,* is that you are driving the wrong way down a one-way street. Unless you can prove you are legally blind, you are in trouble.' He pointed to the sign at the entrance. 'The street is clearly marked. Motorists are expected to respect a sign like that. That is the reason it has been placed there.'

Jaime said apologetically, 'A thousand pardons. My friends and I were in such a serious discussion that I did not see the sign.'

The policeman was leaning into the driver's window. He was studying Jaime, a puzzled expression on his face.

'You will be so good as to let me see your registration, please.'

'Of course,' Jaime said.

He reached down for the revolver which was under his jacket. Felix was ready to spring into action. Megan held her breath.

Jaime pretended to be searching his pockets. 'I know I have it here somewhere.'

At that moment from across the Plaza came a loud scream and the policeman turned to look. A man on the street corner was beating a woman, hitting her about the head and shoulders with his fists.

'Help!' she cried. 'Help me! He's killing me!'

The policeman hesitated for only an instant. 'Wait here,' he commanded.

He raced back down the street towards the man and woman.

Jaime put the car into gear and slammed down on the accelerator. The car shot down the one-way street, scattering traffic headed towards them, horns angrily blaring at them. When they reached the corner, Jaime made another turn towards the bridge that led out of town on the Avenida Sanchez Arjona.

Megan looked at Jaime and crossed herself. She could hardly breathe.

'Would you – would you have killed the policeman if that man had not attacked the woman?'

Jaime did not bother to answer.

'The woman wasn't being attacked, Sister,' Felix explained. 'Those were our people. We are not alone. We have many friends.'

Jaime's face was grim. 'We're going to have to get rid of this car.'

They were leaving the outskirts of Valladolid. Jaime turned on to N620, the highway to Burgos, on the way to Logroño. He was careful to stay within the speed limit.

'We'll get rid of the car as soon as we get past Burgos,' he announced.

I can't believe this is happening to me, Megan thought. *I escaped from the convent, I'm running away from the army, and I'm travelling in a stolen car with terrorists who have just robbed a bank. Lord, what else do You have in mind for me?*

Chapter 31

Colonel Ramón Acoca and half a dozen members of the GOE were in the middle of a strategy meeting. They were studying a large map of the countryside.

The scarred giant said, 'It's obvious that Miró is heading north towards Basque country.'

'That could mean Burgos, Vitoria, Logroño, Pamplona or San Sebastian.'

San Sebastian, Acoca thought. *But I've got to catch him before he reaches there.*

He could hear the voice on the phone: *You're running out of time.*

He could not afford to fail.

They were driving through the rolling hills that heralded the approach to Burgos.

Jaime was quiet behind the wheel. When he finally spoke, he said, 'Felix, when we get to San Sebastian, I want to make arrangements to get Rubio away from the police.'

Felix nodded. 'It will be a pleasure. It will drive them crazy.'

Megan said, 'What about Sister Lucia?'

'What?'

'Didn't you say that she had been captured, too?'

Jaime said wryly, 'Yes, but your Sister Lucia turned out to be a criminal wanted by the police for murder.'

The news shook Megan. She remembered how Lucia had

taken charge and had persuaded them to hide in the hills. She liked Sister Lucia.

She said stubbornly, 'Since you're going to rescue Rubio, you should save them both.'

What the devil kind of nun is this? Jaime wondered.

But she was right. Smuggling Rubio and Lucia out from under the noses of the police would be wonderful propaganda and would make headlines.

Amparo had sunk into a sullen silence.

Suddenly, in the distance, on the road ahead of them were three army trucks filled with soldiers.

'We'd better get off this road,' Jaime decided.

At the next intersection he turned on to Highway N120 and headed east.

'Santo Domingo de la Calzada is up ahead. There's an old deserted castle there. We can spend the night in it.'

They could see its outline from the distance, high on a hill. Jaime took a side road, avoiding the town, and the castle loomed larger and larger as they approached it. A few hundred yards from it was a lake.

Jaime stopped the car. 'Everybody out, please.'

When they were all out of the car, Jaime pointed the steering wheel down the hill towards the lake, jammed the accelerator down, released the handbrake and jumped clear. They stood there watching as the car disappeared into the water.

Megan was about to ask him how they were going to get to Logrono. She stopped herself. *Foolish question. He will steal another car, of course.*

The group turned to examine the abandoned castle. There was a huge stone wall circling it, with crumbling turrets on each corner.

'In the old days,' Felix told Megan, 'princes used these castles as prisons for their enemies.'

And Jaime is an enemy of the state, and if he is caught, there will be no prison for him. Only death, Megan thought. *He has no fear.* She remembered his words:

I have faith in what I'm fighting for. I have faith in my men, and in my guns.

They walked up the stone steps that led to the front gate. The gates were iron and had rusted away so badly that they were able to push them open and squeeze through into a courtyard paved in stone.

The inside of the castle seemed enormous to Megan. There were narrow passageways and rooms everywhere, and facing the outside were gun ports, where the defenders of the castle could repel attackers.

Stone steps led to a second floor and there was another *claustro*, an inner patio. The stone steps narrowed as they walked up to a third floor, and then a fourth. The castle was deserted.

'Well at least there are plenty of places to sleep here,' Jaime said. 'Felix and I will go forage for food. Pick out your rooms.'

The two men started downstairs again.

Amparo turned to Megan. 'Come on, Sister.'

They walked down the corridor and the rooms all looked alike to Megan. They were empty stone cubicles, cold and austere, some larger than others.

Amparo picked out the largest. 'Jaime and I will sleep here.' She looked at Megan and asked slyly, 'Would you like to sleep with Felix?'

Megan looked at her and said nothing.

'Or perhaps you'd rather sleep with Jaime.' Amparo stepped closer to Megan. 'Don't get any ideas, Sister. He's much too much man for you.'

'You don't have to concern yourself. I'm not interested.' And even as she said it, Megan wondered whether Jaime Miró was much too much man for her.

When Jaime and Felix returned to the castle an hour later, Jaime was clutching two rabbits and Felix was carrying firewood. Felix bolted the front door behind them. Megan watched as the men made a fire in the large fireplace. Jaime skinned and cooked the rabbits on a spit over the fire.

284

'Sorry we can't offer you ladies a real feast,' Felix said, 'but we'll eat well in Logroño. Meanwhile – enjoy.'

When they had finished their meagre meal, Jaime said, 'Let's get to sleep. I want to make an early start in the morning.'

Amparo said to Jaime, 'Come, *querida*. I have our bedroom picked out.'

'*Bueno*. Let's go.'

Megan watched them go upstairs, hand in hand.

Felix turned to Megan. 'Have you chosen your bedroom, Sister?'

'Yes, thank you.'

'All right, then.'

Megan and Felix walked up the stairs together.

'Good night,' Megan said.

He handed Megan a sleeping-bag. 'Good night, Sister.'

Megan wanted to ask Felix about Jaime, but she hesitated. Jaime might think she was prying, and for some reason, Megan wanted very much for Jaime to have a good opinion of her. *That's really odd*, Megan thought. *He's a terrorist, a murderer, a bank robber, and heaven only knows what else, and I'm worried about whether the man thinks well of me.*

But even as Megan thought it, she knew that there was another side to it. *He's a freedom fighter. He robs banks to finance his cause. He risks his life for what he believes in. He's a brave man.*

As Megan passed their bedroom, she heard Jaime and Amparo inside laughing. She walked into the small, bare room where she was to sleep and knelt on the cold stone floor. 'Dear God, forgive me for –' *Forgive me for what? What have I done?*

For the first time in her life, Megan was unable to pray. Was God up there listening?

Megan crawled into the sleeping-bag Felix had given her, but sleep was as remote as the cold stars she could see through the narrow window.

What am I doing here? Megan wondered. Her thoughts drifted back to the convent . . . the orphanage. And before the orphanage? *Why was I left there? I don't really believe that my father was a brave soldier or a great bullfighter. But wouldn't it be wonderful to know?*

It was almost dawn before Megan drifted off to sleep.

At the prison in Aranda de Duero, Lucia Carmine was a celebrity.

'You're a big fish in our little pond,' the guard told her. 'The Italian government is sending someone to escort you home. I'd like to escort you to my house, *bonita puta*. What bad thing did you do?'

'I cut off a man's balls for calling me *bonita puta*. Tell me – how is my friend?'

'He's going to live.'

Lucia said a silent prayer of gratitude. She looked around the stone walls of her grim, grey cell and thought: *How the hell do I get out of here?*

Chapter 32

The report of the bank robbery was handled through regular police channels, and it was not until two hours after the robbery occurred that a police lieutenant notified Colonel Acoca about it.

An hour later, Colonel Acoca was in Valladolid. He was furious at the delay.

'Why wasn't I informed immediately?'

'I'm sorry, Colonel, but it never occurred to us that –'

'You had him in your hands and you let him get away!'

'It wasn't our –'

'Send in the bank teller.'

The bank teller was filled with a sense of self-importance. 'It was my window he came to. I could tell he was a killer by the look in his eye. He –'

'There is no doubt in your mind that the man who held you up was Jaime Miró?'

'None. He even showed me a wanted poster of himself. It was –'

'Did he come into the bank alone?'

'Yes. He pointed to a woman in the queue and he said she was a member of his gang, but after Miró left I recognized her. She's a secretary who's a regular customer and –'

Colonel Acoca said impatiently, 'When Miró left, did you see in which direction he went?'

'Out the front door.'

The interview with the traffic policeman was no more helpful.

'There were four of them in the car, Colonel. Jaime Miró and another man and two women in the back.'

'In what direction were they headed?'

The policeman hesitated. 'They could have gone in any direction, sir, once they got off the one-way street.' His face brightened. 'I can describe the car, though.'

Colonel Acoca shook his head in disgust. 'Don't bother.'

She was dreaming, and in her dream there were the voices of a mob and they were coming for her to burn her at the stake for robbing a bank. *It wasn't for me. It was for the cause.* The voices grew louder.

Megan opened her eyes and sat up, staring at the unfamiliar castle walls. The sound of voices was real. They were coming from outside.

Megan rose and hurried over to the narrow window. Directly below, in front of the castle, was an encampment of soldiers. Megan was filled with a sudden panic. *They've caught us. I've got to find Jaime.*

She hurried to the room where he and Amparo had slept and looked inside. It was empty. She ran down the steps to the reception hall on the main floor. Jaime and Amparo were standing near the bolted front door, whispering.

Felix ran up to them. 'I checked the back. There's no other way out of here.'

'What about the back windows?'

'Too small. The only way out is through the front door.'

Where the soldiers are, Megan thought. *We're trapped.*

Jaime was saying, 'It's just our damned bad luck that they picked this place to camp.'

'What are we going to do?' Amparo whispered.

'There's nothing we can do. We'll have to stay here until they leave. If –'

And at that moment there was a loud knock at the front door. An authoritative voice called out, 'Open up in there.'

Jaime and Felix exchanged a quick look, and without a word drew their guns.

The voice called out again, 'We know there's someone in there. Open up.'

Jaime said to Amparo and Megan, 'Get out of the way.'

It's hopeless, Megan thought, as Amparo moved behind Jaime and Felix. *There must be two dozen armed soldiers out there. We haven't got a chance.*

Before the others could stop her, Megan moved swiftly to the front door and opened it.

'Thank the Lord you've come!' Megan exclaimed. 'You must help me.'

Chapter 33

The army officer stared at Megan. 'Who are you? What are you doing in there? I'm Captain Rodriguez, and we're looking for –'

'You're just in time, Captain.' She grabbed his arm. 'My two little sons have typhoid fever, and I've got to get them to a doctor. You must come in and help me with them.'

'Typhoid fever?'

'Yes.' Megan was pulling on his arm. 'It is terrible. They are burning up. They are covered with sores and are very sick. Bring your men in and help me carry them out to –'

'*Señora*! You must be mad. That is highly contagious.'

'Never mind that. They need your help. They may be dying.' She was pulling on his arm.

'Let go of me.'

'You can't leave me. What will I do?'

'Get back inside and stay there until we can notify the police to send an ambulance or a doctor.'

'But –'

'That's an order, *señora*. Get inside.'

He called out, 'Sergeant, we're moving out of here.'

Megan closed the front door, leaning against it, drained.

Jaime was staring at her in stunned amazement. 'My God, that was brilliant. Where did you learn to lie like that?'

Megan turned to him and sighed. 'When I was in the orphanage, we had to learn to defend ourselves. I hope God will forgive me.'

'I wish I could have seen the look on that Captain's face.' Jaime burst into laughter. 'Typhoid fever! Jesus Christ!' He

290

saw the look on Megan's face. 'I beg your pardon, Sister.'

From outside they could hear the sounds of the soldiers packing their tents and moving out.

When the troops had departed, Jaime said, 'The police will be here soon. Anyway, we have an appointment in Logroño.'

Fifteen minutes after the soldiers had departed, Jaime said, 'It should be safe to leave now.' He turned to Felix. 'See what you can pick up in town. Preferably a sedan.'

Felix grinned. 'No problem.'

Half an hour later they were in a beat-up grey sedan heading east.

To Megan's surprise, she was seated next to Jaime. Felix and Amparo were in the back seat. Jaime glanced at Megan, a grin on his face.

'Typhoid fever,' he said. And burst out laughing.

Megan smiled. 'He *did* seem eager to get away, didn't he?'

'Did you say you were in an orphanage, Sister?'

'Yes.'

'Where?'

'In Ávila.'

'You don't look Spanish.'

'So I've been told.'

'It must have been hell for you in the orphanage.'

She was startled by the unexpected concern. 'It could have been,' she said. 'But it wasn't.' *I wouldn't let it be*, she thought.

'Have you any idea who your parents were?'

Megan recalled her fantasies. 'Oh, yes. My father was a brave Englishman who drove an ambulance for the loyalists in the Spanish Civil War. My mother was killed in the fighting and I was left on the doorstep of a farmhouse.' Megan shrugged. 'Or my father was a foreign prince who had an affair with a peasant girl and abandoned me to avoid a scandal.'

Jaime glanced at her, saying nothing.

'I –' she stopped abruptly. 'I don't know who my parents were.'

They drove on in silence for a while.

'How long were you behind the walls of the convent?'

'About fifteen years.'

Jaime was astonished. 'Jesus!' Hastily, he added, 'I beg your pardon, Sister. But it's like talking to someone from another planet. You have no idea what's happened in the world in the past fifteen years.'

'I'm sure that whatever changed is only temporary. It will change again.'

'Do you still want to go back to a convent?'

The question took Megan by surprise.

'Of course.'

'*Why?*' Jaime made a sweeping gesture. 'I mean – there is so much that you must miss behind the walls. Here we have music and poetry. Spain gave the world Cervantes and Picasso, Lorca, Pizarro, DeSoto, Cortez. This is a magical country.'

There was a surprising mellowness about this man, a soft fire.

Unexpectedly Jaime said, 'I'm sorry for wanting to desert you earlier, Sister. It was nothing personal. I have had bad experiences with your Church.'

'That is difficult to believe.'

'Believe it.' His voice was bitter.

In his mind's eye he could see the buildings and statues and streets of Guernica exploding in showers of death. He could still hear the screams of the bombs mingling with the screams of the helpless victims being torn apart. The only place of sanctuary was the church.

The priests have locked the church. They won't let us in.

And the deadly hail of bullets that had murdered his mother and father and sisters. *No. Not the bullets*, Jaime thought. *The Church.*

'Your Church stood behind Franco and allowed unspeakable things to be done to innocent civilians.'

'I'm sure the Church protested,' Megan said.

'No. It wasn't until nuns were being raped by his Falangists and priests were being murdered and churches were being burned that finally the Pope broke with Franco. But that didn't bring my mother or father or sisters back to life.'

The passion in his voice was frightening.

'I'm sorry. But that was long ago. The war is over.'

'No. Not for us it isn't. The government will still not permit us to fly the Basque flag or celebrate our national holidays or speak our own language. No, Sister. We're still being oppressed. We'll keep on fighting until we gain our independence. There are half a million Basques in Spain and a hundred and fifty thousand more in France. We want our independence – but your God is too busy to help us.'

Megan said earnestly, 'God cannot take sides, for He is in all of us. We are all a part of Him, and when we try to destroy Him, we destroy ourselves.'

To Megan's surprise, Jaime smiled. 'We are a lot alike, you and I, Sister.'

'We are?'

'We may believe in different things, but we believe with a passion. Most people go through life without caring deeply about anything. You devote your life to God; I devote my life to a cause. We care.'

And Megan thought: *Do I care enough? And if I do, why am I enjoying being with this man? I should be thinking only of returning to a convent.* There was a power in Jaime Miró that was like a magnet. *Is he like Manolete? Risking his life taking daring chances because he has nothing to lose?*

'What will they do to you if the soldiers catch you?' Megan asked.

'Execute me.' He said it so matter-of-factly that for a moment Megan thought she had misunderstood.

'Aren't you afraid?'

'Of course I'm afraid We're all afraid. None of us wants to die, Sister. We'll meet your God soon enough. We don't want to rush it.'

'Have you done such terrible things?'

'That depends on your point of view. The difference between a patriot and a rebel depends on who is in power at the moment. The government calls us terrorists. We call ourselves freedom fighters. Jean Jacques Rousseau said that freedom is the power to choose our own chains. I want that freedom.' He studied her a moment. 'But you don't have to concern yourself with any of these things, do you? Once you're back in the convent, you'll no longer be interested in the world outside.'

Was that true? Being out in the world again had turned her life upside down. Had she given up her freedom? There was so much she wanted to know, so much she had to learn. She felt like an artist with a blank canvas about to start sketching a new life. *If I go back to a convent*, she thought, *I will be shut away from life again.* And even as she thought it, Megan was appalled by the word *if. When I go back*, she corrected herself hastily. *Of course I'm going back. I have nowhere else to go.*

They camped that night in the woods.

Jaime said, 'We're about thirty miles from Logroño and we aren't supposed to meet the others for two days. It will be safer for us to stay on the move until then. So tomorrow we will head toward Vitoria. The next day we'll go into Logroño and just a few hours after that, Sister, you'll be at he convent in Mendavia.'

For ever. 'Will you be all right?' Megan asked.

'Are you worried about my soul, Sister, or my body?'

Megan found herself blushing.

'Nothing will happen to me. I'll cross the border into France for a while.'

'I will pray for you,' Megan told him.

'Thank you,' he said gravely. 'I will think of you praying for me and it will make me feel safer. Get some sleep now. We'll make Leon tomorrow.'

As Megan turned to lie down, she saw Amparo staring at

294

her from the far end of the clearing. There was a look of naked hatred on Amparo's face.

No one takes my man from me. No one.

Chapter 34

Early the following morning, they reached the outskirts of Nanclares, a small village west of Vitoria. They came to a filling station with a garage, where a mechanic was working on a car. Jaime pulled into the garage.

'*Buenos días*,' the mechanic said. 'What is the problem?'

'If I knew,' Jaime replied, 'I would fix it myself and charge for it. This car is as useless as a mule. It sputters like an old woman and has no energy.'

'It sounds like my wife,' the mechanic grinned. 'I think you may have a carburettor problem, *señor*.'

Jaime shrugged. 'I know nothing about cars. All I know is that I have a very important appointment in Madrid tomorrow. Can you have it fixed by this afternoon?'

The mechanic said, 'I have two jobs ahead of you, *señor*, but –' He let the rest of the sentence hang in the air.

'I will be glad to pay you double.'

The mechanic's face brightened. 'Will two o'clock be all right?'

'Wonderful. We'll get something to eat and come back at two.'

Jaime turned to the others, who had been listening to the conversation in amazement. 'We're in luck,' Jaime said. 'This man is going to fix the car for us. Let's go eat.'

They got out of the car and followed Jaime down the street.

'Two o'clock,' the mechanic said.

'Two o'clock.'

When they were out of earshot, Felix said, 'What are you doing? There's nothing wrong with the car.'

Except that by now the police will be looking for it, Megan thought. *But they'll be looking on the road, not in a garage. It's a clever way to get rid of it.*

'By two o'clock we'll be gone, won't we?' Megan asked.

Jaime looked at her and grinned. 'I have to make a phone call. Wait here.'

Amparo took Jaime's arm. 'I'll go with you.'

Megan and Felix watched them walk off.

Felix looked at Megan and said, 'You and Jaime are getting along well, yes?'

'Yes.' She felt suddenly shy.

'He is not an easy man to know. But he is a man of great honour and great bravery. He is a very caring man. There is no one like him. Did I tell you how he saved my life, Sister?'

'No. I would like to hear.'

'A few months ago the government executed six freedom fighters. In revenge, Jaime decided to blow up the dam at Puente la Reina, south of Pamplona. The town below was headquarters for the army. We moved in at night, but some-one tipped off the GOE, and Acoca's men caught three of us. We were sentenced to die. It would have taken an army to storm our prison, but Jaime figured out a way. He set the bulls loose in Pamplona, and in the confusion got two of us away. The third one was beaten to death by Acoca's men. Yes, Sister, Jaime Miró is very special.'

When Jaime and Amparo returned, Felix asked, 'What is happening?'

'Friends are picking us up. We'll have a lift into Vitoria.'

Half an hour later, a truck appeared. The back of it was covered by canvas.

'Welcome,' the driver said cheerfully. 'Hop in.'

'Thank you, *amigo*.'

'It's a pleasure to be of assistance to you, *señor*. It's good that you called. The damned soldiers are swarming around like fleas. It is not safe for you and your friends to be out in the open.'

They climbed into the back of the truck, and the huge vehicle headed northeast.

'Where will you be staying?' the driver asked.

'With friends,' Jaime said.

And Megan thought: *He doesn't trust anyone. Not even someone who is helping him. But how can he? His life is in danger.* And she thought of how terrible it must be for Jaime to be living under that shadow, running from the police and the army. And all because he believed in an ideal so much that he was willing to die for it. What was it he had said? *The difference between a patriot and a rebel depended on who was in power at the moment.*

The drive was a pleasant one. The thin canvas cover offered security, and Megan realized how much tension she had felt when they were out in the open fields, knowing that they were all being hunted. *And Jaime lives under that tension constantly. How strong he is.*

She and Jaime talked, and the conversation flowed easily as though they had known each other for ever. Amparo Jiron sat listening to them, saying nothing, her face impassive.

'When I was a boy,' Jaime told Megan, 'I wanted to be an astronomer.'

Megan was curious. 'What made you –?'

'I had seen my mother and father and sisters shot down, and friends murdered, and I couldn't face what was happening here on this bloody earth. The stars were an escape. They were millions of light years away, and I used to dream of going to them one day and getting away from this awful planet.'

She was watching him, silent.

'But there is no escape, is there? In the end, we all have to face up to our responsibilities. So I came back down to earth. I used to believe that one person could not make a difference. But I know now that that is not true. Jesus made a difference, Muhammad and Gandhi and Einstein and Churchill.' He smiled wryly. 'Don't misunderstand, Sister. I'm not comparing myself to any of them. But in my small way, I do what I can. I think we must all do what we can.'

And Megan wondered whether his words were meant to have a special meaning for her.

'When I got the stars out of my eyes, I studied to be an engineer. I learned to build buildings. Now I blow them up. And the irony is that some of the buildings I've blown up are ones that I've built.'

They reached Vitoria at dusk.

'Where shall I take you?' the truck driver asked.

'You can drop us off here, at the corner, *amigo*.'

The truck driver nodded. 'Right. Keep up the good fight.'

Jaime helped Megan down from the truck. Amparo watched, her eyes blazing. She allowed her man to touch no other woman. *She's a whore*, Amparo thought. *And Jaime is horny for that bitch of a nun. Well, that won't last. He will soon find that her milk is thin. He needs a real woman.*

The group took to the side streets, keeping a wary eye out for trouble. Twenty minutes later, they arrived at a one-storey stone house nestled in a narrow street and surrounded by a high fence.

'This is it,' Jaime said. 'We will stay here tonight and leave tomorrow when it is dark.'

They entered through the front gate and went to the door. It took Jaime but a moment to slip the lock and they all went inside.

'Whose house is this?' Megan asked.

'You ask too many questions,' Amparo said. 'Just be grateful we've kept you alive.'

Jaime looked at Amparo a moment. 'She's proved her right to ask questions.' He turned to Megan. 'It's the house of a friend. You're in Basque country now. From here on our journey will be easier. There will be comrades everywhere, watching and protecting us. You'll be at the convent the day after tomorrow.'

And Megan felt a small chill that was almost a sorrow.

What is the matter with me? she wondered. *Of course I want to go back. Forgive me, Lord. I asked that You bring me home to Your safety, and You are.*

'I'm starved,' Felix said. 'Let's see what's in the kitchen.'

It was completely stocked.

Jaime said, 'He left plenty of food for us. I will make us a wonderful dinner.' He smiled at Megan. 'I think we deserve it, don't you?'

Megan said, 'I didn't know men cooked.'

Felix laughed. 'Basque men take pride in their cooking. You are in for a treat. You will see.'

Handing Jaime the ingredients he asked for, they watched as he prepared a piperade of fresh roasted, peeled green peppers, sliced white onions, tomatoes, eggs and ham sautéed together. As it started to cook, Megan said, 'It smells delicious.'

'Ah, that's just the appetizer. I'm going to make a famous Basque dish for you, *pollo al chilindrón*.'

He didn't say 'for us', Amparo noted. *He said, 'for you'. For the bitch.*

Jaime cut up slices of chicken, sprinkled salt and pepper over them and browned the chicken in hot oil while in a separate pan he started cooking onions, garlic and tomatoes. 'We'll let it simmer for half an hour.'

Felix had found a bottle of red wine. He passed out glasses. 'The red wine of Rioja. You will like this.' He offered a glass to Megan. 'Sister?'

The last time Megan tasted wine had been at communion. 'Thank you,' she said.

Slowly Megan raised the glass to her lips and took a sip. It was delicious. She took another sip and she could feel a warmth moving down her body. It felt wonderful. *I must enjoy all this while I can*, Megan thought. *It will be over soon.*

During dinner, Jaime seemed unusually preoccupied.

'What's troubling you, *amigo*?' Felix asked.

Jaime hesitated. 'We have a traitor in the movement.'

There was a shocked silence.

'What – what makes you think that?' Felix demanded.

'Acoca. He keeps getting too close to us.'

Felix shrugged. 'He's the fox and we're the rabbits.'

'It's something more than that.'

'What do you mean?' Amparo asked.

'When we were going to blow up the dam at Puenta la Reina, Acoca was tipped off.' He looked at Felix. 'He set a trap and caught you and Ricardo and Zamora. If I hadn't been delayed, I would have been captured with you. And look what happened at the *parador*.'

'You heard the manager telephoning the police,' Amparo pointed out.

Jaime nodded. 'Right. Because I had a feeling that something was wrong.'

Amparo's face was sombre. 'Who do you think it is?'

Jaime shook his head. 'I'm not sure. Someone who knows all our plans.'

'Then let's change our plans,' Amparo said. 'We'll meet the others at Logroño and skip Mendavia.'

Jaime glanced at Megan. 'We can't do that. We have to get the sisters to their convent.'

Megan looked at him and thought: *He's already done enough for me. I mustn't put him in greater danger than he's already in.*

'Jaime, I can –'

But he knew what she was going to say. 'Don't worry, Megan. We're all going to get there safely.'

He's changed, Amparo thought. *In the beginning he wanted nothing to do with any of them. Now he's willing to risk his life for her. And he calls her Megan. It's no longer Sister.*

Jaime was going on. 'There are at least fifteen people who know our plans.'

'We have to find out which one it is,' Amparo insisted.

'How do we do that?' Felix asked. He was nervously picking at the edges of the tablecloth.

Jaime said, 'Paco is in Madrid doing some checking for me. I've arranged for him to telephone me here.' He looked at Felix for a moment, then looked away.

What he had not said was that no more than half a dozen people knew the exact route that the three groups were taking. It was true that Felix Carpio had been imprisoned by Acoca. It was also true that that would have provided a perfect alibi for Felix. At the propitious moment, an escape could have been planned for him. *Except that I got him out first*, Jaime thought. *Paco is checking on him. I hope he calls soon.*

Amparo rose and turned to Megan. 'Help me with the dishes.'

The two women began clearing the table and the men went into the living room.

'The nun – she's holding up well,' Felix said.

'Yes.'

'You like her, don't you?'

Jaime found it difficult to look at Felix. 'Yes. I like her.' *And you would betray her along with the rest of us.*

'What about you and Amparo?'

'We're cut from the same cloth. She believes in the cause as much as I do Her entire family was killed by Franco's Falangists.' Jaime rose and stretched. 'Time to turn in.'

'I don't think I'm going to be able to sleep tonight. Are you certain there's a spy?'

Jaime looked at him and said, 'I'm certain.'

When Jaime came downstairs for breakfast in the morning, Megan did not recognize him. His face had been darkened and he was wearing a wig and a moustache. He was dressed in scruffy clothes. He looked ten years older.

'Good morning,' he said. And his voice coming out of that body startled her.

'Where did you –?'

'This is a house I use from time to time. I keep an assortment of things here that I need.'

He said it casually, but it gave Megan a sudden insight into the kind of life he led. How many other houses and disguises did he need to stay alive? How many other close calls had he had that she knew nothing about? She remembered the ruthlessness of the men who had attacked the convent and she thought: *If they catch Jaime, they'll show him no mercy. I wish I knew how to protect him.*

And Megan's mind was filled with thoughts she had no right to be thinking.

Amparo prepared breakfast. *Bacalao* – steamed, salted cod-fish – goat's milk, cheese and thick, hot chocolate with *churros*.

As they were eating, Felix asked, 'How long are we going to stay here?'

Jaime replied casually, 'We'll leave when it gets dark.'

But he had no intention of letting Felix use that information.

'I have some errands to do,' he told Felix. 'I'll need your help.'

'Right.'

Jaime called Amparo aside. 'When Paco calls, tell him I'll be back shortly. Take a message.'

She nodded. 'Be careful.'

'Don't worry.' He turned to Megan. 'Your last day. Tomorrow you'll be at the convent. You must be eager to get there.'

She looked at him a long moment. 'Yes.' *Not eager*, Megan thought. *Anxious. I wish I weren't anxious. I'm going to shut myself away from this, but for the rest of my life, I'm going to wonder what happened to Jaime and Felix and the others.*

Megan stood there watching as Jaime and Felix left. She sensed a tension between the two men that she did not understand.

Amparo was studying her, and Megan remembered her words: *Jaime is too much man for you.*

Amparo said curtly, 'Make up the beds. I'll prepare lunch.'

'All right.'

Megan went into the bedroom. Amparo stood there watching her, then walked into the kitchen.

For the next hour, Megan worked, busily concentrating on cleaning and dusting and polishing, trying not to think, trying to keep her mind off what was bothering her.

I must put him out of my mind, she thought.

It was impossible. He was like a force of nature, taking over everything in his path.

She polished harder.

When Jaime and Felix returned, Amparo was waiting for them at the door. Felix looked pale.

'I'm not feeling too well. I think I'll lie down for a bit.'

They watched him disappear into a bedroom.

'Paco called,' Amparo said excitedly.

'What did he say?'

'He has some information for you, but he didn't want to discuss it on the phone. He's sending someone to meet you. This person will be at the town square at noon.'

Jaime frowned, thoughtful. 'He didn't say who it is?'

'No. Just that it was urgent.'

'Damn it. I – never mind. All right. I'll go and meet him. I want you to keep an eye on Felix.'

She looked at him, puzzled. 'I don't un–?'

'I don't want him using the telephone.'

A flash of understanding crossed her face. 'You think that Felix is –?'

'Please. Just do as I ask.' He looked at his watch. 'It's almost noon. I'll leave now. I should be back in an hour. Take care, *querida*.'

'Don't worry.'

Megan heard their voices.

I don't want him using the telephone.

You think that Felix is –?

Please. Just do as I ask.

So Felix is the traitor, Megan thought. She had seen him go into his bedroom and close the door. She heard Jaime leave.

Megan walked into the living room.

Amparo turned. 'Have you finished?'

'Not quite, I –' She wanted to ask where Jaime had gone,

what they were going to do with Felix, what was going to happen next, but she did not want to discuss that with this woman. *I'll wait until Jaime returns.*

'Finish up,' Amparo said.

Megan turned and went back into the bedroom. She thought about Felix. He had seemed so friendly, so warm. He had asked her many questions, but now that seeming act of friendliness took on a different meaning. The bearded man was looking for information that he could pass on to Colonel Acoca. All their lives were in danger.

Amparo may need help, Megan thought. She started towards the living room, then stopped.

A voice was saying, 'Jaime just left. He will be alone on a bench in the main plaza. Your men should have no trouble picking him up.'

Megan stood there, frozen.

'He's walking, so it should take him about fifteen minutes to get there.'

Megan listened with growing horror.

'Remember our deal, Colonel,' Amparo said into the telephone. 'You promised not to kill him.'

Megan backed into the hallway. Her mind was in a turmoil. So Amparo was the traitor And she had sent Jaime into a trap.

Backing away quietly, so Amparo would not hear her, Megan turned and ran out the back door. She had no idea how she was going to help Jaime. She knew only that she had to do something. She stepped outside the gate and started down the street, moving as fast as she could without attracting attention, heading towards the centre of the town.

'Please, God. Let me be on time,' Megan prayed.

The walk to the town square was a pleasant one, with side streets shaded by towering trees, but Jaime was unaware of his surroundings. He was thinking about Felix. He had been like a brother to Felix, had given him his full trust. What had turned Felix into a traitor willing to put all their lives in jeopardy? Perhaps Paco's messenger would have the answer. *Why couldn't Paco have discussed it on the telephone?* Jaime wondered.

Jaime was approaching the town square. In the middle of the plaza was a fountain and shady trees with benches scattered around. Children were playing games. A couple of old men were playing *boule*. Half a dozen men were seated on park benches, enjoying the sunshine, reading, dozing, or feeding the pigeons. Jaime crossed the street, slowly moving along the path, and took a seat on one of the benches. He looked at his watch just as the tower clock began chiming noon. Paco's man should be coming.

Out of the corner of his eye, Jaime saw a police car pull up at the far end of the square. He looked in the other direction. A second police car arrived. Officers were getting out, moving towards the park. His heart began to beat faster. It was a trap. But who had set it? Was it Paco, who sent the message, or Amparo who delivered it? She had sent him to the park. But why? Why?

There was no time to worry about that now. He had to escape. But Jaime knew that the moment he tried to make a run for it, they would shoot him down. He could try to bluff it out, but they knew he was there.

Think of something. Fast!

A street away, Megan was hurrying towards the park. As it came into view, she took in the scene at a glance. She saw Jaime seated on a bench, and the policemen closing in on the park from both sides.

Megan's mind was racing. There was no way for Jaime to escape.

Megan was walking past a *groceria*. Ahead of her, blocking her path, a mother was pushing a pram. The woman stopped, set the pram against the wall of the shop and went inside to make a purchase. Without a moment's hesitation, Megan grabbed the handle of the pram and moved across the street into the park.

306

The police were walking along the benches now, questioning the men seated there. Megan elbowed her way past a policeman and went up to Jaime, pushing the pram ahead of her.

She yelled, '¡*Madre de Dios!* There you are, Manuel! I've been looking everywhere for you. I've had enough! You promised to paint the house this morning, and here you are sitting in the park like some millionaire. Mother was right. You're a good-for-nothing bum. I never should have married you in the first place!'

It took Jaime less than a fraction of a second. He got to his feet. 'Your mother is an expert on bums. She married one. If she –'

'Who are you to talk? If it wasn't for my mother, our baby would starve to death. You certainly don't bring any bread into the house . . .'

The policemen had stopped, taking in the argument.

'If that one was my wife,' one of them muttered, 'I'd send her back to her mother.'

'I'm damned tired of your nagging, woman,' Jaime roared. 'I've warned you before. When we get home, I'm going to teach you a lesson.'

'Good for him,' one of the policemen said.

Jaime and Megan noisily quarrelled their way out of the park, pushing the pram before them. The policemen turned their attention back to the men seated on the benches.

'Identification, please?'

'What's the problem, officer?'

'Never mind. Just show me your papers.'

All over the park, men were pulling out wallets and extracting bits of paper to prove who they were. In the midst of this, a baby began to cry. One of the policemen looked up. The pram had been abandoned at the corner. The quarrelling couple had vanished.

Thirty minutes later, Megan walked in at the front door of the house. Amparo was nervously pacing up and down.

307

'Where have you been?' Amparo demanded. 'You shouldn't have left the house without telling me.'

'I had to go out to take care of something.'

'What?' Amparo asked suspiciously. 'You don't know anyone here. If you –'

Jaime walked in through the door. The blood drained from her face. She quickly regained her composure.

'What – what happened?' Amparo asked. 'Didn't you go to the park?'

Jaime said quietly, 'Why, Amparo?'

And she looked into his eyes and she knew it was over.

'What made you change?'

She shook her head. 'I haven't changed. You have. I've lost everyone I loved in this stupid war you're fighting. I'm sick of all the bloodshed. Can you stand hearing the truth about yourself, Jaime? You're as bad as the government you're fighting. Worse, because they're willing to make peace, and you're not. You think you're helping our country? You're destroying it. You rob banks and blow up cars and murder innocent people, and you think you're a hero. I loved you, and I believed in you once, but –' Her voice broke. 'This bloodshed has to end.'

Jaime walked up to her, and his eyes were ice 'I should kill you.'

'No,' Megan gasped. 'Please! You can't.'

Felix had come into the room and was listening to the conversation. 'Jesus Christ! So she's the one. What do we do with the bitch?'

Jaime said, 'We'll have to take her with us and keep an eye on her.' He took Amparo by the shoulders and said softly, 'If you try one more trick, I promise you you'll die.' He shoved her away and turned to Megan and Felix. 'Let's get out of here before her friends arrive.'

Chapter 35

'You had Miró in your hands and you let him escape?'

'Colonel – with all due respect – my men –'

'Your men are assholes. You call yourselves policemen? You're a disgrace to your uniforms.'

The chief of police stood there, cringing under the withering scorn of Colonel Acoca. There was nothing else he could do, for the Colonel was powerful enough to have his head. And Acoca was not yet through with him.

'I hold you personally responsible. I'll see that you're relieved from duty.'

'Colonel –'

'Get out. You make me sick to my stomach.'

Colonel Acoca was boiling with frustration. There had not been enough time for him to reach Vitoria and catch Jaime Miró. He had had to entrust that to the local police. And they had bungled it. God alone knew where Miró had gone to now.

Colonel Acoca went to the map spread out on a table in front of him. *They will be staying in Basque country, of course. That could be Burgos or Logroño or Bilbao or San Sebastian. I'll concentrate on the north-east. They'll have to surface somewhere.*

He recalled his conversation with the Prime Minister that morning.

'Your time is running out, Colonel. Have you read the morning papers? The world press is making us look like clowns. Miró and those nuns have made us a laughingstock.'

'Prime Minister, you have my assurance –'

309

'King Juan Carlos has ordered me to set up an official inquiry board into the whole matter. I can't hold it off any longer.'

'Delay the inquiry for just a few more days. I'll have Miró and the nuns by then.'

There was a pause. 'Forty-eight hours.'

It was not the Prime Minister whom Colonel Acoca was afraid of disappointing, nor was it the King. It was the OPUS MUNDO. When he had been summoned to the panelled office of one of Spain's leading industrialists, his orders had been explicit: 'Jaime Miró is creating an atmosphere harmful to our organization. Stop him. You will be well rewarded.'

And Colonel Acoca knew what the unspoken part of the conversation was: *Fail and you will be punished.* Now his career was in jeopardy. And all because some stupid policemen had let Miró walk away under their noses. Jaime Miró might hide anywhere. But the nuns . . . A wave of excitement coursed through Colonel Acoca. The nuns! They were the key. Jaime Miró might hide anywhere, but the sisters could find sanctuary only in another convent. And it would almost certainly be in a convent of the same order.

Colonel Acoca turned to study the map again. And there it was: *Mendavia.* There was a convent of the Cistercian order at Mendavia. *That's where they're headed,* Acoca thought triumphantly. *Well, so am I.*

Only I'll be there first, waiting for them.

The journey for Ricardo and Graciela was coming to an end.

The last few days had been the happiest that Ricardo had ever known. He was being hunted by the military and the police, his capture meant certain death, and yet none of that seemed to matter. It was as though he and Graciela had carved out an island in time, a paradise where nothing could touch them. They had turned their desperate journey into a wonderful adventure that they shared together.

They talked endlessly, exploring and explaining, and their words were tendrils that drew them even closer together.

They spoke of the past, the present, and the future. Particularly the future.

'We'll be married in church,' Ricardo said. 'You'll be the most beautiful bride in the world . . .'

And Graciela could visualize the scene and was thrilled by it.

'And we'll live in the most beautiful house . . .'

And she thought: *I've never had a house of my own, or a real room of my own.*

There was the little casa she shared with her mother and all the uncles, and then the convent cell, living with the sisters.

'And we'll have handsome sons and beautiful daughters . . .'

And I will give them all the things I never had. They will be so loved.

And Graciela's heart soared.

There was one thing troubling her. Ricardo was a soldier fighting for a cause he passionately believed in. Would he be contented living in France, withdrawing from the battle? She knew she had to discuss it with him.

Ricardo – how much longer do you think this revolution is going to go on?

It was a question she had not asked.

It's already gone on too long, Ricardo thought. The government had made peace overtures, but ETA had rejected them. It had done worse than reject them. It had responded to the offers with a series of increased terrorist attacks. Ricardo had tried to discuss it with Jaime.

'They're willing to compromise, Jaime. Shouldn't we meet them half way?'

'Their offer is a trick – they want to destroy us. They're forcing us to go on fighting.'

And because Ricardo loved Jaime and believed in him, he continued to support him. But the doubts refused to die. And as the bloodshed increased, so did his uncertainty. And now Graciela was asking, *How much longer do you think this revolution is going to go on?*

'I don't know,' Ricardo told her. 'I wish it were over. But I will tell you this, my darling. Nothing will ever come between us – not even a war. There will never be words enough to tell you how much I love you.'

And they went on dreaming.

They travelled during the night, making their way through the fertile, green countryside, past El Burgo and Soria. At dawn, from the top of a hill, they saw Logroño in the far distance. To the left of the road was a stand of pine trees and beyond that a forest of electric power lines. Graciela and Ricardo followed the winding road down to the outskirts of the bustling city.

'Where are we going to meet the others?' Graciela asked.

Ricardo pointed to a poster on a building they were passing. It read:

CIRQUE JAPON!
THE WORLD'S MOST SENSATIONAL CIRCUS FRESH FROM JAPAN!
24 JULY FOR ONE WEEK
AVENIDA CLUB DE PORTIVO

'There,' Ricardo told her. 'We'll meet them there this afternoon.'

In another part of the city, Megan, Jaime, Amparo and Felix were also looking at a circus poster. There was a feeling of enormous tension in the group. Amparo was never out of their sight. Ever since the incident at Vitoria, the men treated Amparo as an outcast, ignoring her most of the time and speaking to her only when necessary.

Jaime looked at his watch. 'The circus should be starting,' he said. 'Let's go.'

At police headquarters in Logroño, Colonel Ramon Acoca was finalizing his plans.

'Are the men deployed around the convent?'

'Yes, Colonel. Everything is in place.'

'Excellent.'

Acoca was in an expansive mood. The trap he had set was foolproof, and there would be no bungling policemen to spoil his plans this time. He was personally conducting the operation. The OPUS MUNDO was going to be proud of him. He went over the details with his officers once again.

'The nuns are travelling with Miró and his men. It's important that we catch them *before* they walk into the convent. We'll be spread out in the woods around it. Don't move until I give the signal to close in.'

'What are our orders if Jaime Miró resists?'

Acoca said softly, 'I hope he does try to resist.'

An orderly came into the room. 'Excuse me, Colonel. There is an American here who would like to speak to you.'

'I have no time now.'

'Yes, sir.' The orderly hesitated. 'He says it's about one of the nuns.'

'Oh? An American, did you say?'

'Yes, Colonel.'

'Send him in.'

A moment later, Alan Tucker was ushered in.

'I'm sorry to disturb you, Colonel. I'm Alan Tucker. I'm hoping you can help me.'

'Yes? How, Mr Tucker?'

'I understand that you're looking for one of the nuns from the Abbey Cistercian – a Sister Megan.'

The Colonel sat back in his chair, studying the American. 'How does that concern you?'

'I'm looking for her too. It's very important that I find her.'

Interesting, Colonel Acoca thought. *Why is it so important for this American to find a nun?* 'You have no idea where she is?'

'No. The newspapers –'

The goddamn press again. 'Perhaps you could tell me why you are looking for her.'

313

'I'm afraid I can't discuss that.'

'Then I'm afraid I can't help you.'

'Colonel – could you let me know if you find her?'

Acoca gave him a thin smile. 'You'll know.'

The whole country was following the hegira of the nuns. The press had reported the narrow escape of Jaime Miró and one of the nuns in Vitoria.

So they're heading north, Alan Tucker thought. *Their best bet to get out of the country is probably San Sebastian. I've got to get hold of her.* He sensed that he was in trouble with Ellen Scott. *I handled that badly*, he thought. *I can make up for it by bringing her Megan.*

He placed a call to Ellen Scott.

The Cirque Japon was held in Logroño's outlying district of Guanos, in a huge tent, and ten minutes before the circus was due to begin, the tent was filled to capacity. Megan, Jaime, Amparo and Felix made their way down the crowded aisle to their reserved seats. There were two empty seats next to Jaime.

He stared at them and said, 'Something's wrong. Ricardo and Sister Graciela were supposed to be here.' He turned to Amparo. 'Did you –?'

'No. I swear it. I know nothing about it.'

The lights dimmed and the show began. There was a roar from the crowd, and they turned to look at the arena. A bicycle rider was circling the ring, and as he pedalled an acrobat leaped onto his shoulder. Then, one by one, a swarm of other performers jumped on, clinging to the front and back and sides of the bicycle until it was invisible. The audience cheered.

A trained bear act was on next, and then a tightrope walker. The audience was enjoying the show tremendously, but Jaime and the others were too nervous to pay any attention. Time was running out.

'We'll wait another fifteen minutes, Jaime decided. 'If they're not here by then –'

A voice said, 'Excuse me – are these seats taken?'

Jaime looked up to see Ricardo and Graciela, and grinned. 'No. Please sit down.' And then, in a relieved whisper, 'I'm damned glad to see you.'

Ricardo nodded at Megan and Amparo and Felix. He looked around. 'Where are the others?'

'Haven't you seen the newspapers?'

'Newspapers? No. We've been in the mountains.'

'I have bad news,' Jaime said. 'Rubio is in a prison hospital.'

Ricardo stared at him. 'How –?'

'He was stabbed in a bar fight. The police picked him up.'

'*Mierda!*' Ricardo was silent a moment, then sighed. 'We'll just have to get him out, won't we?'

'That's my plan,' Jaime agreed.

'Where's Sister Lucia?' Graciela asked. 'And Sister Teresa?'

It was Megan who answered. 'Sister Lucia has been arrested. She was – she was wanted for murder. Sister Teresa is dead.'

Graciela crossed herself. 'Oh, my Lord.'

In the arena a clown was walking a tightrope, carrying a poodle under each arm, and two Siamese cats in his capacious pockets. As the dogs tried to reach the cats, the wire swayed wildly and the clown pretended to be fighting to keep his balance. The audience was roaring. It was difficult to hear anything over the noise of the crowd. Megan and Graciela had so much to tell each other. Almost simultaneously, they began to talk in the sign language of the convent. The two men looked on in astonishment.

Ricardo and I are going to marry . . .

That's wonderful . . .

What has been happening to you?

Megan started to reply and realized there were no signs to convey the things she wanted to say. It would have to wait.

315

'Let's move,' Jaime said. 'There's a van outside waiting to take us to Mendavia. We'll drop the sisters off there and be on our way.'

They started up the aisle, Jaime holding Amparo's arm.

When they were outside in the car-park, Ricardo said, 'Jaime, Graciela and I are getting married.'

A grin lit up Jaime's face. 'That's wonderful! Congratulations.' He turned to Graciela. 'You couldn't have picked a better man.'

Megan put her arms around Graciela. 'I'm very happy for you both.'

And she thought: *Was it easy for her to make the decision to leave the convent? Am I wondering about Graciela? Or am I wondering about myself?*

Colonel Acoca was receiving an excited report from an aide.

'They were seen at the circus less than an hour ago. By the time we could bring up reinforcements, they had gone. They left in a blue and white van. You were right, Colonel. They are headed for Mendavia.'

So it's finally over, Colonel Acoca thought. The chase had been an exciting one, and he had to admit that Jaime Miró had been a worthy opponent. *The OPUS MUNDO will have even bigger plans for me now.*

Through a pair of high-powered Zeiss binoculars, Colonel Acoca watched the blue and white van appear over the crest of a hill and head for the convent below. Heavily armed troops were hidden among the trees along both sides of the road and around the convent itself. There was no way that anyone could escape.

As the van approached the entrance to the convent and braked to a stop, Colonel Acoca barked into his walkie-talkie, 'Close in! Now!'

The manoeuvre was executed perfectly. Two squads of soldiers armed with automatic weapons swung into position, blocking the road and surrounding the van. Colonel Acoca stood watching the scene for an instant, savouring his moment of glory. Then he slowly approached the van, gun in hand.

'You're surrounded,' he called out. 'You haven't got a chance. Come out with your hands up. One at a time. If you try to resist, you'll all die.'

There was a long moment of silence, and then the van door slowly opened and three men and three women emerged, trembling, their hands raised high above their heads.

They were strangers.

Chapter 36

High on a hill above the convent, Jaime and the others observed Acoca and his men move in on the van. They saw the terrified passengers get out, hands raised, and watched the scene played out in pantomime.

Jaime Miró could almost hear the dialogue:

Who are you?

We work at a hotel outside Logroño.

What are you doing here?

A man gave us five thousand pesetas to deliver this van to the convent.

What man?

I don't know. I never saw him before.

Is this his picture?

Yes. That's him.

'Let's get out of here,' Jaime said.

They were in a white station wagon, heading back to Logroño. Megan was looking at Jaime in wonder.

'How did you know?'

'That Colonel Acoca would be waiting for us at the convent? He told me.'

'*What?*'

'The fox has to think like the hunter, Megan. I put myself in Acoca's place. Where would he set a trap for me? He did exactly what I would have done.'

'And if he had not shown up?'

'Then it would have been safe to take you into the convent.'

'What happens now?' Felix asked.

It was the question uppermost in all their minds.

'Spain isn't safe for any of us for a while,' Jaime decided. 'We'll head directly for San Sebastian and into France.' He looked at Megan. 'There are Cistercian convents there.'

It was more than Amparo could bear.

'Why don't you give yourself up? If you keep on this way, there will be more blood spilled and more lives taken –'

'You've lost the right to speak,' Jaime said curtly. 'Just be grateful you're still alive.' He turned to Megan. 'There are ten mountain passes across the Pyrenees leading from San Sebastian to France. We'll cross there.'

'It's too dangerous,' Felix objected. 'Acoca's going to be looking for us in San Sebastian. He'll be expecting us to cross the border into France.'

'If it's that dangerous –' Graciela began.

'Don't worry,' Jaime assured her. 'San Sebastian is Basque country.'

The station wagon was approaching the outskirts of Logroño again.

'All the roads to San Sebastian will be watched,' Felix warned. 'How do you plan for us to get there?'

Jaime had already decided. 'We'll take the train.'

'The soldiers will be searching the trains,' Ricardo objected.

Jaime gave Amparo a thoughtful look. 'No. I don't think so. Our friend here is going to help us. Do you know how to reach Colonel Acoca?'

She hesitated. 'Yes.'

'Good. You're going to call him.'

They stopped at one of the telephone booths along the highway. Jaime followed Amparo into the booth and closed the door. He was holding a pistol to her side.

'You know what to say?'

'Yes.'

He watched her dial a number, and when a voice answered, she said, 'This is Amparo Jiron. Colonel Acoca is expecting

319

my call . . . Thank you.' She looked up at Jaime. 'They're putting me through.' The gun was pressing against her. 'Do you have to –?'

'Just do as you were told.' His voice was ice.

A moment later, Jaime heard Acoca's voice come over the phone. 'Where are you?'

The gun pressed against her harder. 'I – I'm – we're just leaving Logroño.'

'Do you know where our friends are going?'

'Yes.'

Jaime's face was inches from her, his eyes hard.

'They've decided to reverse themselves to throw you off. They're on their way to Barcelona. He's driving a white Seat. He'll be taking the main highway.'

Jaime nodded at her.

'I – I have to go now. The car is here.'

Jaime pressed down the receiver. 'Very good. Let's go. We'll give him half an hour to call off his men here.'

Thirty minutes later they were at the railway station.

There were three classes of trains from Logroño to San Sebastian: the *Talgo* was the luxury train; the second class train was the *Ter;* and the worst and cheapest trains, uncomfortable and dirty, were misnamed the *expresos*, which stopped at every little station from Logroño to San Sebastian.

Jaime said, 'We'll take the *expreso*. By now all of Acoca's men will be busy stopping every white Seat on the road to Barcelona. We'll buy our tickets separately and meet in the last compartment of the train.' Jaime turned to Amparo. 'You go first. I'll be right behind you.'

And she knew why, and hated him for it. If Colonel Acoca had set a trap, she would be the bait. Well, she was Amparo Jiron. She would not flinch.

She walked into the station while Jaime and the others watched. There were no soldiers.

They're all out covering the highway to Barcelona. It's going to be a madhouse, Jaime thought wryly. *Every other car is a white Seat.*

One by one the group purchased their tickets and headed for the train. They boarded without incident. Jaime took the seat next to Megan. Amparo sat in front of them, next to Felix. Across the way Ricardo and Graciela sat together.

Jaime said to Megan, 'We'll reach San Sebastian in three hours. We'll spend the night there and in the early morning we'll cross over into France.'

'And after we get to France?'

She was thinking of what would happen to Jaime, but when he replied, he said, 'Don't worry. There's a Cistercian convent just a few hours across the border.' He hesitated. 'If that's what you still want.'

So he had understood her doubts. *Is that what I want?* They were coming to more than a border that divided two countries. This border would divide her old life from her future life . . . which would be . . . what? She had been desperate to return to a convent, but now she was filled with doubts. She had forgotten how exciting the world outside the walls could be. *I've never felt so alive.* Megan looked over at Jaime and admitted to herself: *And Jaime Miró is a part of it.*

He caught her glance and looked into her eyes, and Megan thought: *He knows it.*

The *expreso* stopped at every hamlet and village along the track. The train was packed with farmers and their wives, merchants and salesmen, and at each stop passengers noisily embarked and disembarked.

The *expreso* made its way slowly through the mountains, fighting the steep gradients.

When the train finally pulled into the station in San Sebastian, Jaime said to Megan, 'The danger is over. This is our city. I've arranged for a car to be here for us.'

A large sedan was waiting in front of the station. A driver wearing a *chapella*, the big, wide-brimmed beret of the

321

Basques, greeted Jaime with warm hugs, and the group got into the car.

Megan noticed that Jaime stayed close to Amparo, ready to grab her if she tried to make a move. *What's he going to do with her?* Megan wondered.

'We were worried about you, Jaime,' the driver said. 'According to the press, Colonel Acoca is conducting a big hunt for you.'

Jaime laughed. 'Let him keep hunting, Gil. I am out of season.'

They drove down the Avenida Sancho el Savio, towards the beach. It was a cloudless summer day and the streets were crowded with strolling couples bent on pleasure, and the harbour was alive with yachts and smaller craft. The distant mountains formed a picturesque backdrop for the city. Everything seemed so peaceful.

'What are the arrangements?' Jaime asked the driver.

'The Hotel Niza. Largo Cortez is waiting for you.'

'It will be good to see the old pirate again.'

The Niza was a medium class hotel in the Plaza Juan de Olezabal, off San Martin Street on the corner of a busy square. It was a white building with brown shutters and a big blue sign on the top of the roof. The rear of the hotel backed on to a beach.

When the car pulled up in front of the hotel, the group got out and followed Jaime into the lobby.

Largo Cortez, the hotel owner, ran up to greet them. He was a large man. He had only one arm as the result of a daring exploit, and he moved awkwardly, as though off-balance.

'Welcome,' he beamed. 'I have been expecting you for a week now.'

Jaime shrugged. 'We had a few delays, *amigo*.'

Largo Cortez grinned. 'I read about them. The papers are full of nothing else.' He turned to look at Megan and Graciela. 'Everyone is supporting you, Sisters. I have your rooms all prepared.'

'We'll be staying overnight,' Jaime told him. 'We'll leave first thing in the morning and cross into France. I want a good guide who knows all the passes – either Cabrera Infante or José Cebrian.'

'I will arrange it,' the hotel owner assured him. 'There will be six of you?'

Jaime glanced at Amparo. 'Five.'

Amparo looked away.

'I suggest that none of you registers,' Cortez said. 'What the police don't know won't hurt them. Why don't you let me take you to your rooms, where you can refresh yourselves? Then we'll have a magnificent supper.'

'Amparo and I are going to the bar to have a drink,' Jaime said. 'We'll join you later.'

Largo Cortez nodded. 'As you wish, Jaime.'

Megan was watching Jaime, puzzled. She wondered what he planned to do with Amparo. Was he going to cold-bloodedly –? She could not bear even to think about it.

Amparo was wondering, too, but she was too proud to ask.

Jaime led her into the bar at the far end of the lobby and took a table in the corner.

When the waiter approached them, Jaime said, 'A glass of wine, *por favor*.'

'One?'

'One.'

Amparo watched as Jaime took out a small packet and opened it. It contained a fine, powdery substance.

'Jaime –' There was desperation in Amparo's voice. 'Please listen to me! Try to understand why I did what I did. You're tearing the country apart. Your cause is hopeless. You must stop this insanity.'

The waiter reappeared and set a glass of wine on the table. When he walked away, Jaime carefully poured the contents of the packet into the glass and stirred it. He pushed the glass in front of Amparo.

'Drink it.'

'No!'

323

'Not many of us are privileged to choose the way we die,' Jaime said quietly. 'This way will be quick and painless. If I turn you over to my people, I can't make any such promise.'

'Jaime – I loved you once. You must believe me. Please –'

'Drink it.' His voice was implacable.

Amparo looked at him for a long moment, then picked up the glass. 'I'll drink to your death.'

He watched as Amparo put the glass to her lips and swallowed the wine in one gulp.

She shuddered. 'What happens now?'

'I'll help you upstairs. I'll put you to bed. You'll sleep.'

Amparo's eyes filled with tears. 'You're a fool,' she whispered. 'Jaime – I'm dying, and I tell you that I loved you so –' Her words were beginning to slur.

Jaime rose and helped Amparo to her feet. She stood up, unsteady. The room seemed to be rocking.

'Jaime –'

He guided her out of the door and into the lobby, holding her up. Largo Cortez was waiting for him with a key.

'I'll take her to her room,' Jaime said. 'See that she's not disturbed.'

'Right.'

Cortez watched as Jaime half-carried Amparo up the stairs.

In her room, Megan was thinking how strange it felt to be by herself in a hotel in a resort town. San Sebastian was filled with people on holiday, honeymooners, lovers enjoying themselves in a hundred other hotel rooms.

But what had Jaime done to Amparo? Could he possibly have . . . but no, he could never have done that. Or could he?

And suddenly Megan wished Jaime were there with her, and wondered what it would be like to have him making love to her. All the feelings that she had been suppressing for so

324

long came flooding into her mind in a wild torrent of emotions. *I want him*, she thought. *Oh, Lord, what's happening to me? What can I do?*

Ricardo was whistling as he dressed. He was in a wonderful mood. *I'm the luckiest man in the world*, he thought. *We'll be married in France. There's a beautiful church across the border in Bayonne. Tomorrow* . . .

In her room, Graciela was taking a bath, luxuriating in the warm water, thinking of Ricardo. She smiled to herself and thought: *I'm going to make him so happy. Thank you, God.*

Felix Carpio was thinking about Jaime and Megan. *A blind man can see the electricity between them*, he thought. *It is going to bring bad luck. Nuns belong to God. It's bad enough that Ricardo has taken Sister Graciela from her calling.* But Jaime had always been reckless. What was he going to do about this one?

The five of them met for supper in the hotel dining room. No one mentioned Amparo.

Looking at Jaime, Megan felt suddenly embarrassed, as though he could read her mind. *It's better not to ask questions*, she decided. I know he could never do anything brutal.

They found that Largo Cortez had not exaggerated about the supper. The meal began with *gazpacho*, the thick, cold soup made from tomatoes, cucumbers and water-soaked bread, followed by a salad of fresh greens, a huge dish of *paella* – rice, shrimp, chicken and beef in a wonderful sauce, and ended with a delicious flan. It was the first hot meal Ricardo and Graciela had had in a long time.

When the meal was over, Megan rose. 'I should be getting to bed.'

'Wait,' Jaime said. 'I've got to talk to you.' He escorted her to a deserted corner of the lobby. 'About tomorrow . . .'

'Yes?'

And she knew what he was going to ask. What she did not know was what *she* was going to answer. *I've changed*, Megan thought. *I was so sure about my life before. I believed I had everything I wanted.*

And Jaime was saying, 'You don't really want to go back to a convent, do you?'

Do I?

He was waiting for an answer.

I have to be honest with him, Megan thought. She looked into his eyes and said, 'I don't know what I want, Jaime. I'm confused.'

Jaime smiled. He hesitated, choosing his words carefully. 'Megan – this fight will be over soon. We'll get what we want because the people are behind us. I can't ask you to share the danger with me now, but I would like you to wait for me. I have many Basque friends living in France. You would be safe with them.'

Megan looked at him a long time before she answered. 'Jaime – give me time to think about it.'

'Then you're not saying no?'

Megan said quietly, 'I'm not saying no.'

None of the group slept that night. They had too much to think about, too many conflicts to resolve. Megan stayed awake, reliving the past. The years in the orphanage, and the sanctuary of the convent . . . The sudden expulsion into a world she had given up for ever. Jaime Miró was risking his life fighting for what he believed in. *And what do I believe in?* Megan asked herself. *How do I want to spend the rest of my life?*

She had made a choice once. Now she was forced to choose again. She would have to have an answer by morning.

*

Graciela was thinking about the convent, too. *They were such happy, peaceful years. I felt so close to God. Will I miss that?*

Jaime was thinking about Megan. *She mustn't go back. I want her at my side. What will her answer be?*

Ricardo was too excited to sleep, busily making plans for the wedding. The church at Bayonne . . .

Felix was wondering how to dispose of Amparo's body. *Let Largo Cortez take care of it.*

Early the following morning, the group met in the lobby. Jaime approached Megan.

'Good morning.'

'Good morning.'

'Have you thought about our conversation?'

She had thought of nothing else all night. 'Yes, Jaime.'

He looked into her eyes, trying to read the answer there. 'Will you wait for me?

'Jaime –'

At that moment Largo Cortez hurried up to them. With him was a leathery-looking man in his fifties.

'I'm afraid there won't be any time for breakfast,' Cortez said. 'You should be leaving. This is José Cebrian, your guide. He will take you across the mountains into France. He's the best guide in San Sebastian.'

'I'm glad to see you, José,' Jaime said. 'What's your plan?'

'We're going to take the first part of the journey by foot,' José Cebrian told the group. 'On the other side of the border, I've arranged for cars to be waiting for us. We should hurry. Come along, please '

The group moved out into the street, painted yellow by the rays of the bright sun.

Largo Cortez came out of the hotel to see them off. 'Safe journey,' he said.

'Thank you for everything,' Jaime replied. 'We'll be back, *amigo*. Sooner than you think.'

'We go this way,' José Cebrian ordered.

The group started to turn towards the square. And at that moment, soldiers and members of the GOE suddenly materialized at both ends of the street, sealing it off. There were at least a dozen of them, all heavily armed. Colonel Ramón Acoca and Colonel Fal Sostelo were leading them.

Jaime glanced quickly towards the beach, looking for an escape route. Another dozen soldiers were approaching from there. There was no escape. They would have to fight. Jaime instinctively reached for his gun.

Colonel Acoca called out, 'Don't even think about it, Miro, or we'll shoot all of you down where you're standing.'

Jaime's mind was racing furiously, looking for a way out. How had Acoca known where to find him? Jaime turned and saw Amparo standing in the doorway, a look of profound sorrow on her face.

Felix said, 'What the bloody hell! I thought you –'

'I gave her sleeping pills. They should have knocked her out until we got across the border.'

'The bitch!'

Colonel Acoca walked towards Jaime. 'It's over.' He turned to one of his men. 'Disarm them.'

Felix and Ricardo were looking towards Jaime for guidance, ready to follow his lead. Jaime shook his head. Reluctantly, he handed over his gun, and Felix and Ricardo followed suit.

'What are you going to do with us?' Jaime asked.

Several passersby stopped to watch the proceedings.

Colonel Acoca's voice was curt. 'I'm taking you and your gang of murderers back to Madrid. We'll give you a fair military trial and then hang you. If I had my way, I'd hang you here, now.'

'Let the sisters go,' Jaime said. 'They had nothing to do with this.'

'They're accomplices. They're as guilty as you are.'

Colonel Acoca turned and gave a signal. The soldiers motioned to the onlookers to move aside to let three army trucks drive up.

'You and your assassins will travel in the middle truck,' the Colonel informed Jaime. 'My men will be in front of you and at the back of you. If any of you makes one false move, they have orders to kill all of you. Do you understand?'

Jaime nodded.

Colonel Acoca spat into Jaime's face. 'Good. Into the truck.'

There was an angry murmur from the growing crowd.

Amparo watched impassively from the doorway as Jaime and Megan, Graciela and Ricardo and Felix climbed into the truck, surrounded by soldiers with automatic weapons.

Colonel Fal Sostelo walked up to the driver of the first truck. 'We'll head straight for Madrid. No stops along the way.'

'Yes, Colonel.'

By now, many people had gathered in the street to watch what was happening. Colonel Acoca started to climb into the first truck. He called out to those in front of the truck, 'Clear the way.'

From the side streets more people began to emerge.

'Move along,' Colonel Acoca called. 'Out of the way.'

And still they came, the men wearing the wide Basque *chapellas*. It was as though they were responding to some invisible signal. *Jaime Miró is in trouble.* They came from shops and homes. Housewives dropped what they were doing and moved out into the street. Shopkeepers about to open for business heard the news and hurried on to the hotel. And still they came. Artists and plumbers and doctors, mechanics and salesmen and students, many carrying shotguns and rifles. They were Basques, and this was their homeland. It started with a few, and then a hundred, and within minutes it had swollen to more than a thousand, filling the pavements and streets, completely surrounding the army trucks. They were ominously silent.

Colonel Acoca observed the huge crowd in desperation. He screamed, 'Everybody get out of the way or we'll start shooting.'

Jaime called out, 'I wouldn't advise it. These people hate you for what you're trying to do to them. A word from me and they'll tear you and your men to pieces. There's one thing you forgot, Colonel. San Sebastian is a Basque town. It's my town.' He turned to his group. 'Let's get out of here.'

Jaime helped Megan down from the truck, and the others followed. Colonel Acoca watched helplessly, his face tight with fury.

The crowd was waiting, hostile and silent. Jaime walked up to the Colonel. 'Take your trucks and get back to Madrid.'

Acoca looked around at the still growing mob. 'I – you won't get away with this, Miró.'

'I have got away with it. Now get out of here.' He spat in Acoca's face.

The Colonel stared at him for a long, murderous moment. *It can't end this way*, he thought desperately. *I was so close. It was checkmate*. But he knew that it was worse than a defeat for him. It was a death sentence. The OPUS MUNDO would be waiting for him in Madrid. He looked at the sea of people surrounding him. He had no choice.

He turned to his driver, and his voice was choked with fury. 'We're moving out.'

The crowd stepped back, watching as the soldiers climbed into the trucks. A moment later, the trucks began rolling down the street, and the crowd began to cheer wildly. It started out as a cheer for Jaime Miró, and it grew louder and louder, and they were cheering for their freedom and their fight against tyranny, and their coming victory, and the streets reverberated with the noise of their celebration.

Two teenagers were screaming themselves hoarse. One turned to the other. 'Let's join ETA.'

An elderly couple held each other, and the woman said, 'Now maybe they'll give us back our farm.'

An old man stood alone in the crowd, silently watching the army trucks leave. When he spoke, he said, 'They'll be back one day.'

Jaime took Megan's hand and said, 'It's over. We're free. We'll be across the border in an hour. I'll take you to my aunt.'

She looked into his eyes. 'Jaime –'

A man pushed his way towards them through the crowd and hurried up to Megan.

'Excuse me,' he said breathlessly. 'Are you Sister Megan?'

She turned to him, puzzled. 'Yes.'

He breathed a sigh of relief. 'I've had quite a time finding you. My name is Alan Tucker. I wonder if I could speak to you for a moment?'

'Yes.'

'Alone.'

'I'm sorry. I'm just leaving for –'

'Please. This is very important. I've come all the way from New York to find you.'

She looked at him, puzzled. 'To find me? I don't understand. Why –?'

'I'll explain it to you, if you'll give me a moment.'

The stranger took her arm and walked her down the street, talking rapidly. Megan glanced back once at where Jaime Miró was standing, waiting for her.

Megan's conversation with Alan Tucker turned her world upside down.

'The woman I represent would like to see you.'

'I don't understand. What woman? What does she want with me?'

I wish I knew the answer to that, Alan Tucker thought. 'I'm not at liberty to discuss that. She's waiting for you in New York.'

It made no sense. There must be some mistake. 'Are you sure you have the right person – Sister Megan?'

'Yes. But your name isn't Megan. It's Patricia.'

And in a sudden, blinding flash, Megan knew. After all these years, her fantasy was about to come true. She was finally going to learn who she was. The very idea of it was thrilling . . . and terrifying.

'When – when would I have to leave? Her throat was suddenly so dry that she could barely speak the words.

I want you to find out where she is and bring her back as quickly as possible.

'Right away. I'll arrange a passport for you.'

She turned and saw Jaime standing in front of the hotel, waiting.

'Excuse me a moment.'

Megan walked back to him in a daze, and she felt as though she were living a dream.

'Are you all right?' Jaime asked. 'Is that man bothering you?'

'No. He's – no.'

Jaime took Megan's hand. 'I want you to come with me now. We belong together, Megan.'

Your name isn't Megan. It's Patricia.

And she looked at Jaime's strong, handsome face, and she thought: *I want us to be together. But we'll have to wait. First I have to find out who I am.*

'Jaime – I want to be with you. But there is something I have to do first.'

He studied her, his face troubled. 'You're going to leave?'

'For a little while. But I'll be back.'

He looked at her for a long time, then slowly nodded. 'All right. You can reach me through Largo Cortez.'

'I'll come back to you. I promise.'

And she meant it. But that was before the meeting with Ellen Scott.

Chapter 37

'*Deus Israel vos; et ipse sit vobiscum, qui, misertus est duobus unicis plenius benedis cere . . .* The God of Israel joins you together, and He be with you and now, Lord, make them bless Thee more fully. Blessed are all they that love the Lord, that walk in His ways. Glory . . .'

Ricardo looked away from the priest and glanced at Graciela standing at his side. *I was right. She is the most beautiful bride in the world.*

Graciela was still, listening to the words of the priest echoing through the cavernous, vaulted church. There was such a sense of peace in the church. It seemed to Graciela to be filled with the ghosts of the past, all the thousands of people who had come here generation after generation, to find forgiveness and fulfilment and joy. It reminded her so much of the convent. *I feel as though I've come home again,* Graciela thought. *As though I belong.*

'*Exaudi nos, omni potens et misericors deus; ut quod nostro ministratur officio tua benedictione potius impleatua per dominum . . .* Hear us, Almighty and merciful God, that what is done by our ministry may be abundantly fulfilled with Thy blessing . . .'

He has blessed me, more than I deserve. Let me be worthy of Him.

'*In te sperav, domine: Dixi: Tues deus meus: in manibus tuis tempora mea . . .*'

'In Thee, O Lord, have I hoped; I said: Thou art my God; my times are in Thy hands . . .'

My times are in Thy hands. I took a solemn vow to devote the rest of my life to Him.

'*Suscipe quaesumus domine, pro sacra connubii lege munus oblatum . . .*'

'Receive, we beseech Thee, O Lord, the offering we make to Thee on behalf of the holy hands of wedlock . . .'

The words seemed to reverberate in Graciela's head. She felt as though time had stopped.

'*Deus qui potestate virtutis tuae de nihilo cuneta fecisti . . .*'

'Oh, God, who has hallowed wedlock to foreshadow the union of Christ with the church . . . look in Thy mercy upon this, Thy handmaid, who is to be joined in wedlock and entreats protection and strength from Thee . . .'

But how can He show me mercy when I am betraying Him?

Graciela was suddenly finding it difficult to breathe. The walls seemed to be closing in on her.

'*Nihil in ea ex actibus suis ille auctor praevaricationis usurpet . . .*'

'Let the father of sin work none of his evil deeds in her . . .'

That was the moment when Graciela knew. And she felt as though a great burden had been lifted from her. She was filled with an exalted, ineffable joy.

The priest was saying, 'May she win the peace of the kingdom of heaven. We ask Thee to bless this marriage, and –'

'I'm already married,' Graciela said aloud.

There was a moment of shocked silence. Ricardo and the priest were staring at her. Ricardo's face was pale.

'Graciela, what are you –?'

She took his arm and said gently, 'I'm sorry, Ricardo.'

'I – I don't understand. Have – have you stopped loving me?'

She shook her head. 'I love you more than my life. But my life doesn't belong to me any more. I gave it to God a long time ago.'

'No! I can't let you sacrifice your –'

'Darling Ricardo . . . It is not a sacrifice. It's a blessing.

334

In the convent I found the first peace I had ever known. You're a part of the world I gave up – the best part. But I did give it up. I must return to my world.'

The priest was standing there, listening, silent.

'Please forgive me for the pain I am causing you, but I can't go back on my vows. I would be betraying everything I believe in. I know that now. I could never make you happy, because I could never be happy. Please understand.'

Ricardo stared at her, shaken, and no words would come. It was as though something in him had died.

Graciela looked at his stricken face, and her heart went out to him. She kissed him on the cheek. 'I love you,' she said softly. Her eyes filled with tears. 'I will pray for you. I will pray for us both.'

Chapter 38

On a late Friday afternoon, a military ambulance drove up to the emergency entrance to the hospital at Aranda de Duero. An ambulance attendant accompanied by two uniformed policemen went through the swing doors and approached the supervisor behind the desk.

'We have an order here to pick up a Rubio Arzano,' one of the policemen said. He handed over the document.

The supervisor looked at it and frowned. 'I don't think I have the authority to release him. It should be handled by the administrator.'

'Fine. Get him.'

The supervisor hesitated. 'There's a problem. He's away for the weekend.'

'It's not our problem. There's our release order, signed by Colonel Acoca. Do you want to call him and tell him you won't honour it?'

'No,' he said hastily. 'That won't be necessary. I'll have them get the prisoner ready.'

Half a mile away, in front of the city jail, two detectives emerged from a police car and entered the building. They approached the desk sergeant.

One of the men showed his badge. 'We're here to pick up Lucia Carmine.'

The sergeant looked at the two detectives in front of him and said, 'No one told me anything about this.'

One of the detectives sighed. 'Goddamned bureaucracy.

The left hand never tells the right hand what it's doing.'

'Let me see that release order.'

The detectives handed it to him.

'Colonel Acoca signed it, huh?'

'That's right.'

'Where are you taking her?'

'Madrid. The Colonel is going to question her himself.'

'Is he? Well, I think I'd better check it out with him.'

'There's no need to do that,' the detective protested.

'Mister, we've got orders to keep a tight grip on this lady. The Italian government is having an orgasm over getting her back. If Colonel Acoca wants her, he's going to have to tell me himself.'

'You're wasting time, and –'

'I have a lot of time, *amigo*. What I don't have is another ass if I lose mine over this.' He picked up the phone and said, 'Get me Colonel Acoca in Madrid.'

'Jesus Christ!' the detective said. 'My wife is going to kill me if I'm late for dinner again. Besides, the Colonel's probably not even in, and –'

The phone on the desk rang. The sergeant reached for it.

'I have the Colonel's office on the line.'

The sergeant gave the detectives a triumphant look. 'Hello. This is the desk sergeant at the police station in Aranda de Duero. It is important that I speak to Colonel Acoca.'

One of the detectives looked at his watch impatiently. '*Mierda!* I have better things to do than stand around and –'

'Hello. Colonel Acoca?'

The voice boomed out over the phone. 'Yes. What is it?'

'I have two detectives here, Colonel, who want me to release a prisoner into your custody.'

'Lucia Carmine?'

'Yes, sir.'

'Did they show you an order signed by me?'

'Yes, sir. They –'

'Then what the fuck are you bothering me for? Release her.'

337

'I just thought –'

'Don't think. Follow orders.'

The line went dead.

The sergeant swallowed. 'He – er –'

'He has a short fuse, hasn't he?' the detective grinned.

The sergeant rose, trying to retain his dignity. 'I'll have her brought out.'

In the alley at the back of the police station, a small boy was watching a man on the telephone pole disconnect a clamp from a wire and climb down.

'What are you doing?' the boy asked.

The man ruffled his hand through the boy's hair. 'Helping out a friend, *muchacho*. Helping out a friend.'

Three hours later, at an isolated farmhouse to the north, Luciā and Rubio Arzano were reunited.

He was awakened by the telephone at 3.00 a.m. The familiar voice said, 'The Committee would like to meet with you.'

'Yes, sir. When?'

'Now, Colonel. A limousine will pick you up in one hour. Be ready, please.'

'Yes, sir.'

He replaced the receiver and sat on the edge of the bed. He lit a cigarette and let the smoke bite deep into his lungs.

A limousine will pick you up in one hour. Be ready, please.

He would be ready.

He went into the bathroom and examined his image in the mirror. He was looking into the eyes of a defeated man.

I was so close, he thought bitterly. *So close.*

Colonel Acoca began to shave, very carefully, and when he was finished, he took a long, hot shower, then selected the clothes he was going to wear.

Exactly one hour later, he walked to the front door and took a last look at the home he knew he would never see again. There would be no meeting, of course. They would have nothing further to discuss with him.

There was a long, black limousine waiting in front of the house. A door opened as he approached the car. There were two men in the front and two in the back.

'Get in, Colonel.'

He took a deep breath and entered the car. A moment later, it sped away into the black night.

It's like a dream, Lucia thought. *I'm looking out the window at the Swiss Alps. I'm actually here.*

Jaime Miró had arranged for a guide to see that she reached Zurich safely. She had arrived late at night.

In the morning, I'll go to the Leu Bank.

The thought made her nervous. What if something had gone wrong? What if the money was no longer there? What if . . .?

As the first light of dawn inched over the mountains, Lucia was still awake.

A few minutes before nine, she left the Baur au Lac Hotel and stood in front of the bank, waiting for it to open.

A kindly-looking, middle-aged man unlocked the door. 'Come in, please. I hope you haven't been waiting long?'

Only a few months, Lucia thought. 'No. Not at all.'

He ushered her inside. 'What can we do for you?'

Make me rich. 'My father has an account here. He asked me to come in and – and take it over.'

'Is it a numbered account?'

'Yes.'

'May I have the number, please?'

'B2A149207.'

He nodded. 'One moment, please.'

She watched him disappear towards a vault at the back. The bank was beginning to fill with customers. *It must be there*, Lucia thought. *Nothing must go –*

The man was approaching her. She could read nothing in his face.

'This account – you say it was in your father's name?'

Her heart sank. 'Yes. Angelo Carmine.'

He studied her for a moment. 'The account carries two names.'

Did that mean she would not be able to touch it? 'What –' She could scarcely get the words out. '– What's the other name?'

'Lucia Carmine.'

And in that instant, she owned the world.

The account amounted to a little over thirteen million dollars.

'How would you like it handled?' the banker asked.

'Could you transfer it to a bank in Brazil? Rio?'

'Certainly. It will be there this afternoon.'

It was that simple.

Lucia's next stop was at a travel agency near the hotel. There was a large poster in the window advertising Brazil.

It's an omen, Lucia thought happily. She went inside.

'May I help you?'

'Yes. I would like two tickets to Brazil.'

There are no extradition laws there.

She could not wait to tell Rubio how well everything was going. He was in Biarritz waiting for her call. They would be going to Brazil together.

'We can live in peace there for the rest of our lives,' she had told him.

Now, everything was finally set. After all the adventure and the dangers . . . the arrest of her father and brothers and her vengeance against Benito Patas and Judge Buscetta . . . the police looking for her and her escape to the convent . . . Acoca's men and the phony friar . . . Jaime Miró and Teresa and the gold cross . . . and Rubio Arzano. Most of all, dear Rubio. How many times had he risked his life for her? He had saved her from the soldiers in the woods . . . from the raging waters at the waterfall . . . from the men in the bar at Aranda de Duero. The very thought of Rubio warmed Lucia.

She returned to her hotel room and picked up the telephone, waiting for the operator to answer.

There will be something for him to do in Rio. What? What can he do? He'll probably want to buy a farm somewhere out in the country. But then what would I do?

An operator's voice said, 'Number, please.'

Lucia sat there staring out of the window at the snow-covered Alps. *We have two different lives, Rubio and I. We live in different worlds. I'm the daughter of Angelo Carmine.*

'Number, please?'

He's a farmer. That's what he loves. How can I take him away from that? I can't do that to him.

The operator was getting impatient. 'Can I help you?'

Lucia said slowly, 'No. Thank you.' She replaced the receiver.

Early the following morning, she boarded a Swissair flight to Rio.

She was alone.

Chapter 39

The meeting had taken place in the luxurious drawing room of Ellen Scott's townhouse. She paced back and forth, waiting for Alan Tucker to arrive with the girl. No. Not a girl. A woman. A nun. What would she be like? What had life done to her? *What have I done to her?*

The butler walked into the room. 'Your guests have arrived, Madam.'

She took a deep breath. 'Show them in.'

A moment later, Megan and Alan Tucker entered.

She's beautiful, Ellen Scott thought.

Tucker smiled. 'Mrs Scott, this is Megan.'

Ellen Scott looked at him and said quietly, 'I won't need you any more.' And her words had a finality to them.

His smile faded.

'Goodbye, Tucker.'

He stood there a moment, uncertain, then nodded and left. He could not get over his feeling that he had missed something. Something important. *Too late*, he thought. *Too bloody late.*

Ellen Scott was studying Megan. 'Sit down, please.'

Megan took a chair, and the two women sat there inspecting each other.

She looks like her mother, Ellen Scott thought. *She's grown up to be a beautiful woman.* She recalled the terrible night of the accident, the storm and the burning plane.

You said she was dead . . . There's another way . . . The

*pilot said we were near Ávila. There should be plenty of
tourists there. There's no reason for anyone to connect the
baby with the plane crash . . . We'll drop her off at a nice
farmhouse outside of town. They'll adopt her and she'll grow
up to have a lovely life here . . . You have to choose, Milo.
You can either have me, or you can spend the rest of your
life working for your brother's child.*

And now here was the past confronting her. Where to
begin?

'I'm Ellen Scott, President of Scott Industries. Have you
heard of it?'

'No.'

Of course she would not have heard of it, Ellen Scott
chided herself.

This was going to be more difficult than she had anticipated.
She had concocted a story about an old friend of the family
who had died, and a promise to take care of his daughter, and
– but the moment she had looked at Megan, Ellen Scott knew
that it would not work. She had no choice. She had to trust
Patricia – Megan – not to destroy them all. Ellen Scott thought
of what she had done to the woman seated before her, and her
eyes filled with tears. *But it's too late for tears. It's time to make
amends. It's time to tell the truth.*

Ellen Scott leaned across to Megan and took her hand. 'I
have a story to tell you,' she said quietly.

That had been three years earlier. For the first year, until
she became too ill to continue, Ellen Scott had taken Megan
under her wing. Megan had gone to work for Scott Industries,
and her aptitude and intelligence had delighted the older
woman.

'You'll have to work hard,' Ellen Scott said. 'You'll learn,
as I had to learn. In the beginning, it will be difficult, but in
the end, it will become your life.'

And it had.

Megan worked hours that none of her employees could
even begin to emulate.

343

'You get to your office at four o'clock in the morning and work all day. How do you do it?'

Megan smiled and thought: *If I slept until four o'clock in the morning at the convent, Sister Betina would scold me.*

Ellen Scott was gone, but Megan had kept learning, and kept watching the company grow. *Her* company. Ellen Scott had adopted her. 'So we won't have to explain why you're a Scott,' she said. But there was a note of pride in her voice.

It's ironic, Megan thought. *All those years at the orphanage when no one would adopt me. And now I'm being adopted by my own family.*

He has a wonderful sense of humour.

Chapter 40

A new man was behind the wheel of the getaway car, and it made Jaime Miró nervous.

'I'm not sure of him,' he told Felix Carpio. 'What if he drives off and leaves us?'

'Relax. He's my cousin's brother-in-law. He'll be fine. He's been begging for a chance to go out with us.'

'I have a bad feeling,' Jaime said.

They had arrived in Seville early that afternoon, and had examined half a dozen banks before choosing their target. The bank was on a side street, small, not too much traffic, close to a factory which would be making deposits there. Everything seemed perfect. Except for the man in the get-away car.

'Is he all that's worrying you?' Felix asked.

'No.'

'What, then?'

It was a difficult one to answer. 'Call it a premonition.' He tried to say it lightly, mocking himself.

Felix took it seriously. 'Do you want to call it off?'

'Because I have the nerves of an old washerman today? No, *amigo*. It will all go as smooth as silk.'

In the beginning, it had.

There were half a dozen customers in the bank, and Felix held them at bay with an automatic weapon while Jaime cleared out the cash drawers. Smooth as silk.

As the two men were leaving, heading for the getaway car, Jaime called out, 'Remember, *amigos*, the money is for a good cause.'

It was out in the street that it began to fall apart. There were police everywhere. The driver of the getaway car was on his knees on the pavement, a police pistol at his head.

As Jaime and Felix came into view, a detective called out, 'Drop your weapons.'

Jaime hesitated for one split second. Then he raised his gun.

Chapter 41

The converted 727 was flying at 35,000 feet, over the Grand Canyon. It had been a long, hard day. *And it's not over yet*, Megan thought.

She was on her way to California to sign the papers that would give Scott Industries one million acres of timberland north of San Francisco. She had struck a hard bargain.

It's their fault, Megan thought. *They shouldn't have tried to cheat me. I'll bet I'm the first bookkeeper they've ever come up against from a Cistercian convent.* She laughed aloud.

The steward approached her. 'Can I get you anything, Miss Scott?'

'No, thank you.'

She saw a stack of newspapers and magazines in the rack. She had been so busy with the deal that she had had no time to read anything. 'Let me see the *New York Times*, please.'

The story was on the front page and it leaped out at her. There was a photograph of Jaime Miró. Below it the communique read: 'Jaime Miró, leader of ETA, the radical Basque separatist movement in Spain, was wounded and captured by police during a bank hold-up yesterday afternoon in Seville. Killed in the attack was Felix Carpio, another of the alleged terrorists. The authorities had been conducting a search for Miró since . . .'

Megan read the rest of the article and sat there for a long time, frozen, remembering the past. It was like a distant dream, photographed through a gauze curtain, hazy and unreal.

This fight will be over soon. We'll get what we want because

*the people are behind us . . . I would like you to wait for
me . . .*

Long ago she had read of a civilization that believed if you
saved a person's life, that you were responsible for him.
Well, she had saved Jaime twice – once at the castle, and
again at the park. *I'll be damned if I'm going to let them kill
him now.*

She reached for the telephone next to her seat and said to
the pilot, 'Turn the plane around. We're going back to New
York.'

A limousine was there for her at La Guardia, and by the
time she arrived in her office it was 2.00 a.m. Lawrence Gray
Jr. was waiting for her. His father had been the company's
attorney for years and had retired. The son was bright and
ambitious.

Without preamble, Megan said, 'Jaime Miró. What do
you know about him?'

The reply was immediate. 'He's a Basque terrorist, head
of ETA. I think I just read that he was captured a day or so
ago.'

'Right. The government is going to have to put him on
trial. I want to have someone there. Who's the best trial
lawyer in the country?'

'I'd say Curtis Hayman.'

'No. Too much of a gentleman. We need a killer.' She
thought for a moment. 'Get Mike Rosen.'

'He's booked for the next hundred years, Megan.'

'Unbook him. I want him in Madrid for the trial.'

He frowned. 'We can't get involved in a public trial in
Spain.'

'Sure we can. *Amicus curae.* We're friends of the defend-
ant.'

He studied her a moment. Do you mind if I ask you a
personal question?'

'Yes. Get on this.'

'I'll do my best.'

348

'Larry . . .'

'Yes?'

'And then some.' There was steel in her voice.

Twenty minutes later, Lawrence Gray walked into Megan's office. 'Mike Rosen is on the phone. I think I woke him up. He wants to talk to you.'

Megan picked up the telephone. 'Mr Rosen? What a pleasure this is. We've never met, but I have a feeling you and I are going to become very good friends. A lot of people sue Scott Industries just for the target practice, and I've been looking around for someone to take charge of all our litigation. Yours is the one name that keeps coming up. Naturally, I'm prepared to pay you a large retainer for –'

'Miss Scott –?'

'Yes.'

'I don't mind a little snow job, but you're giving me frostbite.'

'I don't understand.'

'Then let me put it in legal parlance for you. Cut out the bullshit. It's two o'clock in the morning. You don't hire people at two o'clock in the morning.'

'Mr Rosen –'

'Mike. We're going to be good friends, remember? But friends have to trust one another. Larry tells me you want me to go to Spain to try to save some Basque terrorist who's in the hands of the police.'

She started to say, 'He's not a terrorist –' but stopped herself. 'Yes.'

'What's your problem? Is he suing Scott Industries because his gun jammed?'

'He –'

'I'm sorry, friend. I can't help you. My schedule is so tight that I gave up going to the bathroom six months ago. I can recommend a few lawyers . . .'

No, Megan thought. *Jaime Miró needs you.* And she was suddenly seized by a sense of hopelessness. Spain was another world, another time. When she spoke, her voice sounded weary. 'Never mind,' she said. 'It's a personal matter. I'm sorry for coming on so strongly.'

'Hey! That's what CEOs are supposed to do. Personal is different, Megan. To tell you the truth, I'm dying to hear what interest the head of Scott Industries has in saving a Spanish terrorist. Are you free for lunch tomorrow?'

She was going to let nothing stand in her way. 'Yes.'

'Le Cirque at one o'clock?'

Megan felt her spirits lifting. 'Fine.'

'You make the reservation. But I have to warn you about something.'

'Yes?'

'I have a very nosy wife.'

They met at Le Cirque, and when Sirio had seated them Mike Rosen said, 'You're better looking than your picture. I'll bet everybody tells you that.'

He was very short, and he dressed carelessly. But there was nothing careless about his mind. His eyes radiated a blazing intelligence.

'You've aroused my curiosity,' Mike Rosen said. 'What's your interest in Jaime Miró?'

There was so much to tell. Too much to tell. All Megan said was, 'He's a friend. I don't want him to die.'

Rosen leaned forward in his seat, his legs swinging in the air. 'I went through the newspaper files on him this morning. If Don Juan Carlos' government executes Miró only once, he'll be way ahead of the game. They're going to get hoarse just reading the charges against your friend.' He saw the expression on Megan's face. 'I'm sorry, but I have to be honest. Miró has been a very busy man. He holds up banks, blows up cars, murders people –'

'He's not a murderer. He's a patriot. He's fighting for his rights.'

'Okay, okay. He's my hero too. What do you want me to do?'

350

'Save him.'

'Megan, we're such good friends that I'm going to tell you the absolute truth. Jesus Christ himself couldn't save him. You're looking for a miracle that –'

'I believe in miracles. Will you help me?'

He studied her a moment. 'What the hell. What are friends for? Have you tried the paté? I hear they make it kosher.'

The Fax from Madrid read: 'Have spoken to half a dozen top European lawyers. They refuse to represent Miró. Tried to have myself admitted to trial as *amicus curae*. Court ruled against me. Wish I could pull off that miracle for you, friend, but Jesus hasn't risen yet. Am on my way home. You owe me a lunch. Mike.'

The trial was set to begin on 17 September.

'Cancel my appointments,' Megan told her assistant. 'I have some business to take care of in Madrid.'

'How long will you be gone?'

'I don't know.'

She planned her strategy on the plane flying over the Atlantic. *There has to be a way*, Megan thought. *I have money and I have power. The Prime Minister is the key. I have to get to him before the trial starts. After that, it will be too late.*

Megan had an appointment with Prime Minister Leopoldo Martinez twenty-four hours after she arrived in Madrid. He invited her to Monclo Palace for lunch.

'Thank you for seeing me so promptly,' Megan said. 'I know what a busy man you are.'

He raised a hand in deprecation. 'My dear Miss Scott, when the head of an organization as important as Scott

Industries flies to my country to see me, I can only be honoured. Please tell me how I can assist you.'

'I really came here to assist you,' Megan said. 'It occurred to me that while we have a few factories in Spain, we're not using nearly enough of the potential that your country has to offer.'

He was listening closely now, his eyes shining. 'Yes?'

'Scott Industries is about to open a huge electronics plant. It should employ somewhere between a thousand and fifteen hundred people. If it is as successful as we think it will be, we'll open satellite factories.'

'And you have not decided in which country you wish to open this plant?'

'That's right. I'm personally in favour of Spain, but quite frankly, Your Excellency, some of my executives are not too happy with your civil rights record.'

'Really?'

'Yes. They felt that those who object to some of the policies of the state are treated too harshly.'

'Do you have anyone in particular in mind?'

'As a matter of fact, I do. Jaime Miró.'

He sat there staring at her. 'I see. And if we were to be lenient with Jaime Miró, we would get the electronics factory and –'

'And a lot more,' Megan assured him. 'Our factories will raise the standard of living in every community they're in.'

The Prime Minister frowned. 'I'm afraid there is one small problem.'

'What? We can negotiate further.'

'This is something that cannot be negotiated, Miss Scott. Spain's honour is not for sale. You cannot bribe us or buy us or threaten us.'

'Believe me, I'm not –'

'You came here with your handouts and expect us to run our courts to please you? Think again, Miss Scott. We don't need your factories.'

I've made it worse, Megan thought, despairingly.

*

352

The trial lasted six weeks in a heavily guarded courtroom that was closed to the public.

Megan remained in Madrid, following the news reports of the trial each day. From time to time, Mike Rosen telephoned her.

'I know what you're going through, friend. I think you should come home.'

'I can't, Mike.'

She tried to see Jaime.

'Absolutely no visitors.'

On the last day of the trial, Megan stood outside the courtroom, lost in a crowd of people. Reporters came streaming out of the building, and Megan stopped one of them.

'What happened?'

'They found him guilty on all counts. He's going to get the garrotte.'

Chapter 42

At five a.m. on the morning scheduled for the execution of Jaime Miró, crowds began to gather outside the central prison in Madrid. Barricades set up by the *guardia civil* kept the swelling mob of onlookers across the wide street, away from the front entrance to the prison. Armed troops and tanks blocked the iron prison gates.

Inside the prison, in the office of Warden Gomez de la Fuente, an extraordinary meeting was taking place. In the room were Prime Minister Leopoldo Martinez, Alonzo Sebastian, the new head of GOE, and the warden's executive deputies, Juanito Molinas and Pedros Arrango.

Warden de la Fuente was a heavyset, middle-aged, grim-faced man who had passionately devoted his life to disciplining the miscreants that the government had placed in his charge. Molinas and Arrango, his hard-bitten assistants, had served with de la Fuente for the past twenty years.

Prime Minister Martinez was speaking. 'I would like to know what arrangements you have made to ensure that there will be no trouble in carrying out Miró's execution.'

Warden de la Fuente replied, 'We have prepared for every possible contingency, Your Excellency. As Your Excellency observed when you arrived, a full company of armed soldiers is stationed around the prison. It would take an army to break in.'

'And inside the prison itself?'

'The precautions are even more stringent. Jaime Miró is locked in a double security cell on the second floor. The other prisoners on that floor have been temporarily transferred. Two guards are stationed at each end of the cell block. I have ordered a general lock-down, so that all prisoners will remain in their cells until after the execution.'

'What time will that take place?'

'At noon, Your Excellency. I have postponed mess hall until one o'clock. That will give us enough time to get Miró's body out of here.'

'What plans have you made for disposing of it?'

'I am following your suggestion, Excellency. His burial in Spain would cause the government embarrassment if the Basques should turn his grave into some kind of shrine. We have been in touch with his aunt in France. She lives in a small village outside Bayonne. She has agreed to bury him there.'

The Prime Minister rose. 'Excellent.' He sighed. 'I still think a hanging in the public square would have been more appropriate.'

'Yes, Your Excellency. But in that case, I could no 'onger have been responsible for controlling the mob outside.'

'I suppose you're right. There's no point in stirring up any more excitement than is necessary. The garrotte is more painful and slower. And if any man deserves the garrotte, it is Jaime Miró.'

Warden de la Fuente said, 'Excuse me, Your Excellency, but I understand that a commission of judges is meeting to consider a last minute appeal from Miró's attorneys. If it should come through, what should I –?'

The Prime Minister interrupted. 'It won't. The execution will proceed as scheduled.'

The meeting was over.

At 7.30 a.m., a bread truck arrived in front of the prison gate.

'Delivery.'

One of the prison guards stationed at the entrance looked in at the driver. 'You're new, aren't you?'

'Yeah.'

355

'Where's Julio?'

'He's sick in bed today.'

'Why don't you go join him, *amigo*?'

'What?'

'No deliveries this morning. Come back this afternoon.'

'But every morning –'

'Nothing goes in, and only one thing is going out. Now back up, turn around and get your ass out of here before my pals get nervous.'

The driver looked around at the armed soldiers staring at him. 'Sure. Okay.'

They watched as he turned the truck around and disappeared down the street. The commander of the post reported the incident to the warden. When the story was checked out, it was learned that the regular employee was in the hospital, a victim of a hit and run driver.

At eight a.m., a car bomb exploded across the street from the prison, wounding half a dozen bystanders. Under ordinary circumstances, the guards would have left their posts to investigate and assist the wounded. But they had strict orders. They remained at their stations and the *guardia civil* was summoned to take charge.

The incident was promptly reported to Warden de la Fuente.

'They're getting desperate,' he said. 'Be prepared for anything.'

At 9.15 a.m., a helicopter appeared over the prison grounds. Painted on its sides were the words: LA PRENSA, Spain's prominent daily newspaper.

Two anti-aircraft guns had been set up on the prison roof. The lieutenant in charge waved a flag to warn off the plane. It continued to hover. The officer picked up a field telephone.

'Warden, we have a copter overhead.'

'Any identification?'

'It says *La Prensa*, but the sign looks freshly painted.'

'Give it one warning shot. If it doesn't move, blow it out of the sky.'

'Yes, sir.' He nodded to his gunner. 'Put a close one in.'

The shot landed five yards to the side of the helicopter. They could see the pilot's startled face. The gunner loaded again. The helicopter swooped up and disappeared across the skies of Madrid.

What the hell is next? the lieutenant wondered.

At 11.00 a.m. Megan Scott appeared at the reception office of the prison. She looked drawn and pale. 'I want to see Warden de la Fuente.'

'Do you have an appointment?'

'No, but –'

'I'm sorry. The Warden isn't seeing anyone this morning. If you telephone this afternoon –'

'Tell him it's Megan Scott.'

He took a closer look at her. *So this is the rich American who's trying to get Jaime Miró released. I wouldn't mind having her work on me for a few nights.* 'I'll tell the Warden you're here.'

Five minutes later Megan was seated in Warden de la Fuente's office. With him were half a dozen members of the prison board.

'What can I do for you, Miss Scott?'

'I would like to see Jaime Miró.'

The warden sighed. 'I'm afraid that is not possible.'

'But I'm –'

'Miss Scott – we are all aware of who you are. If we could accommodate you, I assure you that we would be more than happy to do so,' he smiled. 'We Spaniards are really an understanding people. We are also sentimental, and from time to time we are not averse to turning a blind eye to certain rules and regulations.' His smile disappeared. 'But not today, Miss Scott. No. Today is a very special day. It has taken us years to catch the man you wish to see. So this

357

is a day of rules and regulations. The next one to see Jaime Miró will be his God – if he has one.'

Megan stared at him, miserable. 'Could – could I just look at him for a moment?'

One of the members of the prison board, touched by the anguish in Megan's face, was tempted to intervene. He stopped himself.

'I'm sorry,' Warden de la Fuente said. 'No.'

'Could I send him a message?' Her voice was choked.

'You would be sending a message to a dead man.' He looked at his watch. 'He has less than an hour to live.'

'But he's appealing his sentence. Isn't a panel of judges meeting to decide if –?'

'They've voted against it. I received word from them fifteen minutes ago. Miró's appeal has been denied. The execution will take place. Now, if you'll excuse me –'

He rose, and the others followed suit. Megan looked around the room at their cold faces and shuddered.

'May God have mercy on all of you,' she said.

They watched, silent, as she fled from the room.

At ten minutes before the noon hour, the door to Jaime Miró's cell was opened. Warden Gomez de la Fuente was accompanied by his two assistants, Molinas and Arrango, and Dr Miguel Anunción. Four armed guards stood watch in the corridor.

The warden entered the cell. 'It's time.'

Jaime rose from his cot. He was handcuffed and shackled. 'I was hoping you'd be late.' There was an air of dignity about him that Warden de la Fuente could not help but admire.

At another time, under other circumstances, we might have been friends.

Jaime stepped out into the deserted corridor, his movements clumsy because of the shackles. He was flanked by the guards and Molinas and Arrango. 'The garrotte?' Jaime asked.

The warden nodded. 'The garrotte.' Excruciatingly pain-ful, inhuman. It was a good thing, the warden thought, that the execution would take place in a private room, away from the eyes of the public and the press.

The procession made its way down the corridor. From outside, in the street, they could hear the chant of the crowd: 'Jaime . . . Jaime . . . Jaime . . .' It was a swelling, bursting from a thousand throats growing louder and louder

'They're calling for you,' Pedros Arrango said.

'No. They're calling for themselves. They're calling for freedom. Tomorrow they'll have another name. I may die – but there will always be another name.'

They passed through two security gates to a small chamber at the end of the corridor, with an iron green door. From around the corner a black-robed priest appeared.

'Thank heavens I'm in time. I've come to give the con-demned man the last rites.'

As he moved towards Miró, two guards blocked his way.

'Sorry, Father,' Warden de la Fuente said. 'Nobody goes near him.'

'But I'm –'

'If you want to give him his last rites, you'll have to do it through closed doors. Out of the way, please.'

A guard opened the green door. Standing inside, next to a chair bolted to the floor, with heavy armstraps, was a huge man wearing a half mask. In his hands he held the garrotte.

The warden nodded towards Molinas and Arrango and the doctor, and they entered the room after Jaime. The guards remained outside. The green door was locked and bolted.

Inside the room, assistants Molinas and Arrango led Jaime to the chair. They unlocked his handcuffs, then strapped him in, pulling the heavy straps against his arms, while Dr Anunción and Warden de la Fuente watched. Through the thick closed door, they could barely hear the chanting of the priest.

De la Fuente looked at Jaime and shrugged. 'It doesn't matter. God will understand what he is saying.'

359

The giant holding the garrotte moved to the back of Jaime. Warden Gomez de la Fuente asked, 'Do you want a cloth over your face?'

'No.'

The warden looked at the giant and nodded. The giant lifted the garrotte in his hand and reached forward.

Outside the guards at the door could hear the chanting of the mob in the street.

'You know something?' one of the guards grumbled. 'I wish I was out there with them.'

Five minutes later, the green door opened.

Dr Anunción said, 'Bring in the body bag.'

Following instructions, Jaime Miró's body was smuggled out through a back door of the prison. The body bag was thrown into the back of an unmarked van. But the moment the vehicle pulled out of the prison grounds, the crowd in the street pressed forward, as though drawn to it by some mystic magnet.

'Jaime . . . Jaime . . .'

But the cries were softer now. Men and women wept, and their children looked on in wonder, not understanding what was happening. The van made its way through the crowd and finally turned on to a highway.

'Jesus,' the driver said. 'That was spooky. The guy must have had something.'

'Yeah. And thousands of people knew it too!'

At two o'clock that afternoon, Warden Gomez de la Fuente and his two assistants, Juanito Molinas and Pedros Arrango appeared at the office of Prime Minister Martinez.

'I want to congratulate you,' the Prime Minister said. 'It was executed perfectly.'

The warden spoke. 'Mr Prime Minister, we're not here to receive your congratulations. We're here to resign.'

Martinez stared at them, baffled. 'I – I don't understand. What –?'

'It's a matter of humanity, Your Excellency. We just watched a man die. Perhaps he deserved to die. But not like that. It – it was barbaric. I want no more part of this or anything like it, and my colleagues feel the same way.'

'Perhaps you should give this more thought. Your pensions –'

'We have to live with our consciences.' Warden de la Fuente handed the Prime Minister three pieces of paper. 'Here are our resignations.'

Late that night, the van crossed the French border and headed for the village of Bidache, near Bayonne. They pulled up before a neat farmhouse.

'This is the place. Let's get rid of the body before it starts to smell.'

The door to the farmhouse was opened by a woman in her middle fifties. 'You brought him?'

'Yes, ma'am. Where would you like it – er – him?'

'In the parlour, please.'

'Yes, ma'am. I – I wouldn't wait too long to bury him. You know what I mean?'

She watched the two men carry in the body bag and set it on the floor.

'Thank you.'

'*De nada.*'

She stood there watching as they drove away.

Another woman walked in from the other room and ran towards the body bag. She hastily unzipped it.

Jaime Miró was lying there smiling up at them. 'Do you know something? That garrotte could be a real pain in the neck.'

'White wine or red?' Megan asked.

Chapter 43

At Barajas Airport in Madrid, former Warden Gomez de la Fuente and his former assistants, Molinas and Arrango, and Dr Anunción and the giant in the mask were in the departure lounge.

'I still think you're making a mistake not coming with me to Costa Rica,' de la Fuente said. 'With your five million dollars, you can buy the whole fucking island.'

Molinas shook his head. 'Arrango and I are going to Switzerland. I'm tired of the sun. We're going to buy ourselves a few dozen snow bunnies.'

'Me, too,' the giant said.

They turned to Miguel Anunción.

'What about you, doctor?'

'I'm going to Bangladesh.'

'*What?*'

'That's right. I'm going to use the money to open a hospital there. You know, I thought about it a long time before I accepted Megan Scott's offer. But I figured that if I can save a lot of innocent lives by letting one terrorist live, it's a good trade-off. Besides, I must tell you, I liked Jaime Miró.'

Chapter 44

It had been a good season in the French countryside, with fine weather, showering farmers with an abundance of crops. *I wish that every year could be as wonderful as this*, Rubio Arzano thought. *It has been a good year in more ways than one.*

First his marriage and then, a year ago, the birth of the twins. *Whoever dreamed a man could be this happy?*

It was starting to rain. Rubio turned the tractor around and headed for the barn. He thought about the twins. The boy was going to be big and strapping. But his sister! She was going to be a handful. *She's going to give her man a lot of trouble*, Rubio grinned to himself. *She takes after her mother.*

He drove the tractor into the barn and headed for the house, feeling the cool rain against his face. He opened the door and stepped inside.

'You're just in time,' Lucia smiled. Dinner's ready '

The Reverend Mother Prioress Betina awakened with a premonition that something wonderful was about to happen.

Of course, she thought, *enough good things have already happened.*

The Cistercian convent had long since been reopened, under the protection of King Don Juan Carlos. Sister Graciela and the nuns who had been taken to Madrid were safely returned to the convent, where they were allowed to retreat once again into the blessed solitude and silence.

Shortly after breakfast, the Mother Prioress walked into her office and stopped, staring. On her desk, shining with a dazzling brightness, lay the gold cross.

It was accepted as a miracle

AFTERWORD

In 1978, Madrid tried to buy peace by offering the Basques limited autonomy, allowing them to have their own flag, their own language, and a Basque police department. ETA replied by assassinating Constantin Ortin Gil, Madrid's military governor, and later Luis Carrero Blanco, the man chosen by Franco to be his successor.

The violence keeps escalating.

In a three-year period, ETA terrorists have killed more than 600 victims. The slaughter continues and the retaliation by the police has been equally ruthless.

Not so many years ago, ETA had the sympathy of the two and a half million Basque people, but continued terrorism has eroded their support. In Bilbao the very heart of the Basque homeland, 100,000 people took to the streets to demonstrate *against* ETA. The Spanish people feel it is time for peace, time to heal the wounds.

The OPUS MUNDO is more powerful than ever, but few people are willing to discuss it.

As for the Cistercian convents of the Strict Observance, there are in existence today fifty-four convents, worldwide, seven of them in Spain.

Their timeless ritual of eternal silence and seclusion remains unchanged.

The Stars Shine Down
Sidney Sheldon

A magnificent story of passion, intrigue, ambition and revenge – Sidney Sheldon at his compelling, provocative best.

Lara Cameron seems to possess everything that life has to offer. Young, beautiful, a self-made tycoon, she has outshone her competitors to reach the pinnacle of international fortune and renown. But the real Lara is a lonely figure, driven by a childhood obsession, trying, at all costs to bury the ghosts of her terrible past . . .

With her glittering marriage to a world-famous concert pianist, Lara is sure she has fulfilled her destiny. But what she cannot foresee is that terrifying, uncontrollable forces from her secret past are bent on destroying everything she has created, everything she values in life . . .

'Sheldon shines again . . . a compelling read'   *Today*